THE RULE BREAKER

A BILLIONAIRE BODYGUARD ROMANCE

BEAUFORT BILLIONAIRES
BOOK 2

ELLE NICOLL

Copyright © 2024 by Elle Nicoll

Rose Hope Publishing Ltd.
Lytchett House, 13 Freeland Park, Wareham Road,
Poole, Dorset, BH16 6FA

Visit
www.ellenicollauthor.com
for updates on new releases, exclusive content, and newsletter sign up.

Cover Photography by Michelle Lancaster
Model - Darcie
Person Cover Design by Sara of Sara's PA and Design Services
Discreet Cover Design by BooksnMoods
Editing by The Blue Couch Edits

All rights reserved. This book is protected under international and domestic copyright laws. No part of this publication may be reproduced, distributed, or transmitted in any form or by any means, electronically or mechanically, including photocopying, recording, or by any information storage and retrieval system, without the prior written permission of the author, except for the use of brief quotations in a book review.

This book is a work of fiction. Names, characters, places, and incidents are either products of the author's imagination or are used fictitiously. Any resemblance to actual persons, living or dead, events, or locales is entirely coincidental.

No AI was used in the writing of this book. Without in any way limiting the author's exclusive rights under copyright, any use of this publication to "train" generative artificial intelligence (AI) technologies to generate text is expressly prohibited. This prohibition applies worldwide. The author reserves all rights to license uses of this work for generative AI training and development of machine learning language models.

CONTENTS

Foreword   v

    Sinclair   1
1. Sinclair   5
Present Day
2. Sinclair   11
3. Denver   19
4. Sinclair   31
5. Denver   39
6. Sinclair   49
7. Denver   63
8. Sinclair   69
9. Denver   81
10. Sinclair   93
11. Denver   103
12. Sinclair   113
13. Sinclair   119
14. Denver   123
15. Sinclair   129
16. Denver   137
17. Sinclair   143
18. Denver   157
19. Sinclair   161
20. Denver   171
21. Sinclair   181
22. Denver   191
23. Sinclair   197
24. Denver   217
25. Denver   229
26. Sinclair   235
27. Sinclair   245

28. Denver	253
29. Sinclair	259
30. Sinclair	273
31. Denver	281
32. Sinclair	295
33. Sinclair	303
34. Denver	325
35. Sinclair	335
36. Sinclair	341
37. Denver	347
38. Denver	355
39. Sinclair	361
40. Denver	369
41. Sinclair *One week later*	377
42. Denver *Three weeks earlier*	391
43. Sinclair	401
44. Denver	405
45. Sinclair	415
46. Denver	433
47. Epilogue – The Wedding *Sinclair*	439
Denver	443
Sinclair	447
Denver	455
Also by Elle Nicoll	463
About the Author	465

FOREWORD

Thank you so much for picking up The Rule Breaker.

Although this can be read as a standalone story, **I highly recommend you start with The Matchmaker - Book 1 of Beaufort Billionaires** due to the family's backstory, which will unfold across the series.

The Rule Breaker is Sinclair's story, which begins near to where we left off at the end of The Matchmaker, in those months before Sterling and Halliday's wedding takes place.

Enjoy!

*For everyone who knows Sinclair won't go easy on Denver...
Of course she won't, but that's what makes it so much better.*

And Denver? Well, this man can handle anything ;)

Happy Reading

SINCLAIR
TWO YEARS EARLIER

It's not okay. I need to breathe. I need to... Oh my God.

My lungs burn as I drag in the dank air that's thick with the scent of saturated earth.

I might be sick again.

A raindrop lands on the backs of my fingers where they're curled around my necklace, shielding it from the rain. The diamond is cold to my touch, like a stone.

Stone cold dead.

My father steps toward the newly dug graves, his arm outstretched, hand full of dirt. He opens his palm, letting the dark brown earth fall freely. The sound of it hitting my mother and brother's caskets beneath is like a round of bullets straight through my heart, tearing what's left of it to shreds.

"No!" I sob, turning into Sullivan's chest and fisting his suit jacket for support.

My brother wraps his arms around me and says softly into my hair, "It's nearly over, okay?"

I cry so hard that I tremble in his embrace. If I wasn't clinging so tightly to him, then I'd be on the floor being pummeled into the earth by the beating rain before it washed me away.

Tempting.

My heart thuds in my ears as I stay buried in the safety of his protection. Maybe if I squeeze my eyes shut, it will all be over when I open them again. Like a bad dream. One where I didn't witness my father's yacht explode, taking both my mother and brother with it, stealing them from us.

He didn't even reach his thirtieth birthday. In what kind of world is that fair? I'll never witness his smile again, hear his laugh, watch his face light up as he tells me about whatever latest crazy stunt he wants to do.

And my mom...

I whine, and Sullivan tightens his grip around me. I'll never be able to talk to her again. Ask her advice. Ask her why...

"Let's wait in the car," he says.

I nod, focusing on putting one foot in front of the other as he leads me away. The other mourners give me sympathetic looks as we pass their cloud of black.

Black suits. Black dresses. Black umbrellas.

It's all so dark. So depressing. Like the two deep holes they're buried in.

"Oh God." I clasp a hand to my mouth as acid rises up my windpipe like a swelling tide.

"Not much further," Sullivan soothes.

I try to focus on the cars, lined up like a row of ants, but my vision is blurred by tears. The heel of my shoe sinks into a soggy patch of ground, throwing me off balance. Sullivan's arm jerks around me, his other hand holding an umbrella over our heads. A low curse breaks from his lips as he tries in vain to prevent me from stumbling. But he's too late. My ankle twists, sending a shot of ice up my calf. The pain is welcome. I soak it in, grateful to feel it someplace different, somewhere other than my soul; where the constant hell has been eating away at me since we lost them.

I wait for the ground to take me, swallow me whole, wash away all traces of me with the rain until I no longer feel anything.

I wait...

A large hand grasps above my elbow, encircling my arm entirely and pulling me up before the bliss of nothingness can take me.

I want to scream at it to let me go.

My breath stutters as I look at the strong arm holding me up. Such extreme care with the gentlest touch for something so big.

"You okay?"

"What?" I blink through tears, staring into deep green irises, flecked with gold. I never noticed that his eyes are green like mine. You miss so many things when you aren't looking. Like what Mom was up to before she died. Who she was spending her time with. A man who wasn't my father.

"Thanks, Denver," Sullivan says.

My father's head of security gives my brother a curt nod, then quickly shifts his gaze back to me.

"Are you okay?" he repeats, his hand still wrapped around my arm. He studies me, two thick dark brows pinching together and forming a valley at the center of his forehead.

My throat is too thick and sore from crying to answer.

Dad told me Denver was in the US Special Forces before he came to work for our family a few years ago. I'm guessing he's around thirty, but I've never asked. He's always working with my father and rarely speaks to me. He's a silent wall of muscle, watching everything with a stern expression permanently on his face. I've never seen him come close to smiling.

He glances down, his mouth curling toward his chin at the sight of my heels. Disapproval tightens his jaw as he glares at them. Irritation bubbles inside me that he felt it necessary to intervene, breaking my fall and ruining my chance of feeling a different pain for a change. Because now my grief comes whooshing back, stealing my breath straight from my lungs. The same way it does each time I wake from another nightmare where all I see is the explosion, over and over.

And fire. So much fire.

"I'm fine," I snap, shaking his hand off and dislodging my heel from the mud.

His eyes darken as they rise to meet mine again. But his voice is gentle, a direct contrast to the storm behind his eyes. "Sincla—"

"I said I'm fine!"

I tug Sullivan, ripping my gaze from Denver's. "Keep walking."

I don't need Denver's help.

And I certainly don't want his pity.

1

SINCLAIR
PRESENT DAY

"This has to be the last dance. I can't afford for this to turn into an all-nighter," my friend, Zoey, says, as I pull her onto the dancefloor of the nightclub.

"As if I'd make you stay out all night. I know you and Ashton have that thing tomorrow at the gallery," I shout over the music as I spin and tip my head back, soaking up the beat.

I look back at Zoey when she doesn't say anything and smile at the pointed look she's giving me.

"Nothing happened, and you know it. That guy was a complete gentleman," I say about the brother of one of the models I went home with after a night out a few days ago. "I met his boyfriend and their cat and everything. He drove me to the hospital the next day."

My mood sours immediately at the memory of the following morning. The call from Sullivan. The tone in his voice as he told me there had been a fire.

Another one.

Zoey doesn't miss the way I've stopped dancing, my limbs weighed down as it all comes crashing back. She pulls me over to the bar, signaling the bartender for two glasses of water.

"You okay?" she asks the moment I've gulped mine down.

"Yeah." I side-eye her and then sigh at her worried expression. "Yeah," I repeat, wiping my brow. "Just, that night... Dad's club burning down. It was all too much like..."

She curls her hand over my forearm reassuringly. "Too close to the way you lost your mom and brother. I get it."

I look into her kind brown eyes. "Yeah, too close."

It's been two years since they died on my father's yacht in a freak fire. And I was finally feeling that life had something to look forward to again. My career as a model has skyrocketed from all the extra hours I'm putting in, landing me some huge campaigns. Sullivan took over from my father as CEO of our family jewelry firm, Beaufort Diamonds, and is expanding it. And my father has grown his portfolio of member's only piano bars that he enjoys so much.

We are all learning to survive without them. Or trying, at least.

I even hired my father a sought-after dating expert called Halliday Burton hoping he'd be happier if he let love into his life. He didn't like any of the dates she set him up with, instead becoming smitten with her. I've never seen him like it, not even with Mom. Halliday's twenty years younger than him, and now they're engaged and having a baby together.

I worried about him. Worried that I'd never see him truly happy. But that all melted away when Halliday came along.

Until the fire at his club. When she was inside it.

"Hey. They're doing fine now. You said it yourself," Zoey interrupts me, breaking my thoughts.

"Yeah, they are. I'm going to visit them tomorrow." I force a smile, thinking how lucky we are that Dad was able to get Halliday out safely. Not like two years ago. He tried to save them both but couldn't.

"Good. In that case, maybe we should have one more

dance." She raises her brows as a song we both love plays. "We cannot let those guys have all the fun."

I follow her gaze to the group we've come out with, a mix of models, makeup artists, and photographers. One of the male models, Mikey, has taken his shirt off and is encouraging girls to run their hands over his abs. He catches us looking and throws us a cocky wink.

"We need to save those girls from Mikey, you mean?" I snort out a giggle as I let Zoey pull me back toward the dancefloor.

"We need to save Mikey from Mikey." She laughs.

"Hold up," I call as my phone buzzes in the back pocket of my pants. I pull it out and bring up the text.

> Denver: Do you need a ride home?

I roll my eyes as I punch back my reply.

> Me: No. I have my car back.

I groan, pocketing my phone.

"Let me guess? Denver?" Zoey asks.

"Was it the way my face shifted, like I'd just endured the most boring thing in my life, that gave it away?"

She breaks into laughter. "Girl, he's not that bad."

"Why don't you ride home with Mr. Personality and then tell me that again?"

Dad said having a car covered in white Swarovski crystals was a bad idea, but I refuse to admit he was right. It just looks so pretty. It's not my fault the tiniest little scrape has them pinging off like crazy. But I'm going to be way more careful with it in future. Not only is it a pain being without my car, but it also means Denver ends up being my ride every time it goes into the shop for repairs.

I know Sullivan puts him up to it. Denver couldn't make it clearer he hates chauffeuring me around. When he gave Mikey and me a ride home last week, he didn't even speak—just greeted us with a grunt. He's probably pissed it pulls him away from whatever security stuff my dad always has him doing.

"It's a ride home. Who cares if he doesn't talk? Silence sounds like heaven after a night with these guys." Zoey jerks her head toward the group as we approach.

Mikey pulls me straight into his side, grabbing my hand. "You'll feel my abs, won't you, Sin?" He plants my palm over his stomach. "That pure, solid muscle won me the Michael Kors campaign."

I laugh as Zoey calls him an idiot over the music.

Then I fall back into the beat and let it take me as I dance.

"Holy fuck!" Mikey balks.

I take slow steps toward my car, my legs like jelly in my high heels.

"Lenny! How could they do this to you?" I squeak.

I move closer to my Lamborghini Murcielago and run a loving hand over the white Swarovski crystals on the hood. They're rough beneath my palm. I swallow a lump in my throat as I take in an area of wrecked bodywork where they've been scraped off, leaving the metal beneath shining like an angry slash mark.

"Sin, I'd move your hand—"

Mikey grabs my hand, pulling it away as I spot the brown lump sitting in the middle of the hood.

"Someone defecated on Lenny!" I screech.

I stare at the offensive lump sitting menacingly on the hood, one end of it pointing at the windscreen where 'Beaufort Bitch' has been scrawled in a deep shade of red.

"Don't worry, baby," I soothe, tentatively reaching out and stroking my car again. "I'll get you cleaned up. You'll be as good as new, I promise."

"I can smell it from here." Mikey doubles over and gags.

I step back, glancing up and down the street. It's deserted. I thought I'd parked in a safe spot, beneath a streetlight, not far from the club. It's not the first time someone's left something for me on my car. The crystals and my license plate, *Sin B 1,* make it instantly recognizable. But apart from the odd time recently that it's been something unpleasant, it's been nice. A flower, or a cute note telling me I looked pretty in my latest campaign.

Not a...

"Shit! What are you going to do?" Mikey looks at me, then at Lenny. He presses a fist to his lips and blinks hard.

"I'll text the shop," I say, pulling out my phone. "They'll send a truck to pick him up in the morning."

They'll fix Lenny. They've never let me down before. I'll pay them extra this time though, for dealing with the—

"Turd smell makes me want to hurl. Can we stand further away?" Mikey pleads, pulling me along the sidewalk. "Jesus, it smells like something died, and then they ate it, and then they shit it out on... Sorry," he mumbles, giving me a sympathetic look. "Your poor car."

"Yeah. Lenny doesn't deserve this." I chew on my lower lip as I survey the empty street again.

Mikey and I are the only two who walked this way after we left the club. His apartment isn't far from mine, so I said I'd give him a ride. I wish Zoey and the others hadn't already gone. It's only a disgusting prank, but the hairs on the back of my neck are still standing up at seeing Lenny like this.

"Maybe there's CCTV?" I say, glancing up at the buildings, but I don't see anything that looks like a camera. I blow out a defeated breath. "I'll call Sullivan to give us a lift."

The idea dies as soon as I've said it. Sullivan is at my father's place. We've been taking it in turns to stay with him and Halliday since they were both discharged from hospital with smoke inhalation. I can't ask him to leave them. What if one of them needs him?

I unlock my phone and bring my messages up, my thumb hovering over the keyboard. I could text Denver. It would be an awkward ride home with the silent hulk, but at least it's not standing beside Lenny in the middle of the night, seeing him in this condition.

The evening air makes me shiver, and Mikey wraps an arm around me, rubbing me to warm me up. "It's okay." He taps something on his phone. "I've got us a ride. You can stay at my place. I don't like the idea of you going home alone."

"Thanks, but I'll be fine. Besides, Monty's there, I won't be alone," I say, my heart lifting at the thought of a cuddle from my dog when I get home.

My eyes are drawn to a shimmer of white crystals lying in the dirty gutter, and I shiver again. "We'll be fine," I repeat.

2

SINCLAIR

"So we got juice, muffins, and milk. And that was a good call on the coffee beans. Dad hates running out."

Monty wags his tail as he looks at me with shiny, dark brown eyes. I crouch and rub his ear.

"You're such a handsome boy," I coo, earning myself a lick on the face. How anyone can not like the Chinese Crested breed baffles me. He's so cute with his sporadic patches of hair. And it means that he likes wearing the sweaters I get for him because they keep his hairless tummy clean and warm. Dad got him for me as a surprise the day after the funeral. Monty's been by my side ever since.

"And it's going to be your birthday soon. You need to give me some ideas on what flavor cake you'd like this year, okay? The doggy bakery you like gets busy, you know."

He stares at me, his tail wagging. I scoop him up under one arm, nuzzling the top of his head.

"Let's see how they are, then I'll take you to the park," I say as I juggle the bag I'm holding in my other hand and ring the bell of my father's penthouse.

He opens the door, the silver-flecked stubble on his jaw

catching the light. He smiles when he sees me. He's dressed for work in a shirt and suit pants, and Halliday is behind him in a sweater and yoga pants, her cheeks flushed.

"Oh good, you do both look better." I hand the bag of groceries to my father and walk straight inside, depositing Monty on the polished wood floor. He makes a beeline for Halliday, dancing around in front of her as she bends and fusses him.

She looks up from beneath her platinum blonde hair and catches my eye. I smile, my heart swelling. She's thirty, seven years older than me, and we've become friends. People have commented on the fact she's twenty years younger than my father and they're having a baby together. But I don't give a shit what people say, or what garbage the press like to spin. She gave my father something no one else could. Not me, Sullivan, his granddaughter, Molly, Uncle Mal, his friends. She gave him a reason to keep living. Not going through the motions of it each day like he was doing, but *really* live. She gave him love. And now she's giving our whole family a new baby to love.

"There are some bridal magazines in that bag too. I thought we could take a look?"

"Sure, that would be amazing. Come on through, we just ate, but did you want some breakfast?" Halliday offers.

"No, thanks. I won't stay long, just an hour," I reply as I walk through into the open kitchen and living area, Monty trotting behind me.

I head over to the large marble breakfast bar and sit on one of the stools. Halliday sits next to me as my father fixes me a coffee.

"I was thinking of white flowers for the wedding," I muse, reaching into the bag I brought that my father placed on the counter and pulling out a stack of magazines. "Maybe orchids? Or something delicate."

"Sounds good." Halliday smiles as I place a magazine on

the counter in front of her, opened to a double page spread about bouquets.

"I saw these and thought of you. These ones are made from pearls and things. But you can have one made from anything you like, even crystals."

Her voice lifts. "Crystals?"

"Yeah."

She bites her lower lip and looks back at the page, her face glowing. She covered my father's office with crystals the day she arrived, claiming they all have different properties for helping us. I knew she'd like the idea of an alternative bouquet.

"Of course, you need to make sure it isn't too heavy. Although I guess you'll be able to rest it on…" I survey her flat stomach. "I wonder how big your bump will be on the day."

"I don't know. I think I'll be showing. It's still going to be a few months until we get married," Halliday says.

Dad slides a mug of fresh coffee toward me. The bell chimes, and he mutters something about them being popular this morning as he heads off to answer it.

"I can't believe I get to have baby cuddles again. It feels so long since Molly was tiny enough to hold in one arm." I grin, clasping my hands in front of my face as I think of my niece. "You know I'm going to spoil you," I say to Halliday's stomach.

She laughs as the room fills with suits.

"You look much better. You must have had a good sleep last night," Uncle Mal says to Halliday as he walks over and stands beside the counter.

Sullivan heads straight for my coffee mug, lifting it up and taking a gulp. I huff at him.

"I need it more than you, Sis, believe me," he grunts.

I look at the two of them, then at the dark, looming hulk

in a suit, broader than any other man in the room, who is standing further away, near the back wall.

"We were talking about weddings before you all interrupted. What are you all doing here with faces like that?" My question is aimed at all three of them and their matching sour expressions, but my eyes remain fixed on just one of them.

"We need to talk about business," Denver says, his dark eyes boring into mine.

"Ugh. And it couldn't wait?"

I rub my temples as Sullivan drinks the rest of my coffee and places the empty mug down with a thud.

"It's regarding what we were talking about with Killian and Jenson," Denver tells Dad.

I lift my gaze, my interest piqued at the mention of the other two members of our family's security team. Whatever they're discussing must be important.

"Go on," my father says.

"He's in New York. Killian tracked him on a flight yesterday. We looked over the past two years. He hasn't been back here until now."

"I know some people who could make him disappear," Uncle Mal says, his eyes flicking toward me and Halliday before he seals his lips like he's regretting admitting such a thing in front of us. But this is my family. I'm not stupid. I know they'll go to any lengths to protect one another.

It's what Beauforts do. They stick together.

The men exchange looks and words as Halliday looks at me, puzzled.

"Who?" I interrupt them all. "Stop being so cryptic. They made an arrest over the club fire, so who the hell are you talking about?"

"Neil." My father sighs.

My stomach drops. It's a name I wish I'd never heard. One that created nothing but questions. We found all the evidence of their affair after Mom died. I'll never be able to ask her why she did it to Dad. Why her first love was more important to her than all of us. Why she would risk everything for a man who left her heartbroken when he left her decades ago.

"Why are you keeping tabs on the man Mom had an affair with?" I ask.

"He was there the day we lost them. He couldn't have started the fire but... I want you all to be extra alert."

My father's words blur as blood rushes in my ears. I thought it was all behind us. I prayed that we could finally move on if we could accept that it was a freak accident, and we will never know how that fire started that stole them both from us.

The past won't give up its hold over us.

"... trackers in your phones so I can see your location at all times." Denver's deep voice swims into focus.

"Like hell you will!" I snap.

Everyone's eyes turn to me.

"Sinclair, we're all going to be doing this. And for the time being, I'd prefer you call one of us if you need any rides at night. I don't want you out driving alone after dark," Dad says.

I look around for support but only Uncle Mal looks like he feels like shit as my privacy and freedom is revoked. Driving in Lenny is the only place, apart from my apartment, where I'm safe from prying eyes. Where I have some control over my life. The press is all over me everywhere I go. It comes with the territory of being a well-known model. I'm grateful for my career, but I wasn't even allowed to grieve in private.

I avoid everyone's eyes, sickness washing over me as I picture Lenny's white crystals strewn across the dirty sidewalk.

"Seriously? You damaged your car again?" Sullivan says.

I could slap my brother for having this uncanny knack for

knowing when I'm hiding something. And for usually being correct about what that something is.

"No! God, you always want to blame me." I zone out and flick through a magazine, trying to focus on a page of tulle gowns instead of the accusing tone my brother's words have taken on. "It wasn't my fault. I thought I'd parked in a safe spot," I mumble.

"What are you talking about?" Sullivan asks.

"It's not that much damage. The shop said they'll fix it."

Sullivan scowls, making irritation burst up my spine like tiny bubbles popping. If he'd seen Lenny like that, then he'd know I don't want to talk about it.

"It was vandalized, okay? Someone scraped it and wrote 'Beaufort Bitch' across the windscreen." I leave out telling him about the 'gift' they left me on the hood.

"Oh my god, are you okay?" Halliday asks.

"I'm fine, thanks. It's nothing."

"That's not nothing," Sullivan barks. "Jesus, why didn't you tell us?"

"Because you always overreact, like you are now," I snap.

"No one's ever done anything like that before, Sinclair," Mal adds. "We're just looking out for you."

Dad studies me as I fold my arms and wish I could turn invisible so my family can't psycho-analyze me. "It's not the first time, is it?"

I sigh. "They've never damaged my car before. Usually they just leave a note under the wiper."

"Fucking hell," Sullivan hisses, turning away.

"What kind of notes?" Mal asks.

I shrug. "Just ones saying I should watch my back. Or that I'm not as special as everyone thinks I am. Stuff like that."

I look around the room at the stunned faces. This is exactly why I haven't told anyone about the notes. They started recently and they're only pranks. I should have kept my mouth shut.

"I get nice ones too," I add, so they don't worry. "Someone left me a flower and told me I nailed the runway last week."

"Jesus Christ," Dad rasps.

"It's fine, Dad. It's—"

"It's not fine," he barks.

The air in the room grows thick and the side of my face heats where a pair of stormy green eyes are burning into it.

"Denver?" my father says. "From now until we work out who's been sending these threats and find out what Neil is doing here, you're with Sinclair."

"Yes, Boss."

"What? What does '*with me*' mean?" I shout, despite it being futile. Once my father makes a decision, that's it.

"It means he's your personal bodyguard as of now. You don't go anywhere without him."

I fly out of my seat. "No!"

"Yes."

"Dad, not him. Please, I'll take Killian or Jenson... but not him."

I plead with my eyes. But it's useless.

"Denver's the best we have," he says.

"It'll be like being babysat by a gorilla. He barely talks, just grunts. At least Killian's interesting, and Jenson's fun."

"You've got Denver."

"My life is over." I blow out a defeated breath. I'll have to find a way to ditch him. There's no way I want him going everywhere with me. No way in hell.

"Don't be so dramatic," Sullivan says.

I throw him the stink eye as I scoop Monty off the floor and kiss his head. "I'm so sorry. I know this means you're stuck with him too," I whisper.

"Monty too. No one will touch a single one of the few hairs he does have while you're both under my protection."

Determined green irises burn into mine as I lift my gaze.

"You'll protect him as much as you will me?"

The green flares like he doesn't appreciate his ability being put under question.

"Yes."

I narrow my eyes. I'm still going to ditch him. But knowing he's willing to look after Monty makes my dislike for him thaw half a degree.

"Fine."

He stares back, unfazed, as my father's voice rings out around the room with a finality in it that I feel all the way to my toes.

"I trust you with my life. Now I'm trusting you with my daughter."

3

DENVER

"Jesus, it's a fucking wreck."

I clench my jaw at Jenson's words. He's not wrong. The inside of Sterling's piano bar, Seasons, has been eviscerated beyond recognition. Where there was once a low stage with a baby grand piano, there's now a pile of charred remains, emitting a stench like that of a corpse.

"It's going to need work," I clip as I place my hands on my hips and survey the mound of what's left of the tables and velvet seating that the clean-up team have moved to one side of the shell of a room, ready to be removed. "That fucker."

"Hope he rots in jail," Killian says as he bends and lifts the remnants of a picture frame from the ash, the photograph inside melted to the glass.

The chain of piano clubs is the thing that my boss, Sterling, threw his energy into after his wife, Elaina, and their youngest son died. I know a man clinging on to something when I see one. One so lost in his grief that he needs a purpose to get out of bed every morning.

Seasons was Sterling's.

It became a place where people yearned for a membership,

to be welcomed into its inner circle where you weren't judged on anything other than the type of man, or woman, you were between its four walls. Now it's destroyed. Obliterated by a person with a grudge against Sterling and Halliday.

And I failed to stop it.

"Grayson Global is handling the re-model. Sterling will want to take the reins, no doubt. But we are still to take as much of the strain away from him over this as possible, understand?"

Jenson and Killian nod.

"Good. Our point of contact there is Imogen," I tell them.

"Not the British guy, Drew?" Killian asks, mentioning the guy who did the original design.

"No. He's about to become a father," I say.

"Is everyone knocking people up around here? At least we know ours will still swim when we're Sterling's age. Ouch!"

"Idiot," Killian snorts, whacking Jenson up the back of the head. "That's your boss you're talking about. The guy who paid for your grandmother's surgery and gave your baby-faced ass a job."

"Hey, I know." Jenson throws his hands up. "I didn't mean anything by it. He's a solid guy. I'm actually impressed, and a little in awe. He's fifty and getting laid more than me."

I step over the blackened floor, shards of smoke-stained glass crunching beneath my shoes, ignoring the two guys as they joke with one another. This place needs to be even better than it was before once it's finished. I'll make damn sure they do a stellar job rebuilding it.

I owe it to Sterling.

My phone rings in my jacket pocket and I pull it out.

"Hello."

"Mr. Layne? I'm returning your message about Miss Beaufort's car. I understand you're the one who will be collecting it once it's ready?"

"That's right."

My eyes track to Jenson and Killian who have stopped jerking around and are directing some of the workmen and women who have arrived to where they should start. Sterling placed Sinclair under my protection, which means I need to know when her car is fixed. Something tells me she'd be all too happy to pick it up and go out alone in it without telling me if she gets the chance.

"Well," the guy on the other end of the line sucks in a breath, "It's the crystals... Like I said to Miss Beaufort, the windscreen cleaned up nice, and the shit, well, shit don't stick, does it?" He chuckles. "But those crystals have to be ordered in from Switzerland. I told her it'd take a while."

I stop walking. "Did you say *shit*?"

"Wouldn't be the first time we've known someone to take a dump on a car. Assholes." He sighs. "Like I said, it'll take a while until it's done. I'll call you."

I grind the heel of my shoe into a piece of glass, relishing the way it pops, then splinters beneath my weight.

"Take your time, she won't be needing it."

I end the call and curl my hand around my phone in a fist. If Sinclair thinks she can leave out details like the fact that some fucker with a death wish took a shit on her car without me finding out, then she's got a shock coming. Sterling entrusted her safety to me. And I never break my word. Sinclair Beaufort, no matter how difficult she tries to be, is stuck with me until we work out if she's in any danger, and until we figure out why the hell this Neil guy is back in New York.

Exhaling a tense breath, I open up the tracking app on my phone. Her phone location is showing her in her Park Avenue apartment where she said she'd be. I make another selection and a small blue dot pops up on the screen.

"That's a good girl," I rasp, as the tracker I snuck inside

Monty's collar shows him as being in her apartment too. She hardly goes anywhere without that dog. If he's at her place, then chances are that she listened to her father when he told her she can't go anywhere without me.

"We're heading out to get these guys some coffee," Killian calls, gesturing to the workmen and women as I turn. "You want one?"

I shake my head. "Not this time. I need to be somewhere."

Sinclair rolls her eyes as she opens her apartment door.

"I told you I'd call you when I need you to scare the murderers that are poised, waiting to pounce on me the second I step foot outside."

She huffs when I don't react.

"It's Manhattan. And this is the Upper East Side, not The Bronx. You don't need to be with me every time I leave my apartment. I can take a walk in the neighborhood with Monty and be fine."

"Your father put me in charge of—"

"Ruining my social life, destroying my image, and sucking any fun I might have a hope of experiencing, from me? Yes, I'm aware." She folds her arms and leans against the doorframe. "You're here to check up on me, aren't you?"

I clock the gym bag by her feet, and she kicks it to one side.

"Going somewhere?"

"No."

"Sure about that?"

She tips her head to one side. Her blonde ponytail flows over one shoulder as she narrows her eyes at me. She's dressed in white workout tights and a matching cropped vest, sneakers on.

"You have a workout scheduled with your personal trainer, Brad Garrett-Charles," I say.

She snorts. "Why are you using his full name? And how do you—?"

I hold my phone up, showing her the imported calendar her agent sent me, so I'd know all of the places Sinclair needs to be over the next couple of months.

"Oh, that bitch! I got her diamond earrings for her birthday. Our new collection that isn't released yet. She isn't getting them now." She huffs.

She chews on her lower lip, her gaze skirting back to me and over my black suit in disapproval.

"Monty sits upfront with me. He can get sick in the back," she says, pursing her lips.

"That's fine," I reply.

She mutters something under her breath as she retrieves the bag she kicked away. I hold my hand out for it, and she arches a brow, pausing for a moment before depositing the handle into my palm.

"Monty!" she calls, clicking her fingers.

He appears next to her. The white patches of hair on his small gray body shake as he wags his tail.

"We're going to see Brad. I packed you a chew toy that you like. I'm sorry about the…" Her eyes flick to me "… company."

Monty scampers over to me, tail wagging, and licks my hand as I bend to pet him. Sinclair looks at the two of us, then steps out into the hallway, pulling the door closed.

"My session with Brad is for an hour. You can wait in the car."

She lifts Monty into her arms and strides off ahead of me, talking to him as she goes.

We pull up outside the studio and Sinclair reaches for the door handle on the passenger side the moment the vehicle stops.

I lean over her seat, enveloping her hand as I pull the door closed again with a firm thud.

"What are you doing? I'll be late."

My face is level with hers as I meet her annoyed glare.

"When you're with me, I do that."

"Do what?"

"Stay there." I fix her with a look that makes her frown.

I exit the car and round the hood, making quick work of getting to her door before she can try to open it again herself and really piss me off.

She stares at my offered hand for a beat before taking it and climbing out of the car with Monty cradled in one arm. She blinks at me, the top of her head level with my eyes. She's five foot eleven, and I still tower over her.

"I can get my own door, you know."

"You can. But when you're with me, you won't."

Her lips purse like she's trying to think of a snarky comeback.

"Can I go inside now?" She arches a brow.

I fetch her gym bag from the trunk. "We can now."

She holds her hand out to take the bag from me, but I keep it held firmly by my side.

"Seriously? You're coming in?"

"I gave your father my word I would take care of you."

She stares at me, then snorts. "It gets better."

I wait for the argument, but she turns and walks toward the entrance, and I follow.

The walls in the entryway have large, framed posters of a

guy with blond hair who I recognize from the background checks I did when she started training with him.

"Why don't you take a picture so you can stare at him more later?" Sinclair smirks as she opens another door.

A state-of-the-art fitness studio is set up inside, with wall-to-wall mirrors. No more posters, thank fuck.

"Hey, Sin."

The blond guy sweeps her up into a hug and my fist tightens around the handle of her gym bag. I take a seat on a bench against the wall and place her bag next to me, my eyes fixed on the two of them. Sinclair deposits Monty next to me, then rummages in her bag, handing him a treat and taking out her water bottle and towel.

"Won't be long, baby," she coos.

She rubs Monty behind his ear, her eyes flicking to me for a brief second before she spins and heads over to where Brad Garrett-Charles is waiting for her.

I used his full name when I spoke to Sinclair because it's what he uses on his fitness blog where he posts pictures of himself flexing his muscles, much like the ones in the entryway.

And because it makes him sound like a douchebag.

"What's with him?" Brad asks Sinclair in a low voice the moment she reaches him. "You bringing your boyfriends to my studio now?" He nudges her playfully in her side, and she giggles.

He means the studio his fashion designer mother pays for. Brad acts like he's *it* because he has a few celebrity clients that Mommy sent his way using her connections. I know guys like Brad. It's my job to know who he is and what makes him tick. The background checks we run on anyone coming into the Beauforts' lives only tell us so much. I learn everything else by my own observations.

"Ugh, that's my father's head of security. He's just with

me while my car gets fixed," Sinclair answers, not attempting to keep her voice down like Brad.

He looks over at me and jerks his chin in greeting, pulling his shoulders to puff his chest out.

I stare back, leaning forward and bringing my hands together to crack my knuckles. His brow creases before he looks away, returning his attention to Sinclair as he takes her through a warmup.

She doesn't look my way again for an hour. A whole hour of Brad putting his hands on her hips as he 'helps' correct her already perfect form as she squats. A whole hour of him walking around her in a circle, complimenting her technique as he has her doing burpees, his eyes sliding to her ass more than once. Followed by a longer than necessary warm down where he helps her stretch by pressing her thighs against her chest one at a time and bracing himself above her, using his bodyweight to push them down.

Monty straightens next to me with a low growl as he watches.

"I hear you, Boy," I murmur.

"Oh wow, that was great!" Sinclair gushes as she stands and towels her face once they're done.

"You're doing well with your strength, Sin." Brad grins, all teeth and no shame as he reaches out and runs a hand over her upper arm, his thumb inches from the curve of her breast. "Your triceps have got some killer definition. I think we need to work on your flexibility more though."

"More stretches?" she asks, eyes wide like she's hanging off his every word.

He nods, his eyes flicking down her body. "Yeah. More stretching you out together. But next time, okay? I have Kendall coming in next."

"Kendall Jenner?" Sinclair gasps.

He taps his nose with a wink. "You know I can't tell you that."

Sinclair's glowing as she walks over to her bag on the bench next to me and bends to fuss Monty.

"Brad's great," she says.

"Monty doesn't think so."

She stands with one hand on her hip, looking at me. "You know what your problem is?"

I hold her gaze, waiting for her to enlighten me.

"You don't have anything nice to say about anyone. Is that why you're so quiet? Can't say anything nice, don't say anything at all?"

"Sound piece of advice. Who gave you it?"

"No one," she snaps.

I nod. "No one gave you that advice. Uh-huh."

Her face falls. "Are you... Are you implying that *I* say mean stuff? You think I'm a Beaufort Bitch like the person who wrote on my car, don't you?"

"I didn't say that."

"You didn't have to. It's written all over your face. I'm sorry you're stuck with me, like I'm stuck with you." She sniffs, reaching for her bag.

"I told you, when you're with me, I carry that," I say, lifting it from the bench as I stand.

"Are you going to try to do everything for me?" she snaps.

"If I deem it appropriate."

She stalls as she reaches for Monty, her gaze flicking over me. Then she lifts him into her arms and sinks her face into his hair as she cuddles him.

I follow her out of the studio as she calls goodbye to Brad. He slinks away into a back room after I spot him eyeing her ass again, and he notices me glaring at him.

Sinclair grabs the door handle as we reach my car.

I move behind her, placing my hand over hers.

"I told you, when you're with me—"

"Your job, I get it." She inclines her face, and her eyes meet mine over her shoulder. Hers are full of fire. "I'll just keep quiet like a good little helpless client needing protection."

Our faces are inches apart as she slides her fingers out from beneath mine, the warmth of her body seeping through the fabric of my shirt as I lean closer to open the door.

"I don't think you're helpless, Sinclair. But until the threat against you is neutralized—"

"You promised my father you'd take care of me; I get it." She sighs as she slides into the seat. "Everyone always wants to manage me. No one believes I can do things myself."

"You think I want to manage you?"

She shakes her head with a humorless laugh. "Come on. I know you work for my father, but I see you with him and Sullivan. You're all buddies. They've always tried to wrap me up in cotton wool."

"They love you and want you to be safe."

She sighs, stroking Monty absentmindedly. "I love them too. But it's suffocating. At least when…"

Her face closes off. I can guess what she was about to say. 'At least when her brother was alive, she had an ally.' He was a daredevil, a free spirit like Sinclair. The two of them always had each other's backs. I admired that about him. How he knew how to love and protect her without dimming her personality. She hasn't been the same since he died. She's always had a smart mouth. But her eyes used to light up when she doled out the sass.

Not anymore.

I lean inside the car and hand her the seatbelt. Monty being on her lap prevents me from doing it myself like I'd prefer.

Her face is pinched as she takes it from me.

I clear my throat. "We're going to be spending a lot of time together. You can call me Den if you like."

"I've never heard anyone call you Den before."

"No one does."

"Then why would I?"

"I thought it might make you feel more comfortable."

She studies me with narrowed eyes. "Do you want to call me Sin? My friends do."

"Do you want me to?"

She smiles sweetly. "Nope."

She reaches for the door handle and slams the door closed, then looks at me through the glass, triumphant like she's won a game I didn't know we were playing.

I take a slow breath in and let it out through my nose slowly. Jenson would have traded places with me, given the chance. He's always gotten along with Sinclair the best out of the three of us. She likes his jokes.

But Sterling insisted.

"Denver's the best we have."

He knows everything about me.

And somehow he still trusts me with his daughter.

I can't let him down.

Sinclair ignores me as I sink into the driver's seat, but she stiffens as I reach toward her.

"I already did it." She lifts her eyes from her phone as I check her belt is fastened correctly and there are no twists in it.

Monty licks the side of my face, and the scent of meaty dog breath coats my cheek.

Sinclair snorts. "Monty," she scolds, quickly placing her thumb to my face.

She wipes the damp patch away before her eyes meet mine.

Her pupils dilate and she pulls her hand away as though she didn't realize she was touching me. For a couple of seconds, she just stares at me. Then she snaps her eyes forward to the street.

"Can we go now?"

4

SINCLAIR

It's been two days of Denver being my 'personal bodyguard', and we're on our way back from another workout session with Brad. Denver spent this one staring at us across the room again, taking up the entire bench like a menacing shadow. I'm glad I left Monty with Molly and Sullivan today, otherwise Denver might have tried telling me the same crap about Monty not liking Brad. Like I'd believe he knows Monty's opinion better than I do.

I sneak a sideways glance at him as he drives, one hand on the steering wheel, one resting casually on his thigh. He takes a corner, circling the wheel beneath his palm easily, his fingers relaxed.

"You don't drive like I thought you would," I muse as he lets the wheel pass easily beneath his hand until it slides back into position.

"How did you think I would drive?"

His eyes remain on the road ahead, his square jaw and dark chestnut-colored hair, cut close to his collar, creating a striking profile.

"Like a control freak, I guess." I shrug, turning to look out of the window.

"I can assure you, I'm in control. But if it makes you feel more comfortable…"

I look back at him. He's placed both hands on the steering wheel, his fingers curled around it with a firm grip.

"Being babysat will never mean I feel *comfortable*," I huff. "Thanks anyway."

His jaw ticks and he returns one hand to his thigh, but his grip remains tight with the one that remains on the wheel.

I reach up and toy with my diamond necklace, sliding the pendant back and forth along the chain. My workout with Brad first thing this morning was just what I needed. I always have more energy after. And today I have a runway show for a lingerie brand I've worked with before that I need to be on top form for. Their shows usually have a great atmosphere, and I'll be able to catch up with some models I haven't seen for a while. But they are exhausting. A workout will help, and so would—

"Pull over!" I screech.

Denver swerves across a lane and slams to a halt next to the sidewalk. His hand flies beneath his jacket to his hip.

"What did you see?" His nostrils expand and he sucks in a breath. "Sinclair," he growls, his eyes narrowing to slits as he surveys the sidewalk filled with New Yorkers on their way to work.

A muscle in his jaw ticks as he continues his assessment, then turns to me.

I point out of my window at the small truck set up on the sidewalk, silenced by the sudden burst of testosterone filling the car like a storm cloud. He leans over me, his dark, thick eyelashes fanning over his green eyes as he reads the sign on the truck. He lets out a sharp breath of air and warm mint fills the small gap between my face and his.

"You yelled like there was an immediate threat because you saw a juice truck?"

"It's my favorite one. And it's smoothies, not juice."

His brows lower and he runs his tongue over the edge of his teeth like he needs a moment to compose himself. I suddenly understand how Jenson and Killian know when to quit messing around and be serious.

Because Denver must look like he does now.

The back of my neck grows hot as his huge body continues to crowd the space around me, pinning me to my seat.

"Tell me what flavor you want. And wait here."

He exits the car swiftly and walks around to my door.

I roll down my window. "I need to know what the specials are."

He nods, his jaw rigid. "Close it up, lock the doors."

Shaking my head, I do as he says, closing my window and pressing the button that locks all of the doors. It's only when I'm done that he turns and walks across the sidewalk and stops to face the truck. His eyes flick from me and back to the menu board he's reading every couple of seconds as he checks on me.

"This is ridiculous," I mutter.

I throw open my door, jump out and march toward him.

He's on me before I even make it halfway.

"Sinclair!"

It's a deep, gruff warning. One that does something funny to my stomach as it's coupled with a large solid arm wrapping around my torso like a shield.

"Why can't you do as you're told?"

The vibrations from his voice hit my ear along with the same warm, minty breath. A thrill skates up my spine.

My father never said I had to behave for Denver. Perhaps if my family insists on treating me like a child, I should act like one. Winding up Denver is the closest I'm going to get to having any fun until they drop the whole 'personal bodyguard' nonsense.

"I wanted to watch them make it." I pout.

Denver looks at me, a muscle in his cheek clenching before he glances up and down the street. "Fine. But you stay by my side."

"Thank you." I bop the end of his nose with my fingertip. "You know you're almost cute when you're angry. Almost..."

His nostrils flare, and I swear he's grinding his teeth to powder.

True to his word, he stays a couple of inches behind me, and I can feel the heat emanating from his pissed off face as I take my time pretending to choose.

"Are the berries organic today?" I ask the guy behind the truck's counter.

"Sure are. Great for the complexion, not that you need it, Sinclair." He grins, and I giggle.

"Scott, you're such a flirt," I scold gently, loving the grunt that comes from behind me.

I take longer pondering the menu when really I know all of the regular smoothie combinations they offer. I stop here at least twice a week.

"What are the specials today?" I ask.

Scott leans over the counter, his blond floppy hair falling into his eyes. "I was just about to write them on the board. You want to help me name them?"

"Ooh! I do." I look over my shoulder at Denver, raising my brows like he should join in on my excitement.

He stares back at me, his face a mask of indifference.

I turn back to Scott as he reels off a list of berries and coconut milk and points to a baby pink mixture in one of the blenders.

"It matches my outfit." I smile, doing a mini wiggle in my workout gear. "You think we should call it Sinclair?" I turn to

Denver. "What's the first word you think of when you look at me?"

He presses his lips together, his eyes roaming up and down the street as he studies each person walking by.

"I'll help you," I offer. "Stubborn client, needs babysitting, helpless, treated like a child, difficult, spoiled—"

"Princess."

"Sorry?"

His eyes meet mine and he breathes out the single word again, only the way he says it sounds less like the insult I suspect it's supposed to be.

"Princess."

I turn back to Scott. "One spoiled Princess for me, please." I point at a creamy colored smoothie in another blender. "What's that?"

"This," Scott says proudly, "is a powerhouse. A blend of peanut, pea protein, cacao—"

"Ooh! Let's call that one... 'Brute'. My chatty companion will have one of those." I throw Denver a wink over my shoulder.

I wait for him to make our smoothies and then tip him generously, blocking Denver's attempt to pay.

We walk back to the car, and I peel the tiny cartoon fruit sticker that Scott gave me off its backing paper.

"Not only do they make the best smoothies for miles, but they also have stickers. Molly loves them." I press the smiling strawberry onto Denver's shirt with the caption, *'I've been searching for berried treasure.'*

"Suits you, Brute."

I pat it to make it stick and my fingertips connect with solid heat.

I frown.

"Problem?" Denver clips.

I look up into his darkened gaze.

"I always thought... don't you wear a vest under your shirt?"

"I'm not one for layers."

"That's your actual body?" My eyes roam the rest of his broad torso beneath his suit. I never thought anyone was built that huge.

I pat his pec again and am met with the same warm expanse of muscle.

"I meant like a bulletproof vest, something padded. That's... Wow."

"A bulletproof vest? This is the Upper East Side, Princess, not the Bronx."

My lips twitch as I look into his eyes. But his own give nothing away. He holds my gaze as he opens the car door for me, and I slip into the seat.

He leans in and fastens my belt for me before I can do it myself. The same way he did when he collected me this morning, and when we left Brad's studio. The first time I unclicked it just to see what he'd do. And he calmly refastened it. The second time he gave me a look as my hand reached for the release button, so I stopped.

And now...

Now I'm glued to my seat, dumbfounded.

"You made a joke," I say, taking his smoothie from his hand and placing it into the cup holder for him.

"Did I?"

"You did."

He shakes his head. "You didn't laugh, so it can't have been."

My lips twist into a smile, but his face is so stern I can't tell if he's actually serious, or if he's teasing me.

He hovers in the small space a moment, probably waiting to see if I will unfasten my belt.

"Good," he rasps as I sip my straw instead of reaching for it.

He closes my door and rounds the hood, a vision in black suit, white shirt, and black tie. He scans the street ruthlessly as he walks, checking for danger.

"So paranoid," I mutter before he climbs into the driver's side.

He checks his watch as he starts the engine.

"You need to be at Spring Studios by ten, and we still need to go back to your apartment first. We're behind schedule."

Then he pulls out into the traffic and doesn't speak to me again for the rest of the drive.

5

DENVER

Sinclair's apartment is decorated in pinks, golds, and creams. It's delicate and feminine, and Monty has a dog bed shaped like a throne in the living area. It has Sinclair's personality stamped all over it. I've been inside it before, but never for long. That's going to change now that I'm assigned to be with her every time she steps outside her front door.

I stand inside the open living space, mentally checking off all of the electronic devices. There aren't any I haven't already checked for bugs, so that's one good piece of news.

The sound of the shower running echoes up the hallway as I pull out my phone and text Killian.

Me: SitRep.

Killian: Neil's checked himself into the Lanceford. Doesn't appear to be doing much at the moment except meeting up with one old buddy we already have a file on. Some guy he worked with years ago. Nothing that raises concerns.

Me: Good. Keep watching him.

> Killian: Will do, Boss.

I pocket my phone. A situational report with nothing of concern should ease the tension in my shoulders, but it doesn't. Until we know why Elaina's ex-lover is in New York and rule him out as the person who has been targeting Sinclair, we can't afford to let our guard down. It only takes one second for someone to make a move. And if you don't see it coming, the consequences can be devastating.

A door down the hallway opens and Sinclair walks into the room dressed in white sweatpants and a hoodie, a pair of sunglasses on top of her head. She's carrying a large bag and drops it onto the floor.

"You could have sat down, you know? Or helped yourself to a snack or something. We'll be at the show for hours."

She rests a hand on a table as she pulls on a pair of sneakers.

"I'm good," I reply, waiting until she's finished before I pick her bag up.

"Suit yourself, but don't say I didn't warn you when you're starving later."

♦

I follow Sinclair inside the venue of the runway show. There's a security search area set up where bags are being checked and some people are getting patted down.

"It's worse on the way out," she whispers. "The designer had some pieces stolen and copied. Now he insists anyone with backstage access goes through this. But he's a genius and his pieces are to die for, so we all put up with it."

She steps forward and opens her bag, letting the security guy check inside. He nods and then beckons me forward.

"He's with me," Sinclair says. "He's my bodyguard."

The security guy studies me. "You carrying?"

"One," I reply.

He jerks his chin, and I unbutton my jacket, pulling it aside so he can see the gun in a holster at my hip.

"You'll need to check it into a locker."

"Not going to happen," I reply calmly.

Sinclair's eyes dart between the two of us, then back to the gun. "Den—"

"She doesn't come in without me. I don't come in without this."

I hold the security guy's eyes. Sinclair's the most well-known model they have in the show today. There's no way he'll want to tell his boss that he's the reason she doesn't turn up.

"Go. Just keep it covered, yeah?"

I nod at him and place my hand on Sinclair's lower back, steering her inside.

"You have a gun?" she hisses as we follow signs directing us to where the models are needed.

"Yes."

Her eyes widen. I thought she would have known I carry one. Sullivan and Sterling are aware.

"You can trust me," I tell her, not liking the way she's chewing her lip like she's anxious.

"You drive with your hand near it."

It's not a question, so I don't respond.

"Denver?" she presses.

"It's my job to protect you. I need to be able to do that without hesitation."

"Oh my god," she breathes. "You sound like Sullivan and my father."

She doesn't mean it as a compliment.

"I carry a gun, Sinclair. But you don't need to be concerned about it, okay?"

She shakes her head with a small scoff. "Yeah, whatever you say."

We head backstage, and I find a seat out of the way where I have a direct line of sight to Sinclair. She's sitting, having her hair and makeup done. Once finished, she walks over to her bag to change, removing the necklace she always wears. As she tucks the necklace inside and zips up her bag, another model with long brunette hair approaches and starts chatting with her.

I've been sitting for two hours when everything starts moving faster, and more people cram into the area as it gets closer to the show's start time. Sinclair's changed into a white corset and panties set with stocking and suspender belt and a makeup woman is dusting powder over her cleavage.

A male model wearing a pair of the designer's male underwear briefs and nothing else comes up behind Sinclair and hugs her from behind.

"Mikey!" she shrills with a giggle as she turns and kisses him on both cheeks.

Mikey, twenty-eight, from Wisconsin, dreamed of being a model since he was twelve, new face of the latest Michael Kors campaign, Sinclair's friend of four years and three months. A guy I've given rides home to at Sinclair's request, and he's looked like he's about to barf each time he's seen me.

I do my research.

"You look amazing," he gushes.

"So do you. Oh my god! Have you stuffed those?" She bursts into laughter at the bulge in his pants.

"Want to touch it and find out?" He wiggles his brows.

The weight of my gun presses into my hip as I fight the urge to go over there.

"No!" she shrieks with another laugh.

"Why don't you go on a date with me after the show and find out instead?" Mikey grins.

I lean forward and crack my knuckles.

Sinclair shakes her head. "You're terrible."

"You love me," he sings as he walks away, throwing a similar offer out to the next model who says hello to him.

A woman approaches Sinclair and hands her a foil-wrapped bundle and she thanks them before walking over to me.

"Here." She holds the bundle out to me. "It's not going to kill you," she says when I don't move.

I take it from her and peel back the foil.

"Sullivan told me you liked turkey on wholewheat, so..."

"Thank you." I hold the sandwich in one hand as I look at her.

Someone calls her, signaling she's about to go on and she turns and walks away.

"When did he tell you that?" I call after her.

She glances at me over her shoulder with a hint of a smile. "When I asked him."

People crowd her, fussing over her as they prepare her to walk the runway. I peel back the foil and take a large bite of the sandwich, my stomach growling in appreciation.

It's the best fucking sandwich I've ever tasted.

◆

"Hey, you're with Sinclair, right?"

"That's right," I answer the model with long brunette hair.

I look away from her, my eyes moving back to find Sinclair

on the runway. I've moved to a position where I can see her from backstage. She's glowing beneath the bright runway lights as she walks it, a true professional. You wouldn't suspect she has the need for a full-time bodyguard due to threats against her. She doesn't look worried. Probably because she isn't. She should take it seriously, but even if she won't, I will. Anyone wanting to get to her will have to come through me first.

"She's amazing, isn't she?" the other model says.

I nod, still watching Sinclair.

I've been here for six hours while model after model in lingerie strut past for the show. None have that inexplicable something special about them that makes them shine the way Sinclair does.

The designer was backstage earlier, a guy in his thirties, buzzing with energy as he tutted and huffed, smoothing lace, and tweaking silk. He took one look at Sinclair and grinned without fixing a thing.

Camera lights flash faster than they have for any other model as Sinclair reaches the far end of the runway and does a slow twirl.

Jenson would give his right nut to be here watching all this. But it just puts me on edge. There are so many people around her all the time. Talking to her. Touching her. Obstacles in the way should I need to get to her quickly.

"I'm Theodora."

The brunette holds out her hand as I glance her way. I take it, shaking politely. "Denver."

"I know." She gives me a coy smile. "You usually work with Sin's father. I've seen you with him."

I just nod.

"How are you finding being here?" She looks around the busy space. The show is almost over. Sinclair is modeling the final outfit, and the designer is now out, joining her on the runway, receiving huge applause.

"It's fine."

"Fine," she repeats. "You must be bored waiting around for Sin for so long."

Sinclair and the designer are walking back up the runway toward backstage. I turn toward Theodora to position myself to see the entry point where Sinclair will reappear backstage, just over the top of her head.

"It's my job."

"Do you clock off after the show ends?" She brushes her hair over her shoulder, exposing a sheer lace bra beneath. Her dark nipple is visible through it, and her smile widens when I notice.

"No. He's mine tonight. And tomorrow. And the next day," a familiar voice says.

Theodora spins as Sinclair walks over, dressed in a nude lace bustier and matching G-string.

"Sin," Theodora says with a giggle, "you said you couldn't wait to get rid of him. I thought I could help you out."

Sinclair's eyes meet mine briefly and I hold out a bottle of water to her. She takes it, her fingers brushing mine.

"Sorry, Theo. He's with me all the time, he doesn't have time to date." She smiles sweetly, the same way she did when she asked me if I'd like to call her Sin like her friends do.

"Not forever though, right? See you around, Denver." Theodora throws me a flirty wink before she turns and walks off.

"Can we go?" Sinclair asks, putting her hand over her mouth to stifle a yawn.

"Sure."

She changes into her sweatpants and hoodie, and we walk out together, back through security. We're back in my car before she speaks again.

"Theodora's right. You can't date while you're my bodyguard. Hardly seems fair, does it? I mean, I can date if I want to."

"Goes with the job," I reply.

I reach out to start the engine, feeling her gaze on the side of my face.

"Denver?"

I pause with my hand on the ignition.

"Does it bother you?" she asks.

"No."

I switch the engine on.

Sinclair reaches over and turns it off.

I turn to her with a gruff exhale. "I don't need to date."

"Don't need to, or don't want to?" She studies me and I fight the urge to tell her that she won't like what she sees if she looks too deep.

"Both."

"So you won't date while you're with me?"

"No."

She purses her lips, glancing away and then back at me. "What else won't you do?"

"What *else*?"

She tilts her head, pulling her lower lip into her mouth. "Like, I dunno, maybe if you won't date while we're stuck together, then maybe that means you won't flirt with other women, either? And you won't carry anyone else's bags, or open doors for them? You know, that kind of thing."

She averts her eyes from mine as I study her.

"You want me to only do those things for you?"

She scoffs. "Not the flirting, my god, don't get the wrong idea."

"Noted. But the rest? You want me to—"

"Only do those things for me," she says, her eyes flicking to my face and away again just as fast.

"Anything else?"

She shakes her head. "That's all for now, I guess—"

"Done," I answer without hesitation, then start the engine again.

6

SINCLAIR

"An entire gallery of pictures and I don't need any guesses to know which work of art you're staring at."

"Huh?" I snap my eyes to where Zoey has appeared beside me.

We're at an art gallery for Ashton's latest showing. He draws portraits of both famous people and ones from his imagination. And Zoey. It's how they met. She became his muse before he even saw her face. It's such a romantic story that I love to hear her tell every time we have a few drinks.

The gallery is packed with men in tuxedos and women dripping in jewelry, wearing their best gowns. Ashton's paintings sell for hundreds of thousands. Except the ones of Zoey. He'll show some of them but refuses to sell a single one.

Zoey's eyes twinkle as she tilts her head across the busy space.

"Seriously?" I snort, my eyes settling on Denver standing against a far wall, his eyes scanning the space in the over-the-top suspicious way that he does. He's wearing a tuxedo tonight, instead of his usual black suit. The bow tie sits snuggly against his collar, hugging his broad neck.

"How long have we been friends?" Zoey asks.

"Forever," I reply.

"Forever." She hums. "Exactly. So I know when you're enjoying having a guy at your beck and call, following you around all day. It's okay, you can admit it."

Her smile is teasing as I turn to her.

"It's Denver. I'd rather have a PAP smear every waking hour of my life than have him with me every day."

Zoey arches her brows, and I sigh in frustration. "He's just... there. All the time." My eyes flick back over to where he's watching me. His dark brows lower over his eyes as we stare at one another.

"I can see that."

I break Denver's eye contact and note the smirk on Zoey's face.

"I don't like having him follow me around. I told you already."

"Prove it. Go over there and spend some time with him. If you try and get along with him, maybe he'll feel less like an intense bodyguard and more like a—"

"If you say boyfriend, I might scream."

"I was going to say friend, but..." Zoey shrugs, her eyes sparkling.

I narrow my eyes at her.

"Come on." She laughs. "He must be bored as hell standing by himself all night."

"He's used to it." I sniff, my gaze traveling back to him. "Ah ha! See!" I nudge Zoey. "He isn't alone. Someone's talking to him."

Zoey follows my gaze to where a woman in a black dress with a plunging neckline has commanded Denver's attention. Someone walks past them, making her lose her balance. She wobbles and reaches out, placing her palm over Denver's chest to steady herself.

"Oh, yeah," Zoey says, watching as Denver helps her gain her balance, then smoothly removes her hand from his chest. "What's his story, anyway?"

"He left the SEALs before he came to work for my father. Said he wanted to stay near New York because he has family nearby, but he never takes a day off, so I don't know when he sees them."

The woman he's with tilts her head back, laughing. She's totally faking it and flirting with him. Denver isn't funny and he doesn't make jokes.

"This is the Upper East Side, Princess, not the Bronx."

Okay, maybe he does. But they're rarer than a solar eclipse.

"I caught him on his phone earlier when he was waiting for me to get ready. He was *smiling.* Weird, right? He never smiles at anything," I whisper, leaning closer to Zoey.

She mirrors my posture, whispering, "You sure notice a lot of things about the bodyguard you claim not to like."

"Do not." I pout.

"You've told me he has no personality at least ten times in the past."

I shrug. "I'm just making the best of a bad situation. If we're stuck together then it'd be nice to know something about him. He's worked for Dad for over six years and the most personal thing I know is his last name."

"And that he likes red velvet cake."

"What?" I frown.

"The birthday cake you got for him years ago?"

I almost choke on my laugh. "Please. He got that cake because I wanted one to celebrate my first shoot as the face of the family business. Dad insisted I be eighteen before I worked for Beaufort Diamonds. It looked less self-indulgent if I wrote Denver's name on it and claimed it was for him. The fact he was working with us on his birthday, and it was the same day as the photoshoot was a stroke of divine intervention."

"Uh-huh." Zoey smiles.

I fold my arms. "That's all it was. Don't mistake my craving for cake as any kind of fondness for Denver." His name is drawn out from my lips as the woman tucks a piece of folded paper into his jacket pocket and pats it.

"You know what? I could do with a drink. Denver can get me one. It'll make him feel useful."

"You'll walk past the bar to get to him," Zoey points out.

I wave her comment away as I head across the room, making a beeline for Denver as the woman finally wanders away.

"Who was that?" I snap.

"She said her name was Tiffany," he answers, his green gaze boring into mine as I stop directly in front of him and tilt my chin up to meet his eyes.

I wrinkle my nose as a new name for her springs to mind. *Trampy Tiffany.*

"What did she want?"

"Someone to accompany her to the ballet."

"You're not a hired escort service, did you tell her that?" I splutter. "You're my bodyguard. God, the nerve of some people." I cast my eyes in the direction she wandered off in, staring daggers at her back as I spot her in the crowd.

"She wasn't suggesting she pay me."

I snap my eyes back to Denver's face. "She wanted a date?"

His lips thin, and he delivers a firm nod.

"But you don't date. We agreed."

"We did," he replies, his eyes never leaving my face. "I won't date while I'm assigned to you. You're my priority."

"Obviously," I huff, looking around the full room as the back of my neck grows hot.

Trampy Tiffany keeps glancing our way, trying to catch Denver's eye.

"I won't date while I'm assigned to you." There's no way of

knowing how long that could be. I pray as short as possible but... Trampy Tiffany is smiling now, eye-fucking Denver like he's a piece of prime man-meat.

"I need to make a note of something! Quick!"

Denver pulls out his phone, but I place my hand over his and push it away.

"Not that. A piece of paper or something. I need to actually write it." I roll my hand in a circle, urging him to hurry. "Today would be super helpful."

He slips two long fingers into the breast pocket of his dinner jacket and hands me the folded piece of paper.

"Thank you!" I snatch it off him before he can react and catch the attention of a passing waiter who's collecting empty champagne flutes on a tray.

"Excuse me. Do you have a pen, please?"

"Sorry, Ma'am." He gives me an apologetic smile.

I shrug, returning his smile with a bright one. "Never mind." I drop the piece of paper into one of the half-drunk glasses. It soaks up the golden liquid, swelling inside the bottom of the glass. "Oops."

Denver's eyes are dark when I turn back to him.

"I forgot what it was I needed to write," I say breezily. "Oh, that wasn't important, was it?"

I turn as though I'm about to follow the waiter to get the paper back. A strong hand wraps around my upper arm to stop me, sending the shiver of a memory shooting up my spine.

"You okay?" Green irises flecked with gold. My eyes full of tears. Everyone wearing black. "Are you okay?"

"It wasn't important." His deep voice cuts through my thoughts.

"Good." I glance at his face; his expression is unchanged, giving nothing away. I exhale as his fingers uncurl from my arm. "What do you need to do to get a drink around here?" I ask with a small, forced laugh.

"You're thirsty?"

"A little," I reply. My throat is growing scratchier by the second as more buried memories threaten to surface.

Denver moves fast, his hand finding my lower back through my nude silk dress. He steers us smoothly through the sea of people. They part for him, the men subtly looking at his muscular frame filling out his tux, the women less subtly checking out every inch of him, smiling up at him like freaky baby dolls with long batting eyelashes.

Zoey catches my eye from across the room where she's standing wrapped around Ashton's side as they talk to a group of people who are admiring one of his paintings hanging on the wall. She gives me a wide grin, and I shake my head at her.

"What would you like?" Denver asks as we reach the bar.

The bartender comes immediately when Denver tips his chin at him.

"Champagne, please."

"Certainly," the bartender replies before he walks to the other end of the bar and takes a pre-poured flute from a large display of meticulously stacked glasses.

He returns and offers the glass to me.

"She'll take one from a fresh bottle," Denver clips.

The bartender falters, then nods at Denver. "Certainly, Sir."

As he opens a new bottle, I turn to Denver, finding him clenching his jaw. "What was—?"

"Anyone could have slipped something into one of those glasses. No one's been watching."

"You're right. No one is watching. They're having fun instead... Except you."

His jaw clenches tighter. "It's my job to intercept possible threats to your well-being."

I want to roll my eyes at how serious he looks as he says the words. But I don't. My father and Sullivan have treated me like I'm fragile for the past two years and it's always annoyed me. And having Denver assigned to me has only fueled that annoyance further. But the deep set of his brows, and the genuine concern in his voice is creating a new buzzing sensation inside my stomach. One that's not completely unpleasant.

The bartender hands me my drink and I thank him.

"What are you having?" I ask Denver.

"I'm good."

"Oh, come on. You don't have to dehydrate just because you're working." I fix him with a look as he stares at me, the gold flecks in his irises burning.

"Fine." He signals the bartender. "Water, please."

I turn and lean against the bar, settling next to him as we sip our drinks in silence. It's a great turnout. Ashton must be thrilled. Zoey says he's always nervous before a show. But he doesn't need to be. People fly in from all over the world when they know he's about to offer new paintings for sale. He's a celebrity in the art world.

I spot my father and Halliday entering through the main doors, Uncle Mal and Aunt Trudy in tow. I wait, but the door closes behind them. No sign of Sullivan.

"Figures." I snort. "He's probably at The Lanceford."

Denver tips his head in a greeting to my father as I wave at them all.

"Sullivan?" he questions.

"Come on. You know as well as I do what he does there in the suite he has permanently booked."

Benefits of being a billionaire family; your not-so-secret sex pad in one of the city's finest hotels can be paid for upfront for months at a time.

Denver remains silent.

I sigh. "At least your lack of comment means my secrets should be safe with you too."

I twirl the glass in my hand watching the bubbles rise and pop on the surface of the champagne. The voice that flows over me is deep and husky, a breathed whisper. One that makes me wonder if I even heard it at all, or just imagined it.

"Every part of you is safe with me, Sinclair."

◆

The evening lights of the city flow past the window as Denver drives me home. We stayed much later than I intended to. But once I got chatting with Halliday and Trudy about wedding dress styles and planning the wedding, the evening just flew by. Halliday and my father have decided on Cape Town as the location. I understand their reasons for it. It's a new start. A chance to make happy memories in a place that is shrouded in dark ones. But going back to the place where we lost my mother and brother is going to be tough. I haven't been back since the day I saw them die in front of me.

"I know you all think I'm selfish and act out," I say, my voice breaking the silence in the darkened car.

"I've never once thought of you as selfish."

I shake my head at the easy way Denver says it, like he actually means it and isn't just being polite to the daughter of his boss.

"I just..." My shoulders slump as I stare out of the window. "Dad and Sullivan have always been so protective. I know they're only doing it out of love. But sometimes I feel like I can't breathe. My modeling shoots are the only time I get to travel out of the city. But he..." I swallow the lump in my throat, unable to say my brother's name. "He loved to travel.

The Rule Breaker

He lived for adventure. He'd be so disappointed in me if I didn't fight to maintain my freedom. To have those possibilities. To chase after my dreams."

"Sinclair," Denver breathes. "You're grieving. I've seen you battle with it every day since they passed. You're strong. And you have more zest for life in your pinky than most people have in their entire body. He could never be disappointed in you. Ever."

His deep voice and soft words are like a tonic to my soul, bringing a warmth to me in places where there's only been frost for years. I think it's the most I've ever heard him speak.

"Thank you," I whisper.

We pull up outside my apartment building and Denver switches the engine off.

"You're going to insist on walking me up, aren't you?" I let out a soft sigh.

I know the routine. He walks me to my door and won't leave until I'm inside my apartment and he's heard me bolt the door. I tested my theory two nights ago, leaving the bolt undone for the first fifteen minutes that I got home. Denver was still standing in the hallway, guarding my door when I peered through the peephole. He never knocked or called me out on it. He just waited until I slid that bolt into place before he turned and walked away.

"It's my job to—"

"Your job, yeah, I get it."

I turn toward my door as I purposefully reach out as quickly as I can and grab the handle.

The rough growl that's expelled by my ear as he shoots across me and wraps his hand over mine has me holding back a shiver of excitement.

"Sorry, I forgot," I say innocently, biting back my smile as Denver's warm breath skates down the side of my neck.

"When you're with me, I do that," he rasps.

"Sure," I reply, sliding my hand out from beneath his and sneaking a glance at him. But he's already moving, exiting the car swiftly and rounding the hood to get to my door.

I take the hand he holds out to me, climbing out into the evening air. His large fingers splay out across the base of my spine as he maneuvers me toward the entrance of my building, his head swiveling as he scans the sidewalk.

We ride the elevator up to my floor in silence. His hand doesn't leave my back until I open my front door and step inside.

"Hey, baby," I sing to Monty as he sprints over to me, his paws skidding on the polished marble floor of the entryway. I bend to pick him up, dropping my clutch on the floor. He wriggles in my arms and licks at my face. "I missed you too."

I give him a kiss on his head and put him on the floor. His butt shakes side to side and he whimpers as he pushes past me, impatiently.

Denver's crouching, rubbing Monty's ears as I turn. Monty looks at me, his brown eyes hooded in ecstasy as Denver's giant hand engulfs his head. He looks so small next to Denver as he gently fusses him.

"Monty," I call.

He ignores me, his back leg starting to bounce up and down as Denver hits a good spot.

I reach down to undo the ankle strap on my shoe. My heels are new and so high, I've been itching to take them off and give my feet a rest.

"Ugh," I mutter as the silk hem of my dress snags on my bracelet.

"Hold still."

Denver moves in front of me, bending on one knee. He expertly frees my bracelet and I straighten up.

"Thanks."

My breath catches as a warm hand slides around my ankle, lifting my foot. I stare at him as he places my heel onto his thigh.

"They've made your skin red," he grumbles as he eases the strap undone.

He slides the shoe from my foot, placing it onto the floor next to him, before bringing my foot back to rest against his thigh again. A warm pressure eases my aching muscles as he massages my ankle with strong fingers.

A tiny whimper slips from my throat as his thumb slides to the arch of my sole and traces a slow caress over it. I swallow down a lump of disappointment as he places my foot on the floor. But it's only to switch sides. I bite my lower lip as he lifts my other heel, placing it onto his thigh.

"I never knew being on your knees like you're worshiping your client was part of a bodyguard's description," I say with a teasing tone.

Denver looks at me from beneath his dark brows as he frees my other ankle from my shoe and gives it the same careful attention as the first.

"How's that feel?"

The warmth from his breath seeps through the thin silk of my dress, climbing its way up to the apex between my thighs.

I suck in a breath.

"It feels... weird."

His thick brows flatten over his eyes, and he frowns, looking at my shoes like they're the cause.

My phone chimes with an incoming text inside my clutch bag.

"It's fine. Better," I add quickly, slipping my foot from his thigh.

He passes my clutch to me as he stands. I pull my phone out and smile as a text pops up on the screen.

"Brad said he can squeeze me in for a session in the morning."

I type back quickly, happy for the distraction from the weird sensation that's dancing low in my core. A workout is exactly what I need. I didn't have any plans tomorrow except going to see Sullivan and Molly. Brad's usually fully booked. He must have had a cancellation.

"What time?"

I look up at Denver. A muscle in his cheek tightens as our eyes meet.

"Eight," I answer.

"I'll be here at seven thirty." He bends to pat Monty on his way out, stopping at the door like he usually does and waiting for me to come and close it behind him.

"Sure, sounds good." My eyes travel back to my phone, and I click send on my message.

"Lock the door," Denver instructs gruffly.

"I know." I give him a tiny salute as I close the door.

Monty sits at my feet, watching the door as I secure the lock. He's just hoping for another ear rub from Denver's giant hands.

"Come on, baby. Bedtime," I say.

He doesn't move, except to lower his head and sniff at the base of the door.

I tiptoe over and check the peephole. Denver is still standing outside, hands on his hips, head bowed like he's deep in thought. Why hasn't he gone? I did the lock. My hand hovers over it, considering undoing it and asking if he's forgotten something. But then a low curse breaks from his lips and he turns, walking away.

The sound of the elevator dinging outside signals his departure. I bend down and pick up my shoes from the floor. The crystals covering them shine like tiny shards of glass. I turn them in my hands, the recent memory of warm fingers against my skin coming back full force.

"Bedtime, Monty," I repeat.

I glance back at the door.

This time, Monty comes.

7

DENVER

"He looks even more of a jerk than the first time I saw him." Jenson chuckles.

I grunt, and Jenson moves back, away from where he was looking over my shoulder at my laptop.

"Why are you checking on him again, anyway?" he asks.

My eyes flick up from the image of Brad flexing his pecs in another Instagram image to Jenson, who's pacing up and down the length of the meeting room, tapping on the back of each of the chairs as he passes. We usually have our meetings at Seasons. But since the fire, we've been holding them at Beaufort Diamonds' head office.

"Yeah, Boss. Any reason you're repeating work you've already done?" Killian smirks from his position on the opposite side of the meeting table. I clench my jaw, throwing him a warning look.

"Our work is never *done*. We have to be vigilant at all times," I hiss.

Killian arches his brows at me, looking like he's about to speak.

"She's under my protection. Which means any man who

so much as looks at her is on my radar. And I'll find out every damn thing there is to know about them if I see fit. Got it?"

"Yes, Boss," they echo.

I suck in a breath as I return to my dissection of Brad Garrett-Charles' Instagram profile. It's picture after picture of him posing like a jackass. He's mostly alone. But there are some with models and actresses. None of Sinclair. Her agent wouldn't allow her to be tagged for privacy reasons. Thank fuck they have some sense.

The door to the meeting room opens, and I snap my laptop shut and stand as Sterling, Sullivan, and Mal walk inside.

"Gentlemen," Sterling greets first, his silver-flecked hair catching the light against his dark blue suit.

"Boss," the three of us reply.

"Everyone all right?" Mal asks, pulling out a seat at the table and dropping into it. He's Elaina's older brother, a few years older than Sterling. But even though the guy dyes his slicked back hair back to its original sandy blond, he looks at least ten years older than his years. Grief has aged him, creating deep lines at the corners of his mouth and eyes, pulling them down and making him appear permanently sad.

"We're fine," I reply.

There's a knock at the door and Sullivan answers it. A woman says something to him before he shakes his head and says something in reply. She walks off and he closes the door.

"Let's get to it, shall we?" he says as he unbuttons his suit jacket with one hand and takes a seat at the table.

"Problem?" Sterling asks him.

"No." He waves a hand. "Just someone calling for me. I'll call them back."

"Right. In that case, let's get the first thing on the list out the way... Neil?" Sterling says.

He pins his eyes on Killian and Jenson where they've taken

seats opposite me. I'd usually be the one he asks for updates. But now that I'm with Sinclair the majority of the time, keeping tabs on Elaina's ex-lover has fallen on them.

"He's paid upfront for another week at The Lanceford," Killian says.

"Damn it," Sterling mutters, running a hand around his jaw. "He's not planning on going anywhere, is he?"

"Doesn't look like it, Boss," Killian answers.

"What's he back in New York for? Have we figured that out?" Mal asks, leaning over the table. "He hasn't been here since he and Elaina..." He glances at Sterling who gestures for him to go on. "He left after she died. Why come back now?"

"Could be a coincidence," Jenson says.

"Or it might not be," Killian adds. "Whatever it is, we'll find out. We've got the guys watching him twenty-four-seven."

Sterling nods. "Good. Keep it that way. We need to know what he's doing here." His eyes pinch as he thinks. But they're bright in a way they haven't been in all the years I've known him.

He's a changed man since he met Halliday. Jenson jokes about her being twenty years his junior, and even Killian was skeptical when she blew into the Beauforts' lives with all her crystals and talks about energetic vibrations and manifesting your dreams. But I saw the change in him immediately. It was there the day he first told me that Sinclair had hired him a dating expert to find him love. And it's grown brighter every day since they became a couple and got engaged. It's almost blinding now they're expecting a baby together. Something Sinclair's so excited about that she was showing me baby clothes on her phone this morning when I drove her to her workout with Brad.

Brad Garrett-Charles. The name makes sourness roll over my tongue.

"Denver? How's my daughter? Any idea on who's been sending her these threats?"

"No, Boss," I answer. "I'm checking out everyone she knows. But so far it's brought up nothing. There have been no further causes for concern since her car was damaged."

And shit on.

I keep that to myself. The men at the table have matching grave expressions. They're worried about her. Telling them some asshole or crazy fan took a dump on her car isn't going to make it any better. Sinclair still hasn't admitted as much to anyone. So for now, the information is for me and me alone.

"Good. She seems to be taking it well," Sterling says.

"She giving you hell?"

Sullivan's eyes meet mine as I look along the table to him.

I purse my lips. "She's—"

"That's a yes." His eyes glint. "You know my sister. The harder she is on you, the closer you're getting to her."

"Denver must be about in her panties then judging by the shit she gives hi—"

One swift elbow to the ribs has Jenson's cheeks puffing out as he holds back a curse. Killian flashes me a look, leaning back in his chair next to Jenson.

"Just look after her," Sullivan says, ignoring Jenson as his phone starts ringing in his pocket and he pulls it out.

"I will," I reply, my eyes meeting Sterling's as he studies me.

"I trust you, Denver," Sterling says, pinning me with a cool blue gaze.

"I know, Boss. I won't let you down."

He nods, then his face softens. "Now that business is out of the way, I wanted to discuss something else."

"You're hiring the rest of us out to Sinclair's model friends to be their bodyguards?" Jenson quips, having made a speedy recovery from his winding.

The Rule Breaker

Sterling chuckles. "They'd eat you alive, Boy."

Jenson drops back in his seat, defeated. "And I'd hand them the fork to do it... Can't blame a guy for wishing, though, hey?"

We chuckle, and the mood in the room lifts.

"It's about the wedding," Sterling continues. "Hallie and I have chosen Cape Town. And I know you're all expecting to be there."

I glance over at Killian and Jenson's matching frowns. They've spent a lot of time in Cape Town searching for answers over why Sterling's yacht caught on fire that day. I know they've made friends there and were looking forward to a work trip taking them back there since Sterling called off their hunt, saying it was time to move on and accept there might not be any answers to find.

"But..." Sterling spreads his palms. "I don't want you there as our family's security team."

Jenson shifts in his seat and I swear if he tries to say anything stupid, I'll shut him up in a nano second. Sterling has been nothing but good to us since we came to work for him. He does things no normal boss ever would.

"... I want you there as our family."

My attention turns to him, and his eyes are waiting for me, twinkling.

"You've all worked with us for years, especially you, Denver. You're family as much as if we shared blood. So you'll be there as guests. We'll get other guys in to cover the security."

I nod. "I'll handle it. I know the best guys. I'll give them a call."

"Good." He stands. "Now if you'll excuse me, I have a pregnant fiancée and my granddaughter to take for an early dinner before they both get tired."

"And I've got a call to make," Sullivan clips, rising from his chair, typing into his phone.

"And I..." Mal looks at their retreating backs as they leave the room. "I'm going to check in on the team at Seasons, see how the re-model is going." He sighs wearily and stands.

He takes care of the diamond and gemstone imports from Africa, meaning he spends a lot of time away from home. But ever since the fire at Seasons he's stayed in New York. I think the whole family has felt the need to be close together.

"I'll give you a ride," I say, standing and gathering up my laptop. Killian and Jenson have assured me it's all fine, and Sterling is there every day. But I still want to make sure they're doing it as well and as fast as they can.

I owe it to Sterling.

Seasons is also on route to Sinclair's place. She said she was staying in today after her workout this morning because she wanted to relax after yesterday's runway show. But I want to check in on her, see if she needs anything.

My phone buzzes with an incoming text. The screen fills with an image that instantly makes my heart melt.

"You must be proud of her. Look at that smile," Mal says, looking at the picture.

"I am." I admire the light brown braids in her hair, framing her cheeks. She's grown since I last saw her and held her in my arms, smelled the sweet strawberry scent of her hair.

"How old is she now?" Mal asks.

"Six," I reply. "Dixie's six."

8

SINCLAIR

Smiling, I step out of the small discreet door that hides one of Manhattan's best kept secret wine bars behind it.

"Thank you. Tonight was just what I needed."

"Me too." Julian grins. "You're a wonderful woman, Sinclair. Come on, let's get you a cab."

"It's okay, you go. I'll grab one."

Julian looks uneasy, so I raise my arm as we walk along the sidewalk, signaling a cab, which pulls over.

"See? I'm good." I smile, and he leans in to kiss my cheek.

"I'll call you soon, okay?"

"Okay." I beam as he walks down the sidewalk.

It's later than I intended to stay out, the night sky a deep inky black. But once Julian and I got talking, time just flew, like it always does. Every time I see him, I feel better. Our meetings bring something to life inside me. I can't explain it, but I feel like meeting him six months ago was one of the best things to happen to me in a long time.

I turn back to the cab, but someone else has jumped inside and it's already pulling away.

"Damn it," I mutter.

I walk along the sidewalk looking for another cab, but every time one drives past its light is out, signaling it's already picked up a fare.

Something grabs me from behind, spinning me around until my back presses into the wall of a building. The air is pushed from my lungs in a surprised yelp. A body looms over me, leaning in close.

Holy shit, I'm being mugged.

Blood rushes in my ears as the dark-hooded shape towers over me, so close I can taste mint on the tip of my tongue.

"What. The. Fuck?" a voice growls.

"D-Denver?" Relief washes over me, and I wilt against the wall, pressing a hand to my chest. "You scared me."

He pulls the hood down that was hiding his face in shadows. Harsh green eyes penetrate me, making me feel naked.

"You should be scared! I could have been anyone, Sinclair!" he roars, banging his fist on the wall next to me.

I flinch. I've never seen him so mad. His eyes are boring into mine like two green flames.

"What are you doing here?" I choke out.

He places both palms against the brick on either side of me, leaning toward me until he's so close our noses almost touch.

"I went to your apartment, and you were gone. You were fucking gone!"

"I'm fine, I—"

His nostrils flare. "Who was he?"

"What?"

"You know I'll find out. Who was he? Your boyfriend?"

"What? No, he's—"

"A guy you're fucking, then?"

I reel back, but it only makes my back press harder against the wall. "Excuse me?" I scoff.

"Are you having sex with him?" Denver's tone has lowered to a whisper, but it only makes him sound more menacing.

"That's none of your business!" I snap, finding my bite again. "How dare you follow me and then ask me that."

His chest expands as he sucks in a breath. But he doesn't move away. He stays firmly fixed in front of me, caging me in between his arms.

"It's my job to pro—"

"Your job! God, that's all you care about, isn't it?" I shove at his chest, but he doesn't budge.

"Sin—"

"I just needed to do something alone. Can't you understand that?" I search his eyes. Maybe there's a glint of guilt there, but he blinks it away before I can be sure.

"It's not safe," he growls.

"How did you find me? You can't have followed that stupid tracker you put in my phone because I left it behind on purpose so you wouldn't be able to."

A muscle in Denver's cheek twitches so hard I'm surprised he doesn't burst a blood vessel.

"You mean you planned this? You wanted me not to know you were out, with some guy I haven't run any checks on? How could you be so stupid? How do you know you can trust him?"

"I'm not stupid," I spit, shoving his chest again. "I know Julian."

Denver's eyes narrow at my slipup. Still, there must be thousands of Julians in the city; he won't know who he is or how to find him. Julian will be in one of the last places Denver would think to look.

"How did you find me?" I ask again.

Denver shakes his head, glancing up the street.

"Den—"

"I will always find you, Sinclair." He turns back, pinning me under his gaze. "Do you know why?"

"No," I whisper.

His brows pull together and he leans even closer.

"Because you're my responsibility. I'm your bodyguard. And that means I have to know where you are at all times. You won't be going anywhere without me again. Got it?"

"You expect me to be with you all the time?"

"You *will* be with me. No more playing games and sneaking out, Sinclair. This is your safety we're talking about. If I have to cuff you to me, then I'll do it. You don't want to test me."

"Excuse me?" I scoff.

He parts his lips again, the straight edge of perfect white teeth glinting in the moonlight.

"You belong with *me*," he rasps.

He pushes away from the wall, freeing me from the shield his arms had made around me. I take in a big gulp of air as he turns his back on me. My heart gallops in my chest from the shock of him grabbing me. But it's also beating somewhere lower too… deep between my thighs.

Leaning against the wall, I catch my breath, taking him in. He's wearing a black hoodie and sweatpants. I've only ever seen him in suits. Somehow it makes his broad back look even wider than usual.

He clears his throat and extends a large hand behind him, toward me. I stare at it until he looks back at me, his eyes darkening. Wordlessly, I slide my fingers inside his. They're immediately enveloped in solid warmth as he closes his hand around mine. I trail behind him as he marches me over to his car parked at the curb.

He opens my door for me and pulls me toward it using our joined hands.

"Get in."

I blink at him, hovering by the opening. He looks down, his pupils dilating as if he's barely keeping the storm within them at bay.

"In," he growls.

I swallow nervously and move to climb in, but he jerks me back with our joined hands, pulling me into him. My other hand flies up to his chest to steady myself. His heart is pulsing in a deep steady rhythm beneath the muscle, and I press my fingertips into his flesh on instinct, like I need to feel more.

His eyes lock on mine.

"Don't ever pull a stunt like this again."

He lets go of my hand, and I slide into the seat, breathless. He doesn't give me a moment to get comfortable before he leans in and fastens my seatbelt, pulling it tight across my hips. The door closes surprisingly softly. I was expecting him to slam it. Then he takes long purposeful strides around the hood, climbing into the driver's side, his face like thunder.

"I wasn't in any danger," I whisper as he pulls out into the lane.

His expression remains taut as he stares out of the windscreen.

"I really wasn't. I took a cab right to the door. And I was about to get another one back when you... when you grabbed me."

"Did I hurt you?" His face is still rigid, a direct contrast to the concern creeping into his tone.

"What? No. You have this way of touching me that's strong and in control, but so gentle at the same time. I should have known it was you the second I felt your hands on me."

His jaw ticks.

"Denver?" I press, wanting a response. *Needing* a response.

He still won't look at me.

My shoulders sag, and I sink into my seat, folding my arms.

"He's not my boyfriend," I mutter.

But my words don't make Denver look any less pissed. In fact, he looks more murderous. I resort to silence for the rest of the drive.

It's a tense ride up in the elevator to my apartment. Denver chooses to hold my hand again instead of placing it on my lower back like he usually would. Maybe he's worried I'll bolt and try to go somewhere without him again.

I open my apartment door and Monty races over to greet me, quickly going to Denver after. Denver's already standing back up from petting him when I turn around.

"Den—"

"Lock the door," he instructs gruffly.

He holds my eyes. There's no warmth in them, and something about it makes my stomach drop to my feet. I nod and close the door and fix the lock.

He's already walked away by the time I look through the peephole.

I wake up at seven-thirty to the sounds of scratching and whimpering.

"Monty?" I yawn as I sit up in bed and stretch.

He's not in his usual place at the end of the bed where he likes to creep up and sleep in the middle of the night. He's done it since he was big enough to climb up himself. But I've never stopped him. I think we both needed the comfort of not sleeping alone.

I swing my legs out of bed and go in search of the noises he's making. The marble floor in the hallway is cool beneath my feet as I pad over to the front door where he's lying on his tummy, his nose stuck to the base of the door, taking long sniffs.

Something in my gut twists as I step closer and look through the peephole. I don't see anything to start with, until I look down.

Denver's sitting with his back against the door, legs out in front of him, giant arms folded over his chest. I can't make out much more from this angle, but I think he's asleep.

"Monty, speak," I whisper.

Monty looks at me, then barks, like I've taught him to on command.

"Good boy. Speak," I command again.

He barks again, his tail flying around in circles as he looks at me with bright eyes.

I peer back through the peephole and the dark mass has moved and is now standing up.

I fling the door open.

"Did you sleep there in case I snuck out again?"

Denver's rubbing his eyes with his thumb and forefinger, but stops to take me in. His eyes slide down my bare legs then back up over the T-shirt I'm wearing with 'I love my Chinese-crested dog' printed on it. He stares at it and my nipples pebble beneath the thin fabric. He's seen me walk around in lingerie at work, yet somehow my dog T-shirt is the thing that's gotten his attention.

"You've got a meeting with your agent at ten. It's on your schedule," he says. The usually bright white in his eyes is dull. He looks drained. "I've got fresh clothes in my car. I'll come back and wait for you out here."

He turns to walk away, but I reach out and grab his sleeve.

"You need a shower. And coffee." I wrinkle my nose. "Preferably in that order."

"Sin—"

"Don't argue with me. I'm not taking you to a meeting

with my agent when it's obvious you've spent the night sleeping on the floor."

Denver holds my steady gaze, and my heart pounds against my ribs in anticipation of the argument. But I don't care what I have to say to make him come inside, take that shower, and have a drink. After all, he slept on my hallway floor—it's the least he needs. He tips his chin at me. A silent agreement.

I lean against my doorframe and purse my lips. "Good. Hurry up, then. Go get your stuff from your car." I flick my fingers in a shooing motion.

He steps forward, and my nipples pull even tighter.

"You know what you need to do first," he rasps.

I move back and close the door on him slowly, sliding the bolt into place.

The deep husk of his morning voice carries through the wood. "Good girl."

I lean back against the door, sucking in a sharp breath.

Then I wait for him to come back.

◆

"We leave in eight minutes," Denver clips as I walk into the open living area with my purse and shoes in my hand.

"I know." I throw him a small smile which he doesn't return.

I thought him coming in and having a shower would thaw him a bit. But his moodiness has remained frosty since he came back up to my apartment with his duffel bag of clothes. I left him to use my shower in peace, but the clouds of man-scented body wash filling my bedroom had me hovering outside, breathing in the notes of bergamot and mint.

Only one other man has ever used my shower, and it didn't smell like that when he did.

His phone buzzes and he pulls it out of his jacket pocket. His deep brown hair is neat again, but still damp above his collar, and his jaw is freshly shaven. When he woke up this morning, there was a dust of stubble that I've never seen on him before. It suited him. Made him look more intimidating if that's possible.

"You hungry?" I ask.

"No," he replies, his eyes fixed on his phone.

I don't believe him. A guy his size can't survive on thin air. I still remember the giant breakfasts my brother would eat when he was alive. He was muscular and always working out, but he still wasn't as large as Denver.

I should have been scared when he grabbed me last night. And for a second, I was. But the fear vanished as soon as I saw it was him. Seeing him so mad was intimidating, but also oddly comforting, knowing he cares about my safety. But the way he pinned me inside his arms with that wild look in his eyes like he could devour me with one bite prevented me from getting straight to sleep last night.

I laid awake in my bed thinking about him. About whether he fucks women with the same dangerous intensity that oozed from him last night. Whether he holds their eyes as he thrusts inside them. Whether he growls their name when he comes.

And while I was imagining it, he was sleeping against my front door.

A rare smile lifts his lips as he types something into his phone before pocketing it again.

"Killian?" I ask as I walk over to the kitchen counter.

"No."

A single, worded grunt from Denver shuts down any hope of conversation as his expression returns to stony seriousness. I steal small glances at him while turning on the coffee machine and gathering what I need from the cupboards. He stands statue-like, staring out the floor-to-ceiling windows in the living area that offer an impressive view down Park Avenue.

"Okay, I'm ready."

I slip on my shoes and reach down to clip Monty's leash onto his collar, then pick up my two travel cups and walk over to Denver.

I hold one out to him. His eyes flick to it like it's an unstable explosive.

"It's the way you like it." I move the cup closer, urging him to take it.

His long fingers curl around the sides, brushing mine.

"Black with a splash of vanilla... and stirred with an olive branch."

His eyes meet mine, but I can't tell if there's amusement hiding in them. He'd win an award for the world's best poker face.

"Thank you."

He lifts my purse to carry, and my heart sinks as he moves toward the door, not saying anything else. I follow him out into the hallway, and he holds my purse and coffee in one hand as he pulls the door closed behind us.

"Is it okay?" I gesture toward the coffee.

He takes a sip, his Adam's apple bobbing in his neck against his white collar.

"It is."

"Okay then." I shrug. He's obviously someone who likes to stew after an argument. But it's still an improvement. We're up to two syllables.

I walk ahead of him with Monty and press the button for the elevator. We step inside the empty cart once it arrives, and I stare at the numbers going down on the display as we ride it to the lobby.

Denver clears his throat. "Vanilla?"

"You're not the only one who pays attention," I reply, not looking at him. I bite my tongue to stop myself from adding that in my case I'm not paid to notice, like he is. I just like to remember things about people. Like the way Molly's face lit up when I gave her that first fruit sticker from the smoothie truck. And how Halliday loves crystals so much that I'm planning on taking her to this crystal themed restaurant in London as part of her bachelorette celebrations. And the way Denver has always ordered vanilla in his coffee whenever we've stopped to get one.

"We need to stop at the deli on the corner on the way," I say breezily.

"Okay."

His hand finds my lower back once the elevator doors open, like usual. Part of me wishes I'd never made the coffees at all so that I'd have a free hand.

Because a tiny part of me wonders if he'd hold it as tight as he did last night if he could.

9

DENVER

"You sure you don't want something to eat?" Sullivan asks as I sit at his kitchen counter.

I tear my gaze away from Sinclair, who is lying on the floor in the living area, caught in a fit of giggles with Molly. Monty barks excitedly at them, his tail whipping around as Molly pets him.

"No, thanks. I ate before Sinclair's meeting."

"That was hours ago," Sullivan comments, sliding a mug of coffee over the counter to me.

"I'm good," I say.

The truth is, Sinclair went into that deli and ordered the largest breakfast sandwich. Then she handed it straight to me.

"All right, Mr. Moody, you're getting fed whether you like it or not. I'm not entertaining a hangry episode from you while we're meeting with my agent."

She even made us sit inside at a window table for two, scrolling on her phone while I ate, glancing at me every now and then.

"Good boy," she'd cooed when I was done, reaching over,

and brushing a crumb from my lips that I'm sure was never there.

I grip my mug hard.

"You all right?" Sullivan asks, glancing at my white knuckles.

"I'm fine." My gaze travels to Sinclair and Molly. Monty has laid with them and is playing dead.

"She's giving you shit, isn't she? I know she's a handful, but—"

"No, she's fine," I reply, forcing my eyes away from her again.

I'm not going to tell Sullivan about last night. He'd only tear into Sinclair for taking a risk. And the way she'd looked so desperate when she told me she just needed some time alone... She doesn't deserve him laying into her.

Plus I can't be sure of what I might do to Sullivan if I see him try.

I sat in a dark corner of that bar for fifty-seven minutes last night, watching her with that guy, Julian. She has no idea how much danger she could have gotten into. She has a smart mouth, but any person with a bit of strength could lift her off her feet and take her. She wouldn't know what to do in that situation.

I lift my mug and make myself drink before I grind my teeth so hard they'll break.

The sound of Molly's giggles floats over. "Den-va?" she calls.

I turn and am captured by bright blue innocent eyes.

"You okay, Mol?"

"Come play with us."

Sullivan smirks. "You've been summoned."

"Denver's coming, Sweetheart," Sullivan replies as he types into his laptop on the kitchen counter.

I rise from my seat and take the gun from my belt,

removing the magazine, before handing it to him discreetly. He takes both pieces from the room to put in the safe inside his office.

"What are we playing?" I ask as I walk over to join them.

Molly beams as I crouch.

"You go there." She points to a spot on the cream rug behind Sinclair. "You a lion."

My eyes flick to meet Sinclair's.

"Sleeping lions," she explains. "One of us is the hunter, and the rest are lions. The hunter has to wake the lions up. They can't touch them, but they can whisper things like jokes to make them laugh."

"Got it," I reply as Molly tugs on my jacket sleeve.

I lie down behind Sinclair as instructed.

"Close your eyes," Molly says.

I close them as far as I'm comfortable with, keeping a slit open that I can see the main entrance into Sullivan's apartment through.

Molly walks around Sinclair, Monty, and I, her little round cheeks glowing. She's so much like Dixie was at age two and a half. My heart pangs as I picture her. She's getting so big and I haven't seen her properly in weeks.

"Cats!" Molly shrieks, clapping her hands over her mouth as Monty flies from his playing dead position to his feet, barking wildly.

Sinclair breaks into laughter beside me. "Good one, Molly. You got him." She climbs up to standing. "My turn now. Lie down."

Molly drops to the floor, covering her eyes with her hands as Sinclair tiptoes around us.

"Hmm, look at these lazy lions I've found," she muses, pretending to be the hunter. "There's a cute little cub." Molly's face breaks into a grin, but she keeps her hands glued over her eyes. "And there's this big old grumpy looking one."

Sinclair stops next to me, then crouches. I keep still, but each breath I take is filled with her scent. It's light and sweet. Delicate.

Her breath tickles my ear as she leans in close. "Wakey, wakey, big lion," she purrs.

I stiffen.

She blows lightly against my ear, and I unintentionally let out a faint grumble of warning.

Her breath dusts my neck as she giggles. "This big lion snores, does he? Let's see... How about you wake up and I'll give you something sweet to eat?"

I don't move.

"I think you'll like it," she hums. "When was the last time you had something delicious melting on your tongue? Filling your mouth with its flavor?"

I fight the urge to move and pin her beneath me for her teasing tone.

She moves again until her face is in front of mine. "I'll even feed it to you myself," she whispers.

I peel one eye open. Her pupils dilate as she looks at me. I open both eyes fully, staring into her green eyes. She bites her lower lip, her gaze dropping to my mouth and she shuffles close enough that our lips almost touch.

Then she smiles. "Gotcha."

She laughs and moves to Molly, tickling her until she giggles and curls up into a fetal position.

"Denver was cheating," she declares, pointing at me. "He had his eyes open a little."

"Bad," Molly says through her giggles as I sit up.

"Yes. Bad boy, Denver." Sinclair smirks, looking over at me.

She stops her assault on Molly and pulls her into her lap, hugging her tight.

"The cookies look good, though. Did Arabella make them?"

Arabella is Sullivan's PA, formerly Sterling's. She's worked for the family for longer than I have. She's one of the few people he trusts to watch Molly on occasion, but she's been away visiting her sick mom recently.

Sinclair reaches over to a plate of iced cookies shaped like cats wearing colored sweaters and takes one, handing it to Molly.

"Tate," she says, taking a bite.

"Tate?" Sinclair's eyes shoot to Sullivan who's striding back into the room looking pissed. "Who's Tate?"

"She's no-one," Sullivan snaps.

"Who's Tate?" Sinclair asks Molly.

"Daddy's friend," Molly replies with a mouthful of crumbs.

"Daddy's friend?" Sinclair's eyes light up.

"She's not a friend," Sullivan clips, glancing up from his phone. "She happened to be here yesterday, helping with Molly, that's all."

"Is she your new nanny? It's about time you got one. I know Arabella loves Molly, but you can't expect her to work full time for you and help you out in the evenings too."

Sullivan shakes his head, his eyes tracking to me. He hasn't asked me or the boys to run any checks on anyone. And I know he would have if he'd taken on a new nanny.

"I'm not hiring a nanny. Tate was here and I had to make a call. I was in the room the entire time. I wouldn't leave Molly with someone I barely know." He grunts.

Sinclair's face drops and she wrinkles her nose up, looking disgusted. "I didn't realize your friends from The Lanceford came here too."

"They don't." Sullivan pockets his phone. "Like I said, Tate isn't a friend, and she won't be coming back." He tilts his head, gesturing toward Molly. "Let's leave it at that, shall we, Sis?"

Sinclair huffs. "Whatever."

Molly giggles as Sinclair sinks her face into her neck and alternates between blowing raspberries and kissing it.

"I've got to go, Molly-kins," she says. "I love you lots. Look after Daddy, okay?"

"Okay," Molly replies, grinning as Sinclair hands her another cookie.

Sinclair kisses her round cheek, then stands, looking at me.

"Come on, grumpy lion. You could do with an early night after your new friendship with my hallway floor. I promise I'll stay in." She raises her brows, saying it quietly enough that Sullivan can't hear.

I stand and hold her gaze for a beat. "You were supposed to stay in last night."

She sighs. "You don't need to worry about Julian. And I mean it, I'll stay home tonight. I promise, okay?"

She won't tell me who he is, that much is clear. But she won't need to. I'll find him anyway. And if she thinks I won't, then she's underestimating exactly what her being under my protection means. Because not only will I find Julian, but if I deem him to be a threat to her in any way, then not only will she never see him again. No one will.

She hugs Sullivan and he retrieves my gun. I push the magazine inside it before tucking it into my holster. Sinclair watches me the entire time with a frown.

"You done, Brute?"

I meet her fiery gaze.

"Lead the way, Princess."

The Rule Breaker

"Did Sullivan ask you to run a check on a woman named Tate?"

Killian and Jenson's blank faces confirm he didn't.

I lean back in my seat, my grip on my beer tightening. Sinclair's spending the night at Halliday and Sterling's place. Girl's night, she said. Sterling chuckled when I dropped her off, saying he was going to get some work done in his home office while the two women talk weddings and babies. He told me he'd take care of them both and gave us all the night off.

I've been away from her for two hours and the knots in my neck are embedding themselves deeper.

Sterling can handle himself. They're in good hands with him should anything happen. I know that. And yet... I pull out my phone and bring up my tracking app. Sinclair and Monty's dots are together, placing them in Sterling and Halliday's penthouse.

I purse my lips as I place my phone on the table.

"Why?" Killian asks.

I tune back in, shaking my head. "Don't worry about it."

Sullivan's not one to take security lightly, so whoever this Tate is, he trusts her to be in his home and around Molly. I'd still feel calmer if he'd let me run a check on her, though.

"Why are we talking about work?" Jenson says, lifting his beer and swigging from the bottle.

"Yeah, rare night off," Killian adds as his eyes roam the room, settling on a curvy redhead near the bar. She glances away shyly after he smiles at her.

"We've got to make the most of it." Jenson's gaze follows Killian's, meeting the redhead's friend. The blonde isn't as shy and holds Jenson's gaze for a beat with a flirty smile.

"Fuck yeah, we're in there." He smirks at Killian.

"What about the photos in the press today? The ones of Sinclair with Brad Garrett-Charles." I spit out his name before the inside of my mouth turns sour with it.

Killian and Jenson exchange a look.

"I'll get us some more beers," Jenson says, heading over to the bar. He leans on it cockily and starts chatting to the blonde and redhead after he orders. Their gazes keep bouncing over to our table and within seconds he has them both giggling.

"You think it's the baby face? They want to mother him?"

I shake my head as I answer Killian. "It's his terrible jokes."

"At least Killian's interesting, and Jenson's fun." Sinclair's words from when she was told I'd be her bodyguard echo in my head.

"They really are shit. But somehow he pulls them off." Killian looks away from where the girls are giggling again at something Jenson's said.

"The photos?" I say, fixing him with a look.

He holds his hands out. "It's just the press being the press. They're always speculating over Sinclair's love life, you know that."

I grind my teeth. I do know that. They've been running stories about Sinclair and any man she's spotted with for as long as I can remember. Only this time it was Brad Garrett-Charles when she met him for coffee. A coffee she invited me to join them for, knowing full well I'd decline. I sat at a nearby table instead, watching the slimy fucker abuse every opportunity he could to touch her hand on top of the table.

"I still want you to look into it. It could have been a tip-off, like before."

Killian leans back in his chair, exhaling. He knows what I'm referring to. Sinclair went shopping with Halliday a couple of months ago. They were buying baby gifts for a friend of Halliday's, but the press went wild, ambushing them. Both of them ended up needing to go to hospital to get checked over. Thank fuck they were both fine.

The press still ran stories insinuating Sinclair was hiding her own pregnancy. The gossip sites were stuffed with articles, all speculating over who the father could be until it all died down. *Assholes.*

"Sure, I'll take a look."

I nod at Killian, the tension in my neck loosening a fraction.

"You need me to do anything else?"

Julian flashes into my mind. I know who he is now. But why Sinclair didn't want me to know she was meeting a lawyer, I'm still in the dark about. Maybe she really is fucking him.

"No. I can handle the rest."

Killian leans over the table, eyeing me like he's unsure whether moving closer is a wise move or not.

"What?" I ask.

"Just... You and Sinclair. You know, the way you are together."

I stare at him.

"If I can see it, then it's only a matter of time until Sterling will as well. I'm just saying."

"What the fuck are you talking about? I'm her bodyguard. It's my job to be with her all the time."

He sits back, holding his palms up. "That's not what I meant. You know what? Forget I said anything. You know what you're doing."

Three beer bottles are hastily slammed into the middle of our table.

"Jessica and Liana want to meet you." Jenson gives us a shit-eating grin.

"Both of us?" Killian questions, looking over at the girls.

This time, the redhead smiles at him.

"Apparently the blonde over there... Liana"—Jenson rolls her name off his tongue—"likes extra attention on her."

He looks at me pointedly, and Killian puts his fist to his mouth and laughs. "Fuck me."

"Not you," Jenson says, his face serious. "Denver. And me. A double act."

Killian laughs harder.

"I'm not having a threesome with you. You can forget it," I snap.

"You sure? She seemed up for it. It's okay, I'm sure yours won't look *that* small next to mine."

The look I give him kills anything else he might say to try to convince me.

His brow creases, and he glances back at the girls. "All right, then. Looks like I've got some extra work to do. Show Liana that I'm more than enough for her."

Killian smirks at me. "You sure you don't want a little taste of Jenson's coc—"

"Fuck off," I growl.

He chuckles and stands, clapping his hand on my shoulder. "You okay if we...?"

I place my hand over his and pat it. "Go, have fun," I say, meaning it. They're right. We shouldn't be using our one rare night off together to talk about work. They deserve to blow off some steam.

"Call you tomorrow," Killian says.

Jenson slaps me on the back and the two of them head over to the girls at the bar. The blonde catches my eye, pouting in disappointment as Jenson whispers in her ear.

I look away, bringing up the tracking app on my phone again. Both dots are in the same position they've been in since I last checked. The cinema room by the looks of it.

I close it and pull up the website for Sutton Law instead. I drink my beer as I stare at the man called Julian. The one who kissed Sinclair on the cheek like he had the fucking right to touch her.

"What is she doing meeting up with you?" I grit.

My phone rings as I'm studying his image like it might provide answers.

"Lizzie?" I answer, seeing her name on the call.

"Denver?" she says in a rush.

"What is it?" The hairs on the back of my neck stand up at the waver of panic in her voice.

"It's Dixie," she sobs. "There was an accident and—"

I stand instantly. "I'm on my way."

"Okay," she sniffs. "I'm sorry. She was asking for you and—"

"Never apologize," I say as I grab my jacket and stride toward the exit. "Now tell me where you are."

10

SINCLAIR

I open the door to my apartment.

"Oh." My smile falls at the sight of Jenson standing in a black suit on the other side.

"All right, Sinclair?" He grins and walks inside.

I check the empty hallway behind him before I close the door.

"Where's Denver?"

"It's your lucky day, you've got me instead." He bends to fuss Monty as he trots over to him. "Nice sweater, bro."

"The Vivienne Westwood team sent it to him. We were doing pictures for his Instagram account," I say as Monty soaks up Jenson's attention.

"Workout with Brad today, then? Followed by a casting?" Jenson says, glancing at me.

"Yeah," I murmur. "So... Denver?"

"Family emergency." He continues ruffling the hair on Monty's head.

"Family emergency?"

Jenson chuckles at Monty. "You're looking sharp, bro. I'm digging it."

"Denver hasn't mentioned any family to me." I stuff my water bottle into my gym bag as I study him.

"He's a private guy." Jenson stands and looks at me. "You ready?"

"Yeah, one sec." I falter as my two travel mugs catch my gaze.

"Ooh, nice. For me?" Jenson lifts up one and sniffs it. "Ah, of course, for our man, Denver. Well, he's not here, so I'm sure he won't mind." He winks before sipping it and wincing. "You got any milk?"

"Sure." I point at the refrigerator. Jenson strides over and fixes the coffee.

"You and me are going to have fun today. You won't even miss him," he says as he walks over and takes my bag for me.

I arch a brow. "Like there's a chance I'd miss him. This is me and Denver, remember? My father forced us together. It wasn't by choice."

The words feel deceitful as they leave my mouth, even though they'd have felt so natural only weeks ago. I press my lips together.

Jenson slurps his coffee noisily as he looks at me. "That's exactly what he said."

"What?" I scoff. "Seriously? He complained about being with me?"

My stomach drops, and I shove the weird sinking feeling away, instead replacing it with a burst of fire. How dare he?

"I asked for you or Killian if you recall? So if Denver's going around saying—"

"Nah, I'm just messing." Jenson grins. "He didn't say anything. But I'll be sure to tell him you didn't miss him one bit after the amazing day you had with me."

I roll my eyes and shove playfully at his chest as I pass him to get Monty. "You're a jackass."

"Told you you'd have fun with me." He chuckles behind

me. "Now let's go see Brad Garett-Charles. Because Denver sure as hell did have a word or two to say about him. I want to meet this douche."

I snort. "Brad's great, I don't know what Denver's issue with him is."

"He said Monty doesn't like him."

"Monty loves him," I lie. "You'll see."

I can hear Jenson's chuckles as Monty shifts on the bench seat of the studio, his muzzle exposing his teeth as he growls.

"That sweater making him hot or something?" Brad asks, readjusting his hands on my hips as I hold a weight in one hand and lower into another lunge.

"No, he likes wearing clothes," I pant as I hold my position for three counts.

"He's an animal," Brad says.

"So?" I lift my eyes to his, and he plasters a smile onto his face.

"You know, actually, I like it. Suits him."

I look away and perform another lunge, holding for three counts again.

"You're doing really well," Brad praises, squeezing my hips and straightening them a little. "One more."

I finish the set and put the weight down, lifting my towel to dry off.

"Where's your usual guy?" Brad asks.

I glance over at the bench Jenson and Monty are sitting on. Jenson's wearing a cocky grin and Monty's staring at Brad with his ears pulled back like he wants to run over and bite him.

"You mean Denver?"

"That his name? The big guy that doesn't say much?"

"He's got the day off." It's all I can say because I don't know where Denver is, or which family member has gotten an emergency. Because he's never once told me about anyone close to him despite all the time we've been spending together.

"Thought you might have gotten rid of him."

"Why would I do that?"

Brad shakes his head. "No reason."

"Come on. This is me you're talking to," I say, slinging my towel over one shoulder and placing my hands on my hips.

His eyes soften as he studies my face. "Sure is you, Sin."

My cheeks heat as he reaches up and takes my towel, swiping it over the top of my chest above the swell of my breasts.

"It's the way he stares at you all the time. Like he wishes he had a chance," Brad muses, his eyes traveling to my cleavage as he lets my towel go.

"He doesn't."

"I know he doesn't. He's just a bodyguard. You're way out of his league."

I gape at Brad's back as he returns my weight to the rack.

"What? I meant; he doesn't stare at me all the time."

Brad shrugs. "I'm just telling it like I see it. When we had coffee the other day, he couldn't take his eyes off you."

"He's my bodyguard. That's his job," I huff.

"Yeah, maybe. Dude over there seems more chilled though."

I look over at Jenson, who's chuckling to himself as he types something into his phone.

"You ready for some stretches?" Brad grins as he grabs a mat and throws it on the floor.

"So this guy tried to sell me a casket the other day."

I bite the inside of my cheek as Jenson pauses for effect.

"Told him that's the last thing I need."

I snort. "That's even worse than the last one! Where the hell do you get these from?"

"My Uncle Perry was a comedian." Jenson grins as I throw one of my couch cushions at him.

"Liar."

He throws his hands up. "I swear on Monty's life."

"Don't bring my baby into this," I shriek.

He holds my eyes until we both burst into laughter.

He's right. We have had a fun day. I always do with Jenson. He's silly and makes everything seem like a game. And I think he secretly loved taking me to my casting. He grinned and said hello to every model we saw, before asking me their name, then repeating it to himself like he was memorizing them all.

"You want another soda?" I ask.

Jenson's eyes widen as the sound of my front door slamming shut echoes through the hallway. He leaps to his feet, and I whip my head around, peering over the back of the couch. Only my father has a key to my apartment.

"Stay here," he instructs. But he's barely taken two strides before a dark hulk comes tearing into the room.

"You. Out. Now." The harsh growl that comes along with it has me jumping up from the couch.

"Denver? What the hell? How did you get in?" I ask.

Dark green eyes meet mine for a millisecond, and my core clenches at seeing him again. He's in his usual suit, but where he's usually composed, his chest is heaving, and his eyes are wild like he's about to lose it any second.

"Now," he hisses at Jenson. "We need to talk."

"Woah? What's the problem?" Jenson says.

Denver advances on him, stopping inches from his face.

"You had one job today. What was it?"

Jenson glances at me with uncertainty.

"Don't look at her, look at me," Denver snaps.

Jenson's face hardens, and he squares up to Denver. "I did my job. She's safe, isn't she?"

"I heard you laughing from the elevator."

"So we're not allowed to have fun now?" Jenson scoffs. "Come on, man. This is Sinclair. She's not just a client. She's a frien—"

"I've been gone for one day. One day!" he rages. "And I come back and find you laid out eating popcorn." He sneers as his eyes snag on the large bowl that's tipped over on the couch.

"I asked him to stay," I snap, trying to step between the two of them. But Denver wraps a strong hand around my waist and somehow maneuvers me to one side whilst keeping his eyes pinned on Jenson.

"This doesn't concern you, Sinclair."

"Of course it damn well does." I fight to get between them again, but Denver stands firm, ignoring me.

"You texted me while she was working out to tell me that jackass had his hands on her again."

Jenson juts up his chin. "Yeah. He did. You told me not to smack his face in because she likes him."

Denver curses, his eyes flicking guiltily to mine.

"You texted me," he grits at Jenson. "You took your eyes off her."

"You text when you're with her," Jenson says, lifting both brows.

"Not when we're in public. When there's any chance of anyone else being near her, she is *all* I focus on."

"We were in Brad's studio. Relax, man."

I stare at the two of them, facing each other like bulls, nostrils flaring.

I'll give it to Jenson; he doesn't back down easily when Denver's in scare-you-until-you-shit-your-pants mode. Even Monty is looking uneasy and comes to stand beside me.

"How did you get in?" I ask Denver.

He finally drops his glare from Jenson for longer than a second to look at me. The tension eases a fraction in his brow as he meets my eyes. "I picked the lock. Took me seconds. You didn't put the extra bolt in place."

The accusation in his words makes heat spread in my stomach. His attention snaps back to Jenson. *He's going to rip into him again if I don't stop him.*

I fake a light giggle. "Oops."

I study the side of his face for a reaction. A pulse throbs in his temple and I swear he growls from the back of his throat. Something about the way he's so caveman over my safety, even though I know it's just his job is... *not unpleasant*.

"Oops?" he hisses, his lips curling from his perfect white teeth as Jenson is forgotten and he turns his body, raining the full force of his pent-up inferno down on me like green fire. "Oops?" he repeats, towering over me like he's about to swallow me whole. "Is that all you've got to say?"

"It's fine, relax." I pout, trying to shrug it off.

"This isn't a joke, Sinclair. Someone out there might mean you serious harm. Jesus, do you want to end up kidnapped, or worse? Do you want your father to bury another child?"

His eyes widen the second it leaves his mouth.

"Jesus," Jenson utters.

I pull back my arm and slap Denver hard across the face.

"How dare you!"

My palm stings, but not as much as my chest does. I suck in shallow breaths as my lungs tighten. Memories swim in front of my eyes. Of my brother's smile. Him laughing. Of fire. And two graves, side by side.

I whimper, my throat on fire. "Of all the things, how could you say that?"

Monty whines at my feet and Denver's entire demeanor shifts from white hot anger to icy desperation.

"Sinclair, I didn't mean—"

"Get out!" I cry. "Both of you. Leave me alone."

I scoop Monty into my arms, my tears falling onto his neck as I hold him close and flee to my bedroom. I slam the door and lean against it, erupting into sobs. Monty nuzzles and licks at my face, trying his best to give me comfort.

The deep rumble of their voices carries from the living area. Then the sound of the front door opening and closing is followed by silence.

I walk over and sit on the end of my bed, one hand reaching up to touch my diamond necklace, as I keep Monty wrapped inside the other.

"Sinclair?" There's a gentle knock at the door.

"Go away, Denver. Unless you want another slap."

His sigh bleeds through the door. "I'm sorry. I should never have said that."

"No, you shouldn't. Now, get lost." I sniff.

"You know I can't do that."

I squeeze my eyes closed as hard as I can. So that's what this is. He isn't staying because he feels bad. He's staying because he has to. Because it's his job.

"I'll come out and bolt the door after you. Just go away."

"I'm not going anywhere."

I let go of my necklace and wipe my cheeks. He's so goddamn stubborn.

"Go and sleep in the hallway again then. I don't want you near me."

I stare at the door when there's no answer. Maybe he's

gone. I stand and walk over to it, clutching Monty to my chest as I reach for the handle.

"I am sorry. And I'll leave as soon as you open the door, I promise."

His soft words fall against the wood and seep underneath the door.

"I need to know you're okay. I can't leave until I can see you're okay. Please, Sinclair. You're... I... Just open the door, *please*."

I swallow around the lump in my throat as I slowly open the door.

Denver's shining eyes are waiting to meet mine. He studies me, his eyes pinching at the tear tracks skating down my cheeks.

"I'm so sorry. I just *need* you to be safe." He scrubs a hand around his jaw with a rough curse. "God, if anything were to happen to you, I..."

We stare at one another, and something shifts in my chest at the sheer devastation on his face.

"If you want Killian or Jenson instead, I'll understand. I'll speak to your father." A muscle in his cheek pulls tight.

"No."

My breath catches at the flare of hope in his eyes.

"I don't want someone else... It might..." I search for a reason to give him. "... it might be confusing to Monty."

He nods.

"But that hurt," I whisper, my voice shaking.

The realization settles in my gut like a lead weight. He's supposed to protect me. Yet he's just cut me deeper than any of those stupid notes that were left on my car.

He moves closer and hesitates before he places both of his hands on my upper arms.

"Sinclair?"

I sniff and look down at Monty.

"Look at me."

But I can't because I'm afraid my tears will start all over again. I shake my head.

"*You* hurt me," I whisper.

The heaviness in his exhale runs through my entire body, so when his strong arms tentatively slide around me, I sink into them.

He pulls Monty and me against his solid chest, and I press my cheek over his heart, listening to its deep pulse. And despite what's just happened, I close my eyes as he holds me in the safest embrace I've ever been inside in my life.

His breath falls into my hair and he strokes my back.

"I know I did, Princess," he breathes. "And I am so fucking sorry for that."

11

DENVER

"It's looking mighty fine, Boss," Jenson tells Sterling as we stand at the bar inside the newly refurbished Seasons.

"Sure is." The corners of Sterling's blue eyes crinkle as he surveys the space.

It's been transformed. I swore we'd do whatever we had to do to make it better than before. All those late nights here helping the team out after I left Sinclair's apartment. All the extra check-ins Killian and Jenson have been doing.

It was all worth it to see it finished.

"What's she doing?" Killian asks Sterling as Halliday floats around the room waving something in her hand that's emitting a light gray smoke.

Sterling chuckles. "Being my beautiful, unique fiancée."

Halliday smiles as she passes us. "They're sage leaves. It's called smudging. It will help to cleanse the energy and make way for only joy."

She carries on, approaching Sinclair and Molly who are slow dancing together to the music Vincent is playing on the new Grand piano. Sullivan's standing watching them with Monty at his feet. Molly reaches up and pats Halliday's stomach lovingly as she approaches them.

"Hello, baby," she says.

"Too cute." Jenson wipes at his eyes.

Killian nudges him in the shoulder. "One day if you can actually talk a woman into dating you, maybe you'll be a dad."

"Women love me," Jenson replies. "I'm knocking back more proposals than a New York Ranger's goalie."

Sterling and Killian break into chuckles.

"How's Dixie doing?"

"Good. She's got all her friends to sign her cast now. She shows me a new drawing on it every time we video call. She'll be disappointed when it comes off."

"The benefits of youth, healing fast," Sterling muses with a smile. "You're a lucky man, Denver. These women of ours are precious." Halliday looks over, catching his eye. "Give Dixie and Lizzie my love, won't you? Now, please excuse me." He leaves us to walk over to her, pulling her into his arms for a kiss.

"Fuck, he really does get laid more than me," Jenson mutters.

"What about Liana? I thought you were seeing her again?" Killian says.

"I did. But then her boyfriend came home from work, and I had to go down the fire escape."

"Damn." Killian chuckles. "She never mentioned him."

"No, but he knew about me all right." Jenson shakes his head, looking horrified. "She wanted to watch him fuck me. I was a sacrificial lamb. The guy was fucking huge… and ugly."

He shoves Killian as he breaks into laughter. "Don't laugh, man. My ass would have been shredded. You'd have had to do all my work for a month while I sat on an ice pack."

My eyes track Sinclair as Killian snorts with laughter. She

twirls Molly toward Sullivan, and he pulls Molly into his arms. Sinclair turns with a bright smile that falters the moment her eyes meet mine. She looks away immediately, talking to Vincent as he plays the piano instead.

"She still not forgiven you?" Jenson asks.

I roll my neck to ease the tightness in it. "She says she has."

"Women say one thing and mean another," Killian says.

I exhale slowly as I watch her lean over the piano, her smile so easy as she talks to Vincent. It's been two weeks since I said those stupid fucking words. And I've torn myself apart every day. She's distanced herself from me. The teasing is gone. The eye contact is gone. The vanilla coffee is gone.

The part of herself she was starting to trust me with is gone.

Now our car rides are silent again.

"You hurt me."

Me. Those were her words. *I* hurt her. And I was meant to fucking protect her.

"She'll come around," Killian says. "Everyone screws up sometimes."

"We can't afford to screw up," I hiss. "This is our job. If we make a mistake, people get hurt." *And die.*

He and Jenson look at me in understanding.

"It's better this way," I murmur.

They shake their heads like they know I'm talking shit. But it is better this way. Sinclair doesn't fight to open her own door anymore or roll her eyes when I insist on doing something for her. She just accepts it.

In silence.

She says goodbye to everyone and gives Monty a kiss before handing his leash to Molly. Then she walks over to us, smiling at Jenson and Killian before looking at me with a flat expression.

"We should go."

She's got a shoot for a fashion magazine booked. I collect her bag from near the doorway and gesture for her to go first. She walks a couple of steps ahead of me. Close enough for me to do my job. But far enough that it's obvious she doesn't want my hand on the base of her spine, guiding her.

I haven't touched her since that hug. Since she cried the tears I was responsible for, and they soaked into my shirt as I held her.

Since I was a fucking asshole.

Maybe the boys are right, and she'll come around, forgiving me completely.

But even if she does, I'll never forgive myself.

"Beautiful, amazing! Lift your chin a little. That's it. Stunning."

The photographer clicks away as Sinclair leans back against the wall, her blonde hair tousled and falling around her shoulders in the black pant suit she's wearing.

"Makes a change to see us with so many clothes on, huh?"

I flick my attention up to Theodora.

"I love the runways, but shoots are my favorite. Especially if they're for commercials and not editorials. There's something exciting about walking down the street and seeing yourself on a billboard, you know?"

"I'm sure there is." I nod, my gaze already back on Sinclair.

"Have you ever thought about modeling? You'd kill it in men's sportswear." She reaches out to squeeze my bicep through my jacket. "Yeah, totally kill it," she muses.

Sinclair finishes up and glances our way, before walking

over to the wardrobe assistant who starts helping her to get undressed.

"Hmm, she didn't come and stake her claim on you this time. Maybe that means you're free later?" Theodora smiles at me seductively.

I clear my throat. "I'm working."

"He gets off at eight," Sinclair says as she walks past us in her own dress and over to where her bag is.

Theodora's eyes light up. "You giving him permission then, Sin?" She giggles. "I'll take good care of him."

The muscles in my shoulders stiffen as Sinclair stops rummaging through her bag and flicks her gaze over to us. "Do what you like together, I really couldn't give a shit."

Theodora raises both brows at me. "That sounded like an invitation to me." She grabs a pen from the table next to us and gestures to my arm.

I stare at her.

"For God's sake, just let her give you her number. Then we can get out of here," Sinclair snaps as she continues the assault on her bag, turning it upside down and shaking out the contents.

My eyes are glued to the fraught lines marring her brow as her search grows more frantic and she curses.

"Here you go." Theodora grabs my hand and starts scrawling a number on the back of it.

"Oh my god," Sinclair whispers. "No, no, no! Where is it?"

I rise from my seat, causing Theodora's final digit to end in a jerk. I stride over to Sinclair.

"What are you looking for?"

Her eyes meet mine, and she blinks, shaking her head in a panic.

"It was here. I always put it in this pocket inside. See?" She wrenches her bag open and shows me the empty inner pocket.

"Your necklace?" I ask. I've seen her take it off before every shoot and runway we've gone to. And it's the first thing she takes out of her bag once she's done.

She makes a strange sound like she's about to cry. I take the bag from her hands gently and run a hand around the inside, feeling around the silk lining.

"What are you doing?"

"Seeing if it's fallen through," I say.

Sinclair watches me, holding her breath, but her shoulders sag the second I come up empty.

"It's got to be here." Her eyes dart around, and she starts lifting the other models' bags, searching under them. "Everyone, get everything out of your bags! We have to find it," she screeches.

"Sorry, Honey, I have a cab waiting." Another model grabs her bag and starts to walk away.

"It'll take you one minute!" Sinclair yells at her.

"You lost it, not me. Just get another one." The model shrugs like she couldn't care less.

"It's irreplaceable!"

Sinclair's eyes have taken on a wild sheen as she steps closer to the other model.

"Not my problem. You should take better care of your shit."

Sinclair steps toe-to-toe with her. "Empty. Your. Ugly. Fake. Chanel. Now!" she spits.

The other model tilts her head to one side. "What you going to do if I don't? Call Daddy Beaufort to throw his money around and make me?"

"Quit being a bitch and just do it." Sinclair seethes.

"What did you call me?" the other model snaps.

"I called you a bitch. Need me to say it louder?" Sinclair says.

"Why you—!" The other model advances on Sinclair, but

The Rule Breaker

Sinclair launches herself at her before she can take the first swing.

"And you can thank me when I rip those god-awful extensions out of your hair, bitch!" Sinclair screams.

All hell breaks loose. Gasps echo around us as Sinclair grabs the model by the hair and yanks it until the model stumbles, swiping for her bag with her other hand.

"You crazy psycho!" the other model yells, sinking her nails into Sinclair's arm.

I'm on them in a flash, knocking the girl's hand off Sinclair and lifting Sinclair off the ground, pulling her away. She fights against me, arms and legs punching and kicking out into the air.

"Put me down, Denver. I swear to God, I'll—"

"I'm not letting you go until you calm down," I growl in her ear as she puts all her energy into trying to escape me.

"Fuck you, I hate you!" She throws her head back, trying to hit me in the face, but I've got her clasped so hard against me that it thuds uselessly against the base of my shoulder. "Denver!" Her voice takes on a more desperate edge as the model scurries away, slamming the door on her way out. "Denver, please."

She sags against me, letting out a wail.

"It's all right. I've got you," I say in her ear so only she can hear.

"You don't understand," she cries. "It's him…" Her body trembles as sobs overtake her. "It's all I have of him."

◆

I stand further away than I'm comfortable with, giving Sinclair the space she asked for. Her cries carry over to me in the open air as she kneels beside one of the two graves. Her head is bowed, and her slender frame is shaking with the force of her tears.

And all I can do is stand and watch.

Her mouth is moving, and I can make out the words, *Sorry*, and *I love you*, as she tends to the flowers that have been placed in planters around both graves. Sterling told me she comes here often, asking him to bring her, instead of Sullivan, who hasn't been here since the day they were both buried.

Today was the first day she's ever asked me to come with her. But I know there's nothing more to it on her part than desperation.

Desperation over losing her necklace. Now I understand why she was so distraught.

"It's all I have of him."

I called Sterling the minute Sinclair went to freshen up in the restroom after her outburst and he confirmed what I suspected the minute she collapsed into my arms, all her fight leaving her.

The diamond in that necklace was made from her brother's ashes.

Sullivan was able to get what he needed from the medical examiner, and have it made before the funeral because the bodies were already so badly burned. Sterling said Sullivan hadn't liked the idea, but he'd gotten it made for Sinclair when she insisted.

She's worn it every day since.

Bringing her hand to her lips, she kisses her fingertips, then presses them to the headstone. She rises, walking around to the other and repeating the gesture. Then she frowns, reaching down to pick something up.

I walk closer and her eyes flick up to mine. They're red-rimmed and the sight makes my stomach clench.

"Neil left Mom a note," she whispers.

"May I?"

She hands the piece of paper to me.

> *"I'll always live in the 'what could have been'. If only you'd chosen differently, my darling, Elaina, then maybe you'd be living here with me."*

My jaw hardens. We don't need a signature to know that it's from him. It's the note of a lover. One whose reasons for coming back to New York are still unclear.

"Do you think it's…?" Sinclair chews her lower lip. "Forget it," she adds, looking away.

"Do I think it's threatening?" I ask, knowing exactly what the look in her eyes means. "I don't know. But we need to go straight to your father and show him."

"I want to go to Sullivan's and collect Monty, and then go home," she says in a weak voice.

I fold the note and put it inside my jacket pocket.

"Okay, let's go. I'll go and see your father after."

I follow her back toward the car and she wobbles a little as her heel hits uneven ground. My hand curls around her elbow, steadying her.

"Are you okay?"

She blinks at me as if she's remembering something.

"Are you okay?" I ask again, more softly as I look at her tear-stained cheeks.

She nods and swallows. "I want to go home."

I let go of her elbow and she takes a couple of steps before pausing, inclining her face over her shoulder to see if I'm following her. But I'm right here, one step behind her. I'm always right here.

Her body is tense, and she holds her breath. As I draw level with her, she walks again, her pace matching mine so that I stay beside her instead of one step behind.

I place my hand on the base of her spine, and her shoulders soften.

And she breathes again.

12

SINCLAIR

Denver doesn't say anything as I open the door to him two days later and he follows me inside my apartment, witnessing the chaos Zoey and I have created.

"Hey, Denver," Zoey calls from across the room, half hidden by a pile of couch cushions that are in a tower.

"Zoey," he greets.

She stands with her hands on her hips, looking around the ransacked room. "Okay, so we can rule out the living area now."

"That just leaves the guest bathrooms," I say. "We'll need a plumber to check the pipes."

"I'll sort it," Denver says.

I glance at him. "Thanks."

I've been searching my apartment for two days straight. Zoey turned up on my doorstep within thirty minutes of getting back from picking up Monty from Sullivan's after we left the graveyard. I know Denver called her. He waited until she arrived and then he left. I haven't seen him since. I texted him and told him Zoey was staying over and that we were spending the day at my place together. I half expected him to show up here anyway, full of his usual deep growly energy like he didn't believe me. But he didn't, and that only worries me more. Because it means he's been with my father, Sullivan, and Mal, talking about that note.

Trying to figure out what Neil, my mother's dirty little secrets, motive is.

"It'll turn up, Sin," she says, giving me a reassuring smile. "It can't have gone far."

"Thanks," I reply as she comes to hug me.

"You sure you don't want me to stay another night?"

"No." I squeeze her hard before letting her go. "I've kept you long enough. Ashton will be missing you."

She looks at me, then at Denver, and back again, her voice softening. "I'll come by tomorrow, yeah? We can get takeout."

"Sounds good." I try my best to return her smile, but all I feel like doing is crying, then screaming and throwing things.

I lost it. The one part of him I had. The only times I take my necklace off are when I'm working. And I always put it inside my bag in the same pocket. Always. It can't have just vanished.

My chest burns again, so I rub at it as I follow Zoey to the door and let her out. Denver's crouched, petting Monty when I return.

"I can walk him by myself if you like. But I think the air will be good for you." His green eyes meet mine, a rare gentleness in them like I'm a scared animal that needs coaxing out.

I nod meekly and fetch Monty's leash. "I'm coming. He won't walk well for you without me."

Denver stands, taking the leash from my hands and carefully clipping it to Monty's collar.

"Get what you need. We'll wait."

Fifty minutes later and I feel a little better. We've walked in silence, but watching Monty's tail fly around in excitement when we saw another Chinese Crested in the park made my heart lift a little. At least I know it's still there. It's felt broken beyond repair the past forty-eight hours.

My hand reaches up on instinct as we walk past one of my brother's favorite benches to stop and stretch against when I would sometimes run with him. But all that's there is an empty space above my heart where my necklace used to rest.

We exit the park, heading out onto Fifth Avenue. Denver's quiet next to me, but I feel his gaze on me constantly.

"Can we head back now? I think Monty's had enough."

"Of course." His deep voice is grounding, providing something strong and solid to hold on to.

"Thank you for taking me to the... to see him the other day." I sniff. "We were a long time and—"

"We can go whenever you want, for however long as you want."

I swallow the thick lump in my throat. "I appreciate that."

His attention is fixed on something further up the sidewalk. I spot Theodora strutting toward us in a tight cream dress like she's on her way somewhere.

"Sin," she gushes as she reaches us. "How are you? I've been worried." She smiles at Denver. "Hi."

He nods at her before she looks back at me.

"Have you found it?"

I shake my head and her face falls. When I came out of the restrooms at the shoot, Theodora made all of the other models empty and search their bags incase my necklace had fallen inside. It hadn't, but I appreciated her trying.

"Oh, it'll be somewhere. Maybe you should post about it online? Tell people to look out for it. Your followers will recognize it. You've always got it on. We could turn over Manhattan together until we find it."

"Yeah, maybe."

Her eyes move to Denver when it's obvious I'm not in the

mood for a conversation. "Three times in two days. I'll start thinking it's me you're following around, and not Sin."

His eyes flick to mine and away, his jaw clenching.

"Three?" I ask.

"We had coffee together this morning." Her gaze moves back to Denver, and she bites her lip shyly. "I'll get vanilla for next time now that I know you like it."

Denver clears his throat and a prickling sensation inches up my spine.

"Nice to see you, Theo," I say. "Sorry we can't stop. Monty's just got out for his walk and he's so desperate he might relieve himself on your Louboutins if we stay and chat any longer."

Her face falls as she eyes Monty with horror. "They're new."

"Even more of a reason then." I breeze past her, Monty trotting happily next to me. "Sorry, baby," I tell him in apology for using him as my scapegoat.

Denver's back beside me immediately, matching my increasing pace.

"I went to ask her if she'd heard anything else about your necklace. She said she was friends with the model that left first. She was going to ask her to check her bag for it."

I roll my eyes dramatically. "I told you; I don't give a shit what the two of you do. Go on a date with her if you like. Screw her into the mattress all night and then marry her for all I care."

"Okay."

I stop immediately and glare at him. "Okay?" I spit.

His eyes darken as he holds mine. "I don't need your permission to do those things, but thank you for giving it, anyway."

I recoil. The thought of Denver and Theo is just... yuck.

"You're my bodyguard! *I'm* supposed to be your priority."

"You are."

"Not if you have time to fuck around with Theodora."

"I didn't fuck her."

The way fuck sounds as he says it makes me pause as a shiver runs up my inner thighs, leaving a delicious heat behind it.

"But you want to. It's obvious. So just go ahead and get it over with. Then I won't have to keep watching her fawn all over you like a rash. It's gross—"

Denver moves so fast my brain has to catch up with what's happening. Monty goes wild, barking and snarling at top volume and my arm is yanked hard.

Denver's fist flies past my ear, delivering a bone-crunching punch to a person who has grabbed Monty's leash.

I'm swept behind Denver's hulking frame, Monty's leash pulling tight inside my grip.

"Monty!" I screech.

He's barking and growling but I can't see him. Denver lunges forward again, and Monty's lead goes slack.

I claw air into my lungs as a man in a ski mask runs to a van and jumps inside. It's already driving off before the door closes.

"Where is he?" I cry. "They took him!"

Denver turns.

Monty is wrapped inside his arms, shaking so much his tufts of hair are quivering against Denver's black jacket.

"Oh my god," I sob.

I take him from Denver, bundling him inside my arms. His leash falls from my fingers and hits the sidewalk. The end of it has been cut clean through.

"They had a knife," I cry. "Th-they—"

"We need to move." Denver's eyes have taken on a trained hardness as he surveys the street.

He wraps one arm around me and marches me straight

over to a cab that he hails. He opens the back door, and I scramble inside, my heart hammering as I scan for signs of the man coming back.

Denver climbs in and gives my address, pulling his phone out at the same time. I cry softly into Monty's fur, kissing him over and over while he licks my face and Denver calls my father and tells him what just happened.

"We'll come to you," Denver says.

I grab his arm and shake my head violently. "I want to go home. Please."

Denver nods. "Sinclair wants to go home... Okay... I will. You have my word."

Denver ends the call and looks at me. I cry harder as I meet his eyes.

"Not Monty," I whisper. "I'd rather they try and take me."

His mouth is set in a grim line as I sink my face back into Monty's fur.

13

SINCLAIR

Denver says goodbye to my father and Halliday, then slides the bolt into place on my front door.

I reach down to pet Monty. He's recovered much better than I have. He came in from his walk and ate a whole bowl of scrambled eggs that Halliday made for him, then curled up on the couch with his head in my lap and dozed while my father asked Denver to go over the attack again and again. Denver put a call into some friends who are NYPD officers, and they came to take statements too.

"You okay?" Denver asks, walking over to me.

I nod, but my lower lip trembles. "Just cold. I haven't been able to get warm since we got back."

He studies me. "It's the adrenaline. I'll run you a bath."

He walks past me, and I follow him through my bedroom and into my bathroom.

"I'm fine."

"I never said you weren't. But it's okay if you're not."

He leans over the bath and sets the tap going.

"How do you do it?" I ask, leaning against the doorframe, watching as he checks the towel heater is on.

"Do what?" He glances at me from beneath dark brows as he goes into my bathroom cabinet and takes out some bath salts. He sprinkles them into the tub and rolls his shirt sleeve up to his elbow so he can swirl them around until they dissolve. I'm not used to seeing him without his jacket on. It's strange seeing him on his knees doing something as domesticated as running a bath while his gun is in its holster by his hip.

"All the danger."

He pulls his hand from the water and wipes it on a spare towel. "It's my job." He looks at me, then exhales. "You get used to it. And when you've got something worth protecting, it's simple, because not doing whatever you can to keep it safe isn't an option."

He pauses in the doorway as I stand aside to let him pass. We're so close that I can smell the mint on his breath as I blink up at him.

"Get in the bath, Sinclair. I'll wait out here for you."

"Will you fetch Monty?"

His eyes soften. "I'll bring him in."

I lie in the bath staring at the ceiling while Monty snoozes in his throne bed next to the bath. Denver brought it in for him before I got in. I never thought he'd noticed it in the living area. But this is Denver, he's paid to notice everything.

"You okay in there?" Denver's deep rasp floats through the door. I can tell by where it's coming from that he's sitting on the floor on the other side.

"I'm still okay," I reply.

The Rule Breaker

I've lost track of how long I've been lying here. But it's been long enough for Denver to ask me that six times.

I sigh as I sit up and step from the water, wrapping a towel around myself. Monty stirs in his bed and watches me as I dry.

"I love you, baby. You can sleep under the covers tonight."

He tilts his head, then whines until I go and pat him.

"I'm coming out," I call to Denver.

"I'll be in the other room."

I wait until I hear the sound of him closing my bedroom door before I hang up my towel and open the bathroom door, walking out into my bedroom and into my walk-in closet. I'm pulling on a clean pair of lace panties when my phone buzzes on my bed. I walk over and open the message.

> Zoey: I'm on my way over.

> Me: It's okay, I'm fine. I'm about to go to bed. And Denver's here.

> Zoey: I'll be there in the morning then. Love you.

I was going to call her after my bath. It's been non-stop with my father and the cops since we got back.

"Denver? Did you call Zoey?" I shout.

His answer comes immediately from outside the door. "No. But I can call her now for you."

"It's fine," I say, clicking onto the internet.

I don't even have to search for it. It's top of the news site I open first.

Sinclair Beaufort in dog-napping scare.

"Where's your phone?" Denver asks suddenly. "Sinclair?" He knocks on the door. "Sinclair, don't go online."

My eyes ping-pong over the report. Attached is a video

filmed on a passerby's phone. The guy has grabbed Monty by the scruff of the neck and lifted his front paws off the ground. You can't tell who he is because of his ski mask. But you can see the moment he's almost knocked out by one punch as Denver hits him square in the face.

Screams echo from the video. *Mine.*

It cuts out as Denver lifts a barking Monty into his arms.

"Sinclair." Denver's warning rolls through the door as he presses down on the handle.

"Stop. I'm not dressed," I screech, running over and holding the door shut.

But it's an excuse. The fingers on my free hand are scrabbling as fast as they can as I read comment after comment beneath the video.

"Poor dog, I hope he's okay."

"She deserved to lose her dog. Did you hear how she attacked that other model?"

"Screeching bitch, my ears hurt."

"What's with the stupid sweaters she makes him wear? Animal cruelty. #Takeherdog"

"You should all be ashamed. He's an animal. They were probably going to kill him."

Denver growls, "I'm coming in. Move back from the door."

I step back, my hand flying to my mouth as I read the last comment.

"Next time, we won't fail. RIP Monty."

"Sinclair!"

Green eyes burn into mine.

Then my legs give way.

14

DENVER

"I've got you."

Her eyes roll in her head as she crumples inside my arms.

"Sinclair?"

Her body is a dead weight as I lift her beneath her knees, cradling her to me.

"You fainted. You're okay," I soothe as I carry her over to her bed and lay her down on it. I place a pillow beneath her knees to raise her legs to get the blood back to her head.

"Denver?"

It's a weak whisper that tears at my heart.

"Monty, they're going to—"

"They're not going to do anything without getting through me first."

She looks at me with wide eyes, her cheeks pale as she comes around. She wants to believe me. She needs to have that to hold on to. That hope. That trust. I've seen her broken before. I can't see it again.

"I'll go and fetch him," I tell her.

She sits up in a rush, pulling me to her. Her naked breasts

sink against my shirt and her pebbled nipples penetrate the fabric against my chest like we're skin to skin.

"Promise me you'll protect him over me if you have to." Her breath skates over the side of my neck as her lips brush my earlobe. "Promise me, Denver," she pleads.

She pulls back with shining eyes.

"Denver?" Her eyes ping-pong between mine frantically as she moves at the same moment I lift my hand to calm her.

Her nipple brushes my palm, sliding over my thumb until the puckered tip grazes the pad.

I freeze, sucking in a sharp breath.

"Promise me!" She moves closer, oblivious to her breast filling my palm before I pull my hand away.

I yank my tie from around my neck and rip my shirt open, pulling it off and wrapping it around her shoulders.

"I'll put both of your lives before mine, I promise you." I keep my eyes on hers as I pull the edges of my shirt around her until they meet, covering her up.

She nods, her lower lip quivering.

I fetch Monty from his bed in the bathroom where he's fallen asleep and carry him into the bedroom. Sinclair breaks into sobs when she sees him, and he stirs and wriggles inside my arms until I put him down on the bed. He scampers straight up to her, licking and nuzzling at her face and neck as she holds him close.

I stand, ready to go into the other room. I need to call Killian and Jenson and check in with the police. See what everyone has on this guy who tried to take Monty. The boys will already be running checks on the Instagram account the comment was made from. But the chances of it bringing up anything useful are slim.

Sinclair's hugging Monty, looking into his eyes as she lovingly rubs his ear. Sterling bought him as a puppy for her after she lost her mom and brother. *"God help us if anything ever happens to that dog."* Those were his words. And I knew he was right.

But now I see it.

If anything happens to Monty, Sinclair might never recover from it.

"I need to make some calls," I say.

"Stay," Sinclair croaks, her voice hoarse as she wipes the tears from her cheeks. She's looking at Monty, so I lift the comforter over them both, tucking him into bed with her.

"Of course he can stay," I say. "He can sleep in here with you."

"No," she whispers, lifting her green eyes to mine. "I mean you, Denver. *Please.* Just for a bit. I don't want us to be alone."

I falter. I'm shirtless and need to go to my car and get some clothes from the trunk. And I need to talk to the team. I glance at her bedroom doorway like it'll give me answers.

"Please." She reaches out and touches my hand, her fingertips like silk sliding over my palm.

I look into her eyes, at the desperation swirling in them.

Killian and Jenson will have it covered. I can spend half an hour with her until she falls asleep.

She lets out a deep sigh as I remove my gun, placing it onto the bedside table, then climb on top of the covers beside her. My head hasn't even touched the pillow before she curls herself and Monty into my side, resting her head near my shoulder.

Her warm breath fans over my chest, lightly teasing my nipple. I gently place one arm around her with my hand against her back. She sinks into me like it's the first time she's been able to relax since the incident.

"Thank you," she breathes.

Monty rests his head on my rib cage, staring at me. His long pink tongue extends, and he licks me over and over as Sinclair strokes his head with a soft laugh.

"I think he's saying thank you too."

The rough grate of his tongue leaves wet patches on my ribs that turn cold in the air before he licks them again.

I tighten my arm around them both.

"You're welcome, Monty," I rasp, then I dip my nose into Sinclair's hair for a second, breathing her in. "You both are."

Soft cries shake her body in her sleep. I stroke her hair from her face, shushing her. Monty's moved lower down the bed and is now sleeping across the bottom.

Sinclair's been restless since she fell asleep, toeing a line between dreams and memories as she whimpers out Monty's name. But the one that tore into me the most was when she cried out her brother's name. She had rubbed at her neck as she'd cried it, like she was searching for comfort. *And there was nothing I could fucking do.*

I always liked her brother. Everyone did. Losing him was like losing a friend. Something I know the pain of all too well.

My phone lights up with another text as I lean against the headboard, where I've positioned myself since Sinclair fell asleep. I've been talking to Killian and Jenson. And I called Sterling too. He told me to stay with Sinclair tonight. But even if he hadn't instructed me to, there's no way I would have left her like this.

> Killian: No links to Neil with the attempt on Monty. The guy is either smarter than we give him credit for, or he's not involved.

I curse under my breath. The last meeting we all had about Neil, we came up with the same answers.

None.

We patched Mal in, who's back in Botswana, checking on business. But between him, Sterling, Sullivan, Killian, Jenson, and I, we have nothing.

Sterling's family are relying on us to give them answers. And we've got shit. For more than two years, all we've had is shit. Sterling might have ordered Killian and Jenson to stop going back to Cape Town to try to find out what happened that day, but I can't let it go. Yachts don't burst into flames like that. Fires don't spread that fast. Not unless something, or someone, feeds them.

The Beauforts are one of the wealthiest families in the world. There are plenty of people who could see them as a target. But before the fire, there was nothing. No threats, no demands for money. Nothing. And after was the same. No one took credit for the deaths. No sick bastard came forward to gloat about their ability to get close to the family undetected.

Sterling needs to move on and live his life. He's got Halliday and the baby. I get how a baby can change you. How you need to put their needs before your own.

But I won't give up looking, even if Sterling has told us to.

I owe it to him.

And if there's even a chance that it's connected to Neil, and the things that have been happening to Sinclair are too, then he's going to wish he never came back to New York.

Sinclair cries softly, her face screwed up as her dreams haunt her.

I clench my jaw and text Killian.

> Me: Keep looking. Whoever went after Monty is going to pay.

15

SINCLAIR

Denver looks so calm when he sleeps. A direct contrast to the tension that's usually streaking across his brow in precise lines.

I lie on my side watching him as the morning sun casts a glow over his skin. His torso is so tanned. Considering I only ever see him in suits, I have no idea when it sees the sun. His eyelashes are frustratingly long and thick. Why do men get such good natural ones?

The dips and grooves of all his muscles lift and drop with his rhythmic breathing. I can't believe I thought he wore a bulletproof vest. Part of me still didn't believe that was really his strong, solid body beneath his shirts, even when I'd felt his heart beating against my palm. But now I can see that it is.

He's huge.

And beautiful.

Annoying, assigned to be with me at all times, grumpy, occasionally harsh, stupidly stubborn, and sometimes far too silent for his own good...

But beautiful.

Gentle and strong.

I wrinkle my nose as I stare at him. Zoey would be laughing her head off if she could see me, convinced that there's something to it. But there isn't. After yesterday, I'm just grateful to have him around, that's all.

He saved Monty.

He could do a million awful things to me. Hurl a billion mean words at me. But I'd still be grateful to him for that.

I inch closer, the scent on his shirt I'm wearing matching the one that's coming from his warm skin as he sleeps. Maybe I should tell him he snores like a pig when he wakes up. He'll get all grumpy, pissed that he fell asleep in my bed. He takes everything so seriously. Him falling asleep in here is probably crossing some huge client/bodyguard line that he has.

I prop myself up on his pillow with one elbow, stifling a yawn. I slept terribly, but I'm grateful that I don't remember my dreams. I know enough to be certain that they were horrid and dark. And somewhere I don't want to return to now that I'm awake.

Something hard digs into my arm beneath his pillow.

My eyes flick to Denver's sleeping face.

I slide my hand beneath his pillow, understanding what it is the second my fingers graze the cool metal.

"No!"

My back hits the soft mattress as he pins me to it, one hand curled around each of my wrists, holding them against my pillow, either side of my head.

"Don't touch that," he growls, his green eyes burning into mine, all hints of sleep evaporated.

My lips part as he hovers over me, close enough that I'm breathing in each tense exhale from his mouth. My legs are open wide, and his thick body is pressed between my thighs from where he's spun me so fast.

He shifts a little, his brows scrunching together as something long, hard, and thick moves away from where it was pressed against my inner thigh.

"You don't touch that," he rasps. "Ever."

I lick my lips, gazing at him.

"Are you talking about the gun under your pillow or that hard monster in your pants?"

"Jesus Christ," he snaps, letting go of me and pulling back in a shot. "My fucking gun, Sinclair."

I sit up as his chest heaves with angry breaths.

"Relax. I'm joking with you. I have—*had* two brothers. I know all about morning wood. I won't get ideas that it's because you like me," I say, trying to lighten the tension that's engulfed the room. "God," I huff when Denver won't even look at me. "You're so much easier to like when you're asleep."

His jaw flexes, and he retrieves his gun from beneath the pillow and holsters it by his hip.

"I'm going to get some fresh clothes from my car. Will you be okay for five minutes?"

My smile falters.

Denver studies me. "I don't need to go just yet," he says. "You want a coffee?"

I nod.

He rises from the bed, giving Monty a quick fuss as he passes. He walks over to my bedroom door. His naked back looks even broader when he's standing wearing just suit pants... and a gun.

"The vanilla's in the cabinet above the sink."

He looks back at me over his shoulder and nods.

I lean back against the pillow as he leaves, blowing out a breath. Monty gets up from the foot of the bed and flops himself down next to me, putting his head on the pillow where Denver slept. He whines until I fuss him.

"You're a good boy," I coo. "I'm going to make sure

nothing ever happens to you, okay? Denver and I are both going to look after you."

He licks at my face, and I sink my nose into one of his patches of hair as I reach up to touch my necklace.

But it's gone. My brother's gone.

"I can't lose you too," I sniff, kissing Monty's head. "Not you."

"What's the likelihood that the people responsible for trying to take Monty are the same ones who trashed Sinclair's car?"

I sit on my couch rubbing at my temples as my father stands with Denver, Killian, and Jenson, going over last night again.

"From experience, I'd say it's highly likely," Denver tells my father before his gaze tracks to me.

He's standing across the room, the furthest away from me, but his eyes have never left me for more than a few seconds since they all arrived.

"You okay?" he mouths.

I nod, trying not to show that I'm surprised by him speaking to me. It's the most words he's directed at me since he woke up and threw me down into my mattress like I was in danger from touching his gun. I thought at first it was anger that I'd touched something of his. But the way he hulked his grumpy frame around my kitchen as he made us both coffee when I snuck out of bed to watch him, cursing to himself when he thought he was alone, I realized the truth.

He's angry at himself. Angry that he let his guard down and that I could have gotten hurt if I'd handled it incorrectly. It was the way he'd grumbled *"She's yours to protect, idiot,"* to himself as he stood, hands braced on the kitchen counter, huge shoulder muscles taut and straining, that I'd really understood something about him.

Denver's never just mad. He's always mad at himself when something could have ended differently. When he thinks he almost allowed something bad to happen.

And now I have even more questions about who he was before he came to work for my father six years ago, because I still know nothing about him except that he likes vanilla in his coffee... and that he has a huge dick that's hard as steel when he wakes up.

I look away from him, as I tune back into their conversation.

"Those comments are trending online," my father says. His eyes meet mine, softening as I reach for Monty by my feet and pull him up into my lap. "I'm sorry you had to see them, Sweetheart. But they're not going away. We need to deal with them."

He looks at Denver. "Killian said the posting from fans has ramped up too?"

"What?" I ask.

Denver glances at me guiltily, then answers my father, "They have. Her session times with Brad Garrett-Charles have been leaked. The groomer Monty goes to—"

I gasp and clutch Monty tighter.

"They know where Sinclair goes to buy coffees in the mornings. Where she likes to walk Monty. The stores she's seen in most regularly," Killian adds.

Jenson offers me a strained smile when my father curses.

"Goddammit. They know all her movements. She won't be able to step foot outside without an audience," my father snaps.

"At least if the press is on her even more than usual, no one else can get close without witnesses," Jenson offers.

"He's right," Killian adds, and I could jump up and kiss him for the way he's trying to ease the worry that's creasing my father's forehead. Because when my father gets worried, he makes decisions that there's no talking him out of. Like when he assigned Denver to be my bodyguard and—

"You need to get out of the city for a while, Sweetheart."

My father's warm blue eyes meet mine, but where they're full of love, I also recognize the steely determination in them. My stomach knots.

"It's New York fashion week next week. I have my big runway show. I'm walking it for Stella McCartney!" I shriek, snapping my eyes between all the men.

Killian and Jenson give me sympathetic looks, then avert their eyes. My father shakes his head with regret.

I turn to Denver for support.

"Please. Tell him, Den—"

"I agree," Denver says to my father, his eyes flicking to meet mine.

I snap my mouth closed and glare at him with all the hate I can muster, but he doesn't even flinch.

"Can you take her to your place out of the city?" my father asks.

Denver nods. "Yes, Boss. No one will find us. Don't worry."

"Like hell I'm going to some cave with him in the middle of nowhere!" I jump to my feet, flashbacks of being told he was going to be my bodyguard hitting me at full force as my father gives me the same look he did that day.

"It's not up for discussion. Until we know more about who these people are, it's for the best," my father says.

"When do I get to decide what's best for me, huh?" I stab a finger into my chest. "When do I get a say in my own damn life?"

The thought of being in the city when Monty could be at

risk makes my stomach twist. But it's not the point. It's that my life is being dictated to me. That I'm being told where I can be and who I can be with. That I'm letting whoever this is win, by running away.

If my brother was here, he would have my back. He would stand up for me. I never felt alone when he was here, like I do now. I reach for my necklace out of habit, but stop halfway, dropping my hand.

I swirl my gaze side to side, but it's useless. None of the men in the room will listen to me. None.

My shoulders slump as Dad pulls me into a hug.

"I'm supposed to be shopping for baby things with Halliday tomorrow," I say into his neck as I hug him back, hating fighting with him even more than I hate being ordered around.

"I know, Sweetheart. And I'm sorry. Halliday was looking forward to it as well. But it won't be for long. You can go when you and Denver get back. It's just until we figure this out."

I squeeze him hard and open my eyes. My gaze meets Denver's over my father's shoulder.

"I trust him," my father says quietly into my ear. "And you can too. He's got your best interests at heart."

I narrow my eyes at Denver, still so mad at him for not stepping in. For not doing anything other than being a model employee for my father. But I guess that's what this is to him. His job, as he likes to remind me.

"He's a brute," I whisper in my father's ear.

He chuckles, his chest vibrating. "Sweetheart, he's the best at what he does. You'll be safe with him. And so will Monty."

Denver stares back at me as my father's words sink in. Monty. I have to think about him. Dad's right. He will be safer out of the city.

"I'll be back for the runway show next week," I announce

as I slip out of my father's embrace. "If Denver's as good as you say he is"—my eyes stay glued to Denver's darkening ones as I talk to my father—"then this will all be sorted by then and Monty and I can come home."

Jenson lets out a low whistle. "It's not as simple as that, Sin—"

"Fine," Denver clips. "This gets sorted by next week. And if it isn't—"

"If it isn't?" I arch a brow at him.

"If it isn't, then I'll make sure you're prepared before we come back."

I roll my eyes, feigning indifference as my stomach dances in victory.

"Fine," I huff.

"Fine," Denver counters, staring back at me with an intensity that could burn.

"Good," my father says. "You leave this morning. Go and pack, Sweetheart."

16

DENVER

The wind's blowing Sinclair's golden strands around her face as she sits with her face by the open window of my car.

"So where is this top-secret place of yours?" She sighs and closes her eyes against the sun, breathing in the fresh air.

We left the city over two hours ago. All signs of Manhattan and skyscrapers are firmly behind us.

"Close," I reply, running my hand over my chin as I rest one elbow on the open window frame and hold the wheel with my other hand. The familiar feeling seeps into my muscles, loosening them a little. It's not relaxation exactly, but it's the closest thing I get to it being out here, away from it all.

"When do you even come here? I thought you had an apartment in the city?"

"I do," I say to Sinclair.

She pops open her eyes and turns to me with interest.

"I've never seen your place. Do you live with Killian and Jenson."

"Fuck, no."

"Jenson's jokes?" she asks with a smile.

"As well as the sounds I'm subjected to when either of them has company," I reply. Because Sinclair's guess was good. I have lived with them both in the past. But it was short-lived, thankfully. I'm too old for the shit that comes along with having two horny guys with boundless energy and a taste for regular female company as roommates.

"Oh. I guess it's easier for you to have your own place... for when you're dating and not having to spend every minute of your life with me," she adds, looking out of the window again.

Her phone rings in her lap and she breaks into a smile as she answers it, putting it on speaker.

"Brad," she gushes.

"Hey, Sin. You okay? I heard about what happened. Is that why our session got canceled today?"

My grip on the wheel tightens. He knows that's why I canceled her sessions with him. I explained it all to the jackass when I called him this morning while Sinclair was packing.

"Yeah. It's nothing. Just Dad being cautious."

"So where are you?"

Sinclair's gaze flicks to mine, and I jerk my head at her in warning. No one except family can know where she is.

"Oh, nowhere special, just taking some time out. I'll be back in a few days."

"He with you?"

"Who?"

Sinclair holds my gaze.

"That huge bodyguard of yours. The one who thinks he has a chanc—"

"Yes, I'm with Denver," she replies.

My nostrils flare with my deep inhale as I focus back on the road. Brad Garrett-Charles. That fucker's name is enough to make me want to smash his nose up into his brain. There's something about the way he looks at her, the way he touches her when she's with him. All checks on him have come up clean, but I still don't like the guy.

"He's the one who saved Monty. I trust him," Sinclair says.

I glance back at her, but she's staring out of the window again.

"You know who else you can trust? Me," Brad says, his voice dripping with smarminess that Sinclair doesn't notice.

"You're sweet." She giggles.

"Come on, Sin. You know I care for you. Tell me what I can do."

She looks at me, puzzled, as I pull over on a patch of dirt at the side of the road.

"Nothing right now," she replies. "I'll call you when I'm back in the city, okay?"

"You do that, beautiful."

"Bye, Brad."

She smiles and hangs up.

"Why did we stop?" She surveys the deserted road we're on that twists up the side of a large hill, then looks out over at the forest beneath us.

"Give me your phone," I instruct.

"Why?" She wrinkles her nose but hands it over.

I open it up and take out the SIM card. Sinclair reaches for it, but she's too late.

I snap it in half and toss it out of my window where it drops off the side of the road and disappears into the forest below.

"What the hell?" She gapes after it. "Why did you do that?"

I hand her phone back. "Be grateful it wasn't the whole thing."

"What?"

"Your phone can be traced. And until we know how

advanced these guys are, we aren't taking any chances. You can call your father and Zoey from mine while we're away. It's untraceable."

"Oh, thanks so much, you're so fucking generous." She scoffs, slamming back into her seat and folding her arms. "It's Brad. It's not like he's in on it."

"No, he's not. I already checked him out."

She whirls her head in my direction to glare at me.

"But I don't trust him," I add.

"You've never given him a chance. You decided that you didn't like him the moment you met him."

I don't correct her to the fact I didn't like him *before* I met him.

"I never told you I don't like him. I told you that Monty doesn't like him," I say.

Sinclair snorts.

"How do you know? Did Monty tell you?" Her eyes travel to Monty, who's asleep on the backseat. She said he gets sick in the back sometimes, but she begrudgingly admitted an hour into our trip that he seems to be okay when I drive, after he clambered into the backseat and made himself comfortable on a sweater of mine I'd left there.

"Well, did he?" She fixes me with a look.

"He doesn't like him," I say. "He likes to roll in cat shit, though. I've seen him do it."

"Are you likening Brad to cat shit?"

"No. I said Monty *likes* cat shit."

"Oh my god, you're so…"

I wait for her choice insult, but nothing comes. Instead, she sighs and looks down at her phone.

I pull onto the road, leaning back in my seat as I drive.

"The cabin Wi-Fi will be disabled. The only thing your phone will be good for will be as an alarm clock for our morning sessions," I inform her.

"You're kidding? Denver?" she presses when I don't reply. "Seriously? What am I supposed to do without Wi-Fi?"

"You won't need it."

"Wait? What sessions?" She shoves at my ribs. "Den—"

"I'm going to train you." I sneak a look over at where she's fallen into silence. "You want to go back to the city for your show next week? Then you're going back prepared."

"Prepared?" She scrunches up her face. "So what? You're training me in how to be a Brute?"

"I'll teach you how to defend yourself and get out of a situation you don't want to be in."

She sags into her seat, her face twisting over in thought. "You're teaching me?" she muses.

"That a problem?"

"No," she mutters. "Because I'll kick your ass."

I glance at her, but she's still staring out of the window.

"Boot it to the fucking moon." She flicks her hair over her shoulder.

My lips tilt up. "Good. Keep that fire. You're going to need it to fight me."

"Uh-huh, Brute, whatever you say," she sing-songs. "You'll get your ass handed to you."

I run my tongue over my teeth, amusement bubbling in my chest. "We'll see, Princess. We'll see."

17

SINCLAIR

"Ugh!" My breath is forced from my lungs as Denver lays me out on my back on the mat with a thud.

"Again," he clips, holding out his hand to help me up.

I stand, ignoring his offered hand and climbing to my feet. I wipe the sweat from my brow with my forearm.

"I'm just warming up," I pant, fighting to catch my breath.

"I know," he replies. "You want to take a minute?"

I narrow my eyes at him. My warmup has consisted of him making us run a three-mile trail through the woods that surround his secret cabin, and then having my legs kicked out from under me by him five times in as many minutes. We only arrived a couple of hours ago, but he said we should get straight on with it. And true to his word, the Wi-Fi in this secret lair of his has been disabled. Even Monty's no company. He's been sleeping on a rug in the living area since we arrived. So I have nothing else to do. It's either count treetops or start training so I can get back to the city as soon as possible.

"No," I huff.

I kick out at him again and he expertly sidesteps, then grabs me around the knees, hoisting me over his shoulder.

"You're cheating!" I slap his back with my palm before he puts me down.

"These assholes won't play fair," he says, taking a step back from me.

"Uh-huh. Neither will this Brute that I'm stuck with," I say as I grab his vest and pull him toward me, lifting my knee and jabbing it toward his crotch at the same time.

He grabs my waist, lifting me like I weigh nothing, and using the fact I have one foot off the floor to manipulate my balance. I'm thrown up into the air, and he pulls my body to his until I'm straddling his waist, our faces inches apart.

He wraps his giant arms around me so tightly I'm pinned to him, my arms held behind my back. I'm unable to do anything except keep my thighs banded around his thick torso. I squeeze them, trying to dig my knees into his ribs, but it's pointless.

"I know you don't want to hear it, Sinclair. But you're vulnerable. Look at the way I'm holding you and I'm not even out of breath."

I scream into my cheeks in frustration and wriggle in his arms. All it does is rub my nipples in my cropped workout top against his vest and make them pucker into tight peaks from the friction.

"I could do whatever I want to you, and you'd not be able to do a thing about it."

Green irises burn into mine, and I stop fighting. Denver's grip on me loosens a tiny amount as I lean closer to him. His eyes remain locked on mine as I move closer.

"Anything you want, huh?" I dust my lips against his and his breathing stalls.

Then I grip his bottom lip between my teeth and bite hard enough to make a point. His warm, minty breath entwines with mine and his hold on my wrists tightens behind my back.

I expect him to let me go, to flinch, curse, something.

But he doesn't.

I pull back, and he runs his tongue over his red lip, his lids hooded as he stares at my mouth.

"Good," he clips.

"Good?" I echo with a frown.

"If you can surprise your opponent, then it can give you a window to escape." He places me onto my feet and picks up my towel, handing it to me. "Let's take five. Grab a drink."

I do as he says, grabbing my water bottle and walking out of the gym, following him down the hallway and into the main living area of the house. He's striding ahead of me, and he steps outside onto the giant porch that juts out from the side of the house into the treetops. I get the impression he doesn't want company.

I lean against the back of one of the couches as I watch him, hands gripping the railing, shoulders tense as his gaze fixes into the distance on the sunset.

His 'cabin' is a secret mountain mansion. It's huge and decorated in a modern, yet understated way. Lots of bare wood and natural textures. It's fully furnished with an open log fire in the giant living space that Monty has claimed as his area, and huge floor-to-ceiling windows that look out over the treetops. It's also fitted with the most state-of-the-art security system I've ever seen, rivaling the vault at Beaufort Diamonds flagship store on Fifth Avenue. Denver had to scan his retina to grant us access to the built-in garage that the house sits on top of.

We could be anywhere. It's peaceful, surrounded by forest for miles. The roads are small and twist beneath the trees, leading to small country towns that are a world away from the city lights of Manhattan. We passed through one a few miles back on the drive here. If I'd blinked, I would have missed it. It's probably the closest civilization for hours.

I don't get it. He must come here more than I realized. Or at least, he did before he got assigned to me.

Lifting one of the photo frames that caught my eye when we arrived, I study it as I sip my water. The woman in it is beautiful. Blue eyes, light brown hair in a ponytail, a smattering of freckles on her nose. Freckles that match that grinning little girl in her arms. Her hair is darker, a deep chestnut like Denver's. And her eyes... they're the same green as his too.

He walks inside, and his eyes drop to the frame.

"Sorry." I place it down on the bookshelf behind the couch.

"It's fine." He walks past me and to the kitchen, filling a glass with water and downing it in one. He fills it back up again and drinks the second one, the muscles in his neck contracting with each gulp.

"Who are they?" I ask.

"Dixie." His expression softens. "And her mom's name is Lizzie."

"How old is she?"

His eyes meet mine. "She'll be seven soon."

"Oh." I look back at the photo. Seven years ago would have been just before he came to work for my father. "Who is she—?"

"We've rested long enough. Let's go again." He puts the glass he's finished down on the side heavily. The bang makes me jump.

My muscles are already screaming at me that they've had enough, but there's no way I'm admitting that to him. If he tells my father, then I'll be lucky to make it out of here this year, let alone in time for my show next week.

"Sure. Bring it," I say as I walk toward the gym ahead of

him. "I was going easy on you before, just so you know. I won't this time."

"I know," he clips. "Time for you to get serious with me."

Something about the deep promise in his words makes warm tingles shoot up my spine as I walk onto the matted area where we've been training. I spin to face him, but he's not there.

"You can't give your opponent any weakness they can exploit," he scolds as he kneels at my feet and does up the lace on my sneaker that has worked its way loose.

He finishes tying it and then stands, his eyes fixing on mine. "You ready?"

But I'm already lunging for him.

The room spins as he takes me off my feet for the sixth time today and brings his full body weight down on top of me as my back hits the mat.

"Sinclair," he tuts like he's annoyed.

I shove at his face, pushing my palm over it and forcing his head back, my nails resting against his forehead where I could scratch his eyes if this were real.

"That's better," he praises. "Fight me."

I push with all my might, my body thrashing beneath his as he presses down onto me harder, pinning me beneath him with his hips. No matter how much I buck and push at his face, he doesn't move. It's like having a stone wall against me.

"You need to find a weakness," he says calmly, completely unaffected by my attack. "You were on the right track going for my groin earlier. Eyes are another target. Dig your fingers in, gouge them, ignore the blood."

"Eww." I wrinkle my nose.

"Sinclair," he growls, his eyes intent on mine as he flexes his hips, pushing me harder into the mat to make his point. "If they're on you like this, do whatever you can to get back onto your feet where you're less vulnerable. Got it?"

I ball my hands into fists and pummel at his solid chest, but all it does is leave me panting.

"God! I hate you!" I squeal in frustration.

His eyes burn into mine. "Quit throwing pathetic punches at my chest and think," he grits. "On size alone, I have the advantage. What else can you—"

The hiss that leaves his lips as I grab the hair at the back of his head and yank it is an impressed one.

"That's better. Good girl."

"Ugh. Don't be so fucking patronizing!"

I swear his lips curl into the ghost of a smirk. And something about it coupled with his words spurs me on. I wrench my arm so hard that I'm surprised I don't pull the soft strands straight out of his skull.

"That's my girl," he grits, his eyes flashing darkly as his head is yanked back.

"I'm not your girl!" I scream.

"No, you're not. But someone attacking you might force you to be. They could try and do whatever the hell they wanted to you."

My eyes widen and my grip on his hair loosens as what he means sinks in.

"Don't stop," he instructs, so infuriatingly calm, knowing he has me at his mercy.

I stare up at him as anger courses through me, setting my muscles on fire.

"Fuck you!" I snarl, yanking his hair again. I shove at his face with my other hand and manage to get my fingers inside his mouth. I curl them around his lower jaw and pull. The air leaves my lungs and I fight to keep up the pressure as my body screams at me to take a break.

The weight of his body leaves mine as he extracts himself from my grip easily. I stare up at him, my chest heaving as he stands.

"That's good. You've got fight, Sinclair. Now we need to channel it to where it'll benefit you the most. You don't need to be the strongest in a fight. You need to be the smartest."

I roll over and leap to my feet.

"You let me go!" I snap.

"You needed a rest." Denver's eyes hold mine as I struggle to control my panting, hating that he's right. I'm nowhere near as fit as him.

"Don't do that again. I don't want you handing me passes. You need to act like it's real. I wouldn't get a rest if it was real. The guy wouldn't stop until he got what he wanted, would he?"

Denver's jaw tightens.

"Exactly," I huff. "He wouldn't. So you're not helping me by going easy on me. Besides, they wanted Monty, not me. They're not going to be trying to assault me."

"We can't assume anything about these guys and the lengths they'll go to. Attacks can escalate in their objective following a failed one. And it triggered you. You fought harder when you thought my MO was sexually motivated."

"Because..." I search for the reason, but I can't come up with anything. "It was just instinct. Once you started talking like that, I wanted to knock your lights out even more."

"Good. Hold on to that feeling. Imagine that's my goal."

"Fine," I snap.

Denver waits another minute while I walk around the edge of the mat, catching my breath. Then I nod at him that I'm ready to start again.

This time he spins me so my back is to his chest, one arm holding my arms down by my sides, the other clasping his hand over my mouth.

"Now think," he says in my ear. "What can you do?"

I wriggle in his hold, making frustrated sounds that do nothing to help me.

He lets me go and I spin to glare at him.

"You can do better than that. You were trying to tear my hair out a few minutes ago."

"Because you were being a bigger asshole before."

He runs his tongue over his teeth as he studies me with his hands on his hips.

"What? Why are you looking at me like that?" I snap.

He shakes his head, looking at the floor like he's contemplating something.

"You respond to roleplay," he says.

"What?"

"You fight harder when acting out a scene. Some people do. It's because it feels more real. It helps them."

"So let's roleplay." I rub my hands together, grounding my feet and setting my stance wider as I wait for him to advance toward me again.

His face is serious as he remains still.

"What? Come on," I urge. "I'm ready."

"It can get intense." The dark note of warning in his tone has excitement bubbling in my gut.

"Good. I already want to kick your ass more. Let's get to it."

I move closer, but Denver doesn't move, just holds my eyes beneath his creased brow.

"Come on."

"You can trust me, Sinclair. I'll never hurt you. But if we do this properly, then there might be moments where you question that. Seconds where you truly believe what we're doing is real. Where you're scared."

I straighten up and hold his eyes.

"I can handle it."

He stares back at me.

"Denver! I. Can. Handle. It." I step closer until I'm toe to toe with him. "I'm going back to the city next week for my show whether you damn well like it or not. So you can either stand there looking like some serious statue, or you can train me in a way that I'll get the most out of it. Okay?"

His nostrils flare. He's still looking at me like he's trying to decide whether I can deal with it or not.

"Okay?" I say again, waiting until he jerks his chin in a swift nod like he's being forced into doing something that wasn't his idea in the first place.

I pat his chest with my palm. "There's a good boy." I smile sweetly. "Now can we please get on with it?"

There's a deep grunt from his chest as he spins me easily, like I'm a doll, putting me back into the same position he had me in before. I suck in deep breaths through my nose as his hand clamps over my mouth.

"You wanted to get on with it?" His breath is warm against my ear as he whispers in a hoarse voice. *"How about I get on with you, baby?"*

I freeze as his words seep into me. His grip on me remains steady as he waits for my reaction. Seconds pass until the heat of his lips so close to my ear snaps something inside me.

Everything happens fast. I drag the heel of my sneaker down his shin, scraping as hard as I can, then I seize the opportunity to bite his hand as it loosens its grip on my mouth. He lets me go, and despite being sure it's just to give me some confidence and he could have easily kept his grip on me, I'm grinning as I spin around to face him.

"Oh my god, you're right! It's working. Let's go again. Make it worse this time. I want to feel the need to obliterate you running through me."

I lunge toward him eagerly, but Denver moves back, holding his hands up in front of him.

"We should start slow."

"Forget slow. Do your worst." I move toward him again,

but he moves back, and I huff. "Come on. I'm getting somewhere. Please, Denver. You want to help me, don't you?"

His eyes hold mine and I blow out a small, frustrated scream. "What? You're worried I can't take it? Because I'm stronger than you think."

"I know you're strong," he says, his eyes darkening.

"Then do it! Come for me. I'm ready." I bounce on my toes, brimming with adrenaline as I picture the look on his face when I really manage to escape him, and not because he's gone easy on me. "Don't be a pussy," I taunt.

"A pussy?" One of his thick brows arches.

"You heard me." I smirk. "A big muscly Brute like you, and you're just a pussy really."

His lips twitch and then he comes for me. I forget to react for a heartbeat, momentarily stunned by how hot his hands are on my flesh as he curls them around my sides beneath my cropped workout vest. He lifts me off the floor, bringing me down onto my back on the mat. I prepare to go for his hair and face again, but his eyes glint before he spins me onto my front, pinning me beneath him.

"I know what you're thinking," he rasps. "But you don't want me going easy on you, remember? So let's try a new position for you to get out of."

"Fuck you," I snarl, jerking my head back to try and hit him in the nose.

He pins my hands together at the base of my spine and uses a knee to knock my thighs wider. Then his body is back against mine, pressing down.

"You look good from this angle, *baby*," he rasps, running his nose up the side of my neck and making me shiver.

"I'm going to ruin you!" I yell as I struggle, thinking of what I can do to get some control back. I don't have many options. He's got my hands pinned, and now that my thighs are spread wide on either side of his legs, I can't kick him. I just have my mouth. I need him close enough to bite.

His mouth presses against the shell of my ear and he inhales slowly like he's savoring my scent. "The only thing that's getting ruined here is you, baby."

I turn my head fast, trying to knock his face, but he's already moved his mouth to my other ear. His free hand finds my hip and squeezes, pulling my ass back against him.

"I'm going to ruin this pretty model pussy of yours real fucking good. Better than your boyfriend does."

I suck in a breath, ready to fight back, to bite, spit, headbutt.

Then a deep heat spreads in my core as Denver presses his mouth to my neck in a kiss laced with menace. "You'll go back to him with me dripping down your thighs."

I throw my head back fast and there's a satisfying smack as it connects with something.

"That's it, baby. Fight back. It only makes me harder."

My breathing quickens as Denver buries his face into my neck, groaning out the words, *"Yes, baby, you're getting my dick so hard."* I struggle against him, bucking my ass up, trying to get some leverage, but he presses with more force, pinning me down.

"It's so fucking small I can't even feel it!" I spit back.

"You'll feel every inch of it inside your cunt in a minute."

He grabs at the waistband of my workout tights like he's going to yank them down, over my ass cheeks.

I throw my head back again, but this time it's useless. I try to shove my hips up instead. Maybe if I can hit him in the groin, I can make him let go of my hands. Something big is pushed between my ass cheeks as I buck.

"So eager for it, aren't you?" he rasps.

I swallow thickly as his huge dick nestles itself against me.

It's almost as big as it felt when I touched his gun in my bed, and he pinned me to the mattress.

Only then it was hard... this time it's soft.

"You feel how hard you make me?" he groans as he grinds his hips into me, pushing his soft dick against my ass.

My cheeks burn. *Asshole.*

This is roleplay. He's playing his part so well. It's time I did too.

My chest heaves as I force out a sob. I suck it back in, then cough out another, whining at the same time so it sounds like I'm crying.

"Stop," I beg. "You're scaring me." I do a good job of making my voice shake as I splutter out another cry. "I want you to stop."

He turns me so fast beneath him that I'm gazing up into concerned green eyes before I can blink.

"Sinclair?" A warm hand holds my cheek and his eyes dart all around my face like he's checking me over.

I shove at his chest, and he moves back easily, slumping back onto his knees.

"I won that one," I announce as I stand.

Denver looks up at me, his brows lowering as he continues to check me over.

"I'm fine! I won because you went easy on me. Again! I told you I could handle it," I snap, more annoyed than I can put into words. I'm not sure why I'm suddenly so riled up. But Denver looking at me, his jaw stiff with concern, isn't helping.

"You're fine?"

"Yes!"

"Okay. I won't check on you next time," he says, still studying me.

"Thank you!" I snap.

We stare at one another for a few seconds before I shake my head. "Are we done for today?"

He runs a hand around his jaw, looking at me, puzzled. "Yeah, we're done."

"Thank fuck for that."

I stomp down the hallway and up the stairs toward the guest room. I know I'm being a brat, but Denver isn't doing me any favors by going easy on me. We were getting somewhere. The role play was helping. Him whispering all those things to me... it was helping.

I storm into my room and slam the door behind me.

We were getting somewhere.

Then his giant soft dick had to ruin it.

18

DENVER

The security sensor for the kitchen beeps, and I look up from where I'm chopping firewood and to the tablet resting on top of the bench nearby. I place my axe down and walk over to it, wiping sweat from my brow with my forearm.

"And so she awakens," I murmur as Sinclair appears on the screen in her 'I love my Chinese Crested' T-shirt and walks to the refrigerator. She opens the door and takes out a packet of cheese before peeling a slice away and handing it to Monty who's standing beside her, wagging his tail.

"I'll go to the store and get him some food," I say, pressing the button that's linked to the speaker.

Sinclair looks around, her eyes narrowing as she follows my voice to the security camera fixed to the ceiling.

She flips me off.

"The sound works both ways."

"Oh, I thought it would. But I just didn't have anything to say to you." She smiles sweetly, her middle finger still extended before she spins, sticking her head back inside the refrigerator.

I sigh and head back inside the house, climbing the stairs

up to where the living area and kitchen are. She's studying the contents of the cupboards as I walk in.

"Protein powders?" She frowns as she scans the flavored tubs.

"They go well in smoothies. I'll make you one," I say.

"Don't bother. I'm not hungry."

She turns and leans against the counter with a sigh, staring out of the window at the treetops.

"You sure? You went to bed without dinner last night."

I bend to fuss Monty as he scampers over to me.

"I wasn't hungry then either," she says, folding her arms, still not looking at me.

I rub behind Monty's ear, and he licks at my wrist. "You want some of the corned beef again?" He turns his head to one side, his tail going mad as I fetch him some and put it on a plate for him.

"I gave him some last night," I explain as Sinclair watches me, her lips pursed. "I know you fed him before we left, but he looked hungry."

"It's fine." She sniffs. "He seems to like it."

The only sound in the room is Monty's happy chewing as we both stand on opposite sides of the kitchen.

"You okay?" I ask.

"Fine." Her lips press tightly together as she avoids my eyes.

"Sinclair?" I press. "Yesterday. I—"

"You what?" She finally looks at me, but it's only to glare like she thinks I'm the biggest jerk in history.

"I read the situation wrong. Role-play was a bad idea."

She scoffs, shaking her head. "You think I can't handle it. But I told you I can."

"That's not it."

"Then what is?"

The defiance burning in her gaze has me scrubbing a hand around my jaw.

"I think it went a little far for the first time, that's all."

She stares at me like she's trying to figure out what I'm not telling her. Because there is a great big fat piece of information missing from my statement. And that's that I'm the one who couldn't handle it.

I couldn't handle the sound of her crying. That's what did it to me. Made me turn her in my arms so fast to check on her that my brain shook in my goddamn skull. I've heard her cry so many times. I've heard it enough to last a lifetime.

I thought I'd hurt her or scared her. For real.

"Stop treating me like I'm fragile. I'm used to it from Dad and Sullivan, even Uncle Mal. But with you—"

"I'm sorry."

The genuine regret in my voice must be evident because her eyes soften a little as she looks at me.

"It's fine." Her shoulders sag.

It falls silent between us again as Monty makes a show of licking the plate clean and then looking up between both of us, licking his lips.

"I'll head to the store in town, get some supplies. I didn't know anyone would be coming here," I say, looking at the bare cupboards.

"*You* can head there?" Sinclair sneaks a look at me. "Are me and Monty staying here?"

I press my lips together. The security system would alert me to her trying to leave. But it's not like she could go anywhere if I had my car. There's nothing for miles.

She cocks a brow at me and the memory of backing her up against that wall after I caught her sneaking around with Julian, the lawyer, pushes to the front of my thoughts. I wouldn't put anything past her. She'd be out of here in a flash and back to New York if she thought there was a way.

"Fifteen minutes, then we leave," I clip, pushing away from the counter. I'm dirty and sweaty from chopping firewood and need to take a shower.

"Twenty," she counters to my retreating back.

"Fifteen," I repeat.

Something about her muttered curse of asshole sounds good. It lacks venom, like she doesn't really mean it. Like we're back on track again. Like she doesn't hate me for what went down yesterday.

I was right. Roleplay makes her fight better. She was putting everything into it, bucking beneath me, trying to headbutt me, bite me. Grinding her ass back against me like she was going to strike my groin, given the chance.

I've never been so grateful for all the years I spent serving. For the discipline it gave me. For the control it's given me over my mind and body. Because if Sinclair had any idea of the basic urges my body wanted to express in reaction to having her beneath me like that, there'd be hell to pay.

With her father, her brother, but most of all with her.

The worst thing that could have happened was if I'd gotten hard when I was training with her. If I'd lost control and let her affect me. If I'd let her down by making it about anything other than teaching her how to defend herself.

I'd be as bad as the creeps I'm trying to protect her from.

Only, I'd be worse. Because they'd all have to go through me to get to her.

There's no one here right now to save her from me.

No one except myself.

19

SINCLAIR

"It's pretty here. Ashton would love it. He could find you a waterfall to bathe in while he drew you looking all wet and sexy."

Zoey laughs down the phone as I sit in the passenger seat of Denver's car and gaze out of the window as we drive. Monty sighs happily from his position in the backseat where he's curled up on Denver's sweater again. I roll my eyes. Denver's probably rubbed corned beef smell over it to get him to like it or something.

"Well, don't get too comfortable there. I miss you, and we want you home. Mikey was asking after you. And Brad was too when I bumped into him."

"Brad?"

I steal a glance at Denver as he drives. His jaw is set with his mouth in a grim line.

"Yeah," Zoey says. "I ran into him getting coffee this morning. He was with a girl. They looked cozy."

"Really?" I bite my lower lip, wondering who she could be. Brad's never mentioned a girlfriend before. Maybe she's just a new client he's going to work with.

The trees lining the road start to thin out and glimpses of rooftops start to peek through.

"Zoey, I've got to go. We're almost there. I love you. I'll call again, okay?"

I squint through the windscreen, wondering where 'there' is as Zoey says she loves me too and hangs up.

"Thanks." I hold Denver's phone out to him after he parks the car on a patch of dirt that's supposed to represent a parking lot.

"You're welcome. Do you feel better now that you've spoken with her?"

"Uh-huh," I reply, frowning at the tiny rundown store through the windscreen. "You're not always an asshole. I appreciate you lending me your phone."

"Not always?"

I flick my eyes to him as he sits relaxed in the driver's seat, his face straight as he looks at the store as well.

"That's what I said. Of course, if you hadn't broken my SIM card in half, or turned off the Wi-Fi, then you might even progress to 'barely ever an asshole'."

"I see," he says, still looking out of the windscreen. "I guess 'barely ever' would be an improvement."

"It would," I agree. "Are we going in?"

"We are," he replies, his attention traveling to a small blue pick-up that's parked nearby.

"Great," I say with fake enthusiasm as I reach for the door handle.

Denver's head whips to the side like he has a sixth sense for what I'm doing.

"I told you," he grits, leaning across me and grabbing my hand before it reaches the handle. "When you're with me, I do that."

I study the tense line in his brow as he stays inside my

space, his large body crowding mine as my fingers remain wrapped inside his.

"Won't that look suspicious here?" I ask, my breath fanning over his cheek and causing a muscle in it to clench.

"What? A man looking after his girl? If anything, it's more expected out here in the country. Just because folk work with their hands here, doesn't mean they don't know how to be gentlemen."

He moves back quickly and exits the car, walking around the hood. He's wearing jeans and a black T-shirt today. A look I've never seen on him. It's like the Hulk met Hollister and had a giant muscly baby.

It suits him.

I take his hand as he helps me from the car.

"Am I then?"

"Are you what?" A line forms between his brows and he frowns.

"Your girl? For the purpose of our cover, I mean?"

The line deepens and a perverse satisfaction heats inside me. I might not make him hard when we fight. But I know how to piss him off.

"Let's get what we need," he grunts, opening the rear door for Monty to jump out.

We walk across the dirt toward the store with Denver's hand resting on the base of my spine like it does when we're in the city surrounded by people. But there's no danger here. The store is deserted as we walk in and a rusty old bell chimes over our heads.

Denver looks around like he's casing out the place before his shoulders soften a little.

"Go and grab what you want for yourself and Monty. I'll come and find you in a minute."

"What if we get lost? There's probably another realm back there," I tease, widening my eyes as I gesture to aisles that stretch on surprisingly far, spilling over with random cans and packets.

He shakes his head with a hint of a curl to his lips. "I'll have my eyes on you, Sinclair. Now go."

I pick up a plastic basket from a stand and wander off happily down the first aisle with Monty.

"What do you fancy, baby? Steak? Some eggs? I know you like scrambled eggs for breakfast. How about some smoked salmon too?"

Monty trots along happily beside me as I toss things into my basket. I stop at a display of syrups, running my finger along the glass bottles until I find the one I'm looking for.

"We don't want him having any more reasons to be so surly all the time," I tell Monty as I add the vanilla syrup to my haul.

I glance up and my eyes meet Denver's over the top of the low shelving. He's standing, talking to the shop owner, a small, kind-looking man with glasses. He says something to the man that makes him chuckle, but his eyes remain on me.

"He's not funny," I whisper, blowing out a confused breath.

Monty and I head up the next aisle and I take my time looking at the fruit, hovering where I can hear what Denver and the man are talking about.

"She's strong," Denver says.

My ears prick up and I pick up a melon giving it a squeeze as I pretend to study it.

"She's coped with it really well. I'm so proud of her."

Warmth fills my chest at the admiration in Denver's voice.

"He's proud," I whisper to Monty, raising my brows. Monty stares back, his tail wagging. I bite my lip to stop a stupid smile forming on my face. I don't care what Denver thinks about me. But it's always nice to receive a compliment.

"Dixie's a treasure. Bring her in next time she's with you."

"I will," Denver replies.

I place the melon back down, the warmth in my chest moving to my cheeks in humiliation. Thank god he's too far away to see. Of course he's not talking about me. He's talking about Dixie, the almost seven-year-old that he has photos of all around his cabin.

His eyes are on me as I glance up, but I turn and stroll back down the aisle in the opposite direction.

I recognize what I heard in his voice now. The admiration. The pride. *The love.*

All the same sounds that Sullivan has when he talks about Molly.

Dixie's Denver's daughter. But I don't get why he never talks about her to me. We're together all the time. I sigh as I wander around the store, my enthusiasm gone.

Denver's no longer at the cash register when I walk up to it and place my basket down.

"Having a feast?" The old man chuckles as he starts ringing everything up and placing it into a brown paper bag for me.

"My dog is." I gesture to Monty, and the man leans over the counter, peering down at him.

"That a wool sweater?"

I lift my chin in preparation to defend Monty's wardrobe choices.

"No, it's fleece."

The man purses his lips. "Our cat doesn't like wool, makes him itch. He's one of them hairless ones. My wife can't stand the shedding." He scrubs a hand around his jaw. "Fleece, you say?"

"It's really soft. Monty likes it." I lift Monty up so the man can see.

He fusses Monty, admiring his outfit.

"I'll bring you a couple next time Denver and I come in," I say, giving him a bright smile.

"That's kind of you...?"

"Sinclair," I say, kissing Monty on the head as I hold him.

"Sinclair." The old man's eyes crinkle. "I'm Buck. It's nice to meet one of Denver's friends."

"Does he not have many?" I giggle.

Buck chuckles, wagging a finger at me. "I can see why he likes you, young lady. Bet you keep him on his toes."

"Where else would I want him?" I reply, happily, watching Buck as he bags up my groceries, his eyes moving to something behind me.

I turn and spot the source of his attention. Denver's talking with a woman with bright pink lipstick and a laugh that has a weird screechy pitch to it. She touches his forearm as he says something to her.

"Excuse me," I say to Buck.

Denver's voice is low as I get closer. "Georgia, now's not a good time."

"It's been too long, Denny," she purrs, stroking his arm. "I know we're not... dating, but we have fun together when you're here. Don't you miss me?"

His response is so quiet that I can't hear it, but whatever it is, it makes *Grabby Georgia* take her hand off him and pout.

"Hey." I beam, coming to stand right beside him. "Who's your friend, Denny?"

I blink up innocently and Denver's eyes darken as he looks down at me.

I smile brightly at the woman. Her attention is fixed on Monty in my arms, so I step closer. "He's really friendly. Do you want to stroke him?"

"Is that...? Is that a piglet from the farm? I thought they drowned the wrong ones at birth." She stares at Monty, her face screwed up in disgust.

I pull him close to my body, sucking in a sharp breath. "They drown them? God, that's barbaric."

"It's nature, Sweetie," Georgia replies, still eyeing Monty like he could be riddled with disease. "And it can be cruel."

"So can dating in the middle of bumfuck nowhere, I imagine," I snap, rubbing Monty's ear reassuringly.

Georgia looks up at me. Her eyes assess me with the same distaste she gave Monty.

"I've not seen you around here before."

She glances at Denver, then back at me. I lean a little closer to him and smile as her eyes narrow and she purses her over made-up lips. An ugly pink matching her ugly words.

"Oh. It's my first time here. I'm Sinclair, Denny's girl," I say, batting my eyelashes up at him like I think he's the most amazing man I've ever laid eyes on. "We're here on a romantic break. Aren't we, *baby*?" I coo.

Denver's brows lower and he stares at me like he's going to make me pay during our training later. But my muscles are already aching. He can't make them any worse.

"All the forest, the privacy. It's so fun!" I widen my eyes with a giggle, looking back at Georgia.

She scowls at me, then focuses an accusing glare on Denver. I balance Monty in one arm and slap Denver's butt playfully with the other one. He stiffens, clearing his throat.

I've got to give it to him; he really is good at the whole poker face thing. He didn't even flinch. I keep my hand on his ass and squeeze a muscular chunk of it inside my palm.

He'll thank me later.

"You almost done, baby?" I pout. "I'm going to go and pay for our stuff."

I throw a fake smile in Georgia's direction and spin on my heels. Her low hiss starts the second I walk away toward the cash register.

"You have a girlfriend now? Since when?"

"I—"

"Who is she?" she interrupts Denver, making my spine prickle with irritation.

"She's someone I've known a long time," he says.

Georgia huffs. "Well, is it serious?"

His answer is muffled by Buck's sigh as he looks at the black Amex I'm holding out to him.

"Sorry, cash only. Machine's busted again."

"Oh. Um." I reach into the back pocket of my jeans like I'll find a hidden stash of money. But I only brought my card. I only ever need my card. And sometimes I don't even need that. I have accounts at all my favorite stores in the city and they just send a bill each month.

The bell above the door chimes loudly as I give Buck a sympathetic smile. "I'm sorry. I'll have to leave everything—"

"Here, Buck." Denver passes him a fold of bills as he steps up behind me, his large body like a furnace against my back.

"What was that?" he grits quietly as Buck opens the register.

"What was what?" I glance up at him. His jaw is rigid. I swear his teeth are in real danger of cracking, given the way he's clenching it so hard.

He inhales slowly as we thank Buck. Denver carries our groceries in one arm as I place Monty onto the floor, and we head outside.

"You know what," he says as we walk toward his car.

"I was just making friends."

Georgia's opening up the blue pick-up truck that Denver was looking at earlier. I wave at her, but she's too busy recoiling at Monty walking alongside me to notice.

"She seems..." I narrow my eyes. "She seems awful. You could do so much better. I did you a favor."

Denver places the grocery bag on the roof of his car. "A favor?"

"Yeah. She supports the drowning of piglets. Didn't you hear her? What else would she think is okay?"

I stare at Georgia who's still looking at Monty like she wants to snatch him up and dispose of him herself. My stomach tightens at the memory of someone trying to take him. And how Denver saved him. He opens the rear door, lifting Monty onto the back seat with care.

Something ignites in my gut as Georgia climbs into her truck but keeps staring at us. She rolls down her window as she drives toward us, as though she's going to say something to Denver. Whatever it is, it's not going to be useful to him if it's coming out of her mouth.

I grab the front of his T-shirt, leaning close. His brow furrows as I place my finger to his lips.

"Trust me," I purr.

I wait until Georgia's pulling up alongside us, then I crush my mouth to his.

20

DENVER

She's everywhere. Her taste on my lips, her scent in the breath I take, her hot body pressed up against mine.

"Sinclair," I warn, the word muffled by her lips on mine.

She ignores me and wraps a hand around the back of my neck, pulling me closer. A breathy sigh passes from her to me as she keeps her soft kiss pressed to my lips. There's no tongue. No movement. Barely anything other than her soft mouth against mine.

But *barely anything* feels like the whole damn world just shook beneath me.

"That ought to do it." She pulls away, smiling triumphantly as she watches the taillights of Georgia's truck drive away.

She turns back to me, rolling her eyes. "Come on. You can get your sex on with someone much nicer. I'll help hook you up when we're back in the city if you like?"

"Get my sex on?"

"Uh-huh."

I slide my hand around her hip as she tries to walk away,

turning her so she's pinned in-between me and the side of my car. She comes easily, used to me caging her in between my arms. I can't seem to stop needing to do it. She's always putting us in situations where I have to fight to make her listen to me.

"Why would you do that?" I growl.

"Relax. Sullivan has a suite at The Lanceford especially for it. I know single guys might want to fuck but not date, I've got girlfriends who feel the same. Like I said, I'll hook you up. They'll bring a smile to your serious face better than Georgia ever could." She pats my chest, humming happily like she's pleased with herself.

"Fuck, Sinclair!" I slam my hand against the side of the car. "I meant you kissing me! Your father trusts me with you. Sullivan trusts me with you. What if other people had seen us?"

She shrugs, her face closing off like my words have struck a nerve. "Like who? Bigfoot?" She snorts. "It's not like there's many people around here."

"That's not the point. It's my job to—"

"Your job. Oh, here we go." She throws her hands up. "I know. It's your job to babysit me. Well, you're welcome for me giving you a great excuse to cut ties with little Miss Bitchface. Maybe once we're free of each other, you can find someone nicer instead."

"When we're free of each other?" I grit.

She averts her eyes from mine, wrinkling her nose. "No one saw us, and like I'd tell anyone I kissed you, either. Don't be ridiculous. You're worrying over nothing."

She shoulders me out of the way, but I move in front of her, opening her car door for her before she can.

"When you're with me—"

"You do it! I get it!"

She plonks into her seat with a huff.

"No," I correct her. "When you're with me, I worry." I lean into the car and calmly take her seatbelt in my hand. "I worry about you. About Monty. I worry about keeping you safe. Protecting you. If I stop worrying, then my guard could slip. And I won't ever put you at risk like that. So I'll continue to worry, okay? I do it so you don't have to."

"Because it's your job since my father made it your job. I know," she mutters.

"Because *I* worry, Sinclair." I fix her with a look as I click the belt into place. "Because I've *always* worried about you, Since the first day I saw you, before we even spoke."

She stares at me through the window as I close the door. I stare back, one hand resting on the roof as I exhale heavily, unable to make my feet move away from her to get back inside the car just yet.

Instead, I allow myself the indulgence of looking at her face and into her deep green eyes. It was that brightness I noticed the first time I met her. One that reached out and grabbed hold of me, captivating me in its beauty. Its brilliance. Making it hard to look away.

But it's the sadness that's been in them for the past two and a half years that's made it *impossible* to look away.

"You've no idea how much I worry," I murmur.

She frowns as I tighten my fist against the roof of the car before cursing and stepping back.

And I always will, Princess.

◆

"Your hands are like mitts," Sinclair says, hands on her hips as she surveys me fastening her sneaker for her again.

"I should get you some new ones, with Velcro," I clip as I

lace them tightly. They're always coming undone. We've spent two more days training together, and I've needed to fasten them for her at the start of every session.

"Can you get gloves big enough?"

I look up at her from beneath my brows. "Gloves?"

"For your hands," she muses. "If they got cold and fell off, you'd take out half of downtown."

"Good job we're out of the city then, isn't it?" I stand and look at her. "You ready?"

"Yeah." She shrugs. "But can we step it up a bit this time?"

"Step it up?" I frown. I've been getting her in all sorts of holds that she's had to think about the best way to try to escape. I've kept them varied to help her understand it's the thought behind her defense that's important at this stage. Not the strength she uses.

"I mean, with the roleplay." She twists her lips, muttering when all I do is stare at her. "It's helping, it really is. It fuels my desire to punch your lights out." She smirks, but it falters quickly. "But like... I know you're going easy on me. You can be... worse, you know?"

"Worse?"

"Yeah, like... I don't know. Grabbier. More realistic. Like you actually mean it."

"Grabbier?" I arch a brow. "You want me to touch you more?"

She shrugs. "Yeah?"

I step closer until I can see her pulse fluttering in her neck. "Sinclair, if you want me to touch you in a certain way, you need to ask me to. And you need to be sure."

"It'll help me," she says, lifting her eyes to mine. "What? You think it's a bad idea? That I can't handle it?"

"I didn't say that."

"No, but you're thinking it." She snorts. "Look, I know I

can do better. I want to do better. But I need you to feed that part of me that responds to you."

I run my tongue over my teeth as I look into her eyes. She's got them narrowed in her usual defiance, but there's also fear in there, pleading with me. Fear that I'll say no and leave her alone and unprepared.

My chest burns with memories. Lifeless eyes. Blood on my hands.

The consequences of being unprepared.

"We do this, and we need a safe word. So if you're really upset, I'll know."

"I won't be. You can do whatever you like to me." She lifts her nose, but sighs when I don't back down. "Fine. Mine can be mitt. What's yours?"

"What's mine?"

"You need one too, for when I really hurt you and you can't take anymore." She curls her lips, waiting.

"Okay." I nod. "Mine's sneaker."

"Is that because you can cry it more easily?" She smirks and takes a couple of steps backward, preparing for me to come at her.

"No. It's because yours are undone again, baby."

She looks down, and I take it as my opportunity to grab her, snaking one hand around her waist and placing the other against her throat.

"Cheat," she spits, her windpipe pushing against my palm as I hold it.

"I told you; assholes don't play fair."

Her eyes burn into mine as I lift her like she weighs nothing and get her on her back beneath me within seconds. There's no point escalating my attack slowly. We've done this so many times now, we get straight to it.

Only this time, I'm supposed to be 'grabbier'.

I slide my hand over her hip, my thumb dusting over each

rib as I inch higher toward the hem of her cropped workout top.

"Want to use that safe word yet?" I ask.

"Fuck you," she spits, bucking beneath me.

I stroke over her thundering pulse with the hand that's wrapped around her neck.

"Keep up the struggle, baby. It'll make it more fun breaking you in." I slide my other hand higher until the tip of my thumb grazes the underside of her breast through the thin material.

I pause, looking into her eyes as I wait for her to react. She's going to say it any minute. *Mitt.* She's going to say it and then it'll all be over. She'll race out of here, full of anger like she was the first time we crossed this line. The last few sessions we've had have been tamer. She's right. I have stepped it down. I've held back, not wanting to push her too far. Not wanting to face the consequences of what might happen if I did. The way she might look at me after. Or worse, not be able to look at me at all.

We stare at one another, breath mingling. Her pupils dilate.

Then she bucks again.

"I'll rip your dick off if you so much as touch me!"

My hand moves before my brain catches up, and I cup it over her breast, closing my palm over it, taking the weight of it in my grasp.

"Now there's an invitation, baby," I hum.

Sinclair fights me, clawing and scratching at my arm, pulling at my hair. But I don't feel a thing except the way her nipple hardens for me beneath her top as I drag my thumb around it in circles.

"You wet for me too?" I ask, letting go of her neck and grabbing a handful of her ass and lifting her thigh so it wraps around my hip.

"Asshole!" she thunders as she slaps at my face.

I bury it into her neck, away from her attack, and kiss beneath her ear.

"Shall we find out, baby? I know that's what you're waiting for."

Her nipple is so hard beneath my thumb that heat threatens to race to my dick. I force all thoughts of it away.

This is just roleplay. It's what she wanted.

She bucks again, pressing her breast into my palm. "Get your dirty hands off me!" she yells as she delivers an impressive blow to my temple. I'll have to commend her on that one when we're done. She was so fast I didn't have time to block it.

I squeeze her breast, pinching her nipple.

The next buck of hers has even more power behind it, and she manages to lift my weight off her a little.

She's right. This does help her. She's putting everything she has into it.

"Such a little fighter," I muse as I snake a hand between our bodies and place it on her inner thigh, but not too close to where they join.

She could try and get the upper hand over me now. At this part of the attack, I would be distracted. Too lost in her, one hand groping her perfect, soft breast, the other inches from her pussy, to notice.

Come on, Sinclair. You can do it.

Her breathing quickens, and she shoves at my chin. She could go for my eyes or my groin. My throat. Somewhere.

But it's like she's lost, needing something to push her over, to give her that final boost. She grabs at my hair, completely missing an opportunity to hit me in the face as I straighten up and look at her.

"Asshole," she says, her eyes burning.

I hold her eyes, wanting to tip her over that edge. Show her what she's capable of.

I lick my lips. "You going to come on my cock as I fill you, baby?"

Her eyes narrow. She's so close, I can sense it.

"You going to milk me dry with this beautiful cunt?" I stroke her inner thigh with my thumb, still keeping it away from the heat that's seeping through her clothes.

She fights against me, still so close to overpowering me.

But close isn't good enough.

Close won't save her.

Come on, Sinclair.

Her lips part and blood fires through my veins like a shooting cannon, urging me to push her to her limit. To make her see that she's capable and strong. Just like I'm always telling her.

I yank the neckline of her top down roughly, exposing her breast. Her nipple pebbles as the air hits it.

She gasps, but still doesn't use her safe word. Her eyes drop to her breast, then back to my face, her lids hooding as I slide my hand up slowly and drag my thumb over her nipple, taunting her as I click my tongue.

"I think you like me touching you, baby. Admit it."

"Screw you," she hisses. "Your hands on me makes my skin crawl."

She's stopped fighting me. Her eyes are glued to where I'm cupping her breast and teasing her nipple.

But she has to remember what this is all for. She needs to be safe. I'd lay down my own life to protect her, but if there's even a small chance someone could get to her, she needs to fight them with all she has.

I *need* her to be okay.

I need to push her to her breaking point.

"My hands?" I growl, holding her eyes as I lower my head toward her body. "How about my tongue?"

She watches me in silence as I move closer. She's going to

fight back any second. She's going to stop me. I move painstakingly slowly.

Come on, Sinclair.

My lips brush her nipple, and her sharp intake of breath makes her chest rise, pushing the tip between them. I hold her eyes as I take it in my mouth... and suck.

Her eyes widen as an involuntary groan slips from the back of my throat. My grip on her thigh tightens, and I suck harder, rolling my tongue around the tip.

She stiffens beneath me.

Fuck, I've taken it too far.

"M-m..." she pants.

I pull my mouth from her, bracing myself for her scream.

The word that was meant to protect her from this. From me.

"Sinclair, I'm sorry, I—"

But she's screaming, drowning me out as she launches herself at me. I move back just in time before her fingers penetrate my eye sockets.

"M—!"

21

SINCLAIR

"M-motherfucker!" I yell, finally getting the word out. Finally regaining control over my body.

Denver's already off me, but I slap him hard across the cheek.

He grabs my wrist, his eyes wild. "You didn't use your safe word. Why didn't you use it?"

"I didn't need to! I had you. I was going to beat your ass," I snarl, using my other hand to try and hit him again.

He grabs that one too, easily blocking my shot. "Enough. You don't need to keep fighting. If you get them off you, then you run, okay? You get away."

My breath is coming in sharp bursts as my heart pounds. I yank my hands free and shove at his chest, needing to do something with all the energy that's racing through me.

"I had you!" I screech, giving him one final push before dropping my arms to my sides, my breath shuddering as I suck in giant mouthfuls of air. "I had you!"

"Breathe," he instructs.

I stare into his eyes as I get my breath back, my entire body tingling like I've had a shot of adrenaline injected straight into my bloodstream.

Denver searches my eyes before averting his gaze. A muscle clenches in his cheek and I follow his line of sight to my breast.

My nipple is puckered and glistening, damp with his saliva.

I wrench my top up, covering myself.

"I would have gotten away. I got some good hits in. And I was about to go for your eyes like you taught me." I swallow, composing myself as I notice red scratch marks on his neck. "Are you okay?"

Denver looks at me like he can't work something out.

"You did. Some good hits. And I'm fine. But—"

"I think that's enough for today, though." I avoid his eyes, getting quickly to my feet. "I'm going to take a shower," I call as I race from the room without looking back.

I grind to a halt the moment I turn the corner into the hallway, sagging against the wall where he can't see me. My hands drop to my knees, and I drag in a shuddery breath.

What the hell was that?

His mouth was on my—?

A low curse vibrates from inside the gym. A deep thud accompanies it, and I know he's punched something.

A succession of muttered fucks drift out. They're laced with regret, and I squeeze my eyes shut. But I asked him to do it. I *wanted* him to do it.

I just never considered the possibility that alongside the urge to gouge his eyes out, there'd be this other fire. One that was blazing between my thighs. One that made me want to feel his mouth on me everywhere. One that was hotter than anything I've ever experienced.

But it's Denver. This is his job. *I'm* his job. Everything about us being here together is all because he's paid to protect me. Once we find out who trashed Lenny and why Neil is in

New York, things will go back to normal. Denver will be back being my father's right-hand man and I'll barely see him. I doubt we'll even speak. He'll have no reason to talk to me again, just like he didn't before this all started.

I don't know if it's relief or disappointment that makes my stomach twist at the thought.

I take a deep breath and head to my room, needing space. There's not even any Wi-Fi here. I can't use my phone to call Zoey and get her take on what just happened. I have no one to talk to here. Monty listens, but he can't give me advice.

There's no other human being for miles.

Except the man I swore would be the worst person to be stuck with. The man whose touch just sent my brain into freefall.

Denver.

"Morning," I say breezily as Denver walks into the kitchen.

He frowns, looking surprised to see me.

"What? I like to get up early sometimes."

It's six-thirty and I slept a grand total of one hour. The rest of the night, I lay awake replaying our training session in my head. Monty stayed awake with me, knowing I was unsettled. He always knows when something's wrong. He's back asleep on his favorite rug in front of the fireplace now, making up for lost sleep.

I lift a fresh mug of coffee from the side and hand it to Denver.

"Thanks." He takes it, his eyes dropping over my workout gear before his frown deepens.

He's not in his shorts and vest like he usually is first

thing in the morning. Instead, he's wearing khaki cargo pants and a black T-shirt, his hair still damp from his shower. He smells fresh, with hints of herbs and mint, the way he did when he showered at my apartment after sleeping in my hallway.

Disappointment pulls at my stomach. He's obviously in no rush to train together again. Regardless of yesterday, I still want his help. I didn't know how much better fighting physically with him would make me feel about returning to the city. But it does. Monty needs me to be able to fend off anyone who might try to take him again. Denver won't be with me forever. Even when this is all done, there's always going to be a risk that I might need to defend us by myself.

"So, what's the plan for today?" I ask, lifting my mug and blowing steam off the top of it, trying the cheery approach to break through Denver's sour mood.

His brows pinch as he looks at me. "I told Buck I'd drop him off some firewood this afternoon."

"Oh, great. I said I'd take some of Monty's clothes for his cat."

Denver stays silent.

"What about this morning, then?"

I sip my coffee, waiting.

He clears his throat. "We could go for a hike."

I manage to swallow my coffee and not spit it out. A hike sounds like hell. But maybe it'll loosen him up.

"We'll stick to a route I know. Monty will like it," he adds, studying me.

I fake a bright smile. "Okay. Sounds fun," I lie. "I love hiking."

An hour later and we've been marching at Denver's pace for so long that my legs are heavy and sluggish. Monty does seem to like it and has been staying at the front of our pack since we set off.

"You okay?" Denver asks over his shoulder.

"Fine," I reply, avoiding a patch of thick mud.

"We'll reach a clearing soon. We can take a break," he says, striding on in his giant boots.

"Sure."

I keep following him, taking his hand each time he reaches back to help me over an exposed tree root or some rocky ground. He takes it away just as quickly, turning back to face ahead like he can't look at me.

It's ridiculous. One of us needs to clear the air. He's obviously got himself worked up about how far he went. But I don't blame him. It's what I wanted. He was doing what I asked. And I made progress as a result.

But the feeling of his mouth on me was... unexpected. I need to say something. Squash it before it becomes a thing. I've gotten used to it being less awkward between us. I like talking in the car. I like that he isn't always as serious as I first thought he was. I mean, he mostly still is. But I've seen how gentle he is too. With Monty. With me.

"Denver? We need to talk about—"

Something rustles in nearby undergrowth. I whip my head in its direction, losing my footing. I reach out to steady myself, but the only thing in grabbing distance is the branch of a bush. The thorns slice across my palm before I can do anything about it.

"Ouch!"

"Sinclair!" Denver grabs me before I fall.

He steadies me in his arms, and I turn my palm up. There's a red line across the center with small droplets of blood oozing from it.

"Damn it." Denver's deep, worried voice fills the air as he takes my hand inside his and studies it.

"It's nothing. Just a scratch."

He grumbles, frowning at the blood as it drips from my palm and onto the forest floor.

"We'll just patch it up when we get back," I say.

He lets me go and steps back, pulling the checkered shirt off that he's put on over his T-shirt. He spreads it on a dry patch of earth.

"Sit," he instructs gruffly.

He helps lower me down and Monty comes and sits beside me.

"I'm fine," I argue.

But Denver's already pulling the bag off his back and crouching beside me.

I sigh and let him get on with pulling out a medical kit to tend to my hand, a look of deep concentration on his face.

The trees stretch up high above us and small patches of sunlight filter through. Now we've stopped walking, I can appreciate the forest's beauty. It's calm here. Quiet. You could almost believe your worries didn't exist. That real life was another world away. That your heart was still intact.

"Have you ever lost someone you loved?" I ask.

Denver glances up at me from beneath dark brows, then fixes his attention back on my hand, cleaning it with a wipe.

"Yes."

One word. Nothing more. So simple. Straight to the point.

"Oh," I murmur, not sure what I was expecting. Him to avoid the question, maybe. It's not like I've ever known him to share things. At least, not with me. "It wasn't Georgia, was it?" I fail to disguise the disapproval in my tone.

He shakes his head, the tense line of his mouth softening a little. "No, not her."

I exhale in relief. He keeps his attention on my hand, his touch gentle.

"When?" I ask.

He pauses. "Almost seven years ago."

"Before you came to work for my dad?"

He wraps a light gauze around my palm and secures it. "Yes."

"Does it get easier?" I whisper.

His eyes meet mine, and I study the gold flecks in them as he looks at me. Finally, his shoulders drop with a long sigh, and he shakes his head.

"No."

"Oh." I fiddle with the bright white gauze as Denver packs the medical kit away.

"But you find a way to carry on without them. You get stronger," he says.

He wraps his hands around my elbows and helps me to my feet.

I study him as I stand. There's heartache in his eyes that I've never seen. Maybe because he's never spoken about it before, I missed it. Or maybe he hid it so well because he didn't want me to see.

"Was it Dixie's—?"

A flash of pain lances across his face.

"I'm sorry," I say in a rush. I can't imagine what it would be like to be away from your child so much because your relationship with their other parent broke down.

The few times I've seen him on his phone is the only time I've seen Denver almost smile. And now I get it. It's when he's been speaking to Dixie, or her mom has sent a photo to him.

"Have you ever considered the two of you... I don't know? Could you—?"

"No."

It's one harsh word, fired at me. And the matching anger in Denver's eyes as he says it has me clamping my lips together.

"It is what it is," he says more softly, reaching down to grab his shirt. It's got my blood on it.

"I'm sorry, I'll get you a new one," I say.

Denver stuffs it into his bag and tosses it over his shoulder.

"Don't. It's old." He glances at me. "You okay to walk back?"

"What choice do I have? A piggy-back?" I give him a small smile, the knot in my stomach easing as the tension in his shoulders softens.

"You know I'd carry you," he says, his face serious.

We look at one another for a few beats before I shrug.

"I can manage. It's only my hand." I start walking ahead of him, then look back over my shoulder. "I think hikes might grow on me."

"You said you loved hiking."

"I lied."

"I know."

Something about the way he holds my eyes has my core heating.

"But they could actually grow on me after today."

"Really?" He arches a brow.

"No."

He breathes out with what sounds like an almost chuckle. "Come on, Princess. Let's get you back to civilization."

"The city?" I beam.

"The cabin," he counters.

I twist my lips into a smile. "You said civilization?"

Denver wraps his hand around my lower back and steers me back along the trail the way we came.

"I have half of Buck's store in the kitchen after yesterday. What more do you want?"

"Wi-Fi, a SIM card." I tick off on my fingers. "Fifth Avenue. A spa. The Smoothie truck. My own bed. Zoey.

Lenny... Freedom." I grin at him. "You know, spoiled princess essentials."

"Not much then?"

"Not much." I shrug.

I smile as Monty pushes past us both so he can be in front.

"He's getting as bossy as you."

Denver rolls his lips. "It's if he gets as difficult as you we need to worry."

I grin. "You made a joke."

"Did I?"

"You did."

"You're not laughing, so can't have been."

I shove at his chest and force a giggle. "How's that, Brute?"

He nods, his lips twitching. "Then I guess I made a joke."

I fall into step in front of him with a smile. Bringing up yesterday now would pop this bubble. I like this side of him. The side that talks to me. Opens up to me. Jokes with me, in his own way.

It makes a change from the usual terse frown he wears.

Talking about how his mouth felt on me can wait.

22

DENVER

A FRUSTRATED HUFF FLIES OUT OF THE GYM AS I walk down the hallway. We got back from delivering Buck's supplies half an hour ago and Sinclair said she was going to play with Monty. But judging by the way he's spread out on his back, sleeping in front of the fire, I'd say her plans changed.

I stop in the doorway, irritation climbing up my spine.

"What are you doing? You could hurt yourself."

Sinclair flicks her attention in my direction, then turns around and jumps again, trying to reach the pull-up bar I have fixed high where I can reach it.

"You won't train me, so I'll do it myself," she huffs.

I roll my tongue over my teeth as I watch her struggle to grab it. She'll end up pulling a muscle, or worse. She's still wearing the dressing on her palm too. Pull-ups are the last thing she should be doing.

She glances at me, muttering to herself. The earlier bubbly version of her has gone. It seeped away after our hike once we went to see Buck and he told me that Georgia had been into the store asking after me this morning.

Sinclair's back to looking at me like my presence is irritating her. The return of it is not as welcome as it should be, considering it would be easier for everyone if things went back to the way things were.

Back to before I crossed a line. Before I had a glimpse of what she feels and tastes like beneath me.

"You should use a step to get up," I say, walking over to her.

"How about you lie down, and I'll use your face as one?"

I cross my arms, watching her struggle.

She rolls her eyes. "Go on then. Give me a leg up."

"A leg up?"

She gestures to my hands, then the bar, so I slide both hands around her waist, lifting her easily so she can reach it.

"Thanks," she says, managing to pull herself up halfway before she hangs like a rag doll.

"You need some more help?"

"No," she puffs.

I reach up and grab the bar next to her, pulling myself up with one arm.

"Oh god, you're a showoff." She scoffs, looking at my bicep.

"I've just done this lots of times. Pull your core in."

"What?"

I maneuver closer to her so I can wrap my free hand around her from behind.

"Here." I tap her abs with my fingers. "Pull it in."

She does as I say, her stomach drawing in toward her spine.

"Good. Now keep it tight as you pull up. I'll help you."

She hisses as she pulls on the bar. I flatten my hand over her stomach and use my thighs beneath her ass to help push her up as I pull myself up on one arm.

"Don't tell me you think this is fun," she pants as we do it three more times.

"I don't mind pull-ups," I say.

I let go, landing on the floor, then hold her around the waist again, setting her back on her feet.

"I prefer fighting as a workout," she says, wiping her forehead with the back of her hand.

She looks at me when I don't respond.

"I want to train again like we were."

"No." I grab her towel from the bench, passing it to her.

"Yes." She snatches it from me and wipes herself. "What are you worried about? I told you to get grabby. I have a safe word to use. It's fine. It doesn't need to be a big deal. You're making it a thing when we're not... when *it's* not a thing."

She's staring at me with so much fire in her eyes, but I still shake my head. "No."

"Denver," she moans.

"It *is* a big deal, Sinclair. I don't train like that with anyone. I've never done that type of thing with—"

"Ever?" Her eyes widen.

"Fuck no. I don't..." I plant my hands on my hips and inhale slowly. "I've trained with plenty of guys where we roleplay like we're going to kill each other. Women too. But not... I've never done that kind of roleplay before."

"Roleplay where you talk about fucking me?"

"Jesus Christ," I rasp as she steps closer to me, her eyes narrowed in defiance. She isn't going to let this go.

"I can handle it. I told you I could. It's working for me. Who cares if I'm not normal to want to do it like that."

"There's nothing wrong with you doing what helps you. But I can't—"

"Fine. I'll carry it on when I get back to the city, then."

"You'll carry it on?"

She shrugs, pursing her lips. "Yeah."

"With who?" I growl, heat flaring across the back of my neck.

"I don't know. Brad, I guess. He's my trainer."

"Not anymore, he isn't."

"Excuse me?"

"You're not training with him anymore," I grit. "He puts his hands all over you."

"Not his tongue, though. At least not yet." She gives me a fake smile.

"Fuck." My hands clench into fists. "You are not going anywhere near Brad Garrett-Charles." I spit his name out like it's trash.

"We'll see," she hums, turning away and sauntering over to the mat.

She lies on it and starts doing crunches.

"He's a creep," I say as I walk over and stand beside her.

She looks up at me. "What are you worried about? It's just training. It doesn't mean anything."

"I don't trust him."

"I do."

"Sinclair." I drop to a crouch, fighting the urge to lay a hand over her chest so she stops crunching and listens to me.

"Do you mind? You're distracting me and using up the oxygen I need to train with."

"You're not training with him again. I canceled all of your sessions."

She sits up and glares at me. "You had no right to do that."

"I had every right. I'm your bodyguard and your well-being is my priority."

"Just not enough that you'll actually help me be ready for when we go back, though, right?"

"Sinclair," I growl.

"No!" she snaps. "You don't want to train me yourself anymore, but you don't want anyone else to do it, either. What about what I want?"

Tension rolls off her in waves. *What she wants.* I've heard her use those exact words with Sterling and Sullivan multiple times. They want what's best for her. They love her. Their family has been through hell. But she's right. She doesn't get asked what she wants often enough. She gets told instead.

"Not Brad," I say.

"Who else?"

I suck in air through my nose, every muscle coiled tight in my body as I fail to offer up any alternatives. No one else is going to lay their hands on her and live. Not if I have any say in it.

"So it has to be you then." She holds my eyes.

"I..." It tears at me, knowing that I'm letting her down. "Sinclair... I can't."

"Can't or won't? Come on, we don't even have to speak if you don't want to. I'll just imagine you saying those things to me, it'll still work. We can practice me getting out of holds again. Walk through them. I need you, Denver."

I curse as her gaze turns pleading.

"I need *you*. Please."

Her begging me for something, for anything, is more than I can handle. I can't ignore the desperation in her eyes. I can't say no to a damn thing if she's going to beg me with that edge of panic in her voice, should I deny her.

"Sinclair..." I sigh. But it's too late. It's done. She sees the breakdown of my reserve as I lift my eyes to hers.

"Thank you," she breathes. "We'll take it slow, I promise. I'll do it however you want. You can take the lead."

That's what I'm afraid of. Because me taking the lead means staying in control. After yesterday, I know there's a danger that all my control will desert me again when it comes to her. But if it's not me, then she'll find someone else to train her. I know her, she's stubborn. I can't allow that to happen.

I clear my throat. "We take it slow. Tell me your safe word."

"Mitt," she breathes, biting her lower lip. "And I promise

I'll use it if I need to. It's my responsibility, not yours. You don't need to worry." Her eyes light up, making my heart pound in my chest. I put that look on her face by giving her what she wants. But she doesn't understand the potential consequences.

Because I've told her already, when it comes to her, I always worry.

And this time I know beyond doubt that I have every reason to.

23

SINCLAIR

I stand, ready to get started before Denver changes his mind.

"Shoot," I mutter, pouting at my unfastened laces.

Denver bends, tutting as he starts to lace them for me. "How many times have I told you—"

"Don't give your opponent any vulnerabilities to exploit? I remember," I say, before I shove him hard, catching him off guard and making him stumble backward.

His eyes glint as he looks up at me and quickly jumps to his feet. "Good."

"Thought you'd like it." I smile sweetly before blocking his arm as it comes for me.

The impressed look on his face makes my chest swell with pride. I'm a good student, and he might think we shouldn't be doing this, but I've been taking notes, and this time I'm going to show him just how much I'm benefiting from it.

He comes for me again, grabbing me around the waist, but I get an elbow into the side of his face before he can lift me off my feet, buying myself a couple more seconds. He hisses and I struggle hard as he fights to bring me to the ground.

My back hits the mat as once again his size and strength outperforms mine. But like he's taught me, it's about using my head. And maybe he doesn't want to talk this time, but he never said I couldn't.

"Show me then." I stare up at him as he clamps my hands either side of my head.

"Show you?" His brow furrows.

"I know you're going to claim it's the best I'll ever have. So get it out and let me see."

The brief hesitation in his eyes as he tries to work out what my angle is has his grip loosening on my wrists. I take my opportunity and yank them free, using all my strength to shove at his face and push him away.

As soon as he moves an inch, I gain more strength, heat firing in my core as I scream and force him further back. But I'm not done. I keep pushing at his face to disorientate him until I'm able to throw my body onto his, bringing us both down onto the mat again with a thud. Only this time I'm on top of Denver.

I sit up fast, straddling him and grabbing hold of his neck. He looks up at me, his hair ruffled.

He licks his lips. "Good girl. Nice move."

I squeeze his throat. "No talking."

His eyes gleam.

"I could end your pathetic existence right now. Give me one reason why I shouldn't."

My nails dig into the side of his windpipe and his lips curl. Mine lift, matching his as we stare at one another.

I've got him and he knows it.

White flashes past my eyes and my head spins as Denver breaks out from underneath me, rolling us both until I'm wedged beneath him again.

"You want to rethink that?" he rasps.

"Asshole," I spit, bucking as much as the small gap between our bodies allows.

"That was good, though. You did well."

I sag against the mat at his praise.

"What's wrong?"

I blow out a tiny groan. "It's not going to work. *Nice* you doesn't make me want to kill you like *dirtbag* you does."

"Sinclair, we can't."

We look at one another. Denver's huge body is braced over me with my thighs spread around him. Neither of us make any attempt to get up or move away.

"I trust you." I search his eyes, seeing a fraction of give in them. "Denver, I *trust* you. And you can trust me too when I tell you it's fine. We'll stop it if I need to, okay?"

I hold my breath, waiting. I knew if I got him to agree to train with me that this would be my next move. Layer it on again until he's doing what I need him to. But it's not just about the training this time. I need to know what it feels like again. I need to show myself that yesterday was just a moment of madness.

That I didn't get turned on by my bodyguard.

That I don't actually want him after all these years of him being around.

Because *that* would be madness.

"You trust me?" he echoes.

I nod. "With my life. With Monty's."

He drops his head with a curse.

"So, it's a yes?" I ask, hopefully.

He exhales slowly. "You sure you want to do this with me?"

"I can't think of anyone else I'd rather scream at."

He shakes his head. "Okay."

"Okay?"

He looks at me and I hide my excitement. He has no idea

how much I need to get this over with. Then things can go back to the way they were and I won't lie awake all night thinking about him.

"What's your word?" he asks quietly.

"Mitt," I whisper.

He swallows thickly, then nods. "Make sure you use it."

"I promise I will if I need to."

I wait for him to move, and he looks into my eyes one final time before he slowly leans in close. I stay still, not wanting to do anything that could cause him to change his mind. Once we get started, I know we'll be okay. He'll see that. He just has to trust me like I trust him.

He runs his nose up the side of my neck, breathing me in, and I squeeze my eyes shut as something flutters low in my stomach.

"You've got a safe word," he breathes in my ear, making all of the hairs on the back of my neck stand up like they have an electric current running through them.

I should move away from him, but instead, I turn toward him until my lips brush his temple, waiting to see where he goes with this.

"But you won't be needing any words, will you, baby?" he rasps. "Not when all you'll be able to do is cry out as I make you mine... over and over..."

A thrill shoots up my spine.

We're back on.

I suck in a breath and fight back, using all of my strength to pull his hair and try to get to his eyes or his mouth. But Denver preempts every move I make, pressing his giant body down over mine as I struggle.

"Get off!" I scream.

"I'm not an asshole, baby. I'll make sure you get off first."

I wriggle beneath him as he sinks his face into my neck and groans. But he doesn't kiss me there this time. Not like when he had his hand on my breast, teasing my nipple and making it hard for him.

I bite back the words, 'Touch me,' before they leave my lips, instead choosing to thrash beneath him until he pulls back to look down at me.

Green irises flecked with gold dilate as he presses his hips into me.

I whimper as I stare back.

"You're disgusting," I say, disguising my whimper as one of revulsion instead of what it really was.

One of lust.

I arch beneath him, the feel of his torso against my inner thighs creating a delicious friction that my core is screaming out at me to explore.

But it's just the roleplay. I must have a weird fetish for it. The rolling around, being manhandled. Having a huge guy with a huge dick between my legs.

"The way you're squirming about beneath me makes me think you can't wait for me to sink inside you." He watches me carefully, like he knows something isn't the same as the previous times.

I glare at him, not trusting myself to do anything else.

"Do you want that? Do you want me to fuck you?"

His brows scrunch together, and I shake my head sharply.

"I'd rather eat dog sick," I finally spit out.

Denver exhales, his face relaxing. "I can give you something much better to put in that pretty mouth."

"Yeah?" I arch a brow.

He leans closer, baiting me. "Fuck yeah, baby."

The warmth of his breath hits my lips, and I lick them as he hovers mere inches away, waiting for me to react.

What we're doing is filthy. It's degrading. It's wrong.

It's perfect.

"You think I like that idea?" I breathe. "Having your dick in my mouth? What do you think I'll look like choking on it?"

His jaw clenches as I roll my hips beneath him, dragging my pussy over his groin. He sucks in a sharp breath and presses closer. This time the thick length that presses against me isn't entirely soft.

"I think you'd look beautiful," he rasps, his mouth hovering over mine.

I arch up until my lips dust his. "You're deluded if you think that's going to happen," I whisper.

His hips flex, pushing his rapidly hardening dick against me. This time I let my whimper free, biting down onto my lip.

"You wet for me, baby?"

"What do you think?"

"I think I'm going to find out."

I fight against him, but it's half-hearted. He lets go of one of my wrists and slides his hand between our bodies. My pulse thunders in my ears as he reaches between my thighs and his fingers meet the hot, damp fabric of my workout tights.

My back arches off the mat like a bolt of electricity has shot through me.

"You *are* wet," Denver says, his fingers freezing.

I move, causing him to suck in a sharp breath as the evidence of what we're doing pushes harder against his fingertips. He looks at me in hesitation until I dig my heel into his calf and kick him.

"Jesus," he grits, moving his fingers slowly, finding my clit with ease and circling it through the material.

I moan at his touch, parting my thighs wider.

"You like that?" he breathes.

"No," I pant, still pretending to struggle.

"Is that because these are in the way?" He pulls at my workout tights, letting the fabric snap back against my pussy.

I yelp.

His eyes are pinned to mine as he presses a little harder against my clit. "You want me to take them off, don't you?" he whispers.

"Just try to get them off, jerk, and I'll strangle you with them," I snap.

His eyes remain on mine as he moves back, letting go of me long enough that I could easily hit him, deliver a blow that would get him off me so I could escape.

If this were real.

If I *wanted* to get away.

"What was that, baby? You're going to wrap these gorgeous thighs around my ears while I taste what's mine?"

"Fuck you!" I rage, shoving at his hands as he curls his fingertips around the top of the fabric either side of my hips.

But as he starts to pull, I lift my ass away from the mat so the fabric rolls down my legs easily.

"Oh, fuck," he breathes, looking at the tiny black lace panties I'm wearing.

He's back over me in a shot, his breath hot and heavy as I try to roll away. He plants one giant hand on my shoulder, forcing me onto my back beneath him.

"You're not going anywhere."

I shudder, entranced by the intensity his eyes have taken on as he drags the back of his knuckles down the center of my panties.

"You are so wet for me, aren't you?"

He licks his lips, his forehead creasing as he turns his fingers and runs the pads of them over me. I push his hand away, but he puts it straight onto my lower stomach, slipping it beneath the top of the lace.

"Stop," I say weakly.

I'm not even putting any effort into pretending to fight anymore and I'm sure he knows it.

"You want this," he breathes. "You want my hands on you. My mouth. I bet you want my cock too, don't you?"

I bite back a moan as he slides his hand lower. His eyelids hood as his fingertips meet the slick arousal coating my skin. I grab hold of his wrist like I'm going to stop him.

"Say it," he whispers, his pupils dilating as my breathing stutters.

"Get off me," I whisper, but it sounds more like an invitation as I hold his eyes and encourage his hand to slip lower until his fingertips graze my entrance.

"Not that." He shakes his head at the same time as I nod mine.

I tilt my head back and moan as I rub his fingers against me.

"Say it," he warns, his eyes darkening as my wetness smears over him.

"Say what?" I moan louder, circling my hips.

"You know what. Your word. Say your word."

He starts moving his fingers without my encouragement, sliding them over my skin.

"Say it," he groans.

"M..."

His eyes flash as I part my lips.

"Good girl. Say it. You know you have to say it," he rasps.

I slide my hand around the back of his neck, toying with his hair. "You want me to say it?"

"You *need* to say it," he forces out like he's barely holding back.

I pull his face to mine, lifting my mouth to his ear. "Make me."

He yanks back, snapping his eyes to mine. They're on fire, like he's about to give me hell.

"Say it," he hisses, his voice gaining power. "This stops now."

I stare at him, licking my lips as his fingers slide over me, rubbing circles over my swollen clit.

"Say it," he grits again, switching them with the heel of his hand as his fingers curl lower. He makes no attempt to stop what's happening. And I'm not about to help him. Not when my whole body feels alive from his touch.

I stay silent, holding his eyes as the tip of one finger brushes my entrance.

"Say it," he groans.

I shake my head and my mouth parts with a small gasp as he slides his finger inside me slowly. We stare at one another as my wetness pools around it, seeping out into his palm.

"Say it," he repeats. "Before I have you taking more than just my finger."

I shake my head, moaning as he hits a delicious spot inside me.

"Goddamn it," he hisses, sliding it out and then back inside me, but even though my body is stretching for him, he still can't get it all the way inside me.

Heat erupts inside me like a swirling inferno, and I moan. He watches me, the muscles in his neck rigid as he fucks me slowly with his finger.

"This what you wanted? You wanted me to feel how wet and perfect you are? You wanted me to dream about all the ways I'd fuck you and make you mine? The way I'd make you come on my cock again and again until you cried because you needed a rest? Huh? That what you wanted, baby?"

Every last shred of hesitation leaves me as my body ripples around his finger, and I cry out, giving in to the desire taking over my body. "Denver."

He looks at me, his expression a mix of shock and pure heat as I use his name.

I grab his face and pull his lips to mine.

"What are you doing?" He breaks away immediately.

"Kissing you." I press my lips to his again and this time a deep groan is forced from him before he cuts away again.

My lips are tingling with the need to feel what it's like to really kiss him as he stares at me.

"You can't. This isn't pretend anymore, Sinclair. We need to stop."

"Do you want to stop?" I clench around his finger making a muscle contract in his neck.

"Fuck, don't do that."

"What? This?" I do it again.

"You need to stop this," he grits at the same time as he gives me two shallow, but delicious pumps like the temptation is too strong not to.

"You've got a word, too, remember?"

He shakes his head, his eyes on my mouth. "I'd never use it with you, and you know that."

White heat runs through my veins at his admission.

"You want me?" I whisper.

"I'm not allowed to want you."

"But you do?"

"None of that matters. Say. Your. Word."

"No."

I pull his mouth back to mine and this time he kisses me back like he can't physically restrain himself.

He groans into my mouth, all heat and power, kissing like a man who knows how to fuck you all night and make your soul leave and re-enter your body. I open up for him and he slides his tongue into my mouth, owning it, claiming me, like he has every right to do whatever the hell he wants with me, because I'm his and he's been waiting for the moment when I realize it.

I run my fingers through his hair, pulling him closer, kissing him back and whimpering as he keeps fingering me, rubbing my clit with his thumb at the same time.

"Denver," I gasp, climbing higher, trapped beneath the heat of his body.

"Say your word, Sinclair," he rasps, before kissing me even harder so I can't speak even if I wanted to.

I moan around his tongue, my fingers gripping his hair tighter so he can't go anywhere.

"Say it," he repeats.

The rock-hard length of his dick presses against my inner thigh.

"I want to take them off," I pant against his mouth.

"No," he growls.

"Yes."

"If you get naked beneath me, Sinclair, then I can't promise you that I won't fuck you for real right here on this mat. This has gone too far. Say your word."

"I'll never say it, you can't make me."

Denver breaks our kiss. His lips are a darker pink and he licks them like he's savoring my taste. "You need to stop this now."

He pulls his finger from inside me and I whine at the loss.

"Take my clothes off, or I will," I demand.

When he doesn't move, I sit up, forcing him back onto his knees. I peel my crop top over my head and throw it to one side.

His eyes drop to my breasts and darken as he curses.

"You do the rest. Then I'll let you suck them again."

"Fuck, Sinclair. We can't—"

I reach out to pull him to me, but he's already coming anyway. Our lips crash together, and he holds my neck as he kisses me roughly, his other hand dropping to grab my breast.

"You know how beautiful you are to me? How much I want you even though I shouldn't?"

He breaks our kiss and lowers his head, cupping my breast and lifting it to his lips to suck on my nipple. Slickness pools between my thighs. I moan as he switches sides before rising to kiss me again.

"Say your word, Sinclair."

"No." I nip his bottom lip between my teeth, and he inhales sharply.

He's shaking his head, his face a mask of dark turmoil as he uses the hand around my neck to encourage me to lie down. He lets go and holds my eyes as he grabs one of my sneakers. The laces are undone again, and he lifts one with one finger, letting it drop back against the shoe.

"About the only time they've been useful." He tuts.

He pulls it off my foot, followed by the other, then drags my tights down, holding them in his hands as he looks at me laid out in just my panties.

"Not just those," I say.

His gaze drops to my black lace panties, and he drops my tights and scrubs a hand around his jaw.

"Say the word, Sinclair," he growls, his eyes fixed on them.

"Take my panties off, Denver."

His eyes flash dangerously like he's really mad at me. But all it does is make me wetter.

Then he slowly slides them down over my thighs.

He balls them into his fist and stares at me.

"You can keep them if you like?"

His eyes flare and my pussy throbs as he shoves them into his pocket.

I part my thighs wide, and his gaze drops between them.

"What would you do now?" I ask, reaching down with one hand and parting myself with two fingers for him to see how wet I am.

"Say the fucking word, Sinclair," he growls like he's about to completely lose it and never be able to come back.

The threat in his tone makes more wetness run between my legs and he curses as it seeps free.

"Say it," he says again as he slides onto his front, hooking both of my thighs over his biceps.

"No."

He holds my eyes and presses a kiss to my inner thigh.

"Say it."

"No."

His lips drag over my skin as he moves higher, kissing the crease where my thigh meets my body.

"Say it."

"Nu-uh."

His lips part and he sucks just inside the crease, making me shudder.

"Say it."

His breath is warm against my clit as he moves to suck the other side.

"No way," I breathe, sinking both of my hands into his hair as my clit throbs with need.

I'm desperate for him to touch me where I need him to, but he just keeps alternating between sucking and kissing on the outer edges of my pussy.

"Denver, please," I whisper.

"What do you want?"

I look down into his eyes, my breath hitching that he's not telling me to use my word.

"Tell me what you want, Princess," he breathes, kissing me gently on my clit.

I let out a breathy gasp full of desire as I shudder at the contact.

Princess. Not baby this time.

This is real.

"I want you to make me come," I beg. "Please, Denver. Make me come."

"You want to come on my face?"

"Yes." I screw my hands up in his hair, trying to pull him back to my clit. "I want to come for you. Please."

"Fuck," he groans. Then he swipes his tongue over me, the slight roughness of his jaw grazing my skin.

His eyes fall closed and he sinks into me. Licking, sucking, tasting, devouring. He curls his hands around my thighs, spreading my legs wider for him so he can eat me out with an intense determination I've never seen before.

When he does open his eyes again to look at me, the dark, all-consuming depth to them makes me whimper. I can't look away. I can't do anything except watch as he pushes me closer and closer to breaking.

"Denver." I twist my fingers in his hair, pulling hard.

He groans as his head is pulled up, then he sinks back into me again.

"Say the word, Sinclair," he rasps.

"Make me come," I counter.

"Fuck. Say it, Sinclair." One of his balled fists slams against the mat beside my ass.

"I want to come on your tongue," I whimper.

His mouth grows fiercer against me, lapping up every drop of wetness as it leaves me. I shake against him as I coil tighter and tighter.

"Say it, or I'm going to take it from you like it's mine."

"It *is* yours," I gasp, my back arching.

His balled hand hits the mat again.

"You come for me, Sinclair, and there's no going back. You can still stop this."

His tongue circles my clit faster and heat floods to meet it.

"Say the word."

"Denver," I pant.

"Say it."

My lips part as I look down at him. My wetness is all over the lower half of his face.

"Say it," he says again.

I hold his eyes.

"I'm going to come."

His eyes narrow. "No, you're not. Say the goddamn word."

But I'm too far gone. The next swipe of his tongue has me screaming out as pleasure hurtles through me, hitting me full force.

"Denver!"

My nails dig into his scalp as my whole body is taken over by a huge orgasm, ripping me apart. He keeps licking and sucking, swallowing it down like it belongs to him. Just like he said he was going to take it from me. I squirm against his mouth, jerking as he sucks my clit again and everything is intensified and more sensitive.

"Denver," I whimper.

I look into his eyes as he keeps circling my clit with his tongue until my orgasm crests, threatening to roll into another.

"Fuck, I'm going to come again."

He growls and drinks up every drop of wetness that my body sends to him. My bottom lip trembles and I lose control of everything. All I can do is stare into his eyes as I come all over his face a second time.

I'm a panting, hot mess and my ears are ringing as he sucks it from me, stopping while my body is still clenching around nothing, aching to be filled with something it can grip onto.

"Your taste," he groans. "Jesus Christ, the way you taste when you come."

He straightens up and pulls his T-shirt off. Then he rips the button of his pants open and throws them and his boxers off.

"Say the word, Sinclair," he grits as he climbs over me, the heat of his giant naked body like molten lava.

I've seen him shirtless before, but not like this. Not in all his glory. He's magnificent. A giant hulk carved from solid muscle. So huge he should be intimidating. But I know how gentle those giant arms and hands are.

I bite my lip as I glance down. His cock is huge, hard, and angry, shining on the tip as it presses against my wetness.

"Say it," he hisses.

I shake my head, unable to speak.

"Say it, unless you want me to fuck you right now."

"Do it," I manage to choke out in a strained whisper.

"You don't really mean that," he groans, looking tortured.

"Don't tell me what I mean. I know what I want."

He looks into my eyes and his expression melts as I blink up at him. He braces himself on his arms, pressing down to kiss me.

"Tell me, then, Princess," he says more softly. "Tell me what you want."

"You," I say against his lips. "I want you inside me. I want to know what you'll feel like."

"Fuck," he rasps, screwing his eyes shut for a brief second like he isn't going to listen to me. Then he opens them and angles his hips so the tip of his cock pushes against my entrance.

"Last chance," he whispers. "Otherwise this is happening between us right now."

I lift my hips so the head of his cock slips inside me.

"Last chance," he chokes, his biceps trembling.

"I want you," I breathe. "I need you."

"Fuuuck," he groans, thrusting his hips.

"Denver!" I gasp, flinging my arms around his neck as he pushes inside me, making my eyes water.

I sink my teeth into his shoulder and bite.

"Fuck, Princess. You're so tight," he chokes, halting partway inside me. "Are you okay?"

I nod, keeping my face buried in his neck. "You're just big. Keep going."

Despite my pleading, he remains only a fraction of the way inside me. He lifts my leg behind my knee, wrapping it around his waist as he presses a kiss to my hair.

He pushes again, but my body fights him.

"Keep going," I urge, kissing his shoulder.

He circles his hips, trying to stretch me out. Then he thrusts a little deeper. "Fuck, that's it. Good girl. Open up for me. Let me in, Princess."

His words send more wetness from my body to him, letting him push all the way inside me.

The groan that vibrates his chest has my core clenching with need.

We stay still for a moment with him deep inside me. His balls are dusting my ass cheeks as I cling to him, stroking his hair and kissing his shoulder.

"You okay?"

Concern fills his voice, but as he turns his head, I catch him in a kiss before he can look at my face.

"I'm amazing. Now move. Fuck me," I say against his lips.

I keep kissing him, holding his face to mine so he has no choice but to kiss me back as he starts thrusting his huge cock in and out of me. I gasp each time he bottoms out, making me so unbelievably full that I feel like I might tear wide open.

"So good," I pant, burrowing my face into his neck. "Feels so good."

"Fuck, you're beautiful," he groans as he thrusts into me over and over, pushing deeper each time.

I gasp and grab at his hair and kiss him, doing everything I can to show him I'm loving it. But I can't look into his eyes. If I do, then he'll know. He'll stop.

His thrusts speed up and he cups my neck, stroking my jaw with his thumb as he kisses me. I sink into it, concentrating on the way his tongue seeks out mine and he lets out a husky groan like every dream he's ever had is coming true.

"Beautiful," he murmurs, kissing me harder.

I kiss him with everything I have, ignoring the burning between my thighs. I fight to cling on to the way I feel safe and protected in his arms. I don't care that he's my bodyguard and we shouldn't be doing this. Being with him like this feels the farthest from wrong that it could be.

"I'm going to come, Princess. You need to let me pull out."

"No." I shake my head as I kiss him, holding his face to mine.

"Sinclair, I can't come inside you without anything."

"It's okay, I want you to. I want to know how it feels. No one's ever—"

"Ever?" His eyes burn into mine with a possessiveness that makes me clench around him.

I shake my head.

"Jesus," he groans as I pull him into another kiss.

My words are his undoing, and his body expands above me, his cock thickening inside me. He thrusts into me twice more, then breaks our kiss, pressing his forehead against mine.

"Sinclair, I'm going to—"

"Come inside me," I breathe. "Please, Denver."

"Fuck, fuck, fuck. Sinclair... fuck..."

His eyes lock onto mine as he fills me. He keeps pumping into me, groaning out my name like it's his fuel.

The sound of wet skin on skin fills the air around us.

"Fuck, Princess," he growls, shuddering to a halt as his orgasm ebbs away.

He cups my face and kisses me like he's in awe.

"You should have used your word," he murmurs between kisses. "Why didn't you say it?"

"I didn't want to," I whisper.

"We just... I can't believe we just did that..." He looks into my eyes. His brows pull in, making a deep line between them as he studies me. "What's wrong?"

"Nothing." I try to kiss him again, but he pulls back, searching my eyes.

"What is it?"

"Nothing."

"It's something. I know you."

His cock shifts inside me as he moves, making me wince a little.

"Did I hurt you?"

I glance at the deep red bite mark he has on his shoulder. He didn't even notice when I did it.

"Sinclair?" His voice has taken on a hint of concern that I know is only going to increase.

"No. I'm fine."

But Denver's already pulling back, looking down at where our bodies are joined. He starts sliding his cock out from inside me. It's covered in a sheen of mixed arousal, cum... and blood.

His eyes flick from his dick up to my face and back again as more blood-smeared inches appear.

Fuck, he's massive. No wonder it felt like I was being split in two.

The head of his dick finally emerges and there's no hiding the trace of blood on the end of it, or the pink-tinged cum that comes out with it.

His eyes meet mine with an intense worry that makes me swallow. He drops back on his heels, pushing a trembling hand back through his hair.

"Y-you d-didn't tell me... If I'd known, then—"

"Then what?" I snap.

He stares at me, and I press my lips tightly together in shame as his eyes drop to the evidence painted all over his dick.

"Sinclair," he breathes again. "...why didn't you tell me you were a virgin?"

24

DENVER

"I'M NOT!" Sinclair sits up and grabs my T-shirt off the mat, using it to cover herself.

I take it from her so I have an unobstructed view of what I've done to her.

"The blood on my dick says otherwise."

She turns her face away and I hook my fingers under her chin, bringing her eyes back to mine. "You should have told me. Why didn't you?"

She snorts. "Your dick needs its own area code. It was going to hurt the first time no matter what. Besides, I told you, I'm not a virgin."

My gaze drops to the pink-colored cum running out of her.

My cum.

"Jesus." I scrub a hand around my jaw. She follows my gaze, wincing as she sees the mess.

"I've done it before, okay? Kind of."

"Kind of?"

"Yeah, I've done lots of stuff." She grabs my T-shirt from

me and yanks it on over her head, covering up her beautiful body.

"Lots of stuff? With who?" I growl.

"Doesn't matter." Her eyes hold mine, full of her usual fire.

"It matters to me," I grit, failing to rein in the overwhelming urge to pull her to me and demand she never so much as look in another man's direction ever again.

"Just... I'm not a virgin, okay?" She looks away as if she's embarrassed. "The tip went in, so..." She shrugs.

"Just the tip?" My jaw clenches. Who the fuck is this other guy who's been near enough to her to get 'just the tip' in?

The need to tear someone's head off makes my pulse pound in my ears.

"Yeah, it went in you know... a bit. So I'm not a virgin." She meets my eyes and then snaps hers away again.

"Doesn't count," I hiss.

"It does." She glares at me.

"Did he come inside you?"

"What? I told you—"

"Was his cum dripping out of you like mine is right now." My eyes drop to the apex of her thighs where she's covered herself with my T-shirt. I frown, wishing I could still see her, to assess how much I've hurt her. "Was it?"

"Denver!" she gasps.

"Fuck, Sinclair!" I snap my eyes up to her face. "Tell me who he is right now."

"It's none of your business. And no, he didn't. I told you no one ever has."

The inferno inside me is doused, but merely a fraction.

"Tell me," I urge again, more quietly.

"Why?"

I shake my head, my teeth grinding.

"So you can what? Add him to your hitlist? No way."

I run through the possibilities in my head.

"Someone you know?"

She clamps her lips together.

"Someone you see regularly?" I press.

She's silent and dread coils itself around my windpipe.

Fuck no.

"Brad Garrett-Charles?" I spit.

"Why do you always use his full name like that?"

"Sinclair," I warn.

She huffs, rolling her eyes. "So what if it was him. He's my friend."

"He's a sleazebag."

"He's not!" She stares daggers at me. "That's just your opinion."

It's fact. But telling her that will only delay me getting the information I want.

"When?" I grit.

"It's not important." She frowns, unable to meet my eyes once more.

"When?" I repeat, leaning to the side until I capture her gaze with mine.

She presses her lips together, her face pinching like she knows I'm not going to like what she's about to say.

"Two weeks after the funeral."

Rage erupts like molten lava, racing its way around my body, enough to make Brad Garrett-Charles spontaneously combust with just one look from me if he were here now.

"The funeral," I echo, dropping my head into my hand and rubbing at the intense throbbing in my temples.

"Over two years ago, okay? So you can stop acting all pissed about it. And we didn't go all the way. I got upset and we stopped."

"You got upset?"

She shrugs. "It's fine."

"It's not fine. He took advantage of you when you were grieving."

"It wasn't like that."

I drag in a deep breath before I explode. I want to kill the guy. Right this second. I want to get in my car, drive back to the city, and mow the fucker down in the street. Then I want to disembowel him with my bare hands and let the rats eat what's left.

"You may not be able to see it, Sinclair. But it *was* like that," I snap, regretting it as her eyes immediately turn glassy and her bottom lip trembles.

"Are you going to fight with me now? Is that how this goes?" She sniffs, wrapping her arms around herself. It pulls my T-shirt tight, but it still swamps her, making her look vulnerable and anxious.

Jesus Christ, I'm an asshole. I just took her virginity on the floor and made her bleed. And now I'm more concerned about some other guy than taking care of her.

I blow out a slow breath, shaking my head. "No, Princess. No, of course not."

She watches me with shining eyes as I stand. Then I sweep her into my arms, bridal style.

"What are you doing?" she asks, looping her arms around my neck to hold on.

"What I should have done first," I answer, striding from the room with her.

I take us to my bedroom, then straight through into the ensuite before grabbing a towel and placing it onto the counter by the sink.

"Sit," I say, placing her on top of it so it's not too cold for her.

"What are you doing?"

She watches me as I grab a pair of sweatpants and pull them on, then start to fill the giant freestanding bathtub.

"Running you a bath," I murmur, reaching for the Epsom salts I put in after I've had a hard workout, and throwing a generous handful into the water along with some bubble bath.

"There's a bath in my room."

She clamps her mouth shut when I turn to her with a raised brow.

"This is your room now."

I turn back to the bath, checking the temperature once the water is high enough.

"Time to get in, Princess."

I walk over to her, and she stares at me as I inch my fingertips beneath the hem of my T-shirt, gliding it up over her hips.

"Denver," she whispers huskily, making my dick throb.

"Come on," I coax gently, encouraging her to lift her arms above her head so I can undress her.

I keep my eyes on her face as I drop my T-shirt on the floor. We stare at each other for a few seconds before I take her face in my hands. Her soft intake of breath as I press a gentle kiss to her lips has my chest clenching painfully.

No one's ever taken care of her like this. Not the way she deserves.

"Time to get in."

I lift her from the counter and take her over to the water, lowering her in slowly until the bubbles come up over her shoulders.

She leans back with a relaxed sigh as I draw my arms back.

"Are you okay? Sore?"

"I'm fine." She gives me a small smile, narrowing her eyes like she's trying to work my angle out.

"I was rough," I mutter, cursing internally as I reach for a washcloth and put it under the water.

"What are you doing?" Her eyes widen as I press the cloth between her legs beneath the water.

"There was blood," I say.

She watches me as I wipe her gently, her eyelids hooding as she starts to relax and sinks back against the side of the tub.

"I'm fine. You don't need to worry."

"I'll always worry."

"Because it's your job?" she asks.

"Because it's you."

My jaw clenches as I clean her some more, pretending not to notice the small moan that slips from her lips when my fingers brush her skin. Her cheeks are flushed pink when I take my arm from the water.

"Stay here. I'll be back."

"Where are you going?" she asks as I walk to the doorway.

"I'm going to check on Monty. Stay there," I instruct, before slipping from the room and closing the door.

Thirty minutes later, I'm back with a warm towel in my arms, holding it open for Sinclair to step into as she climbs from the bath. I look to one side to give her privacy, even though thirty minutes ago, I was exploring every inch of her body… kissing her, tasting her… making her come for me, before coming so damn hard inside her that I lost all coherent thought, leaving her vulnerable. I re-checked all the security measures around the cabin while she was in the bath. Everything is fine. But I still lost my head without making sure first. If anything had happened to her, it would have been my fault.

Only it did happen to her. I hurt her. I made her bleed.

"Thanks," she says, securing the towel around her chest.

She looks at me shyly, studying my tense expression.

"Come on." I rest my hand on her lower back and open the door that leads into my bedroom, steering her through it.

She whips her head around, looking at me, then turns back to take in the room. Every available surface is covered in candles. I'm so fucking grateful I had a load here in case of a blackout.

"You did this?" she breathes.

"No, Monty did."

She looks at me. "You made a joke."

I gaze at her as she shuffles closer to me. "Did I?"

"You know you did," she teases.

"You're not laughing, so it can't have been."

Her eyes light up. "You get a smile. Keep working on them, Brute." She pats my chest. "Was Monty okay?"

"He's fine. I took him out to the bathroom, gave him his dinner and a treat. He's probably back asleep now."

Worn out from the way I made him march around the property's perimeter with me, checking everything over.

Her lower lip snags between her teeth. "Thank you... So what's this all for?"

I follow her gaze to the candles. Maybe I went overboard. I might pass out when I have to blow them all out.

I clear my throat. "This is how it should have been. And I'm sorry it wasn't."

She chews on her lower lip, a deep line down the center of her forehead. But then it's gone, and her lips tilt into a soft smile.

"No one's ever done anything like this before. Thank you."

"I'm sorry about the way we—"

"Do you regret it?" She struggles to meet my eyes and my chest grows heavy at the wavering in her voice.

"No."

Her shoulders relax and she looks around the room at the candles some more, her face glowing in their light.

"Do you?" I frown, steeling myself for her answer.

"No." She shakes her head, her attention still dancing around the room.

Relief softens every muscle in my body as I lead her over to the bed and pull back the covers.

"Get in."

"What?" Her eyes widen as she looks up at me.

"You're sleeping in here with me. I need to know you're okay."

"I have my own room."

"Not tonight, you don't," I rasp.

She looks like she's going to argue with me, but then she drops her towel to the floor, smirking as I fail to keep my eyes from roaming over her body with a slow appreciation.

"You've seen me on my modeling shoots in lingerie," she says as I drink her in.

"I didn't look then," I say, my eyes honing in on every curve of her smooth skin.

"Really?"

"That was work."

"Okay. So what's this?"

I exhale, biting on my lower lip with a groan as I lift my eyes away from her breasts reluctantly.

"This is... Get in and we'll talk about it." I tilt my chin toward the bed.

Sinclair climbs in and I cover her up, then walk to the other side of the bed, which is closest to the door. I lie beside her.

"Aren't you getting under the covers?"

"Not until after we've spoken."

"Why?"

I glance at her. She's turned on her side to face me.

"Because I can't guarantee I won't touch you if I do."

"What's wrong with that?" she teases.

I exhale, fighting down the stirring heat in my groin.

"You have no idea the battle I'm having in my head right now. But we're... you're sore... and—"

"Stop," she huffs. "Don't wrap me in bubble wrap. Please. Dad does it. Sullivan does it. Uncle Mal does it. They've been so protective over me, keeping tabs on me. And I know it's because they care, but it's no wonder I didn't lose my virginity until a couple of years ago—"

"You lost your virginity thirty minutes ago, Sinclair."

"What?"

"I'm serious. You lost it to me." I can't hide the possessiveness in my tone, but I swear her eyes light up from it.

She gazes at me, unaffected by the way my entire body has bristled at the thought of another man's hands on her.

"You don't think what I did with Brad counts?" she asks.

"I know it doesn't fucking count," I snap. "I've still got the evidence proving it doesn't all over my dick."

She wrinkles up her nose and I scrub a hand around my jaw, forcing myself to calm down.

"I mean, no, it doesn't count," I say more gently. "I don't like the idea of you with anyone, especially him. Half an inch from a jackass who couldn't respect you when you were grieving will never count, okay?"

"Okay."

She rolls her lower lip into her mouth as she watches me. The urge to pull it free and kiss her hits me like a bullet to the chest.

"You said you got upset when you and he were...?" I'm unable to say more. Just the idea makes my blood boil.

"I don't want to talk about him anymore. He's just a friend. Nothing's ever happened between us since."

The way her brow creases makes me think there's more to it than she's telling me. I've seen the way Brad acts with her during their training sessions. I would bet my life on the fact he's tried it on with her since then and she's knocked him back.

"So, I'm sleeping in here tonight?" She lifts her brows, a playfulness in her eyes that makes it almost impossible for me not to reach out and pull her closer.

"I want to know where you are."

"You know, you can just admit it's because you want to play big spoon."

"Big spoon?"

She trails her fingers over my bare chest, circling them around my nipple before she moves up to my jaw and runs them along it.

"I remember you sleeping next to me the night Monty was attacked. You held me all night like I was the little spoon."

A small rumble of amusement rolls out of me. "Did I?"

"You did." She bites her lower lip, her eyes following her fingers as they dust over my lips. "Of course, that was before you woke up and pushed the giant monster in your pants into me."

"That wasn't intentional." I frown.

She leans closer so her breath tickles my ear. "I still liked it," she whispers.

She moves back, smiling as I shift position, glancing at the ceiling in an attempt to make the growing erection in my pants less noticeable. I don't want her to think this is what it's about — that all I care about is getting off again.

"Denver?"

I turn, and she's there, pulling my mouth to hers before I can react. I should be stronger. I should make sure I'm completely convinced that she's okay before I kiss her back. I should do a lot of things.

But fuck, this is Sinclair.

I groan, kissing her back and pushing a hand into her hair until the silky strands spill over my knuckles.

"Sinclair," I breathe against her lips as she sinks into me, nipping my lower lip with her teeth.

"Don't stop kissing me, Denver. You're one hell of a kisser." She smiles against my mouth.

I groan again, tightening my grip on her hair and wrapping an arm around her waist so I can pull her across my chest.

Her hard nipples graze my skin and my dick fights for attention in my sweatpants.

We kiss for so long, like two teenagers who are only just discovering it for the first time, savoring every second, memorizing every pass of one another's lips against the other.

"This is what it would have been like if we'd dated," I say, sliding my lips from her mouth and along her jawline.

"What do you mean?" she says, sounding all breathy.

I kiss along her jaw, before settling on her neck, sucking and kissing it, enjoying the little gasps and moans she makes.

"All the kissing first," I murmur, inhaling the scent of her skin as I kiss beneath her ear. "I'd have kissed you so fucking much. I'd have never done a thing more until you'd told me you were ready. I wouldn't have taken your virginity, Sinclair. You'd have given it to me when you wanted to. I'd have worshiped you through the whole thing."

"Denver." Her voice comes out shaky as she shudders in my arms, her pulse fluttering beneath my lips.

"I'd have made it so good for you, Princess," I whisper.

"Show me," she breathes.

I look at the uncharacteristic shyness in her eyes as she blinks at me. Her lips are swollen and pink where I've kissed her so much.

"Show me now how it would have been."

"No, you're sore. We—"

"I'm not. Please, Denver. You won't hurt me, I trust you."

"Jesus." I exhale, cupping her face and stroking her cheeks with my thumbs. She turns her face and catches one in her mouth, sucking the tip softly.

I should be a stronger man. I should stop this now before it goes any further. Before we cross that line again. But the complete faith in Sinclair's eyes as she watches me is more than I can resist. Because even if every cell in my body is screaming at me that this is against every professional rule I have… it's still her.

It's Sinclair.

And there isn't any lifetime I could live where I would ever be strong enough to say no to her when she's looking at me like this.

"You sure this is what you want?" I ask.

"It is." She presses her lips against mine. "Show me."

25

DENVER

"We do it properly this time. We'll take it slow. And I should have said something before, but you're safe, I've been tested recently."

"Uh-huh."

"Sinclair," I scold.

She snaps her eyes up to mine. "I'm listening."

But her eyes drop straight to where I'm kneeling on the bed beside her, lubing up my throbbing dick.

She sat up the minute I came back from the kitchen with a jar of coconut oil and has been watching me intently ever since.

"Can I do it?"

My dick hardens further inside my palm. "You want to do it?"

She nods eagerly and scoots closer, reaching out and curling her hand around my shaft.

"Fuck." I tip my head back with a groan as she strokes me up and down.

"Do you like it like this?" She jerks me slowly, then lowers her head and wraps her lips around the head of my dick.

She moans softly as she sucks on it, and I almost come on the spot. My abs clench as she gazes up at me and slides the whole thing down her throat. The base of it still has a hint of her dried blood on it, but she doesn't seem to care as she moans and sucks harder.

"That's enough." I pull back so my dick pops free of her lips.

Her face falls. "Do you not like the way I suck you off?"

"Sinclair." I shake my head with a groan, before pulling her face to mine and kissing her. "This isn't about me."

She kisses me but still looks unsure.

"I love the way you suck me off, Princess," I whisper. "Believe me. It's insane how good your lips feel on me."

She smiles against my kiss, her hand dropping to wrap around my dick again.

"And I love the way that feels," I say, taking her hand in mine so she can't touch me anymore. "But you'll make me come too soon."

"You can do it again that quick?"

A rumbled hint of a chuckle leaves me.

"What?"

"Nothing."

I ease her beneath me, making sure the pillow is under her.

"You comfy?" I ask, kissing her.

"Yes," she breathes, widening her legs around my thighs.

"You sure you want to do this?"

"Denver," she huffs.

I kiss her again. "I'm just checking."

She wraps her arms around my neck and kisses me over and over. I wait until she's arching up toward me, grinding herself against me and letting out frustrated moans of my name before I let the head of my dick swipe through her wetness.

"We stop if it hurts, okay?"

"Denver." She squirms beneath me, tugging on my hair impatiently.

"We stop," I repeat, holding her eyes.

"Fine." She huffs.

I move my weight onto one forearm so I can slide my other hand between our bodies. Sinclair gasps my name as my fingers slip through the arousal that's coating her inner thighs.

"Jesus, you're so wet."

"Because I want you," she pants, kissing my throat.

I hold her eyes as I swirl my fingers around her clit, driving her closer and closer to the edge. She wriggles and moans, but I still won't move any nearer.

"You're beautiful," I whisper.

I wait until the pink in her cheeks is in full blush before I slowly start to push inside her.

"Denver." She drops her head back with a moan, as I ease inside her one inch at a time, giving her time to stretch around me. It's easier than the first time, and her body opens up, allowing me to keep pushing until I'm deep inside her and her inner thighs are trembling against me.

"You okay?"

"Yeah." She nods, her cheeks still flushed.

I start to move slowly, keeping my eyes on hers, savoring the way they roll in her head as I alter the angle slightly and hit the special spot inside her. Her breathing changes and she lets out soft little moans and strokes the back of my neck.

"That feels good," she whispers.

I move in and out of her, keeping everything slow and gentle as I slip a hand down to stroke her clit. Her eyelashes flutter as I push into her a little deeper, but her eyes find mine again each time she reopens them.

"Beautiful," I rasp, pressing a kiss to her lips.

My dick is straining with how wet and tight she is. It would be so easy to lose myself in her. But there's no way I'm going to let that happen. This is for her. I want it all to feel good for her. I want her to remember this moment whenever she thinks of me.

"You're going to come while I'm inside you this time, Princess. Okay?"

She nods, her breath coming in shallow pants as I increase the pressure against her clit.

"Good girl."

"Wow, that feels..." Her lips part and the lower one trembles as she gazes at me. I catch it between my teeth and suck on it.

We kiss, only breaking free to look into each other's eyes. The whole time my fingers work her clit, coaxing her orgasm closer and closer to the surface.

"I think I'm going to... Oh my God..."

"You're safe, I've got you."

She pants, arching up beneath me and making my cock sink deeper inside her. I groan as my balls touch her skin.

"Denver," she moans.

"I'm here," I breathe, my eyes glued to her face as her lids hood.

I increase the speed at which I'm pumping into her a little, drawing a gasp of pleasure from her.

Her pussy clenches around my cock and I almost lose it.

"Come for me. You can do it," I urge.

Her grasp on my hair tightens and she pulls hard as her pussy strangles my cock. My balls draw tight to my body, aching with how desperate they are to unload inside her. But there's no way in hell I'm coming before she does.

"Good girl, come on, let it go."

"Oh my God, Denver."

"Let it go, Princess. Come for me. It's right there, I can feel it. Just let it go."

She trembles and my fingers slide all over her clit with how wet she's become.

"Good girl," I whisper. "Good girl."

"Denver," she squeals.

"Good girl," I repeat. "You're such a good fucking girl. Come for me."

The moment her pussy spasms around my cock I lose it. My vision blurs and blood rushes in my ears as she comes for me, her body strangling mine in pulsing waves.

"That's it," I choke. "Just like that. You're doing so well. You're taking me so well." I keep my rhythm, sliding into her in slow, deep thrusts while looking into her eyes.

"Fuck, Denver, I'm coming again," she cries.

"Good girl," I pant, circling her clit faster.

As she comes again, I bury my face into her neck, my own orgasm rushing close to the surface.

"Sinclair, Jesus Christ…"

She pulls my face to hers and then her lips are on mine as I thrust into her, my balls screaming at me to come.

"Inside me," she pants against my mouth.

I look into her eyes, and she nods.

"Come inside me," she breathes.

"Fuck," I groan. "You sure?"

"I want to feel it again," she says against my mouth.

"Fuck, Sinclair…"

I look at her as I come so hard my eyes water.

She's there, kissing me, wrapping her thighs tighter around me as I spill inside her, groaning her name.

Everything is amplified. Her taste, her warmth, the sound of her breath against mine.

It's still slow. It's still gentle and tender.

But it wrecks me more than anything else ever could.

"Sinclair," I murmur, kissing her back, refusing to let her go as I keep thrusting, emptying myself inside her.

"I never knew it could be so... wow," she whispers as I slow down but keep us connected.

"That's how your first time should have been."

"I know, but—"

"Let me have it," I beg. "That part of you can belong to me as long as you agree. I'll take better care of it than he did. I promise you."

She looks into my eyes and my heart stops as I wait for her answer.

She presses the gentlest dust of a kiss to my lips.

"I know you will. And it *is* yours. *You* were my first, Denver."

"Thank you," I choke.

I cup her face and lose myself in her kiss, soaking up every sweet little moan she makes, like they're a melody written just for me. One I could sing for the rest of my life, treasuring every note.

"It's mine, Princess."

"Yours," she agrees with a smile.

I kiss her again, keeping the thoughts racing around my head to myself. Thoughts that have no right to be there. Selfish ones.

I want to be your first and last, Princess. I want to be your only one.

26

SINCLAIR

Denver's side of the bed is empty when I wake up. I smile when Monty crawls up from the end of it, his tail wagging.

"Hey, Boy," I coo. "When did you come and sleep in here?"

It must have been the early hours of the morning because Denver and I didn't sleep until then. Now I understand why he sounded smug and chuckled when I asked him if he could come again so close together last night. Because after that first, gentle time, he made love to me again. Then again. Then again. Each time getting a little faster and rougher than the last.

This morning, I'm aching. But it's a good ache. *A great ache.*

"Do you know where the big grump is?" I ask Monty as I rub behind his ear.

Monty wags his tail at the sound of a phone ringing from outside the room.

"Stay here and be cozy." I kiss him on the head and tuck

him beneath the covers where he lets out a sigh and watches me as he rests his head on Denver's pillow.

I climb out of bed, but all of my clothes are in my room. I literally have nothing to put on, not even a pair of panties. I bite back a smile. Those are still in Denver's pocket.

His white shirt is hanging on the back of a chair, so I saunter over and pick it up, inhaling the scent of him from the collar. How can a man smell so good? It's musky and hot and earthy all at once. So deliciously sexy. I can't believe I've known him for six years and never gotten close enough to discover how incredible he smells.

I slide my arms into the cool cotton and do a couple of buttons up before wandering from his bedroom in search of him.

A deep rumble of voices is coming from behind a closed door further up the hallway. *His office.* I haven't been inside since we arrived at the cabin, but I've peeked through the open doorway once or twice, trying to imagine him sitting in there at the giant rustic wooden desk, the giant windows showcasing the deep forest behind him.

I open the door and slip inside the room quietly. Denver's eyes lift beneath his dark, lowered brows, capturing mine immediately. He's sitting at the desk in a black T-shirt, his biceps straining against the fabric as he rests forward on his elbows, his cell phone lit up with a connected call in front of him.

"They've done a good job," my brother says.

"They have," Denver replies, his eyes roaming over me in his shirt, dropping to my legs where the fabric ends mid-thigh.

"But they haven't been able to find out how he got it?"

"He's refusing to say anything," Denver says.

"I'll inspect it myself before we do anything else."

"Understood," Denver says to Sullivan, his attention fixed

on me as I wander around the room, running my finger along a bookshelf filled with books on military subjects.

There's a picture of a group of men all wearing green combat gear, rifles slung over their shoulders. I pick it up and study it until I find a familiar pair of green eyes flecked with gold.

"Sinclair giving you a hard time?"

I turn around at my brother's question and raise my eyebrows at Denver. He clears his throat, his eyes darkening as I put the photo down and slink over to him.

"She's fine. Her self-defense skills are coming along," he says, watching me as I spin his desk chair so there's space on the floor in front of him for me to drop to my knees.

"Bet she loves having free rein to come at you. You've always had a way of getting under her skin." Sullivan chuckles.

Denver jerks his head, glaring at me as I palm his hardening dick through his sweatpants.

I nod slowly, loving the way his jaw clenches like he's pissed as I pull the waistband down and take his dick out. It's glistening on the tip, and I moan quietly as I lick the drops off, enjoying the flavor on the tip of my tongue.

Denver's hand scrunches into my hair, tilting my head back. His eyes are on fire as they meet mine.

"Stop," he mouths.

"Make me," I mouth back.

He lets out a low curse as I wrap my lips around him and suck the head of his dick, letting the tip of my tongue trail along the slit, licking up the drops of arousal that are flowing from it.

"You still there?" Sullivan asks.

Denver's grip on my hair tightens but all it does is make me suck him with more determination.

"Yeah. Just bad reception here sometimes."

"All right. I've got to go anyway. Tell that sister of mine to take it easy on you."

"I told you, she's good."

Sullivan snorts. "You can admit it, I bet she's busting your balls."

Denver's lips press together as I suck him off faster, my hand tugging on his balls at the same time.

"I mean it. She's... good," Denver grits again, the muscles in his neck tensing as he looks at me with a heated glare.

"See you when you get back to the city," my brother says. Then he's gone.

"What are you doing?" Denver growls the moment the call disconnects.

"What I want to," I reply simply, before continuing.

His grip in my hair is almost painful as he starts thrusting his hips, fucking my mouth, like he's punishing me.

"You can't walk in here looking like that in my shirt and start blowing me when I'm on the phone with your brother. What were you thinking?" he hisses.

I can't reply because my throat is full of him, so I gaze up at him instead, batting my eyelashes as his cock thickens inside my mouth.

"You think you can look at me like that, Princess? And I won't be angry with you?"

I bat my lashes some more.

"Fuck," he groans, holding my eyes. "Fuck," he grunts again, his hips speeding up and his fist clenching in my hair. "Fuuuuckkk...."

Hot cum fills my mouth as his cock explodes over my tongue. I whimper and do my best to swallow it, but there's so much, and it keeps coming. Some spills out of the side of my mouth, running down my chin.

"Jesus, Sinclair," Denver growls, watching as I swallow another mouthful and more escapes the corners of my mouth.

I moan, sucking harder, loving the way his lower abs shudder as the final drops fire over my tongue. I lick them up, gulping them down with a happy sigh as I slide his cock from my mouth.

For a moment, we just look at each other. Then Denver's eyes narrow as he reaches forward and uses his thumb to swipe up his cum from my chin.

"These lips," he says, pushing his thumb up to them and smearing his cum over them. "I shouldn't know how they feel sucking me off, Sinclair. I shouldn't know what they taste like."

He reaches down and hauls me up into his arms, pulling me into his lap.

"I shouldn't fucking know," he repeats before kissing me deeply, sliding his tongue over mine and tasting himself inside my mouth. He pulls back with a throaty groan and sucks and kisses his way up my neck and over my chin, collecting the evidence of himself on his tongue before pressing it back past my lips in another searing kiss.

"But you do," I muse as I kiss him back. "And you're going to have to get used to it, because I like the way you taste when you come."

He grunts, deepening our kiss as I use his own words back at him. We kiss until I break free.

"I thought you were in the SEALs," I say, glancing at the photograph I was looking at earlier. It's the only one in the room.

Denver shakes his head as he presses soft kisses to my neck, breathing me in at the same time.

"I wasn't."

"How did I not know that?" I ask, still studying the photos. I don't know much about the military. But I know enough to see that the green he's wearing with the other men in the photographs isn't a SEAL uniform.

"You never asked," he says against my neck, still kissing me.

Guilt swirls in my gut. This is a huge part of his life, long before he came to work for my family. And I know nothing about it. I always knew he'd done something in the military, but I never bothered to ask because I told myself I didn't care. I didn't see the point in getting to know the man who barely looked at or spoke to me unless his job required it. I was too caught up in my own life, too focused on launching my modeling career.

But look where that's gotten me. I didn't even see my mother's affair coming because I was so damn self-absorbed. Then I lost her and my brother before I could ask her why she did it. Ask her if she loved Neil more than she loved my father. If she was going to leave us all for him.

I push Denver back until he meets my eyes. "I'm asking now. Tell me. *Please*," I add when his lips press together.

"Not much to tell."

A vein in his temple is pulsing and I swear if I hooked him up to a lie detector now, the needle on it would be going haywire.

I look back into his eyes, a spark of hope glimmering in my chest as he lets out a long sigh and starts stroking my thigh absentmindedly with one hand.

"I was part of Delta Force. It's a special missions unit of the armed forces."

"Oh," I breathe. "Sounds serious."

"It was."

"Do you miss it?"

His jaw tightens but he doesn't answer. Instead, his gaze tracks to the photo I'd been studying.

"Do you still see any of them?"

"The ones who are still alive, sometimes, yeah."

"Denver," I whisper.

His eyes come back to meet mine. "Don't be upset for me, Sinclair. We all knew the risks doing a job like that."

"This is why you worry so much," I say, finally beginning to understand. "Why you sleep with your gun under your pillow and always sit facing the doorway."

"Threats are everywhere. That's why I wanted to train you. So you're prepared if you need to be. But at the same time I don't want you overthinking it. That's my job."

"That doesn't mean you're immune to death, though. I mean..." I swallow the lump in my throat that appears whenever I think of my mom and brother. "I'm so sorry."

He sighs, tracing figures of eight over my thigh with his thumb. "No one is immune. But when you've held your friend's bodies together as they've died in your arms, you have to find a way to keep going."

I lift his free hand in both of mine. It's huge in comparison. But despite the power in his hands, I know how gentle they are. I know what it's like to be steadied by them, to be held by them when I've thought I was about to fall apart.

Like when he caught me and asked if I was okay at their funeral.

And I know what it's like to be stroked by them, to have their fingertips pressing into the skin on my hips and thighs as he's driven himself inside me and made me come for him. Then had them cupping my face as he kisses me so tenderly like I'm his one gift he's allowed himself to have.

I press a kiss to the center of his palm and then rest my cheek against it.

"You can always talk to me if you want to. I don't know what that must have been like for you. But I do know grief."

His eyes soften. "I wish you didn't."

I give him a small smile. "I wish you didn't either."

We stare at one another as he strokes my cheek.

"Why didn't you use your word yesterday?" he asks softly.

"Because I stopped not wanting to know what it would be like to feel your hands on my body. And your mouth on mine. I don't know when exactly. Only that I did. And I wouldn't change a thing."

He inhales slowly, studying me. His eyes pinch like he's thinking about something he would rather ignore.

"I can't say no to you. You know that, don't you? I'd do anything you asked of me."

My heart lifts, then immediately drops at the heaviness in his voice. He says it like it's a bad thing. Like it's the *worst* thing.

Like he wished it wasn't true.

"Anything? Like make me eggs for breakfast?" I ask, eager to do something to dispel the seriousness from his expression.

The weight in his shoulders eases and his lips curl up a fraction. I run the tip of my finger over them. "I like your nearly smiles now that I'm starting to see them."

"Do you?" he rumbles, his voice deep and delicious again.

"Yep."

"Well, they're yours."

"Mine," I muse. "I like the sound of that, Brute."

He slides a hand around my neck and pulls me to him, kissing me again. I sink into it, warm and protected in his arms. Butterflies dance in my stomach as his grip on my thigh tightens and his dick starts hardening in the gap between our bodies again.

This can't just be a close proximity thing from being stuck here in the middle of this forest together, can it? Not when it feels like so much more.

I sigh into his mouth as he kisses me, my name a soft groan on his lips. I want to believe it's more. Because this is Denver, and the thought of him not looking at me the way he does, and touching and kissing me like this now that I know how it feels... it's not something I can imagine, or even want to imagine.

But despite how much has happened since we arrived here, I have no idea what will happen once we return to the city.

27

SINCLAIR

For the next few days, Denver and I train more. But without the role play. It's as though now the tension has snapped between us; I don't need it anymore. I'm able to fight with him just for the opportunity to show him how far I've come since he started teaching me. Because as much as I would have once hated to admit it, I love seeing the pride in his eyes each time I almost kick his ass.

But it's only ever almost. Each time I've come close, he's managed to overpower me and get me beneath him again. His favorite place for me to be.

That's when I kiss him.

We've had a lot of sex on that gym mat.

I smile as I lean against the side of the cabin watching Monty sniff around happily in the undergrowth while Denver chops firewood, shirtless, in a pair of faded jeans.

"You okay?" he asks, wiping sweat from his brow with his forearm and placing his axe down as he notices me.

"I am now. Don't stop."

He shakes his head, the closest thing to a smirk I've ever seen on his face as he picks the axe back up and continues.

There's more than enough wood for the fire in the evenings, which is the only time he and I are really in the front room. The rest of the time we're either training, cooking in the kitchen, or in his shower or bed together.

I clench my thighs as he lets out a grunt, his ab muscles rippling as he chops a huge log in half down the center. I know who this firewood is for really. And that's what makes him look even sexier as he goes to so much trouble to chop it.

"You okay, Boy?" Denver says, leaning down to pat Monty as he trots over to him. Monty whimpers at him, so Denver scoops him up, holding him to his naked chest as he fusses him.

"Wait until I tell Zoey about this," I mutter quietly as I take in the scene that looks like it's from a *hot guys who love animals* calendar. If I weren't taking the contraceptive shot, then I might have just gotten pregnant.

Denver places Monty down and he trots over to me.

"I'll start to think you love him more than me," I say, looking down at him.

He wags his tail and I crouch, rubbing his ears. "You like it here, don't you, baby? Walking in the forest, eating all the good treats, sleeping in front of the fire all day long." He licks my face, and I giggle.

Denver walks up to us, brushing his hands off on his jeans. "I'm going to go and clean up, then I'll make us dinner."

"I can do it," I say as I stand, unable to stop my eyes from lingering on the dips and grooves of his pecs.

"Make dinner?" His brow creases. I'm a terrible chef and he knows it. He's the one who's made all of our meals.

"Clean you up," I tease.

He runs his tongue over his lips. "You want to come wash me, Princess?"

"I want to come in the shower with you so you can do that thing to me against the wall again."

The Rule Breaker

"That thing?" he rasps.

"You know the one." I giggle as his eyes darken.

He grabs my hand, wrapping his fingers around it protectively, the same way he did after he caught me out with Julian weeks ago. Everything about home and the city feels so far away here.

I grin as he marches me inside the cabin, locking the door behind us. He pauses in the living area to throw another log into the fire where Monty promptly flops down onto the rug in front of it. Then he pulls me along behind him toward his bedroom and I have to rush to keep up with his large strides.

I shouldn't even call it his room anymore. It's ours. I've been sleeping in here with him every night since what happened between us. I wake up cocooned inside his giant arms while he sleeps beside me with his gun beneath his pillow.

It's funny how quickly you can get used to something like that.

And now I make full use of the huge erection he wakes up with every morning. This morning when he opened his eyes, I was already sinking down onto it. I know he was awake long before I straddled him. This is Denver. He wakes from the slightest sound, always on high alert. But he pretended to be asleep as I trailed kisses over his chest and jerked him off before climbing on top of him. I love that he lets me be in control sometimes. Because most of the time he's on top of me, huge and powerful between my thighs as he makes me come over and over. And I love that, just like I loved when he flipped me over after I'd ridden him for a bit and thrust into me from behind, his giant hands curling around my hips as he told me to come for him. Just like that, *"Come for me, Princess."* And I did.

I always do.

He turns and faces me as we enter the room. I bite my lip,

my nipples already pebbling against my vest. I hope he sucks them again when we get in the shower. Drinks the water off them like he did yesterday, groaning about my taste and how he can't get enough. I loved feeling the vibration of his growl travel over my skin when he had his mouth on me.

I reach down to peel my vest off, but his gaze has dropped to my sneakers. I follow it, finding him scowling at my undone laces.

"You know, at the funeral, you looked at my shoes the same way you're doing now. It's obvious you hate these sneakers, and you looked like you wanted to throw my heels I wore to Ashton's gallery show in the trash too. Do you have an aversion to all footwear, or just mine?" I tease.

"Just yours," he says, his attention still on my feet.

"Oh."

He drops to one knee by my feet and lifts my foot, pulling my sneaker off. I place one hand on his shoulder for balance so he can remove the other. He looks so serious as he rubs my foot before placing it down onto the carpet.

"Are they that bad?" I ask, confused. The sneakers were a gift from Gucci after a shoot I did with them. I think they're pretty.

"The laces come undone too much. I don't like anything that could hurt you."

His face is so serious as he looks from my sneakers back to my feet.

"Even back when it was the funeral?" I ask. It's more than two years since my stilettos sank in that mud and almost made me fall over. Sometimes the grief makes it feel like only yesterday. But Denver wouldn't remember it as clear as I do, surely.

He runs his strong fingers over my ankle, massaging it.

"Even back then?" I ask again.

He looks up and holds my eyes. "Always."

My breath hitches as he stands.

"Do you think everything I've done for you has been because it's my job?"

"Well, I was... I mean, I am your client."

"No." The sharp cut of his jaw catches the light as he says that one word so softly I almost miss it.

"No?"

"You mistake me choosing to do things for you because I want to, for me being at your beck and call because it's my duty. I could have stopped and treated you like any other client."

"Then why haven't you?"

"Because you've never been just a client and I think you know that."

"Ever?" I ask.

He looks away, shaking his head with an exhale like he can't believe I just asked him that.

I'm stunned. I know things have changed between us since he became my bodyguard. But he's talking about before. He's talking about all the years he's worked with my father, barely looking my way, hardly ever speaking to me. All those silent car rides when he had no choice to pick me up because Sullivan or my father had asked him to.

"Then what was I? Before we came here, I mean. Who was I to you?"

His eyes meet mine and the gold glows in them. "You're Sinclair," he breathes out, saying it like it has meaning, like I should understand.

"But who is that?" I whisper, emotion clogging my throat. The last couple of years I'm not sure I even know. Some days I could swear I've almost faded into nonexistence. Everything has felt so... numb.

He slides his hand around my neck, the pads of his thumbs pressing gently over the racing pulse in my neck. "Someone beautiful."

I roll my eyes. "Cameras are all about light and how it hits your face. I have a face that photographs well, that's all. I'm plainer in person, I've been told that more than once."

"By who? Idiots?" Denver grumbles. "It's not the camera that makes you beautiful. It's the light in your eyes, the one in your smile."

I give him a half smile. "You're sweet."

"I'm accurate," he huffs. "But I didn't mean on the outside. I meant the way that you look after others when you're hurting. It takes someone special to do that."

"I don't."

He fixes me with a warning look that tells me not to argue.

"It's easy to be happy for others when you're happy yourself. But to be happy for them on your darkest days... that takes something special. And you have that, Sinclair. You *are* that. You hired your father a dating coach to find him love because you knew he needed it. You're angry at your brother for having a suite at The Lanceford because you want him to find someone too. You convinced Zoey to meet Ashton and now they're getting married. You don't see it, but I do."

"But you called me a spoiled princess when we got smoothies." I pout, loving the tenderness that's crept into his eyes as he gazes at me.

"I called you a princess. Not spoiled. You added that yourself."

I open my mouth to argue, then close it again. He's right. He's never once called me spoiled or treated me like he thinks I am. Not like a lot of people I meet do. I know what they must be thinking, supermodel with a billionaire father, heiress to one of the largest family-owned diamond businesses in the world.

To the outside world, I have it all.

To Denver, I'm Sinclair. And that's all I need to be. Nothing more, nothing less.

"Tell me something about you."

"Me?" He arches one perfect, thick brow.

"Anything. Something I don't know."

His eyes pinch like he's considering how much to share with me.

"My parents died in a car accident when I was five. My grandparents took me in and raised me."

"Oh my god. I'm so sorry. I had… I had no idea." My heart clenches painfully. How can I have spent so many years with Denver in the periphery of my life and know so little about who he really is?

"My grandparents were great. You don't need to get upset for me. I was loved."

The deep sigh that accompanies his words has my breath stalling.

"They *were* great?"

"They're both gone now too. I lost them both when I was eighteen."

I swallow down the yelp that bursts from my lips. "I'm so sorry."

He strokes my cheeks with his thumbs like he's trying to ease my pain. Like I'm the one who deserves to be comforted.

"I'm okay. Don't worry about me."

"That's the thing," I whisper, holding his eyes. "I *do* worry about you. I'm starting to worry a whole lot."

His eyes soften. "I told you, worrying is my job. Now, are you going to come and wash my back for me like you promised?"

I blink at him and fight down the emotions bubbling inside my stomach. He wants to move on. It must be so painful for him to talk about, and as much as I want to ask more, to understand more, to know him better… now isn't the time.

I manage a slow, teasing smile as I tilt my head to one side. "You want me to?"

"I do." His eyes darken. "So...?"

Heat fires low in my belly from the way he's looking at me like he can't wait to get my clothes off.

I trail my fingers up his bare chest. "That depends."

"On?"

"On whether you'll do that thing to me again?"

"Make you come on my fingers?" One of his dark, thick brows arches.

"Uh-huh. And then your tongue... and then your..." I curl my hand around his swelling dick, grateful there's no sadness in his voice anymore, only lust.

"Get in the shower, Princess," he growls, his lips hovering over mine.

I press a gentle kiss to them, squeezing his cock again and making him hiss.

"Now," he adds.

And I swear he smiles.

28

DENVER

"You told Sinclair yet?"

"No," I grumble quietly. "I don't want to upset her," I tell Killian.

"She's going to find out once she comes back to her place and sees the security upgrade you organized."

I roll my lips as I look across the living area and at the deck from my position inside. Sinclair's on it with Monty playing catch with small treats she's throwing in the air for him. Her eyes light up and she claps each time he successfully gets one before it hits the ground.

"It needed upgrading since Neil's sniffing around."

"What do you think he wants with her? He hasn't made any attempt to speak to Sterling or Sullivan."

"I don't know," I answer Killian. "But whatever it is, she won't be alone when he comes back."

"Yeah?" Killian's voice lifts. "You er... you going to be staying at her place overnight? In case he calls late?"

I run my tongue over my teeth as Sinclair bounces on her toes in delight when Monty performs a spin for her on command. She looks so happy and carefree. Almost as much as when her brother was alive. *Almost.*

It tears at my fucking heart.

"I don't think that'll be necessary. Neil won't get inside the building, let alone near her apartment door."

"I thought you might have wanted to be sleeping under the same roof, like you are at the cabin. It's probably been quite cozy there, just the two of you and Monty," he says, a hint of an unspoken question in his tone.

"I'll see you when we get back. Sinclair's show is in two days' time. We'll leave tomorrow."

"All right." Killian chuckles, knowing he isn't going to get any more out of me. "Later."

He hangs up, and my phone rings again immediately.

"Denver?" Sterling clips.

"Boss," I reply, the hairs on the back of my neck prickling at his unusual curtness.

We only spoke a couple of hours ago when I had a video call with him, Killian, Jenson, and Sullivan over the sightings of Neil near Sinclair's apartment. He was calmer then. Because even though Neil is still around, the two guys who tried to take Monty have been identified by the cops. They were a couple of stupid teenage kids who said it was a prank and that they would have returned Monty after a couple of hours. They were looking for their fifteen minutes of fame. But even though Sinclair seemed happy with the cop report, and is eager to let it go, I'm not taking any chances. Kids or not, they threatened Sinclair's happiness when they decided to mess with Monty. Killian and Jenson are keeping tabs on them for me until I'm convinced they're of no further risk.

"I'm going to cut straight to the chase. I'm concerned about you bringing Sinclair back tomorrow. Hallie misses her, and damn, I miss her too. I know she's happy to squash the thing with Monty because she wants to come back to the city, but now there's this thing with Neil..." He exhales and mutters out a curse.

"I'll be with her at all times whenever she leaves her apartment," I assure him, my shoulders tightening as Sinclair looks in from the deck and catches my eye. She blows me a flirty kiss, giggling when I frown back at her.

"I know, I know. Maybe I'm overthinking it. I just... She's my *daughter*."

"I understand," I reply.

"You get it, I know you do." He sighs. "But between you and me, I'm goddamn worried. She's too trusting, always has been. I know she's safe with you. No one will lay a finger on her as long as you're with her, but I still... damnit," he mutters.

My teeth grind as guilt weaves its way around my windpipe and squeezes. Safe with me... He thinks she's safe with me. He's right when he says no one will lay a finger on her. Because I'd gut them for even trying. But that hasn't stopped me from having my fingers all over her... inside her... making her body bend to my every whim.

"I trust you, Denver," Sterling says. "If you think it's safe for her to come back to do this show, then I'll take your word for it."

I scrub a hand around my jaw, holding back the low fuck I almost hiss out.

He trusts me. The man who helped me seven years ago when I needed it most. The man who has been more than a boss to me ever since. The man who's been my friend. Who I'm now deceiving. And using one of the things he cares most about as I do it.

Sinclair.

"Is she safe?" Sterling asks. "Denver? Can you keep her safe if you come back now?"

The concern in his voice makes it hard for me to swallow. Part of me wants to tell him we should stay here indefinitely.

In our bubble away from the real world. But as happy as Sinclair seems on the surface here, I know she misses her family. And I know she wants to go back to work. It gives her purpose. It's what she loves.

I can't keep her to myself any longer. She needs to go back to the city. She needs to go back to her life.

"She's safe," I finally manage, my voice hoarse.

"You sure?" Sterling asks.

My eyes track to Sinclair as she stands holding Monty, hugging him to her and whispering something to him.

"I'm sure. I'll take care of her," I reply.

"I know you will," Sterling replies, sighing in relief. "I know you will."

The complete trust in his voice makes me screw my eyes closed in disgust at myself.

I've spent the past few days fucking her every way she'll have me. Hard and rough. Slow and gentle. Filling her over and over. Growling out her name as I come inside her again and again… or in her mouth… or over her ass… and her beautiful tits. Moving back and watching as my cum runs out from inside her tight, perfect pussy. Then getting hard at the sight and doing it all over again until she's so tired that she's fighting to keep her eyes open.

Then I take her again anyway, telling her she doesn't need to move if she's tired, that I'll do all the work. That she can lie back and relax and just let me make her feel good.

Because I'm too selfish not to.

And the beautiful princess that she is, she lets me. She allows it. She even smiles at me as I hold myself up on my arms above her and push inside her again. She even fucking comes for me when I tell her to, even though I know she's exhausted.

She takes everything I give her and still wakes up looking at me like I hung the damn moon before she kisses me and asks me to touch her again.

I've been ravaging her like she's mine. Like I have the right to.

Yet, her father *trusts me.*

"You don't need to worry. We've stepped up the system at her apartment. And I'll keep an even closer eye on her than before we left. She'll be fine," I say, ignoring the taste of deceit coating my tongue.

"Okay." Sterling sighs. "Then I'll see you both tomorrow."

My fist clenches around my phone as he hangs up.

I know what I should do. Even though it's the last thing I want. She'll hate me for it. She'll probably slap me, lash out at me, hurl abuse at me.

I hope she does. I hope she rips me apart.

Because I deserve it.

29

SINCLAIR

Something about the increased sourness in Denver's expression as he steps out onto the deck has me faltering.

"Was that my father you were speaking to?"

He nods once, his jaw locked tight, a vein throbbing in his temple.

"Are Halliday and the baby okay?" I ask, my heart racing.

"They're fine. Everyone back home is fine."

My shoulders loosen. "Okay, good. Then why do you look so worried?"

"We're going back to the city tomorrow, Sinclair," Denver says simply, looking at me from beneath his dark brows like his words carry extra meaning.

"I know." I smile as I put Monty's brush down and stand. "I've got my show, I can't wait."

"Your father is concerned."

"So he's concerned," I reply, studying the deep line between Denver's eyebrows. "Why are you letting that bother you? You've known him for years. You know what he's like.

He might be concerned, but he'll deal with it, like he always does."

"He trusts me," Denver clips.

I wait for him to say more but am met with stony silence and a harshness in his eyes.

"He trusts me," he repeats, straightening his rigid shoulders as a flash of guilt passes over his face.

And there it is.

I narrow my eyes and study him. His green eyes are dark and impenetrable. Like he's on a mission and can't afford to lose sight of his main objective.

"Uh-huh," I say. "And now you're worried because you've spent the past four days inside his daughter making sure she's definitely not going back to the city a virgin."

"Sinclair!" he snaps.

I shrug, hiding the anger that's flaring inside me. I get it, he thinks he's betrayed my father's trust. But what about my trust? I've never let anyone get close to me like Denver.

"I mean, I'm clearly not, am I? You've had your dick everywhere except in my ass. Was that going to be your next conquest?"

The sharp intake of breath he takes only makes me more determined to piss him off. He's watching me, nostrils flaring like an angry bull.

He's expecting me to fight him. Or to cry, maybe. More likely fight. Maybe he's hoping I'll slap him. Take out some of my anger on him... make him feel better about the cowardly thing he's doing.

I won't give it to him.

"Okay," I say, keeping my voice light as I walk over to him. "Well, thanks for the dick, I guess. You definitely taught me some things I can use with my new boyfriend when I meet him." I smile brightly as he glares down his nose at me, his jaw clenching.

I pat him on the chest, happy to find his heart is pummeling out a fast rhythm against his ribs.

"Sinclair," he growls.

I hold his eyes for a beat. They're like two green flames burning in the night sky.

I spin and sashay to the open door that leads back inside.

"Sin—"

"I'm going to pack. Do you mind taking Monty to the bathroom?" I say, looking back at him over my shoulder.

"New boyfriend?" he spits.

"Oh, yeah." I pout at him. "Did you think this was"—I wave my finger between us both—"like, a thing?" I wrinkle my nose, as if the possibility had never even crossed my mind.

He glares at me like he's about to explode.

"Oh, you did?" I let my face fall in mock pity. "I'm so sorry. Why would you think that? Was it all the romantic stuff we said to one another? The way we've been sleeping in each other's arms every night? Or the fact that you were my first and only and that should mean something?"

His jaw slackens and something akin to panic laced with 'oh shit' tints his gaze.

I hold back all the things I'd like to hurl at him and force a sweet smile. "Like I said, Monty might need the bathroom."

But Monty has already moved back inside to his favorite spot in front of the fire and has sprawled out on his back.

"Hmm," I murmur, looking at Monty. "Maybe not. Thanks anyway, Brute."

I'm barely two steps inside before his voice hits my back, making a shiver scoot up my spine.

"No one else is touching you. Ever."

A joyless smile plays on my lips, but I bite it back as I flick my eyes in his direction. "It's sweet that you care, but you don't get a say in what, or who, I do."

"Sinclair," he growls.

I start walking again, speeding up to put distance between us. He barks out my name roughly behind me, and curses as I stomp through the inner door and down the stairs leading to the lower level and the forest.

I want to get away from him. I'm so fucking angry at him. The blood racing in my veins is pumping adrenaline to my muscles as his heavy footsteps thunder down the stairs behind me.

"Sinclair!"

"I guess I should thank you for breaking me in," I toss back at him casually. "At least now I know I like sex. It'll be interesting to see how other guys do it. I mean, you're ten years older than me. Maybe a guy my age will have even more stamina. I'll barely have time to sleep once we go back to the city and I get out dating."

"Do you mean that?" he barks. "You really want to see what other guys are like?"

I whip around at the foot of the stairs, and he has the sense to stop halfway down them as I glare at him.

"What the hell do you think?" I snarl, unable to hide my true feelings any longer. He looks like he's about to say something, so I throw up a palm. "You know what? I don't care what you think."

I turn and stride to the main door, yanking it open.

"Don't follow me!" I yell as I stomp outside.

"Where are you going?" he shouts after me as I head past the tree stump where he chops the firewood and toward the thick tree line.

"Getting some fresh air, what's it look like?" I yell back, breaking into a run.

"Don't run from me, Sinclair!" he bellows. But unlucky for him, all of the training I've been doing with him since we arrived has made me fitter, and I'm actually a pretty good sprinter. Lighter on my feet than him. A little faster.

"Go to hell, asshole!" I shout back, my earlier façade completely cracking as I put distance between us.

I hate him. I actually hate him. Just like I did before we came here. I should never have stopped. He's just another person in my life who thinks they know what's best for me. Who's trying to make decisions for me.

"Sinclair!" he thunders. "You don't go anywhere without me! Come the fuck back here!"

I ignore him, pumping my arms and legs as hard as I can as I race through the gaps between the trees. I'm wearing a dress, but at least I have my sneakers on. And this time my laces are done up tight in a double knot.

Take that, jerk.

I keep running until my lungs burn and my eyes sting. I hate him. Stupid giant muscly asshole.

Footsteps moving fast behind me make the twigs on the forest floor snap with a loud urgency.

"You'd better run, Princess," he calls from somewhere closer to me than he was moments ago. "Because when I catch you, I'll spank that ass of yours until it wears my handprint. Don't think I won't."

"Fuck off," I holler back, gasping for air as I run faster.

I break through the trees and skid to a halt meters away from the edge of a river.

"Shit," I mutter, spinning back into the trees and running in another direction.

Everything is quiet except for the pounding of my blood in my ears. I slow down to a walk, fighting to keep my breath steady and quiet so I can listen.

Nothing.

I must have lost him. I'll have to go back to the cabin, I know that. But I just need some time away from him. He might be willing to forget about what's happened between us the moment we leave here, but I'm not. I can't go back to the city like nothing ever happened. Go back to him working with my father and barely looking my way. Not when the way he's looked at me since we've been here has made me feel more alive than I've felt in years.

I'd feel like such an idiot. I wouldn't be able to stand being in the same room as him.

I stop and rest my hands on my hips, breathing deeply. Sweat prickles my hairline and runs down the dip between my breasts.

I listen again.

Nothing.

"Stupid jerk," I mutter.

Strong arms grab me from behind, coiling around my torso and pinning my arms to my sides. I'm lifted from the floor like I weigh nothing.

"Get off me!" I screech, kicking my legs out. But it's no use, he's got me held in the air like a doll.

How can he creep up on me like that? Stupid giant hulk with his special ops training.

"You're an asshole!" I snarl, throwing my head back, trying to hit his nose, but missing.

He walks forward and pushes my front against a giant tree, pinning me between it and his body that's burning like an inferno against my back. My tiptoes dance against the floor as I try to get free.

"I told you not to run from me," he whispers, his breath hot and menacing against my ear.

"And I told you not to follow me," I spit back.

I struggle some more, but all it does is make the bark of the tree snag my dress.

"What am I going to do with you?" he grits, taking one arm from my torso, but still easily pinning me in place with the remaining one.

I gasp as he pushes my dress up around my waist. His

large, warm palm slides over the curve of my ass and his breath grows ragged as he grabs a handful of my flesh and squeezes.

"Don't ever fucking run from me, Sinclair," he breathes, kissing my neck beneath my ear.

I whimper at the sensation of his lips on my skin, internally cursing myself for not holding it back.

He kneads my flesh, stroking his thumb along the outer edge of my panties. Then he pushes the fabric into the crack of my ass, leaving one ass cheek exposed.

"Don't ever run," he says again.

Then his palm connects with my skin.

I cry out, my voice hitting the tree and bouncing straight back at me and ringing in my ears.

"So pretty and red," he says, rubbing my stinging skin.

He spanks me again.

Harder.

I grit my teeth and hiss.

"That's one of the things I like most about you, your fire," he rasps, kissing my neck again.

"Fuck you," I snap.

"You know I don't want to let you go, Princess," he says, his voice hoarse as he strokes the burning flesh on my ass. "It's the last thing I want."

He lowers me enough that my feet flatten on the floor, and I spin inside his arms, ready to unleash hell on him. But the second my eyes lock onto fiery green burning with bright gold, I stop, and my voice deserts me.

"You want another man?" His eyes are intent on mine, pinching at the corners like he's bracing himself for my answer. "You want to fuck another guy?"

I tip my chin up. "Maybe," I say, wanting to rile him even more.

"This not good enough for you?"

He grabs my hand and places it over the erection inside his

jeans. The heat of it seeps through the fabric. He squeezes his fingers around mine, until I curl mine around his dick.

A rough hiss leaves his lips, and he plants his hand against the tree beside my head and looks at my hand on him.

"Take it out," he rasps.

I squeeze, digging my nails into the denim. "Why should I?"

He snaps his eyes up to mine, and I clench my thighs together, heat pooling between them at the animalistic dominance in his gaze.

"Take my cock out, Princess," he says slowly.

"Why should I?" I say back even slower.

His eyes blaze and he runs his tongue over his lower lip.

"You're the only one I want, Sinclair. And I need to hear you tell me that I'm the only one you want too."

I hitch a brow, feigning indifference. But the scent of his warm skin is making my pulse race as he leans closer.

"You want to get your dick out in the forest, then do it yourself," I say, my core igniting like fuel on a fire as his pupils blow wide at my defiance.

"Fine," he snaps.

He tugs the button on his jeans open and tears down the zipper, pulling his cock out. I glance at it, making sure my face remains neutral as I take in the thickness of it, the way it's swollen and angry looking. And so impossibly *hard*.

He wraps his hand around it and jerks himself off slowly. My pulse throbs in my pussy as the fat head of it swells and glistening drops ooze out.

"You don't want another cock inside you, Sinclair. Not when this one is all yours. Mine's the only one you'll ever want, isn't it? Tell me."

I shrug, tearing my gaze away from how big he is.

His eyes burn into mine as I look up.

"I don't know. Is it?" I say, letting boredom tint my voice.

"Fuck!" He slams his other hand against the tree, making some bark break off.

Excitement bubbles inside me knowing that I'm about to make him lose it. Knowing I'm the only one who knows how to make him lose his cool. Mr. Never-gets-flustered-can-stalk-you-undetected-in-the-woods-but-is-brought-to-his-knees-by-Sinclair-Beaufort.

"Touch it," he hisses.

I smile slyly. "No, thanks."

"Touch it!"

His nostrils flare, the whites of his eyes growing larger around his pupils.

"Please, Princess." His voice drops to a husky plea. "*Touch me.*"

He stares at me, holding his breath as I lift my hand and dust my thumb over the head of him, swiping up some drops of precum.

"Fuck," he exhales shakily. "Fuuuck."

The muscles in his neck tense as I swirl my thumb around and then run it over his slit. "Good girl," he rasps.

His lids hood, a rough groan coming from deep in his chest like my touch is the one drug that can end his torture.

"Tell me you don't want another man, that you don't need another man."

His eyes are focused on my hand as I replace his fingers with my own and jerk him off slowly.

"Tell me, Sinclair. Please."

He screws his face up as he watches my hand on him. The turmoil in his expression stabs me in the gut. Maybe Dixie's mom left him for another man. Maybe that's why he sounds so desperate to hear me say it.

But he still said those things about my father trusting him. He still implied that this needs to end between us. Whether he meant it or not, I'm still angry at him.

"Maybe I do," I say, causing his jaw to clench tight as he grits his teeth. "Maybe I'm already forgetting what yours feels like inside me."

"No," he rasps.

"Maybe I am." I squeeze him, stroking faster. "Maybe that's the way it's supposed to be."

"Fuck!"

He rips his hand from the tree and grabs me underneath my ass, lifting me against the trunk. My back flattens against the rough bark as he crowds me with his body.

"You won't forget, Princess. Ever. I won't let you." He crushes his mouth against mine, kissing me forcefully until the air leaves my body. "I won't let you."

I grab either side of his face and hold it to mine, grazing his lips with my teeth as I match his fiery kiss with my own savage one.

"You don't want me to forget?" I pant against his mouth.

The muscles in his arms work overtime as he grabs handfuls of my ass, then holds me up with one arm and grabs my breasts. His mouth slides to my neck, sucking it desperately before coming back to my lips with a curse.

It's like he can't figure out where to touch me because he wants all of me at the same time.

"You can't forget," he growls. "I won't leave you alone long enough. I'll make sure there's always a part of me inside you soaking your panties as it drips out. The scent of me will be on you so everyone knows who you belong to."

The possessiveness in his tone makes my nipples pebble and my clit throb.

"You're an asshole." I seethe, biting his lower lip as I kiss him.

"I know," he fires back, shoving up my dress and stuffing his hand between my thighs. "But I'm an asshole who'd fucking die for you. And no... not because it's my job."

I moan into his kiss as his fingers find my wet panties and rub my swollen flesh through them.

"Sinclair," he snaps, like my arousal makes him angry.

"What?"

"Even when I give you a reason to hate me, you're still soaking for me, aren't you? You want me no matter what, don't you?"

"No."

Yes.

He grunts as he slips his thumb beneath the wet lace and my body covers it in slick heat.

"Fuck," he groans.

He tugs my panties roughly, shredding the thin material that covers my pussy. Then he shoves his jeans down over his hips with one hand.

I'm taking all of his cock before I have a chance to breathe.

"Sinclair," he rasps, thrusting into me hard. "Princess... fuck..."

I pull at his hair and bite his lip as we kiss, not caring when I taste blood. I suck on it, swallowing the metallic taste of him as he groans and pumps into me faster.

"You're mine. You belong with me. You know that. Don't ever talk about another man touching you again. Or I'll have to kill him, you understand?"

I cry out as he fucks me deeper. We're loud, our moans echoing off the trees and traveling up to the sky above.

It's wild, messy, desperate.

"You don't get to tell me who I can date if you're going to ditch me like I'm some dirty little secret," I snap as his hips drive his dick up inside me at a delicious angle that has my toes tingling.

"Fuck, you're not some secret," he hisses, forcing his forehead against mine. His eyes burn into mine as he pushes so deep inside me, sliding over the place inside me that sets a familiar heat building.

"What am I then?" I gasp as the undeniable pressure of an impending orgasm makes more wetness coat his cock.

"I told you. You're Sinclair."

I grab a handful of his hair and jerk his head back, enjoying the way his Adam's apple bobs in his thick neck as he swallows.

"You're mine," he rasps. "No one else's. You don't want some other man, do you? Not when I know the way to make you come so hard you cry."

The asshole. He knows he's right. His eyes darken as I glare back at him.

"Do you, Princess?"

I pant, staring daggers at him as he thrusts into me, the head of his cock sliding over my G-spot again and again.

"Do you?" he asks again.

I tighten my grip on his hair, twisting it until his eyes pinch.

"Say it," he urges.

"No."

"Say it."

He fucks into me harder and my eyes roll in my head.

"You're so close. Be a good girl and say it as you come on my cock for me."

I try to keep my lips clamped shut, moaning into my cheeks as the pressure builds.

"Say it."

I screw my eyes shut, blocking him out, but he kisses me hard, making me gasp for air.

"Say it," he breathes.

I open my eyes.

And I explode.

"Yes!" I whine as I come hard on him, my pussy clamping

down around his cock and squeezing it as wave after wave rolls through me, stealing all my control. "Denver! Oh my god!"

He pumps into me, driving me through an earth-shattering orgasm that immediately crests into another without giving me a moment to breathe.

"Denver," I whimper, my eyes watering and blurring my vision.

"You're okay, Princess. I'm here."

I gasp, trying to focus on his eyes as I come. My body hugs his cock as it gets even harder, and his fingers dig into my thighs.

"Fuck, Sinclair. I can't hold back. The feeling of you coming for me..."

"Do it," I choke.

The veins in his neck thicken, and his eyes hold mine as he comes inside me with a gravelly groan. The sound is so raw, husky, and hot that I whimper, parting my thighs wider around his hips so he can push deeper inside me.

"Yeah? You want it deep? You want to be full of me?"

"Yes," I moan, my clit rubbing against his skin as he thrusts.

I come again without warning and tears spring from the corners of my eyes.

Everything gets harder and faster and deeper as he groans out the rest of his orgasm. Our bodies slide together as he empties inside me. Slickness coats my inner thighs where it's running out from inside me.

"Oh, fuck," he chokes, his thrusts slowing to deep, rough jerks of his hips as his mouth finds mine. "Fuck," he grinds out, kissing me roughly, all panting and teeth and sex. "Fuck," he groans again.

I gasp, fighting to get my breath back as my body turns to jelly.

"Don't ever run from me, Sinclair." He grabs my chin and

presses a searing kiss to my lips. "Please don't ever leave me not knowing where you're going or if you're okay. I need to know you're okay... I need to see you... I can't have... *Don't fucking leave me like that.*" He screws his face up as he kisses me.

My anger was ripped out of me with my orgasm. All I want to do is stay in his arms and hold him tight.

"I'm here." I cup his face, kissing him back. "I'm not going anywhere. I'm here."

I press urgent kisses to his lips. One by one. Over and over. Trying to cover the cracks that are opening up and pouring pain out from him.

"Sinclair." He exhales, his eyes closed as he kisses me back.

Something shifts in my chest at the desperate tone creeping into his voice.

I kiss him more gently, stroking the sides of his face.

My big strong Brute.

I don't know what memory I just evoked in him, but whatever it was, it wasn't a good one. He keeps kissing me, his body crushed to mine like he can't bear to let me go.

"I'm sorry," he whispers.

He opens his eyes, and I gaze at the flash of something hiding in their depths. He looks so lost. So broken for a second before he blinks it away. Maybe it's the love he lost years ago, Dixie's mom. Maybe not. But either way I recognize the look in his eyes because I've seen the same one in mine every day since I lost the people I loved too.

Maybe we're both lost in grief.

I press another kiss to his lips, and he relaxes, sinking into me.

"It's okay," I whisper. "It's okay."

30

SINCLAIR

"Feel good to be back?"

I glance at Killian as I place Monty's breakfast bowl down for him and fuss him as he trots over to eat.

"Yeah. I mean the peace was nice. Denver's place is in the middle of nowhere. But I'm not going to lie, I'm glad to have Wi-Fi back."

Killian chuckles as I move around the living area, packing what I need for my runway show into my bag. We got back yesterday, and after dropping me home, Denver showed me how to use my new security system he had installed while we were away, and then he left. My father wanted to have a meeting with him. I haven't seen him since. Even with Monty in bed with me last night, it still felt empty. Killian came over this morning to be my backup for the day incase whatever Denver's doing takes longer than anticipated.

"They're here." Killian pockets his phone after reading the text that just came through.

Butterflies erupt in my stomach. I'm being stupid. It's one night since I saw him. One. Yet I'm buzzing with electricity now he's close by.

A few minutes later, there's a knock at my apartment door, but I let Killian answer it as I move into the kitchen.

Deep rumbles of voices flow down from the hallway, and I clench my thighs together at the deepest one.

"Hey, Sinclair."

I turn, smiling at Jenson as he walks into the room.

"Hey." My eyes immediately move from him to the giant, dark and brooding hulk behind him.

Denver's back in his usual uniform of dark suit and tie, white shirt, gun on his belt... and a serious expression that gives nothing away and just makes him look pissed.

Jenson starts talking to Killian as Denver and I stare at one another. His brows lower over his intense gaze, and something about how cold and detached he is makes me spin back around under the pretense of fixing the drinks I'm making.

I swallow, my throat thick. I recognize that look. He's all business, looking at me like I'm his client.

He clears his throat. "Sinclair? We need to leave in the next five minutes to make it to your show on time."

I squeeze my eyes shut, keeping my back to him. That voice. Those instructions, spoken without any warmth. So clinical. Detached. If he's going to try and tell me we have to stop this, like he did before I ran from him in the forest, I don't know what I'll do. Smack him in the mouth, perhaps? Or burst into tears. The way my heart's racing right now, either is possible.

He can't expect now we're back in the city, we're going to just ignore what happened.

Goosebumps prick up along my upper arms as his breath hits the back of my neck. He's moved so close that the heat from his body seeps through my vest and makes me burn. The sound of his tongue wetting his lips as he leans closer, keeping his voice low so Jenson and Killian can't hear, makes a shiver run up my spine.

"I missed you," he breathes.

Relief and lust entwine together, making heat flood my core. I spin and lean against the counter, gazing up at him.

"Did you?"

His green eyes soften, the gold around his pupils glowing like a sunbeam in the dark.

"More than anything," he murmurs, all delicious and gravelly.

"Then I guess I missed you too," I whisper, aching to slide my arms around his neck and pull his lips to mine. It's the longest I've ever gone without feeling his lips on mine and his hands on me. I hate it.

I bite my lower lip and we stare at one another until the silence grows and I realize Jenson and Killian have stopped talking.

I glance over and they're both watching us. Jenson's wearing a cocky grin, but Killian looks concerned.

"We're going. Sterling needs us to keep looking into something." Killian keeps his eyes fixed on Denver's like he's communicating in some special code.

Denver's jaw tightens and he nods once. "Fine. I'll call you later for an update."

"Enjoy your show, Sinclair," Killian says to me.

"Thanks, I will."

"Later." Jenson grins, before looking at Monty. "Nice bro, always looking so sharp."

I follow his gaze to the new sweater Monty has on and hold back my giggle as Denver zones in on it.

"That's my shirt," he rumbles.

"*Was* your shirt," I say, admiring the way it turned out when I remodeled it into something for Monty. "You threw it in the trash. I didn't want to waste it."

His eyes stay on Monty and the sweater I made from the shirt he got my blood all over on our hike.

"He's grateful to you. He likes it," I add with a smile.

"Wears it better than you," Jenson quips.

Denver's eyes narrow as he takes the travel mug of coffee I'm holding out to him. Our fingers brush and the way his eyes heat when they meet mine, like he's thinking of doing something really filthy to me, has heat pooling between my thighs.

"Wait for us," he calls to Killian and Jenson, keeping his eyes locked on mine. "We'll ride the elevator down with you."

I keep my gaze on the side of Denver's face as we drive. We've just dropped Monty off at my father and Halliday's while I'm at the show. Denver's barely said two words since we left my apartment.

"Are you annoyed about the sweater? Is that why you marched us out of there?"

A muscle in his cheek clenches and he sucks in a breath through his nose. "I don't care about the sweater. I cared about the fact I couldn't be alone with you in your apartment for even a second if there was a chance you were going to make your show today."

"Oh." I grin. "Because you wanted to get me naked?"

He exhales, his shoulders softening. "Because I'm going crazy every second I can't touch you." He places his hand on my thigh, letting out a gentle groan as he squeezes my flesh.

He drives with one hand on the wheel, in relaxed control as he massages my thigh with his thumb. It's so simple, yet something about it makes me wet.

"I could be late?" I suggest, squirming in my seat.

He squeezes my thigh more firmly. "No, you can't. This

show's important to you. It's the reason we're back here earlier than I wanted. You aren't going to be late for it."

I pout as he glances at me.

"Princess," he growls in warning, which only makes me wetter.

"Fine," I huff. "I just... you haven't... since we came back to the city, we haven't..." I fold my arms and stare out of the window like a sulking child.

"I haven't taken care of you?" He squeezes my thigh when I don't answer. "I want to, believe me. It's just been full on since I got back. I had a lot to get caught up on."

"It's fine." I shrug.

"Can I stay with you tonight?"

I whip my gaze back to his, but his eyes are on the road and his face is straight, giving nothing away.

"You want to sleep over?"

"That a problem?" He frowns.

A bolt of excitement jabs me in the stomach. I expected to have to talk him into it. Like being back was going to play with his conscience until we came clean to my father and Sullivan about us. Whatever 'us' is exactly. But a part of me was hoping we wouldn't have to do anything yet. Because even though it's selfish, I'm enjoying having something to myself for a change. So much of my life I've been protected. Decisions have been made for me.

Denver is my decision, and mine alone. And I want to keep it that way a little longer.

"No problem," I answer, turning to the window again so he doesn't see my goofy grin.

"Will Monty be wearing more of my clothes when I wake up, though?" Amusement laces his tone, and I can't help but look back at him.

"He looks good in it, admit it."

Denver's lips twitch. "Yeah, he does. Did you make it yourself?"

"I did." I beam, rather proud of myself. "I've picked up a trick or two working in fashion. I know my way around a needle and thread. Plus, I know where it came from. I'm really careful about the brands I work with. You wouldn't believe some of the workers' conditions that make garments for some fashion houses."

"Child labor," Denver says.

"Exactly. For an industry that's all about beautiful things, it's really ugly. I saw it when I visited a factory overseas on a shoot. I took Monty with me, and the kids there loved him. *Kids,* Denver. They were filthy and overworked and..." I rub at my chest, at the ache there whenever I picture their little faces. "The real beauty was there. In every snotty-nosed cuddle and dirty-handed stroke they gave him and me. I thought of Molly when she's older and I... They don't even get to go to school."

"I know."

I narrow my eyes at him, but he keeps his attention on the road, even though my gaze must be burning into him.

"You know?" I drop my head back against the headrest and roll my eyes. "Of course you do. You know everything because it's your job."

He squeezes my thigh, and I snort.

"How long?"

"How long?" he repeats, glancing at me.

I can't help but smile at the warmth in his eyes as they meet mine.

"How long have you known who Julian really is?" I ask.

Denver presses his lips together. "Since a few days after I saw you out with him that night."

I shake my head and laugh. "Jeez. There's no hiding anything from you, is there? Why didn't you say something?"

"Because it was for you to tell me when you were ready.

We have to be ready to talk about these things. As long as I know you're safe, I don't need to know more until you're ready to share it with me."

I gaze at him. Maybe that's what it's like for him and Dixie, and her mom, Lizzie. And why he hasn't told me more about what happened between them yet. Maybe he's not ready to share that part of himself yet.

"I don't understand why you keep it a secret, though."

I shrug. "People expect me to be a certain way. And I'm fine with that. They don't need to know that Julian's helped me start a foundation to help get those kids out of the factory and into school. It'd look like some vain publicity stunt if I were to share it. Our investors are good people who are helping because they care about the changes they'll make, not because they care what it'll do for their image. And besides, only my family's opinion of me matters, no one else's."

"I admire that, I really do."

"But?"

He glances at me. "No buts, Sinclair. You're doing something great."

"But you think I could use my name to help give it more publicity? To raise more money and awareness."

"I didn't say that."

I reach up and run the backs of my fingers over his cheekbone and down the planes of his handsome face.

"You didn't have to. You're right. I'm just... not ready yet."

He turns and catches my fingertips with his lips, kissing them. It's the first bit of real contact I've had with him since we crossed the Brooklyn Bridge and drove into Manhattan, and my pathetic heart soars at the momentary flash of warmth against my skin before it's gone.

"We're here," he says, taking his hand from my thigh. "Time to get back to work, Princess."

31

DENVER

I crack my knuckles as the make-up artist runs a fingertip over the exposed skin on Sinclair's ass cheek in the lingerie she's wearing.

"You get in a fight with a wild cat or something, darling?"

Sinclair turns her head to look down at him. "What do you mean?"

"Your ass. It's covered in little scratches."

Guilt weaves itself around my throat. The tree. I fucked her against a tree, and I hurt her.

I scrub a hand around my jaw, cursing myself as Sinclair's eyes meet mine.

"I'm fine. I didn't even know they were there," she says to the make-up artist. I know her words are meant for me. To reassure me. But they do nothing to quell the rising tide of nausea I have from my gut from knowing I've left marks on her body.

"Okay, well, now they're gone." The make-up artist stands with a grin, holding a brush and sponge in his hand as he assesses his work. "Beautiful, you're all set."

"Thanks." Sinclair smiles at him before walking over to where I'm sitting on a bench along one wall.

"Are you going to sit there looking sulky the whole show, Brute?"

I look at her face, all golden and dewy with the make-up. They've styled her hair up into a high ponytail with a pink ribbon to match the baby pink bustier and panties she's modeling. My eyes slide over the low waistband of the silk panties. She hooks a finger underneath my chin and lifts my eyes to her face.

"Thought you don't look when you're working?"

"I didn't." I hold her eyes. "But it's kind of hard not to now."

"Now what?" She hitches a brow with a teasing smile. I know she loves to play with me, and damn, I can't help but let her, because hearing the fun flirty tone in her voice, and seeing the way her eyes light up with joy does something to me.

I love to see something other than pain in her eyes.

"Now that you're my girl," I rasp.

She purses her pink, glossy lips, her eyes bright. "You calling me your girl, *Denny*?"

"I'm calling you my girl, Princess."

The smile that lights up her face is enough to make my heart swell.

"Okay," she muses. "I'll consider your request."

She spins on her heels and walks over to where she's needed with a spring in her step, leaving me with my lips curling up in amusement. I'm treading a fine line and I know it. I almost confessed to Sterling on the spot what I've been up to with his daughter when I saw him. But something stopped me.

The threat of losing her.

Because there's every possibility I'll be out of a job when he finds out. And I'll no longer be able to spend every day with her. I know I have to be the one to tell him. But I want to protect that lightness that's overtaken her since we started this thing between us.

I want more time seeing her happy like this.

"I thought you'd decided to retire without telling anyone." Theodora giggles as she comes to stand beside Sinclair to have their outfits checked one final time, ready for the runway.

"What made you think that?" Sinclair asks.

I shift forward in my seat, listening.

"You were gone a long time, that's all."

"Hardly. It wasn't even two weeks. I needed some time out of the city awhile, that's all," she answers as someone sprays her hair with something and fluffs her ponytail.

"It felt like longer. I missed both of you." Theodora looks in my direction and my neck stiffens as she meets my eyes.

"You can't date him, Theo," Sinclair says, following Theodora's attention to me.

"Why? You were the one who told him to take my number."

Sinclair shrugs. "That was then. This is now. He's too busy looking after me to date. Aren't you, Denver?" she calls over.

"Swamped," I reply, holding Theo's eyes.

Theodora bristles, studying me for a few seconds before she looks away, flustered. I return to cracking my knuckles as the girls are ushered to the rear of the stage where they're needed. I need to move positions in a minute so I can see Sinclair when she's out on the runway. But for now, I don't want to let either of them out of my sight.

My phone chimes in my pocket, and I pull it out, scanning the text quickly.

> Killian: I know you don't take calls when you're in public with Sinclair, but you need to hear this.

I hit dial and bring my phone to my ear.

"What is it?" I bark as soon as he answers, standing and moving along the wall so I'm closer to Sinclair.

"Neil."

That one name has my shoulders bunching up in defense.

"What about him?"

"Jenson followed him to two streets away from Sinclair's show before he lost him," Killian says. "It wasn't his fault," he adds when I curse. "A woman got her purse snatched and Jenson intervened."

"He get them?"

"Knocked three of the guys' teeth out."

"Hmm, good," I grunt in admiration.

"Yeah, you should've seen how smug he looked when he told me."

"So, Neil?" I ask, because I know Jenson will be dining out on that story for weeks now and I'll likely hear it thirty more times before the end of the week. But Neil is within the vicinity of Sinclair, and knowing I have potential threats nearby to her has every muscle in my body coiling tight in preparation to unleash hell if necessary.

"He's nearby, that's all. Just wanted you to be aware."

"Fine," I clip. "Thanks."

"Look. Nothing suggests he wants to even speak to her. Maybe he just wants to look at her in the flesh, you know? See if she's like her mom? The guy was in love with Elaina."

"I know," I grit. "She was fucking him behind Sterling's back for months before she died."

Rage boils inside me. I don't know why Elaina cheated on Sterling, and it's none of my goddamn business. But I know what Sterling's done for me in the past. What he's done for Dixie. He didn't deserve that. So whatever Neil's angle is with coming back to New York and showing up near Sinclair, he better be damn well prepared to deal with me.

"He hasn't done anything concerning—"

"Yet," I hiss.

"Okay, yet." Killian agrees. "Maybe he's only interested in seeing Sinclair is all I'm saying. So don't go shooting the guy in the street without thinking it through first, okay?"

"When do I ever not think it through?"

I move further along the edge of the room, closer to the spot I planned out earlier that allows me to see Sinclair on the runway once she steps onto it.

"Just don't kill the guy in broad daylight."

"If he comes near Sinclair..." I growl.

"And the way you just said her name is exactly my point," Killian says. "Look, to you, she's... I get it, believe me. Be careful, that's all I'm saying."

I take in Sinclair as she steps onto the runway. I move so I can see out from backstage and down the length of it. I scan the crowd quickly, making sure no one new has appeared in the front row of the audience.

"I will be," I reply.

"And please, tell Sterling and Sullivan before Jenson shoots off his big mouth by accident. If he can tell you two have something going on, then those guys will see it a mile off."

My shoulders stiffen. "Thanks for the advice."

"I hope for your sake, they don't cut your balls off and feed them to you."

"I'll worry about that," I say as I narrow my eyes on Theodora as she heads out onto the runway and passes Sinclair.

"Fine." Killian sighs. "Tell me how last night went before you go."

I drag in a slow breath to control the anger that's threatening to spike my blood pressure.

"I got him talking," I say about the guy who they found with the identical copy of Sinclair's missing necklace.

The boys took it from him, and Sullivan tested it while Sinclair and I were out of the city. Initially we thought it could be the real one, but Sullivan knew the moment he saw it that it was a good fake. It didn't carry the Beaufort Diamonds signature marking that all their pieces have. The guy wouldn't talk, scared of giving up his forger and getting in deep water. But we don't give a shit about that. We just needed to know how he managed to get such a convincing fake made.

One visit to him myself and I had his tongue loosening.

"Don't tell me how," Killian says.

"I barely touched him. Didn't need to. He would have given up his own mother once I told him I was there for Sinclair because someone is trying to hurt her."

The look on the guy's face when I told him that was all the confirmation I needed. He isn't the one who's been leaving threatening notes on Sinclair's car, or the one responsible for trashing it. He's just a superfan who follows her every move and scrapbooks them. The amount of press clippings he had of Sinclair from various angles made him able to get a copy of her necklace made. And if he hadn't been so vocal about how thrilled he was to have one just like hers, then we might not have found him.

But we did. So of course I paid him a visit.

The guy practically pissed himself when I turned up hammering on his door last night. It's why I was late to get Sinclair this morning. I was giving Sterling and Sullivan an update.

"He might not have had her real necklace, but he did have some useful things to share."

"Yeah? Sterling said you have a lead on who might have taken the real one?"

"I do." I grit my teeth as Sinclair comes backstage and is swept up into an outfit change.

Theodora isn't far behind her, and she looks over at me as she pulls her lace vest up over her head, letting her breasts spill free. The smile on her face falters when I pay them no attention and keep my eyes fixed on hers instead.

"The guy takes photos of himself in all the places where he's waiting to see her. Outside her runway shows and shoots."

I pull my phone from my ear and select the images I showed to Sterling and Sullivan this morning, then click send.

"Is that...?"

"Sure the hell is."

Killian whistles. "Jealousy?"

"Got to be. Sinclair gets the big brands chasing her all the time. This girl doesn't. The work she's done recently, she's been doing for free to try to build her portfolio. They didn't even use any of her shots from the last shoot she was on with Sinclair."

"Cutthroat industry," Killian mutters.

"Yeah. She's about to find out how much."

Theodora's stealing furtive glances over at me. She knows something's wrong.

"Maybe it's not Neil I should be warning you not to kill."

"Maybe," I murmur, staring at her as she starts to look really uncomfortable at my attention.

"All right. Give me an update once you have one."

"Will do," I reply, hanging up.

I walk over to where Sinclair's now in a white bridal set comprising of a corset and stockings and suspender belt.

"Wanted a close up, huh?" She giggles as I stop beside her.

"I'm not looking at this one, Princess," I whisper.

"Why not?" she asks playfully.

"Because the only time I want to admire something like this is when I'm taking it off my wife," I rasp.

"Oh." Her voice falters.

I lean a little closer until the back of my hand brushes hers. No one around us will notice; they're all too busy rushing about, keeping the show running.

"You'll look even better in it when my ring's on your finger," I say, flexing my ring finger against hers.

She shivers and my blood heats from the sound of her breath catching in her throat. I shouldn't be saying it. I'm crossing every damn line there is. But I can't stop myself. It spills out before I can hold it back.

It's what I crave.

Her being mine. Forever.

No matter how wrong or unlikely that might be.

Sinclair's swept toward the runway to line up behind another model who is about to walk out, and I feel the loss of her body next to mine like a limb has been torn off.

Theodora's unsure eyes meet mine as I glare at her.

"You going to give it back nicely, or am I going to have to take it?" I hiss.

"What are you talking about?" Her eyes narrow like she thinks she can play dumb. But I'll shout it out in front of everyone if that's what she wants.

I'll rip her to shreds with an audience.

"You know what."

She glances to the side, checking where Sinclair is.

"She'll know what you did soon. The minute you give it back, you're going to walk out of here and get into the cop car that's waiting outside for you, where they're going to charge you with vandalism, malicious communications, and theft."

"You can't prove anything," she snaps. She looks me up and down, pretending she's unaffected, but her bottom lip is trembling as she blinks fast. "Don't tell me... you're another person who's in love with her?" She snorts. "Why does everyone think Sin's so special?"

"Because she *is* special," I grit. "And that's why roaches like you want to crawl all over her, spreading their poison. But Theodora"—I lean close so my lips are at her ear—"you didn't count on me. I know exactly what kind of girl you are. And soon everyone else will too. You'll never work in fashion again."

She shudders before snapping her chin up to glare at me.

"You're just some paid henchman for the Beauforts. How's it feel knowing they could ditch you at any moment and you'd be on the outside? Then you'd be like the rest of us, living in their shadow," she spits. "Her father owns half the fucking city. What chance does anyone else have?"

"Sinclair is where she is because she works hard. And because she doesn't shit on other people to get to where she is. She's liked. She's respected. She isn't *trash*."

"You're an idiot if you think she won't turn on you once she's fed up. I get it, the whole protective bodyguard vibe is hot. But you're a plaything to her. Everyone in their world is disposable. Rumor has it her father killed her mother because he's always preferred younger women. Just look at who he's marrying now. She's twenty years younger than him."

The venom in Theodora's voice is ripped from her throat as she lets out a garbled gasp.

"What did you just say?"

She looks back at Sinclair and grabs her wrist, which is embedded in Theodora's scalp, pinning her in place by her hair. I catch Sinclair's eye and the look she gives me is a warning. But she doesn't need to worry. She can have her minute with Theodora before the cops take her away. I'm not going to interfere.

I take a step back, cracking my neck as Sinclair yanks Theodora's hair.

"Denver? Did she take it?"

She heard every word. She came closer the moment I had Theodora's full attention on me. She knew something was wrong. The same way I knew I didn't trust Theodora the first time I met her.

Instinct.

"She did."

Sinclair's eyes go wide as she looks back at Theodora, who's flailing about pathetically, at the mercy of Sinclair's iron grip on her.

"Where is it?" Sinclair asks her. "Where is it?!" she shouts when Theodora says nothing.

The entire backstage area has gone deathly silent. All eyes are on Sinclair as she marches Theodora over to her bag and thrusts her toward it, not loosening her grip on her hair.

"I'm not letting go until you give it back. So I hope for your sake it's in that ugly thing."

Theodora struggles some more. "You're a bitch!"

"Yeah? Takes one to know one," Sinclair replies calmly, shoving her toward her bag again. "Now give it back."

Theodora scrabbles to open her bag. She shoves her hand inside and then screeches as she flings something out of it.

The necklace hits the floor and skids across it, stopping near my feet. Sinclair gasps and lets go of Theodora as if she's about to race after it.

"Sinclair?"

Her glassy eyes lift to meet mine and the unshed tears in them gut me. But my girl's a fighter. And she's going to win this one.

"I don't think that's the way to hand someone something precious, do you?" I tip my head toward Theodora who's rubbing at the matted tuft of hair on the back of her hair.

Sinclair turns to her, hatred oozing from her. "Pick it up," she spits.

"No."

"Sinclair. Come here," I say.

She looks at me, her eyes full of fire. But she does as I say, keeping her head high as she walks over to me.

"Don't touch it," I say in a soft voice as she comes to stand beside me.

Her necklace is at our feet, and a tiny whimper shakes her shoulders as she glances at it. She's been through enough. She doesn't deserve this. And bullies like Theodora only learn their lesson when someone has the balls to stand up to them.

"Theodora," I instruct. "Pick it up."

Theodora's eyes dart around the room at the captive audience we've attracted. Even the show seems to have ground to a halt, and an announcement rings out over the speaker system apologizing for a brief 'technical issue'. It's because Sinclair should be on the runway right now.

Theodora's lip curls in disgust in understanding as she listens to it.

The whole show has stopped because they won't do it without Sinclair.

"Fine." Theodora takes a step.

"Stop."

She falters at my command and stares at me.

"On the floor."

Sinclair sucks in a small breath next to me as Theodora's eyes widen.

"You can't be—"

"Serious?" I arch a brow. "If there's one thing I definitely can be, it's serious. Would you agree, Sinclair?"

Her eyes glint as she meets my gaze. "Oh yeah, Denver's always serious. He doesn't make jokes. Ever."

"That's right. I don't. She never laughs, so it must be true."

A couple of seconds pass as we look at one another. Then there's a collective murmur as Theodora drops to her knees.

"Better," I grunt, looking at her sniveling on the ground. I don't take pleasure in humiliating her. But I know it's the only thing that will make her understand the effect of her actions. "Now... crawl."

"What?" she snaps.

"Didn't you hear him?" Sinclair says. "I did."

"So did I," another model pipes up.

"Yeah, me too," calls out another.

"The fine man said *crawl*, dear," the makeup artist who covered up Sinclair's scratches drawls.

Everyone watches as she slowly shuffles along the floor on her hands and knees. She stops in front of me and Sinclair and reaches out for the necklace.

I place my shoe over a tiny piece of the chain before she can pick it up.

"I think you're missing something."

She lifts her head, looking at me through smudged mascara.

"An apology?" I add, moving my foot back.

"I'm sorry," she spits, swallowing hard as she picks the necklace up. She puts it into Sinclair's waiting, outstretched hand.

The shaky exhale of Sinclair's held breath almost makes me miss Theodora's uttered words.

"What?" I snarl.

"I said..." She looks at Sinclair with a cruel smile. "Such a big fuss over something worthless."

I wrap a hand around Sinclair's hipbone, squeezing it gently to stop her taking Theodora out in front of all the camera phones that are now recording us.

"You wouldn't understand," Sinclair says, looking at her in pity. "I bet you've never known anyone as brilliant as my brother in your life." She gazes at her necklace like she can't believe she has it back. "*It's priceless.*"

"Maybe..." Theodora sneers. "If it were actually him in that diamond. But it's not."

"What?" Sinclair jolts. "Of course it is. Sullivan made it himself."

"The ashes used to make that diamond were of someone with African descent," Theodora says, smiling like she's enjoying the wavering that's creeping into Sinclair's voice.

"How would you know?"

"I got it tested. It's why I took it. You're always playing the victim, Sin. Rubbing that thing, getting all the pity. I thought it was a clever touch. Increase your public support while bringing more awareness to your family's business. I expected it to be fake, just a normal diamond, not one made of human ashes. But it's real. You've been carrying a dead person around your neck like a weird shrine, only it's some nobody, not Sl—"

"Don't you dare say his name!" Sinclair cries. "Don't you dare!"

"Get up!" I hiss at Theodora. "And get out of here. Your ride's waiting outside."

She takes her time getting up and pulling her clothes on, a smug smirk on her face as Sinclair turns the necklace over and over in her palm, studying it.

"Denver," she chokes.

"Don't think about it now. We'll get it checked."

But even as I say it, I'm sure that Theodora's telling the truth.

And my biggest fear is what it'll do to Sinclair when she knows it too.

32

SINCLAIR

"She's lying, right? She must be."

"We'll find out," Denver says, his jaw tightening at the despair that's inched deeper and deeper into my voice since the show ended.

I finished it, despite what just happened. There's no way I was going to let everyone down who worked so hard. But my stomach hasn't stopped churning since Theo's words.

It's not him.

I couldn't even bring myself to look at my necklace again after she said it. It's been something I've treasured for so long and now... now I don't know how I feel. I handed it straight to Denver. It's been in the inner pocket of his suit jacket ever since I asked him to take care of it for me.

Denver nods a thank you to the security guard who lets us out of the side entrance. Killian called to inform him that what just went down backstage is already trending online and the main entrance is swamped with reporters waiting for me to exit.

"I can't believe it's been Theo all this time. She acted like she was a friend."

He wraps an arm around me, guiding us out into the alleyway. My head spins as I try to make sense of it all.

"She wrecked Lenny. She... Oh my god, she put..."

"She put shit on your car?"

I shake my head. "Oh my god, you know about that?"

"I do."

"I don't get why she would do it all. We're not super close, but I thought we were friends. She's come out with me, Zoey, Mikey, and Brad so many times. How did you know it was her who took it?"

Denver's arm is like a shield around me, and I lean into his side, the scent of him helping to calm my racing heart.

"I saw photos of her meeting that model you fought with the day it went missing. She was handing it over to Theodora in exchange for cash."

"I can't believe it," I murmur, sinking further into his side as a shiver runs through me. "Do you think she..." I squeeze my eyes shut as my throat burns. "Do you think she paid those boys to try and take Monty too?"

Warm lips dust my forehead. "If she did, Princess, then we'll find out."

I sniff, trying desperately to cling on to the safety of his deep voice.

"I don't know what I'd do without you," I murmur as Denver leads us toward the top of the alley. "I mean it. Not just you being my bodyguard, but just... being you, being there for me like you are. I know we never saw what's happening between us coming, but I want you to know that I think the world of you and I—"

"Get behind me!" Denver barks.

He reaches for his gun, maneuvering me behind him at the same time.

"What's wrong?" I cry.

His gun is pointed at a figure at the head of the alleyway before they even get the chance to take a step toward us.

"I'm armed and I will shoot if you come any closer."

I look out from behind him and take in the man standing frozen to the spot, his palms up in front of his stomach as he stares at Denver's gun. Something about him is familiar, even though I've never met him before. But I've seen photos. I've looked him up online, needing answers, needing to know why she would do what she did to my father.

"Neil?" I gasp.

"Hello, Sinclair." He lowers his hands and tilts his head like he's trying to see me better around Denver's body shielding me.

The click of Denver's safety being released echoes off the high walls around us.

"Is he going to shoot me?" Neil asks me.

"If you move any closer," Denver hisses.

"I wouldn't test him," I say, craning my neck to see him better. He's the same age as my father but looks older with thinning gray hair and sallow cheeks. His eyes are dull, like he hasn't slept properly in months. He looks like he did in the photos of him and Mom that my father found hidden amongst her things after she died.

Only he was smiling in them. He looked like someone in love. And so did my mother.

Now he looks sad and lost.

I swallow the bile that's threatening to creep up my throat.

His eyes widen as he takes me in. "My god, you look so much like her. Elaina told me you were fair like her, and that your brothers were dark. And I've seen pictures, but seeing you now... I—"

"What the hell do you want?" Denver snaps, his gun trained on Neil's forehead.

"I just want to talk." Neil glances uneasily at Denver, then back at me. "Sinclair, please, I just want to talk. Your father and brother will never want to hear what I have to say, but you—"

"Was she going to leave my father for you?" I choke.

Neil's face falls. He looks like he might step closer, but I shake my head at him as Denver stiffens.

"I asked her to," he says wearily, as though admitting it is draining the life out of him. "I *begged* her to. I loved her. All of my life, I loved her. I was a coward when I left her all those years ago. I didn't want to walk away a second time."

Something about the utter devastation on his face and the way his shoulders slump have me placing my hand over Denver's rigid bicep.

"Put the gun away," I whisper.

The corners of his eyes pinch and his gaze remains pinpointed on Neil.

"I don't want to do that, Princess," he grits.

"But I'm asking you to. *Please*."

Denver's brow furrows and his nostrils flare as he glares at Neil.

"I can tear your heart out of your chest so fast that when I crush it in my fist, it'll still be beating."

Neil's face pales at Denver's deathly calm voice. He nods once, his throat bobbing as Denver places the safety back on his gun and holsters it.

"I just want to talk. Just for a minute," he says.

"So talk," Denver growls.

I step out from behind him, but he catches me with a hand to my hip and curls it around me protectively, drawing me into his side. I glance up at the murderous set of his jaw.

"I'm an asshole who'd fucking die for you. And no... not because it's my job."

My eyes rake over his profile for a second and warmth blankets over me.

"It's okay," I breathe.

"When some guy accosts you in an alley, Sinclair, it is not okay."

"I just want to talk," Neil says again.

There's no malice in his voice, no strength. He sounds like a broken man. One who's lost everything.

"She told me she would never leave you," he says.

"She still loved my father?" My heart lifts.

These past two and a half years he's had to live knowing Mom had an affair with her first love. The man who left her pregnant and heartbroken. My father was the one who picked up the pieces and dealt with the wreckage he left behind. My father was the one who held her when she cried after her miscarriage. My father was the one who built a family with her. An empire.

My father was the one she truly loved.

He's beyond happy with Halliday now. But maybe knowing Mom never meant to hurt him will be some comfort to him. Because he never got to ask her himself. He was robbed of those conversations when she died.

"No. Elaina said she would never leave *you*," Neil replies.

I suck in a sharp breath. "Me?"

"She said you were her youngest. Her only daughter. She said even though you were an adult that you still needed her, that a daughter always needs her mom. She would never leave you, even though she loved me."

My eyes burn. Neil's outline gets blurry, and Denver's grip on my hip tightens, supporting me.

"Is that what you came to tell me?" I cry. "The reason you're back in New York? Because you wanted to tell me it was my fault she wouldn't leave to be with you? You came back into her life, and you screwed with my whole family! We were fine before you came back. We were all together."

My chest heaves as sobs threaten to break free.

Denver pulls me into his side, the warmth of his solid chest meeting my cheek as I press it against him.

"Get the hell out of here before I kill you," he snarls.

"I miss her too," Neil says.

"Go!" Denver thunders, reaching for his gun.

"I was there the day they died."

I snap my head up from Denver's chest. "What?"

"I was there," Neil says. "I flew to Cape Town after her. It was my last attempt to get her to leave with me. I'm sorry, Sinclair, but I loved your mother, and I wasn't prepared to let her go without a fight. We talked at the marina, I begged her to leave with me, but she wouldn't. Then she..." He drags a hand down his face, blowing out a breath as his eyes fill with tears. "Then she... she was gone." He clamps a hand over his mouth as he lets out a strange, muffled cry.

"Did you hurt her?" Denver asks slowly, his voice low and commanding.

"No," Neil splutters. "Of course not, I loved her! But that's why I came back. I saw your father's engagement announced. He's moving on, but I... I can't. Not until I know what happened to her."

Every nerve in my body tingles as I stare at him.

"She died in the fire. No one knows how it started, except that the yacht must have had a fault. A fuel leak or something." My voice comes out shaky as images of flames and thick gray smoke rush to the front of my memory.

"No." Neil shakes his head. "I saw a man getting off the yacht. He walked away a few minutes before your brother ran onboard. Then it... Oh God," Neil chokes up.

"My brother *ran* onboard?" I reel back. "No, he was on there with Mom and—"

"I saw him run onboard before it exploded."

"Who was this man you saw?" Denver snaps.

Neil's chest deflates like an old balloon. "I couldn't tell

you. I was too far away at that point to get a good look. It was a man, that's all I know. Dressed smart. I don't even know how old he was. Nothing."

"If you think you can come back here and even suggest that Sterling—"

"No!" Neil throws his hands back up as Denver pulls his gun on him again. "No, that's not what I'm saying at all. It wasn't your father." He glances at me, then looks straight at Denver again. "Sterling ran onboard after the yacht exploded. He came from another direction. It couldn't have been him."

"Denver," I whisper, my chest turning in on itself until breathing is difficult. I just want to get out of here. I squeeze my eyes shut hoping that the memory of the smell of burning leaves me as fast as it's arrived.

"You go back to where you're staying, and you don't move until we come to you," Denver instructs Neil.

"Okay, okay... I'm—"

"I know where to find you," he growls, making Neil's face pale. "Now, get the hell out of my sight."

Neil takes a couple of steps backward, his eyes darting to me. "I'm sorry, Sinclair. I loved your mother. I would never have asked her to leave you if I didn't. But she chose you. She loved you too much to leave."

"Now! Before I shoot you!" Denver barks.

Neil spins and rushes off, and I turn into Denver's embrace, sinking my face into his chest.

"Denver," I whimper.

"It's okay, Princess," he soothes. "It'll be okay."

His lips meet my forehead, and I desperately want to believe him.

33

SINCLAIR

"He only plays like this when he's stressed," I say as we walk inside the bar area of Seasons to the melody of piano music.

Sullivan sits at the piano while Vincent leans on it, nodding in approval as Sullivan plays the closing bars of a Liszt piece with vigor. The club isn't open yet, but Denver called my father and told him about Neil showing up, so my father said everyone would meet us here.

All eyes snap up in our direction as we cross the room.

"Go," I say to Denver, knowing my father will be keen to have a debrief about Neil as soon as possible.

"You okay?"

"I'm fine," I breathe; a warm fuzziness filling my stomach at the way he's always so concerned. "Honestly, go."

He nods, his hand slipping from my lower back, and I immediately miss his touch.

I rush from his side before I find it too hard to move away from him and scoop Monty up as he runs over to me with his tail wagging wildly.

"He missed you," Halliday says, looking up from the table where she's coloring with Molly.

"I missed him too," I say between Monty's licks on my chin. Seeing him is already helping ease the tension that's weaved itself into my muscles since finding out about Theo and then seeing Neil.

"That's good, Molly."

My niece beams at me, her crayon poised over the scribble on the paper. "Monty."

"It looks just like him." My returning smile makes her grin widen as she looks down at her picture with pride.

"Is that me walking him?" I ask, pointing at the pink shape with yellow on top of it.

Molly picks up her yellow crayon and adds more hair. "Mm-hm."

"And who's that?" I gesture to the giant black blob that's twice my size standing beside me.

Molly sticks her lower lip out in concentration as she keeps adding more hair to me until it reaches my toes like Rapunzel.

"That Den-va."

The way she says his name is so cute. I turn to look for him to see if he heard, but he's deep in conversation with my father, Sullivan, Uncle Mal, Killian, and Jenson at a table on the far side of the room.

Halliday follows my gaze to them. "They look so serious," she murmurs.

"I know." I drop into the seat beside her, keeping Monty in my arms. My father's face tightens as he runs a hand over his jaw, then says something to Denver. The men listen, then Uncle Mal speaks, and Sullivan nods. My father's gaze shifts to me, his eyes softening before he says something that makes Denver glance in my direction.

The moment Denver's eyes meet mine, heat blooms in my core.

The Rule Breaker

"What do you think they're going to do?"

"I don't know," I answer Halliday. "Knowing my father, he'll want to go straight to Neil, even if all he'll do is repeat exactly what he told me and Denver."

"What about Denver? He sounded really pissed on the phone earlier."

"You heard him talking to Dad?"

Her cheeks flush. "I was in the office with your father when he called."

"Uh-huh. Helping him work, right?"

"Yeah," she replies.

I narrow my eyes, smirking when she avoids my gaze and picks up a crayon to color with Molly instead.

"You know I'm messing with you. I'm happy for you both. And I know you..." I look pointedly at her stomach where she hasn't started to show her pregnancy yet "... I mean, the baby got in there somehow, didn't it."

Halliday wrinkles her nose up with a soft laugh. "I can't talk about that with you. It's... weird."

"Baby," Molly says, pointing at Halliday's stomach.

"Yes. Baby." I stroke her gorgeous dark curls. "It's exciting, isn't it? A new life."

Halliday reaches over to fuss Monty where he's sitting on my lap, then places her hand on my forearm.

"Are you okay?" she asks as Molly slides off her chair to pick up a crayon that's rolled onto the floor.

"I'm fine. It was just weird seeing him in person. I recognized him from the photos, but he just looked... I don't know... normal?"

"You thought he wasn't going to because you'd made him out to be this monster in your head that your mom was deceiving your father with?"

"Exactly," I say, looking into her understanding gaze. "He just looked sad. I guess I always thought of him as the enemy, but seeing him today..." I blow out a breath. "What they did was wrong. But he loved her. I could tell how by the way he looked like he's been suffering. None of us have survived these past two and a half years without scars."

"Scars are marks of what we've overcome, signs of strength," Halliday says, squeezing my arm reassuringly. "Here." She reaches into her purse on the floor and takes something out. "It helps aid in times of emotional overwhelm."

She presses a crystal into my palm.

"It's beautiful," I say, studying its shiny black surface.

"It's black tourmaline. It creates a protective shield around the bearer."

"Like a bodyguard," I muse, taking in the sensation of it in my hand, and the way it's dark, inky surface matches the suit of a certain hulk who's been by my side through everything.

"How are things between you and Denver? Sterling's been concerned about throwing you both together."

I look up into Halliday's worried gaze.

"It's fine. Dad doesn't need to worry. Denver and I are getting along fine."

Halliday's expression softens and she glances at my father.

"Good. He's been worried knowing it's not what you wanted. But he does everything out of love. You're everything to him. You, Sullivan, Molly, Mal..."

"And you and the baby," I add. "He was a mess before you came along."

"I love him so much," Halliday murmurs, more to herself as she gazes at my father adoringly. "So, you and Denver? It's all okay?" She turns back to me.

"Yep. We've gotten used to each other."

Her eyes thin into slits. "You said he has no personality. I thought you couldn't stand him."

"He's grown on me." I shrug, playing down the way my heart lifts as Denver glances our way again. "And Monty likes him."

"Hmm, okay." Halliday's assessment of me ends and a smile transforms her face as my father and Denver walk over to us.

"We're going to take Molly home with us for dinner. Sullivan's going with Mal and the boys to pay Neil a visit," my father says to Halliday.

"Oh. You don't want to go with them?" she asks.

His eyes soften, and he shakes his head. "No, they've got this. And you said you were tired earlier. I want to make sure you take it easy."

"I'm fine. I'm just pregnant." But as she protests, she fails to hide the weary tinge in her voice.

My father's eyes warm as he gazes at her. "I know, Baby girl. So let's get you and Molly home."

The fact that my father is happy to leave the others to deal with Neil tonight is testament to how much Halliday has changed his life. He's looking forward to the future again, instead of being stuck in limbo with the pain of our family's past.

"Sweetheart, Denver's going to stay with you tonight," Dad tells me.

"Um—"

My father lifts a hand. "I know it's usually only during the day, but please, it'll make me feel better until they've seen Neil."

Denver's brows are lowered as he stands beside my father, all silent and serious.

"Please, Sinclair. Don't argue with me on this," my father adds.

I clamp my mouth shut and nod.

"I'll take care of her," Denver says.

I bite my lower lip.

"Thank you." My father exhales in relief, then ruffles Molly's hair. "Come on, Munchkin, go and say goodbye to daddy, then we'll go."

After they've left, Denver leans close.

"Time to go, Princess."

I turn my face, enjoying the way his warm minty breath cascades over my cheek.

"Back to my place?"

"Later. I have something to show you first."

"Denver Layne, did you get me a surprise?"

He clears his throat, his attention darting to where the remaining men are still talking, but they're too engrossed to be paying attention to us.

"Maybe," he rumbles.

"Maybe?" I squeal as his lips twitch. "You did! Thank you!"

"You don't know what it is yet," he says.

"I don't care what it is. After today, anything is going to be amazing. It's exactly the distraction I need. Thank you." I clasp my hands together in front of my face. "Can I have it now? Where is it?"

I start patting his pockets, searching.

"Sinclair," he warns, but there's warmth in his tone.

"Where are you hiding it?" I slide a hand over his crotch, grazing his dick. "Is it this? Because if it is, then I want to unwrap it now."

"No." His hand closes around my wrist. "You can't do that here," he hisses, his entire body tensing.

I peel my eyes from his dark ones to look across at the table of men.

"They're not looking."

Denver exhales, looking at me like he wants to spank me. I flutter my lashes innocently.

"If it's not this, then can I have my real surprise? Pretty please?"

His thumb traces soft circles over my inner wrist. He wets his lips with his tongue before he rasps quietly, "It's outside, Princess."

◆

"I love this one! Turn it up!"

Denver cranks the radio, and a song called "Unleash" blares from Lenny's speakers.

My grin almost splits my face in two as we hurtle down the freeway.

"I can't believe you got him back." I pat the steering wheel to the beat of the music as I drive. "Thank you!"

I turn to Denver in the front passenger seat.

"See, even Monty is excited to have my car back!"

Monty sits tall and proud on Denver's lap, staring out of the front windscreen. His tail keeps wagging, creating a constant side to side sweep over Denver's shirt.

"Eyes on the road," Denver grunts, grabbing the steering wheel and straightening us up where we're drifting lanes.

"Oh, people are so friendly when that happens. Look." I blow a kiss to the man in the car that overtakes us. He smiles at me, then his eyes move past me, and it falls from his face. He puts his foot down and speeds past us.

I look at Denver who's glowering.

"You didn't have to scare him. He looked worried you were going to kill him."

"The only person who should be worried for their life right now is me," he clips as another car blasts its horn at us.

I throw my head back and laugh. This is exactly what I needed.

"You're getting better! That was funny."

"It wasn't a joke," he grumbles.

"But I'm laughing..." I throw him a smile and his lips quirk a little, matching the gleam in his eyes.

"I guess you are," he murmurs.

I turn my attention back to the road, happiness running through me like warm rays of sun. He knew I needed this. I didn't see him make the call to the garage to ask them to bring Lenny to Seasons. But there he was, all fixed and sparkling, waiting in the street for me when we walked outside.

My fingers curl tighter around the steering wheel, savoring the feel of freedom at my fingertips.

"Where shall we go now?"

"Back."

My shoulders fall. "I don't want to go home yet."

Denver looks out of the window as if he's assessing something. "Until I've had an update on what went down with Neil, I'd feel better if we went home."

"Why? He's not going to be following us." Denver's jaw tightens, and I sigh. "Fine. Back to my gilded cage." He looks at me, and I roll my eyes. "All the extra security you've installed is fine... but..." I shrug. "It's why I love being out in Lenny so much. I don't have any of that here. I can just be me. I can drive wherever I want."

"You don't want to go back to your place?"

"Not yet," I confess.

"Okay. Follow my directions."

I sit up straighter in my seat. "Where are we going?"

"Just do as you're told, Princess."

. . .

Thirty minutes later, I'm bouncing on my toes in excitement as Denver opens the door.

"It's not that exciting," he rumbles in amusement.

"Are you kidding me? I get to see inside the Brute's lair. It's *very* exciting."

Monty follows me as I skip inside, my head on a swivel as I take it all in.

"Oh my god, it's huge! I didn't think you'd have something like this."

Denver walks in behind me and closes the door, locking it.

"I don't mean that in a bad way... Oh god, that sounded so rude, I just meant—"

"That I'm not a billionaire, so I wouldn't have a penthouse? Sinclair, it's fine, I know what you meant."

"I just meant, you're hardly ever home, you're always with my father... well, me now...so I figured you'd have something practical and... I just didn't expect this."

I take in the exposed brickwork and vaulted ceiling. "It's incredible. A trendy artist's loft kind of vibe. Are you going to bring your paintings out next and show me? If they're really ugly, I swear I'll not let it show on my face."

"No paintings," Denver says in amusement.

I continue to take in the space, my eyes ping-ponging over the sleek black kitchen and industrial-looking stools at the breakfast bar. Everything about the space is masculine and neat. There aren't any keepsakes or much of a personal nature at all. It's all so in control. Just like him.

"Oh! Who's that?" I ask, my eyes catching on the one photograph in the living area. I pick it up from the bookshelf and study it. "You're smiling!" I stare at the photo of Denver standing next to another guy who looks familiar. They both have matching smiles on their faces. Denver looks younger, but it's still him. Minus the seriousness and dark broodiness.

"Oh my god, you should do it more, you're one hell of a kisser and one hell of a smiler. Your mouth has skills."

I grin, but it falters when he looks at the photo, a brief flash of guilt crossing his face.

"Who is he?" I ask.

"Rick."

Simple. Straightforward. One word.

Just like he can be when he doesn't want to talk about something.

"Oh. He looks like a nice guy," I say.

"The best." Denver sighs.

He's moved closer and his giant warm body is inches from mine. I place the frame down where I found it carefully, then turn to face him.

"So no paintings?" I feign disappointment as I run my fingers over his shirt buttons, toying with them, when it's obvious he isn't going to say any more about who Rick is.

"No paintings," he rasps.

"Hmm." I trail my fingers up his chest and loosen his tie. "What are you going to entertain and delight your guests with then?"

His darkened eyes flick to Monty, who's already curled up on a beanbag dog bed on the floor.

I frown. "You don't have a dog."

Warm fingers hook underneath my chin and turn my face back to his. "No. But you have Monty."

The delicious deep husk of his voice sets butterflies swarming in my stomach.

"You bought a bed for Monty? When?"

"Two and a half years ago," he says, stroking my hair back from my face.

"That's when I got him," I say in confusion.

"I thought there was a possibility you'd come here with

Sterling or Sullivan one day. I wanted you to feel comfortable knowing Monty was okay."

My breath catches in my throat, mesmerized by the way his pupils blow wide as he gazes at me.

"You did that... for me?"

His eyes pinch at the corners. "I did it for me. I can't stand seeing you sad, or unsure, or worried. I didn't want you to feel that way if you were ever here."

"Because worrying is your job, right?" I breathe.

"I told you, with you, it's what I do. And it's a privilege that I've been close enough to be able to worry about you."

I flick my eyes to Monty on the dog bed and back again. Two and a half years. He's had that dog bed for two and a half years in case of the small chance I might be here one day with Monty.

"But... come on... always?" My voice falters with disbelief. "I'm sure you never used to see it that way. You... you barely spoke to me."

"I *always* spoke to you when you spoke to me first. But I was never going to push for conversations that you might not have wanted."

"But I like talking. I talk a lot."

His eyes hold mine. "I know."

Shock zaps my gut like a lightning bolt. He'd see me chatting with my family, my friends, with colleagues, but he knew I didn't want to talk to him, and he never pushed it.

He's waited all this time while I was busy trying to ignore him.

I rest my palms on his chest, feeling the beat of his heart through them.

"I don't think I'd have been ready for what talking with you would have done to me if we'd started any sooner than we did," I confess.

I wasn't ready for this. For him. I was too consumed with

getting my career started, and then after the accident... too busy grieving.

And he respected that, never pushing for anything I wasn't ready to give.

"I know." His voice is full of tenderness as he cups my face in his huge palms. "And that's okay."

I swallow as I gaze at him. "How did I see you every day for years and not *see* you?"

"Don't make me sound special, Sinclair, I'm just a man."

"You're not, though," I breathe, something shifting in my chest and embedding itself inside my heart as I slide my hands up so I can stroke his jaw. "You're not just anything... *You're Denver.*"

We stare at one another, energy flowing around us in big, billowing waves. It's like magic, just like Halliday is always talking about. It's as though the universe was scheming and planning all this time, intent on bringing us to this exact moment.

"You're Denver," I repeat, rising on my toes to brush his lips with mine with an increased tenderness. "You're exactly who I want to talk to. Every day. Always."

"Yeah?" he murmurs, his voice lifting. He dusts his lips over mine, making me want nothing more than to lose myself in one of his earth-shattering kisses.

"Yeah." I drag the tip of my tongue across his lower lip slowly.

"Sinclair, Princess, I want to take you to bed," he rasps, his fingers tensing against my cheeks.

"And you seem mad about that, why?"

"I'm not mad, I'm..." He exhales heavily, the sound making me press closer to him to offer comfort.

"Because we're back in the city?" I say, pressing a gentle kiss to his lower lip. "Because doing something here will make it real?" I kiss him softly again. "Because it's not just something that happened in the forest anymore, something we can close off?" Another kiss makes him suck in a sharp breath as I leave my lips touching his and whisper, "It's not just a momentary lapse of—"

His mouth crashes into mine, devouring me in a deep and searing kiss that goes on and on until I'm panting.

"It wasn't a momentary lapse of anything," he growls, kissing me again. "Don't ever imply that. I told you I missed you. I've been going crazy since we got back not being alone with you. Not being able to find out how you really feel."

"You thought I'd change my mind?" I gasp between desperate kisses.

"I didn't know."

"Denver." I hold his face close as I kiss him back with everything I have, trying to convey a million thoughts and feelings about the way I feel about him without using words. I kiss him until we have to break apart for air.

"I know what I want," I say as I yank his tie loose and pull it over his head. "I want you. That hasn't changed. It won't ever change."

I push his jacket from his shoulders with urgency and kiss him again, rushing to undo his shirt.

"Did you really think I wouldn't want you again once we got back to the city? That I wouldn't want this?" I kiss him harder, pressing my whole body against him, practically climbing him like a tree as lust and need overtake me.

"I was going crazy," he groans, hoisting me up into his arms so my legs wrap around his waist. He turns and slams me against the wall, devouring me from the inside out as his tongue dances against mine.

My dress is hoisted around my waist, and I tighten my thighs around his thick torso. His gun digs into the underneath of my thigh.

"Your weapon is pushing into me." I smile into another heated kiss.

"Fuck yeah, it will be in a minute."

I giggle, having to physically pull his mouth from mine so I can speak. My eyes meet his, and I giggle harder as I realize he just gave me another Denver joke.

"Not the monster." I arch a brow, biting my lip.

He readjusts his grip on me, lifting my leg higher.

"Fuck, Princess. You. Naked. Beneath me. Now," he groans like he's about to lose control any second.

He strides down the hallway, carrying me like I weigh nothing. I run my fingers through the hair at the back of his head as my lips find new angles to kiss his throat, drawing a gravelly moan from him.

"I want to know how much you missed me," I say, running my tongue over his Adam's apple, then kissing it as it flexes beneath my lips. "I want you to show me exactly how crazy it's made you not being able to touch me in the way you want to. I want you to do whatever you want to me."

"Don't give me free rein like that, Princess," he groans like he's being tortured in the best possible way.

"Why not? I trust you."

His mouth finds mine again as we enter a room that has his scent all over it. But I can't look around because he's already placing me onto a huge bed and pressing down over me.

"You want me?" he rasps, his eyes almost black as he looks at me with desire.

I push his unfastened shirt from his shoulders, allowing my hands to roam over the hot smooth skin that's unveiled.

"I want you so much I can barely think straight," I pant, wriggling in the small gap between his arms. "Please, Denver. I need you inside me."

I arch up into his kiss as he groans into my mouth,

taking my breath like it belongs to him. But his mouth leaves mine too fast, and I huff in frustration as he moves away.

"There's something I need to do first," he says, shoving his hands up my dress and tugging my panties off roughly.

He balls them up inside his fist and presses them to his nose.

"Fuck, Sinclair," he groans as he inhales. "How the hell have I functioned without having you?"

"I don't know," I breathe, parting my legs. "Probably the same way I've struggled without you."

I swear his lips curl into a smile at my words as he drops my panties onto the bed and pushes my dress higher, exposing me to him.

"You're soaking, Princess." He *tsks*, taking me in.

I use two fingers to spread myself wider, loving the husky curse that slips from his lips.

"Am I?" I pout.

He glances at me, his eyes darkening as he places his fingers on either side of mine, opening me wider. I gasp as he bends his head and spits on my clit.

"Soaking... and mine," he declares.

The first sweep of his tongue has me arching off the bed with a cry.

"God! You're so... oh my god... you're so good at that," I mewl, sinking both hands into his hair as he eats me out like a starved man.

His eyes don't break contact with mine as he brings me to a fast, loud orgasm.

"Denver," I moan, as he slides two fingers inside me and fucks me with them, his tongue still lavishing attention on my clit.

"I can feel you squeezing me. So eager for my cock to fill you, aren't you, Princess?"

"Mm-hm," I mewl in agreement, writhing against the sheets as pressure starts building inside me again.

"The only cock you've ever had, and you're addicted to it. Listen to how wet you are for it."

He pumps his fingers, and the accompanying sounds are obscene.

"Denver," I plead.

"Not yet," he says, circling my clit with his tongue again and making my eyes roll. "I want you coming on my fingers first. We need to loosen you up, because if I put myself inside you now, you'll make me come with this perfect, tight cunt."

I scrape my fingers over his scalp, mewling at his crude words. He grunts in approval as they do what they always do... make me even wetter for him.

"Denver," I beg again.

"Come for me again," he coaxes, pushing down on my lower belly.

His fingers curl inside me, hitting a delicious spot that has me feeling like I'm about to lose control. My inner thighs shake, and I look down at him in confusion at the new sensation that's taking over my body.

"You're okay. Let it go," he encourages.

He curls his fingers again, his tongue flattening and pressing harder against me.

"Denver," I whine.

"Do it."

I suck in a breath, all control leaving me as I come hard. A gush of fluid spurts from inside me and spills over his face.

"Jesus Christ, yes," he groans, his eyes closing in ecstasy as he drinks it up, first lapping his tongue in sensual strokes over me, then pressing kiss after kiss over my drenched skin.

"Was that? Did I...?"

He flips me easily so my stomach is on the bed, resting over the soaked sheets.

"That was fucking delicious. You're such a good girl, letting go like that."

My ears ring from the force of the orgasm that's still vibrating its way through my body. The sound of Denver's gun and belt being removed and his zipper being lowered seem far away.

"Did I squirt?"

He chuckles— a rare sound from him. Yet me soaking his face is what's earned me the pleasure of hearing the sound. And I love the way it sends a warm vibration over my skin.

"You sure did, Princess. Now we know you can, we can have you gushing for me all the time."

"Oh my god." I bury my burning cheeks into the mattress.

"Don't you dare get shy," Denver rumbles, pulling me up onto my knees in front of him and running his palms over my ass cheeks. "I love everything you do."

I bite down my smile. That was one hell of an orgasm, and he's right, I shouldn't be shy about the way my body reacts to intense pleasure. Judging from the way his hands are roaming over my ass, squeezing handfuls of it as he murmurs in admiration, I know he's being honest when he says he loves it.

I wriggle inside his grip.

"Please, fuck me now. I want you inside me."

I don't care if I sound needy. I just need to feel him there.

He answers me by surging forward and thrusting into me.

"Fuck," he growls, his hands curling around my hips and holding himself deep. "You're so wet, see how you've taken all of me straight away? Such a good girl."

I hum at his praise, contentment filling my chest now that he's inside me again. I lift my ass higher, my head falling to the mattress as I savor the fullness having him so deep gives me. His balls dust my clit as he grinds into me slowly. I arch my back, pushing back.

"Look at you," he croons. "So eager for me, thighs spread

wide, full of my cock and aching to be fucked." His giant hands encase my ass and tease my cheeks a little further apart, exposing my asshole.

It must look filthy from Denver's angle.

I mewl shamelessly again, completely at his mercy but loving every second. He makes me feel desired and safe. *So comfortable to be his dirty girl.*

"So beautiful. How the hell am I supposed to last with you?"

I clench around him, and he lands a light spank on my ass.

"I don't want to come yet, Princess, so keep this perfect cunt still for me, okay?"

I sigh happily as he continues his perusal of me, his hands roaming over my ass. He keeps his cock nestled deep inside me as he runs a thumb down the seam of it.

Then he slips the tip inside me.

"Denver!" I gasp, pushing back instead of pulling away like I'd expect myself to if I'd known someone was going to finger my ass.

He holds me in place with a firm grip on my hip as he works his thumb in and out of me slowly.

"So beautiful," he murmurs. "Do you want to take my cock here one day?"

I clench around his dick involuntarily, and the sharp inhale of breath joins the awe in his voice. "Fuck, Princess. You do? Okay, we'll work up to it."

"Um," I squeak, not sure what my body has just agreed to on my behalf. But I'm intrigued by the idea. The idea of submitting to Denver like that is... hot.

But his dick is *huge*.

I'm not sure I'll ever manage to do it, no matter how much we work up to it.

"My perfect princess," he rasps, leaving his thumb inside me.

The Rule Breaker

Then he starts to move.

Giant moans of pleasure leave me as he fucks me, but I don't stop. The whole neighborhood can hear for all I care.

His pace is deliberate. Deep, strong strokes, designed to push me over the edge before he loses control. Each pump of his hips sends waves of pleasure hurtling through me like a warm light.

"Denver," I choke. "You're so deep."

"Does it feel good?"

"Amazing," I purr. "Does it feel good for you?"

"Incredible," he groans in agreement, increasing his pace.

The bed shifts, and a deep thud vibrates the wall as he plants one hand on the headboard, his fingers curling around it to grip it hard and use it as leverage.

His thumb slides away from my ass, eliciting a breathy squeal from me as he places one foot, then the other, on the mattress. The heat of his body is like an inferno against my back as he squats over me.

His fingertips bruise my hip, and he pins me in place beneath him.

"Fuck, Sinclair. Fuck…" he groans as if all sense has left him, leaving only pure carnal pleasure.

I cry out, loving how full it feels having him so impossibly deep.

My ass is pulled higher, and I'm folded so obscenely beneath him, completely at his mercy, on display for him like an offering. It's such a degrading position. I'm like an animal being fucked raw by her mate, surrounded by sounds of slapping skin.

I love it.

"Denver!" I gasp, knowing I'm going to come again soon.

"You're strangling me, Princess." He thrusts harder, his cock solid as steel. "You want to come together?"

"Yes," I moan, tiny spasms already starting around his dick as he plows into me.

"Good girl," he rasps.

The headboard bangs against the wall in time with his thrusts.

My vision blurs and my breathing stalls as I twist my face and try to focus on his hand against the headboard.

His balls slap against my clit.

Then I fall over the edge into bliss.

"I'm coming!"

"Fuck, Princess. Me too."

He growls, his knuckles turning white as he almost rips the headboard off, pushing even deeper into me and pitching my orgasm to a whole new height.

"Oh my god!" I cry as wave upon wave make me clench around him over and over.

He pumps into me from behind, deep guttural grunts leaving him each time he drives his hips forward.

"Fuck, Sinclair," he groans, coming hard.

I whimper as my body flutters around his, taking everything he's giving to me.

"Denver!" I squeal.

My eyes spring with tears, my orgasm wringing me out and leaving me reeling for something to grab on to to ground me.

With one final thrust, Denver stills inside me and his hand leaves my hip, gliding up over my head and stroking my hair tenderly. He was right when he said he makes me come so hard I cry. I'm not upset... just overwhelmed by the emotions running through me. It's the way he can make me forget everything until all I focus on is this exact moment we're in together.

And for a few blissful seconds, there's nothing else.

It's the purest kind of freedom.

The Rule Breaker

"You're okay," he soothes. "You're okay."

He's still catching his breath as he pulls out of me and then eases me up and into his arms, cradling me to him like I'm the most precious thing in the world. He wipes up my tears with his thumbs, then his lips, catching the final ones tracking down my cheeks.

I look into his eyes, diving into the gold flecked green as he runs the backs of his fingers down my cheek. He rests his forehead against mine, his soft words leaving him so gently as he holds me close.

"Me too," he whispers, without me saying a word. "Me too, Sinclair, me too."

34

DENVER

"Do you like it?" Sinclair beams as she walks out of my hotel room bathroom wearing only a shirt.

I run my lower lip between my teeth as I allow myself a leisurely roam up her toned legs until I meet the hemline, which is a couple of inches lower than where her panties would be... if they weren't sitting on top of my bedside cabinet.

I lean back against the pillows on the bed, toying with her as I pretend to take my time to consider her question.

"Don't tell me you're still pissed about those guys at the restaurant?" she says, sauntering toward the bed. Her eyes are lit up, waiting for my reaction as she slowly unbuttons the shirt.

"Those guys are lucky to still be breathing," I answer, pushing away the flare of jealousy thinking about the guys who were sending drinks over to her and the girls last night, trying their luck. A few choice words from me when they went to the men's washroom, and they soon called it a night and fucked off.

"They were harmless," Sinclair says, undoing more buttons and arching a brow at me in invitation.

I make myself comfortable as she undoes the last button, then crawls up the bed to straddle me.

It's been five days since we saw Neil. Five days of the whole team working around the clock. Not only keeping tabs on him, but also trying our best to check out if what he says is true.

If there really was a man near the yacht that day.

Whether what Neil says is true or not, we haven't found anything yet. I'm not sure we ever will.

And that's something that's been weighing heavily on everyone. So when Sinclair announced that her, Zoey, and Halliday's friend, Sophie, from London, thought we should bring forward Halliday's bachelorette celebrations to have something positive to focus on, Sterling agreed. I think he was secretly relieved to have the girls in London for a few days, away from it all. It didn't stop him from flying the private jet over from New York last night, though, under the pretense it was to pick the girls up and take them home today—when we all know it's because he missed Halliday so much that he couldn't bear to be apart from her for more than two days without losing his mind.

I can understand that kind of madness all too well.

"I do like it," I say, running my thumbs down the edges of the open shirt, admiring Sinclair in it. My blood heats at the way she shivers as my thumbs dust down the valley between her breasts. "You didn't need to buy me a new shirt, though."

"I owe you one," she says, pouting. "Besides, I like shopping. I got as much out of it as you did."

I run my tongue over my lower lip, unable to take my eyes from her body. "Okay, Princess."

"Of course." She sighs. "If you don't like it..."

She shrugs her shoulders, letting the fabric cascade off her body. Her magnificent tits are presented to me at the perfect height to suck one of her rosy nipples into my mouth.

"Denver," she moans, teasing my hair between gentle fingers.

I'm about to switch to the other side when the hotel phone rings.

Sinclair reaches for it, but I cut her off, giving her a warning look that she bats her eyelashes innocently at, her lips twisting into a coy smile.

My hand closes around the receiver as she slides down my body and pulls my dick free from beneath the covers.

"Hello?"

"Denver?" Sterling's voice hits me at the exact same moment his daughter wraps her lips around the crown of my cock and sucks with a breathy moan.

"Sterling," I say, frowning at Sinclair as she smiles around my dick and takes more of it into her mouth.

The recent worry in his voice has lessened. Theodora was charged and also admitted to paying those two boys to try and take Monty. She said it was to shake Sinclair up, and they wouldn't have harmed him. And we've got Neil under constant surveillance, so Sterling has loosened the reins a little. I'm still assigned as her full-time bodyguard. But he's not insisted I spend the night with her again.

We have just worked out that arrangement all by ourselves.

"Have you seen Sinclair? I went by her room and she wasn't there."

The familiar guilt every time I hear him say her name coils around my windpipe, constricting it until it's hard to breathe.

"We did an early workout together," I say, clenching my jaw as she speeds up sucking on my dick and adds a soft, massaging hand to my balls at the same time. "We just finished. She's actually here now. Do you want to speak to her?"

Sinclair's eyes shine with mischief as she sucks harder, taking me right to the back of her throat and then pulling back and letting a string of saliva connect my cock to her lips before she swallows me back down again.

She knows the sight is a surefire way to make me almost come.

"No, it's fine. We'll see you downstairs for breakfast. Halliday wanted everyone together before Sophie gets picked up."

"Okay, I'll tell her," I force out, sweat breaking along my hairline as I fight down the tightening in my balls as they prime themselves, raring to unload.

I swallow down a groan at Sinclair's determined sucking when Sterling adds, "Thank you, Denver. I know this hasn't been easy for you. Sinclair's got a mouth on her when it comes to voicing her opinion on having you as her bodyguard. But you've done a great job, and I'm grateful for how you've taken care of her."

Sinclair smiles at me wickedly, hearing every word.

She sure does have a mouth on her. But I can't recall the last time I heard it complain about me. It's too busy crying out my name or swallowing my dick that's inside her at every opportunity.

I clear my throat instead of answering. I can't bring myself to thank him or accept his compliment. Not when I'm about to come down his daughter's throat. So much for taking care of her.

"See you downstairs," Sterling says.

Then he's gone.

I toss the phone back on the cradle and it clatters loudly.

"Sinclair!" I bark, my chastising tone going unnoticed by her as she hums around my cock happily, feasting on it like she's having the time of her life.

"Shut up and enjoy it, Denver." She giggles and tugs on my balls, making me curse.

I drop my head back to the pillow, eyes holding hers as I decide to give her what she wants. I let out a grunt and slide both hands into her hair, holding her in place as I thrust my hips.

Her eyes widen as I fill her throat with my cock.

"You wanted it, Princess," I rasp, loving the flare of defiance that lights up her eyes before she makes a gagging sound. "Well, here you are." I fuck her throat for a few pumps before I ease off on my grip.

She glares at me, and I smirk as she doubles down her efforts, taking it out on my dick. It's not long before every muscle in my body is tensing and I'm groaning her name.

"Sinclair... fuck."

Victory gleams in her eyes as she turns me into a wreck for her, losing all semblance of control.

I come in deep spurts, filling the inside of her silky mouth. Her tongue laps them up, sliding over the sensitive head of my cock as more spills inside her.

"That's my girl," I groan as she swallows a mouthful of my cum with a satisfied moan that has my balls drawing up tight and unloading another fresh load across her tongue. "My perfect girl, aren't you?"

I cup her cheek, feeling the head of my dick pushing against it as she continues sucking on me with enthusiasm, teasing my slit with the tip of her tongue and drawing out my sensitivity almost to the point of pain.

Her eyes flash as I hiss.

"Such a fucking princess," I scold as she finally releases me.

She licks her lips and climbs over me.

"Your princess," she muses, leaning down to kiss me.

"Mine," I rumble, sinking a hand into her hair, holding her to me so I can kiss her deeply, taking my time to slide my tongue over hers, exploring all the places my cum just touched.

She's smiling at me when I finally let her go with a sound that's full of regret.

"I hate lying to your father," I say.

Her smile falters, and she runs a finger down my nose and over my lips slowly. "I know you do. The truth is, so do I. I don't like lying to anyone. Especially my family. Lies can ruin everything."

We stare at each other, neither of us knowing what to say. She's still dealing with the fact her mother lied for months before her death, keeping her affair with Neil a secret. They were always close. I know it hurt her that her mother lied to her. To all of them.

Now she's gone, and Sinclair's still coming to terms with it.

We have to tell Sterling, We should have told him weeks ago. And Sullivan. And Mal. They all deserve to know.

But I don't know how to tell the man who has done so much for me that I've betrayed him in one of the worst possible ways. He trusted me.

And I've fallen in love... with his daughter.

I lift her hand and kiss her wrist. I haven't told her how I feel yet. Something's stopped me from saying the words, but I'm sure they must be written in my eyes every time I look at her. Because they feel so damn obvious to me. I don't know how no one else has noticed it.

She looks into my eyes and a soft smile lifts her lips. "We'll tell him when we get back to New York. This is Halliday's weekend. I don't want to do anything that might cause tension on it."

I close my eyes, kissing her wrist again and breathing in the scent of the skin. She's right. This is Halliday's weekend.

And once we tell Sterling... anything could happen.

The Rule Breaker

"I don't think he's lying." Sterling keeps his voice low as we sit together at the front of the jet. Sinclair, Halliday, and Zoey are sitting at the back, laughing over something as they all chat. Sterling's attention travels to them and he smiles.

"Neither do I," I agree.

"But if he is... If he's back for any other reason, trying to get close to them..." Sterling's smile morphs into a murderous scowl as he turns back to me.

I understand the tension radiating through him. It matches mine. Because the thought has crossed my mind. Knowing Neil got that close to Sinclair unnerves me. Part of me wonders if I should have just shot him and had it done with. I could have lived with killing an unarmed man if it meant knowing she will be safe.

"Jenson has one of the other guys with him. They have him under twenty-four-hour surveillance."

"I know." Sterling nods, running a hand over his silver-flecked jaw. "And Sullivan was adamant that he believed his story about..." He curses, the same grief clouding his eyes whenever he talks about that day. "Sullivan thinks he did see someone walking away from the yacht. And I'm inclined to believe it too. My son can tell when someone's lying. Just like I can."

His piercing blue eyes meet mine and I hold back from swallowing around the lump in my throat as he holds my gaze for a beat.

"But I wasn't there." He breaks my eye contact with a sigh. "So I need to trust my son on this."

I nod and look down at my hands, clasped between my spread thighs. My skin prickles with unease. I hope he can maintain some of the level of trust he's had in me over the years once Sinclair and I tell him what's been going on. He's going to notice soon if we don't tell him. That's if he doesn't suspect something already. I'm with her all the time, and it's getting increasingly hard not to slip up and call her Princess or touch her in a way I would never touch a client in front of people.

"It'll be good having you back."

I blink, tension furrowing my brow as I snap my head up.

The relaxed slope of his shoulders as he leans back in his seat and gazes out of the jets window tell me I heard him correctly.

"You don't want me assigned to Sinclair anymore?"

Just her name has my mouth turning dry at the thought of no longer having a reason to use it every day.

At being separated from her.

"You can still accompany her to big events." Sterling tips his head, thinking. "Or Jenson can. She's fond of him."

I can't prevent the crack that comes from my knuckles as I clench my hands into fists.

"But we know it was that other model who was responsible for the notes and what happened to her car. And that's being dealt with by your friends on the force," Sterling continues. "And now that Neil is being watched... well..." He exhales with a chuckle. "... my daughter will be happy to have her overprotective father back off a little."

I can't speak. I can't do anything except give him a curt nod as he studies me for a reaction.

"Good. That's settled, then. You're back with me as soon as we land in New York."

The girls' laughter explodes from the rear of the plane, and a content smile spreads over his face as Halliday shrieks in response to whatever's just been said. Sinclair's accompanying cackle rings out and Sterling shakes his head with a chuckle.

"It's been a long time since I heard her so happy. I appreciate you keeping her safe, Denver."

"Of course," I answer automatically.

Sinclair's laugh pitches again, and Sterling's eyes catch mine, crinkling at the corners as he listens to the sound of her infectious joy.

"She's safe and she's happy."

"She is," I agree, sucking in a breath through my nose as I keep my exterior cool and in control.

But the inside of me is thrashing around like a punctured dingy in a storm.

I press my lips together in a terse line, holding my reaction in at Sterling's next words as he stands and claps me on the shoulder.

"Sinclair will be fine, Denver. She doesn't need you anymore."

35

SINCLAIR

"What do you think it'll be like not having the huge hunk following you around every day?"

My face falls and Zoey pulls herself into a sitting position from where she's been lounging on my bed with Monty as I unpack from the trip.

"Sin, I'm sorry. I didn't mean that to sound so—"

"Honestly, it's fine." I wave away her concern.

It's only been a day.

Of course *I'm fine* without him.

Although, it's a relief that I've been able to talk to Zoey about Denver. I told her everything as soon as I saw her after we got back from the forest. She'd laughed when I stared at her in shock over the fact she wasn't even a little bit surprised that I'd spent my trip to the wilderness getting fucked to within an inch of my life by Denver.

But she's my best friend, and I saw the potential she and Ashton had before she did, so perhaps we were the same for her.

"I mean... I had loads of space in bed last night without him... so there's positives, right?"

Zoey arches a brow.

"Yeah," I mutter, not fooling anyone. "... I totally miss the giant Brute."

We landed yesterday, and I haven't seen Denver since. He managed one phone call to me last night and a text this morning. But my father has him busy working on something, and he's not been alone at all from what I can tell.

Monty rolls onto his back, looking up at Zoey pathetically until she rubs his belly.

"Aww, Monty, what's wrong?" she asks in a baby voice.

"He didn't finish his breakfast this morning," I say, looking at Monty's big brown sad eyes.

He's not been himself since I got back to the city. He ran to greet me the second Sullivan and Molly dropped him off yesterday, then he ran through my place from room to room.

Searching for Denver.

But of course, he wasn't here. He will hardly ever be here now. Not if things go back to the way they were before when he was my father's right-hand man. I saw him once a week then, at most. He was always busy doing something. Sometimes he'd work with Sullivan, and he'd even go to Botswana with Uncle Mal from time to time to check on the mines and business there.

Those trips sometimes span across weeks.

I exhale, my shoulders slumping as I take my lingerie bag out of my suitcase. Most of it doesn't even need laundering. I was naked whenever we went back to the hotel, the girls to their rooms... me to Denver's. I'd grown so used to spending every night together, almost like being back in the forest again. Sleeping inside his big, strong arms, waking up to him. Looking into his deep green eyes as he pushed inside me slowly each morning, increasing his pace as his hands tangled in my hair and he kissed me awake with a passion that made my throat burn.

I was falling.

Deeper and deeper every day.

And now it's all stopped.

Just like that.

"You guys will get more time together once you tell your father though, right? He'll understand Denver needs more time off so you can spend it together now he isn't your bodyguard anymore."

I shrug, not wanting to get my hopes up. "I don't know. We've got to tell him first. He and Denver have always gotten on so well, I don't know how he's going to take knowing that we've been keeping this from him."

"You'll talk him around. He never stays mad at you," Zoey chirps, trying her best to cheer me up.

I pull some clothes from my suitcase and lay them on the bed, ready to hang back up. She's right. My father doesn't stay mad at me. I wrote off his Bentley when I first got my license, and after he made sure I was okay he was only mad at me for a day, tops. Then there was the time I threw a secret party at his and Mom's old place when they were out of town, and someone spilled bleach all the new marble floor. He was mad for two days then, but I'm sure he only stretched it out because Mom was so disappointed.

Since we lost her and my brother, I don't think he's spent one minute being mad at me for anything. He's just been a little overprotective. Assigning me my own personal bodyguard who I'm now missing so much that it's like my chest has a hole in it.

"I thought Denver would have insisted we told him the second we got back from his cabin," I say, abandoning my unpacking and flopping down onto my bed.

Zoey frowns. "You say that like it's a bad thing?"

I reach out and fuss Monty, rubbing his ear as Zoey continues stroking his belly.

"It's not... I just..." I let out a frustrated groan.

"You wanted him to take the initiative to tell your dad? And now because he hasn't insisted at the first opportunity, you're questioning whether he's as all in as you think?"

I look into Zoey's understanding gaze.

"How do you do that?" I huff.

"It's what I would be asking myself in the same situation. But that's because you can't see it when you're the one whose emotions are involved. Because from the outside, there's no question that man is smitten with you. He scared those guys in London so bad they practically ran out of the place."

I purse my lips. "He did that to people before anything happened between us."

"Before anything happened from your side, you mean?" Zoey gives me a pointed look. I know what she's hinting at, that Denver has always gone that extra mile for me. He's always been more protective over me than Sullivan, or my father, or any other person that's connected to our family whose security is entrusted to him and his team.

He's never treated me like just a client.

"You're Sinclair." The memory of his words makes a shiver run up my spine.

"Go and tell your father."

"What?"

"Go and tell him," Zoey repeats, looking at me like she's about to shoo me off the bed and push me out of the door to do it.

"I can't. Not without Denver. He wants to be the one to tell him."

"So ask him to meet you there. Or get in Lenny and go pick him up and go together. Just do it. It'll be like ripping off a Band-Aid. The sooner and quicker the better. Unless you want to keep wondering when the next chance you'll get to be together will be."

I stare at Zoey as my mind starts whirring at lightning speed.

I totally should. We need to tell my father. And if Denver's not going to initiate it, then I will. Okay, so my father and Sullivan might take a while to get used to the idea. And if they try and take it out on Denver, then I'll claim it was me who started it. I mean, it was technically. I'm the one who coerced him into training me the way he did. I'm the one who didn't use my safe word.

I'm the one who asked him to fuck me on that gym mat.

And I'm the one who has been getting drunk on every look, touch, and kiss he's given me since.

This is on me. And it's on me to make us come clean.

I grab my phone and dial him as Zoey looks at me encouragingly.

I frown, staring at the screen as it's diverted to voicemail. "No way! He screened me."

"He's probably in the middle of something important, or driving," Zoey suggests.

I chew on my lower lip, a flare of indignation sparking in my gut. He's never not answered my calls straight away. My phone chimes with an incoming message before I have a chance to overthink it any further.

> Denver: Sorry, Princess. Something's come up I need to deal with. I'll call you as soon as I can.

"See?" Zoey says, reading the message. "He's working, that's all."

"Yeah, you're right," I agree, rolling my eyes at myself for almost getting pissed over nothing.

"He'll probably call you before you even finish unpacking, I bet," Zoey says.

"Yeah, you're right." I jump back to my feet and resume

emptying my suitcase. I want to have it done by the time he calls. Then we can go and see my father the way we should have done already.

Together.

36

SINCLAIR

Monty's tail is wagging as we stand outside Denver's front door. I take a deep breath, trying to push down the annoyance that's fizzing inside my stomach like a shaken bottle of soda.

I'm overreacting. Acting spoiled.

So he didn't call me back last night? So what?

But then I think about the way I called Sullivan after not hearing back from Denver, and he informed me Denver had left work hours before.

I'm pissed. And… worried. But mostly pissed.

I huff in frustration. His text couldn't have been vaguer. That's why I'm standing here at seven a.m. after barely any sleep because I was thinking about him all night.

I've brought our two travel mugs, his filled with vanilla coffee, exactly the way he likes it. Maybe something's wrong and he'll be grateful for it as he lets me inside and I can help him with whatever it is he has going on.

"You ready to bust some balls, Baby?" I ask Monty.

He looks up at me.

"Yeah, some sidekick you are. You're going to lick Denver all over the minute you see him, aren't you?"

His tail wags faster the second he hears Denver's name.

I smile at him and bang on the door.

Nothing happens for ages.

Then the door finally opens.

"Hello."

I stare at the woman who's answered, then glance up and down the hallway, and back at the door, checking the number. But I'm definitely at the correct door.

"Um... Hi," I reply, bringing my attention back to her.

But it's not her face that catches my attention. It's her long, bare legs, and the shirt she's wearing.

The one I bought for Denver in London.

"Are you here to see Denver?" she asks.

She's not wearing any makeup, and her hair is tousled like she's just gotten out of bed. Her cheeks have a glow to them.

She's beautiful.

And familiar.

"Uh... you're Dixie's mom, right?" I ask, still taking her in. She looks exactly like she does in all of the photographs at Denver's cabin. Only better. And less dressed.

"Yeah, I am. I'm Lizzie." She smiles at me, and I force myself to return it out of politeness, when in reality I just barfed a little in my mouth.

"Mommy?"

My eyes move to the little girl who's appeared beside her. Lizzie wraps an arm around her as the little girl looks up at me with big green eyes. *Dixie.*

"I'll go and fetch Denver and tell him you're here...?"

"Sinclair," I offer as Lizzie looks at me.

There's no recognition in her expression. Zero. She has no idea who I am because Denver's obviously never mentioned me.

The realization twists at my stomach, sharp and unexpected.

My grip tightens on the coffee mugs as Lizzie leans back, keeping her hand curled around the door as she calls out Denver's name into the apartment.

"We're here to visit my daddy," Dixie says, smiling at Monty as his butt wiggles at the prospect of more attention. He loves Molly and kids in general.

I loosen my grip a little on Denver's mug, the same hand I'm holding his leash in, so he can move closer to her.

"He's really friendly. You can pet him if that's okay with your mommy," I offer, my attention fixed on her, looking for more similarities to go with the green eyes.

Lizzie nods, and Dixie bends, giggling in delight as Monty licks and fusses around her.

I'm still staring at them both when Lizzie calls for Denver again.

"I'll go and get him," she says when he doesn't appear.

I lift my eyes upward, but I only get as far as her bare thighs in Denver's shirt before Dixie is ushered back inside and the door is closed in my face.

"Oh my god!" I scoff.

She really has no idea who I am. She's probably thinking I'm some weird woman with a crush, or a jilted one-night stand who's turned up uninvited. She's not even comfortable enough leaving the door open as she goes to get him.

I stand like an idiot with Monty, hovering on the doorstep.

A few seconds pass before the door flies open.

"Sinclair?"

Denver's naked except for a towel wrapped low on his hips, one that's doing nothing to hide the outline of his dick. His hair is wet and there are beads of water running down his chest.

The same delicious masculine herbal scent that surrounded him when he showered in my apartment that first time hits my nose as his stormy eyes capture mine.

"I told you I'd call you. What are you doing here?"

His brusque tone is like a slap to the face.

"I'm sorry, I..." He glances back into the apartment, his voice lowering to a soft whisper. "What are you doing here, Princess?"

"I brought you coffee," I say lamely. I regain my composure, jerking it toward him, and snapping, "What's going on?"

Our hands collide and the mug gets knocked to one side. It falls to the floor and the lid shoots off, spraying the dark liquid all over the floor.

I step back, tugging on Monty's leash so he doesn't step in it as it forms a puddle.

"Sinclair."

I look up into Denver's eyes. There are small creases at the corners. The same ones he gets when he's tired because we've been up all night together... fucking.

He reaches for me, but I take a step back, my eyes dropping over his freshly showered torso. "I didn't realize you had company."

"Lizzie and Dixie are..." He glances back into the apartment again, turmoil swimming in his eyes as he looks back at me. "I didn't know they were coming until they showed up last night. I was going to call you, but... they hadn't planned on staying over."

"I figured as much, judging by the fact she's wearing your shirt."

Denver's brows lower. "It's not like that. Nothing happened. I told her to grab something of mine. I didn't know she picked up that one until just now."

"I believe you," I say, rather unconvincingly. "But I get it... she's turned up to see you, and she's Dixie's mom, who is adorable, by the way." I sniff, flicking my eyes away from his as I fight to hold myself together. "You guys must have a lot to talk about. And once you're done, you and I should talk too."

I meet his eyes, faking a composure that is rapidly crumbling.

"Sinclair," he rasps. "Don't... it's not like that. She's not..." He drops a hand to hold the waistband of his towel together as he steps closer to me. "I'm in..." He searches my eyes with a determined intensity, but exhales without finishing what he was going to say.

His minty breath hits my lips, and I ache to lean forward and be kissed by him. And for him to not have the woman he loved and lost half naked in his apartment right now, wearing the shirt I bought for him.

"It's fine." I swallow hard, flicking my hair over my shoulder for something to do that will stop me from touching him. "I only came to see if you were okay. I can see that you are, so we'll talk later, okay?"

"Sin—"

"It's fine, Denver," I lie, meeting his gaze with a final cold flick of my own.

I walk away before he can say another word.

37

DENVER

"Fuck!"

I leave the front door wide open as I race into my bedroom, toss my towel on the floor, and grab a pair of sweatpants and sneakers, tugging them on in a crazed panic.

"I'll be back," I shout to Lizzie as I tear through the living area where they are.

"Everything okay?" she calls after me as I run down the hallway.

"I hope so," I call out as I burst into the external corridor and sprint toward the elevator.

I punch the button. "Come on, come on." I slam a fist against the panel. "Fuck!"

I turn and shove through the door to the stairwell instead, taking them three at a time as I grip the handrail and fucking fly down to street level like my life depends on it.

She depends on it.

I can't allow her to leave thinking something is going on with Lizzie. That's just... Fuck...

I spot her, pressing the key fob for her car as she hurries over to it.

My hand slams the driver door closed before she manages to crack it further than an inch.

"I do that," I pant, my chest heaving as I drag in much needed air.

She whips her face in my direction, her mouth so close to my own as I crowd her body from behind, trapping her between me and her car.

"You're not my bodyguard anymore," she says, turning to open the door again.

I slam it closed again.

Oh, she's pissed. I've seen her like this countless times over the years. Only when she's extra quiet like this, devoid of emotion, it's not only because she's pissed. It's because she's *hurt*.

"Sinclair."

"Let go of my door, Denver. I want to leave."

My jaw clenches as she avoids my eyes. I suck in a deep breath, my nostrils flaring as I open her door for her, standing back so she has space. She puts her coffee mug into the holder and then bends and scoops Monty up from where he's jumping at my legs trying to greet me. She lifts him into the car carefully and tells him to stay.

She straightens back up, stiffening as I step closer to her.

"Please, listen to me. They came to talk to me about something important."

"It's fine. You don't have to explain right now. Go back upstairs. We'll talk later." She finally turns and looks at me properly, taking in the fact I'm shirtless in the street.

"No," I grit. "We'll talk now!" I jab a finger down at the sidewalk to accentuate my point. "We've put off talking for too long. We should have told your father about us by now. And that's the first thing we're going to do as soon as I tell you what's going on with Liz and Dix."

Her pupils dilate, and I swear she looks pleased at my outburst.

"Okay."

"Okay?" I frown, expecting some push back. This is Sinclair. She's always got something to say about everything.

"We tell my father as soon as possible, I agree," she says.

"Right," I murmur, studying her.

"Does she still love you?"

I grimace at her question. "What?"

"Lizzie. Does she still love you?"

"No, it's not like that between us."

"Do you still love her?"

I'm stunned into silence as she stares at me, waiting for an answer. Her eyes grow glassy, and she turns to slide into the car.

"Sinclair?" I pull her up against me, my hand curling around her hip. "I've never been in love with Lizzie. Why would you think that?"

"She's Dixie's mom."

"And?" I search her eyes and understanding dawns on me. "Princess, Dixie isn't my daughter."

Her brows furrow as she processes my words. "But I asked you if you'd ever lost someone you love, and you have photos of the two of them all over your cabin? She's always texting you and it's the closest you ever get to smiling when you open one of her messages."

I ease her a little closer to me so I can wrap my other hand around her opposite hip and look into her eyes. "She's Rick's."

"Your friend in the photo?"

I nod. I've mentioned him by name once, yet she remembers.

"The cabin's his too… or it was. Now it's mine."

"*Was* his?" Sinclair searches my eyes.

"Yeah, was." I let out a sigh. "He was my best friend. We

enlisted together after my grandparents died. He pulled me out of a dark place. I wouldn't be here without him. Dixie's his daughter. And Lizzie was his girlfriend. They're going to visit his grave today."

"You lost him?" Tenderness swirls in Sinclair's eyes.

"I did. We all did."

She parts her lips, then closes them again, all of her fight seeming to evaporate instantly. She's silent as she gazes into my eyes. And I get it. People don't know what to say when you've lost someone.

"Will you tell me about him?" she asks.

I look back into her understanding eyes. Fuck, this is Sinclair. She knows what this feels like—the suffocating grip of grief. How it wraps around you like a dark, heavy cloak some days, catching you off guard. It's not the days you expect. You're ready for those: anniversaries, birthdays. It's the unexpected ones. Like hearing their favorite song on the radio, or catching a scent that reminds you of them. Or picking up your phone to share something with them, only to remember that no matter how many times you call or text, they won't answer anymore.

They'll never answer again.

"What do you want to know?" I ask, softly, reaching up to dust my knuckles across her cheek. My heart somersaults with relief when she leans into my touch instead of moving away.

"Anything. Everything," she whispers.

"Get in the car," I say softly.

She nods and climbs inside. I close her door and walk around the hood, climbing into the passenger seat. The moment my ass hits the fabric, Monty scampers from Sinclair's lap and into mine.

"Hey, Monty," I say, fussing him until he flops happily inside my arms. He rests his head against my chest, his tongue reaching out to deliver slow licks against my flesh.

Sinclair watches him with shining eyes. "He missed you."

"I missed him too."

She bites her lower lip as I rest my head against the headrest, my face turned toward her.

"I love you, Sinclair."

Her eyes widen.

"Before I say anything else I need to say that. I love you. *I'm in love with you.*" I smile softly at her, and she stares at my mouth, her voice failing her. "I love you, Princess," I say again. "I'm so fucking in love with you, it physically hurts me right here when you aren't close to me." I tap two fingers against my chest and Monty takes it as an invitation to lick my chest again.

Sinclair's eyes crease with fondness as she watches him with me.

"You love me?" Her breath falters.

"I do."

"But—"

"I'm smiling, so it must be true," I say, loving the way she's gazing at me in wonder.

"You are," she muses, studying my mouth.

"I've never been in love before," I say.

"Neither have I." She looks at me, and I know I have to keep talking before she says something that I'll want to grab on to and protect with every breath that's in my body.

Because it's time I told her everything. She deserves to know. And if she's about to say what I hope she is, then I'll be too busy feeling like I punched the fucking moon to even speak if I don't get it out first. It's been years since I've told anyone. The last time was when Jenson came to work with me.

"I had no one to go home to after I signed up. My parents were gone. My grandparents were gone. I'm an only child. So I used to spend every holiday with Rick and his family, and Lizzie," I begin.

Sinclair's eyes fill with tears.

"Don't get upset, Princess," I soothe, hating seeing her sad, especially because of me. "I'm fine. Rick and Lizzie became my family. She was studying to become a nurse when we were last on deployment together. She found out she was pregnant before we left. She asked me to look after him, and I..." I roll my lips, pressing my fist to them as I pause.

"It's okay," Sinclair encourages gently.

"... I promised her I'd keep him safe," I whisper.

"Denver," she breathes, suspecting what I'm about to say.

"We were ambushed." I clear my throat, keeping the emotion that's bubbling there from surfacing. "He was hit by shrapnel from a rocket launched grenade. It ripped through him, tore him open and I tried to..." I glance at Sinclair, then shake my head. She doesn't need the mental image of what it's like to keep your friend's guts from spilling out of his body. It's more than I can bear to recall most days. "He didn't stand a chance. He died in my arms before backup arrived."

"I'm so sorry," she whispers.

"I didn't go back. I couldn't. Everything reminded me of this void that losing him had left behind. I lost faith in my ability to do my job. I didn't trust myself to keep my other brothers safe." I scrub a hand around my jaw and stare out of the windscreen at two joggers who run past. "I came back and took time off until Dixie was born. I was the first person to hold her, after Lizzie. She insisted. She never once fucking blamed me for what happened to him. Not once."

"Because it wasn't your fault," Sinclair says.

I lean back against the seat, all the energy draining from me like a bag of water that's been slashed open.

"Denver, it wasn't your fault," she repeats, laying her hand over my forearm. I drop my eyes and stare at it, needing something to focus on so I can get my words out.

"I came to work with your father when Dixie was three

months old. He asked why I left Delta Force, and I told him. I told him everything. How Lizzie had put school on hold, how I wanted to support them financially. Rick would have done the same for me.

"Before I even made it home from the interview, Lizzie had a realtor call her, congratulating her. She had a house with a yard bought for her in a nice neighborhood, and a live-in nanny set up so she could go back to school. And I had a voicemail from your father telling me the job was mine, but that if I didn't want it, I could still keep the 'signing bonus' he'd sent."

"That's..." Sinclair gasps, then breathes out with a soft laugh. "That's exactly the type of thing my father would do."

"He's a good man, a *great* man. And I'm lying to him."

"I'm sorry I put you in a position where you had to."

"Don't." I allow my eyes to rake over her face, taking in every soft millimeter of skin. "This isn't on you. It's on me. And we'll tell him. As soon as Liz and Dix leave, we'll go over and tell him together, okay?"

"Okay." A softness has seeped into her expression, and she's turned in her seat to face me, mirroring my position.

I take her hand in mine and entwine our fingers. Monty sighs, his warm body creating a comforting weight in my lap.

"Do you want to come inside and meet them properly?"

Sinclair's brow wrinkles and she bites her lip, looking unsure. "Don't you have stuff to talk about? You said it was important?"

"They're moving to LA." I don't manage to hide the heaviness in my voice, or the way that my entire body sags. "Liz has a new job offer. It'll be amazing for her. And for Dix."

"But you said they're your family? How can they go and leave you behind?"

I frown. "I..."

"They asked you to go with them, didn't they? That's why they came?"

I flick my eyes to meet hers, then have to look away again. "Yeah."

"Do you...? Do you *want* to go?"

"I..." I inhale slowly. "I'll miss them, that's all." I look back at Sinclair. "I'm not leaving you. Or your family."

Her lips curl into a gentle smile. "I know."

I exhale slowly, the pressure that began in my chest the moment Lizzie told me about her plans easing for the first time. "Good. As long as you know that."

"I do."

She watches me carefully as I lift our joined hands to kiss inside her wrist.

"I love you, Sinclair," I rasp against her silky skin, kissing her again. "I love you so damn much, Princess. I'm not going anywhere."

38

DENVER

The adjacent elevator doors are sliding closed as I step out of the one I've ridden up in. There are only a few apartments whose main doors are on the same level as Sinclair's. It's the first time I've ever seen an elevator getting used by someone else when I've been here.

I knock at her door, one hand holding the travel mug she brought for me this morning. Only now it's filled with a smoothie for her from her favorite truck. My eyes drop to the sticker I've stuck to the mug. It's a cartoon banana, with the text, *'I find you very appeeling.'* My lips quirk. It's Sinclair and Molly all over, they'll love it.

Lizzie and Dixie left not long after Sinclair drove away. I hated letting her go, but we straightened everything out. She knows now. She knows who they are, and she knows the demons from my past. Why I'm extra protective over her. Why I'm obsessed with her safety.

I can't lose her.

I wouldn't survive it.

She's taking longer than usual to answer, so I knock again.

The only thing we need to do now is tell Sterling together. I crack my neck, which does nothing to ease the tension that melds itself to my muscles each time I think about how I'm lying to him. But no matter what he says, I'll handle it. I'll take anything he can throw at me. As long as he doesn't ask me to give up his daughter.

No one could ever make me leave her willingly.

"Denver." Sinclair smiles as she opens the door, and my heart skips a fucking beat at the way my name sounds coming from her lips. But it stops dead like it's had a thousand volts blasted through it as I look at her face.

"You've been crying."

"What? No, I haven't."

"Your eyes are red, don't lie to me." Unease prickles up my spine as she flaps her lips searching for an excuse.

She's never speechless.

She was fine when she left me a few hours ago.

"What's wrong?"

"I'm fine." She takes the travel mug from my hand and looks at the sticker on it. "I've not seen this one before." She tries to smile, but it's weak, too affected by whatever's made her eyes puffy.

"Is it because of Liz wearing my—?"

"No. *No*," she repeats more firmly. "I know nothing was going on. I haven't even thought of that again, it's nothing... I..."

She trails off, probably hoping I'll drop it, so I change tactics. "What were you doing before I got here?"

Her eyes shift to the side, and she shrugs. "Not much."

"Sinclair?" I warn. "Did someone do something to upset you?" The departing elevator as I arrived springs to mind. "Who was just here?"

"What makes you think someone was here?" she asks.

But she can't hold my eyes for longer than a second. Alarm bells blare in my head.

"Was it your father? Sullivan?"

"Denver... it's fine. Just come in."

I stay rooted to the spot, my body expanding as I drag in a slow, deliberate breath to keep my cool. "Who the fuck made you cry, Sinclair?"

"No one."

"Who was here?" I grit.

Her eyes pinch. "It doesn't matter," she whispers.

"Who?" I growl.

She falters, her eyes roaming over me, studying me. She knows I won't let it drop until she tells me.

"Brad," she says quietly. "But it's fine. He didn't upset me. It wasn't—"

I'm spinning on my heels, striding toward the elevators as she runs after me.

"Denver! Stop! He didn't do anything, I swear!"

But her words hit my back as I barrel into the waiting car and punch the street level button so hard the display around it cracks.

"Stay here," I bark as she catches up with me.

The last thing I see is her pale face as the doors slide closed.

The asshole is in the deserted lobby, texting on his phone with a smirk on his face as I fly out of the elevator. His eyes widen as he sees me storming toward him.

"You!" I hiss, jabbing a finger in his direction. "Don't fucking move!"

He tucks his phone into his shorts pocket and does his best to puff out his chest like a prized jerk. My nose grazes his as I slam to a halt, all the blood in my body reaching boiling point.

"What did you do?" I snarl.

He takes a step back, and I take one forward, towering

over the pathetic piece of shit as he looks like he's about to piss himself.

"I..." He gulps. "Nothing. I never touched her. We just talked. She said she's missed me."

I grab him around the neck of his T-shirt, and he chokes out a rough gasp as I lift him onto his toes. "Lie to me again and I'll rip out your fucking tongue."

He pales. "You won't."

"Try me." My lips curl as I tighten my grip on him. "I've never fucking liked you. The way you look at her. The way you try and put your filthy hands on her. Always chasing an opportunity to get that other inch in, hey?"

His eyes narrow. "You know about that? You know that I was her firs—"

"You weren't fucking anything!" I roar, moving us back until Brad's back slams into the wall. "You were *nothing* to her. You are still nothing to her. And you never will be. You tried to take advantage of her when she was grieving."

"Like you're not abusing your position as her *bodyguard*?" He sneers the word. "You're meant to work for her, not pine after her like a pathetic dog. She's way out of your league."

I slam my fist into the wall beside his head, making him flinch. He tries to jerk his chin up, feigning some bravado bullshit.

I lower my voice to a bone-chilling whisper. "Come near her again and I will take you apart piece by piece." I press my forehead against his, pinning his head to the wall. "And if Monty wants, I'll feed him your tiny dick, then let him shit it out in Central Park."

Brad swallows, but his Adam's apple gets stuck above my fist, and he makes a weird gurgling sound instead.

"You don't want to know what my body count is," I snarl. "But you'd be the first one I'd actually enjoy."

I drop him like a sack of shit, and he bends over, coughing and clutching at his neck.

"You're a fucking psycho."

I wait until he lifts his head, his eyes meeting mine. "I'm glad we understand one another," I say calmly.

He stands and his eyes flick to something behind me.

"Denver!" Sinclair yells as she runs out of an elevator. "What the hell are you doing?"

Brad straightens up, his attention bouncing between the two of us. "You need to hire some new fucking help," he says, coughing.

My upper lip curls against my teeth with a snarl as I step toward him.

"I'm going, Sin. Will you be okay?" he asks her.

"I'll be fine," she says, rushing to my side as Brad backs away.

His eyes continue to ping-pong between us. "Be careful with this motherfucker."

"Just go, Brad!" she snaps as I take another step toward him, my fist clenched.

Sinclair wraps an arm around my bicep and pulls me back. "Leave him," she begs. "He didn't do anything. I told you, I'm fine."

I look at her and her eyes have recovered their usual fiery defiance. She no longer looks like she's upset or has been crying. She looks ready to go into battle. I turn my body toward her fully, ignoring Brad as he takes the opportunity to get out of the building at a run.

"Why did you do that?" she snaps. "I told you I was fine. He could report you for assault."

"He won't."

She glares at me. "It would serve you right if he did. I can't believe you!"

"He made you cry," I grit.

"No!" she cries. "He didn't! I don't know why I'm even..." She throws her arms up in the air. "Why didn't you listen to me?"

"Sinclair?" I reach for her, but she's already stomping back toward the elevators. "Tell me what the hell he was doing here?" I snap at her retreating back.

I race after her and get inside just before the doors close.

39

SINCLAIR

I stand with my arms folded and eyes fixed on the elevator display as it ascends.

"You need to trust me," I say quietly.

Denver blows out a rough breath. "I do. But I don't trust him. And I'm right to not fucking trust him. Look how he's treated you."

"He's done nothing," I snap, whirling to face him head-on. "Just... I can't even..." I shake my head, finding it too hard to look at him.

"I'm sorry," he utters after a few silent seconds. The anguish in his voice has me sneaking a glance at him. "I never want to upset you. I love you," he says, his eyes pinned on my face.

I press my lips together, my chest tight at the intensity behind his words.

"But you don't want me to have friends," I whisper.

"Brad's not your friend," he snaps.

It's funny. I liked how I was the one person who could make him lose control. Knowing that I can bring this beautiful strong man to his knees. But all that knowledge does to me now is tear at my heart and make me feel like I can't breathe.

"Princess," he pleads, reaching for me.

I step away, and the way his face crumples is as if someone ripped the air from his lungs.

He loves me.

He loves me and he just wants to protect me.

We stare at one another, the air swirling in the confined space until it's cloying. We're two people who've fallen so deeply for one another that we're vulnerable. I've taken Denver's strength, and I've poked holes in it, one after another.

I've opened him up.

But I'm no longer sure that's a good thing.

He holds my gaze and steps toward me again. And this time, I'm too weak to refuse him. Because the truth is that I want him more than anything. I love him more than anything.

I need him to be *okay*, more than anything.

His arms have barely opened before I'm throwing myself into them, jumping up and locking my legs around his waist.

I crash my lips to his.

"Sinclair," he groans, diving into my kiss like he needs it. Like he can't survive without it.

Then he's in control, kissing me with all the power and skill that I love about him.

"I don't want to fight with you," I gasp as I take control back, meeting his kiss with my own—harder, deeper, more desperate one.

"Fuck, neither do I," he rasps.

He devours my mouth, swallowing down each pant, sliding his tongue over mine and holding me as close as he possibly can.

I offer everything I have to him, begging him to take it.

"Denver," I moan as he pushes me back against the wall of the elevator.

"You belong with me," he hisses. "And I don't want to fight with you, but I *will* kill men like Brad if they come near you in a way that they shouldn't."

"No," I pant.

"Yes," he growls, pressing another bruising kiss to my lips. "I will do *anything* for you, and the sooner you understand that, the better."

He reaches out and pulls the emergency stop lever and the elevator comes to a halt.

"What are you doing?" I gasp.

He keeps his lips hovering over mine. "We're not going anywhere until you understand that as much as I would fucking die for you, I will also kill for you. I won't apologize for feeling that way."

I search his eyes, my gaze catching on the gold flecks in them. They're like bright flames now, dancing amongst the vivid green.

"I do understand," I whisper. "Believe me... I know how far you'd go for me. But I don't..."

His dark brows lower as he frowns, waiting for me to say whatever it is I'm about to.

"... I don't want you to..." I can't say it. My tongue goes dry, and my throat tightens as he looks back at me.

"Tell me," he urges.

I clamp my lips together, not trusting myself to speak. I don't know exactly what I'm going to say. I only know something needs to be said.

"Sinclair," he urges when I don't say anything. "You don't think I know how fucking crazy I get over you? The lengths I would go to for you?"

I run my fingers through the hair at the back of his head and he curses.

"Jesus, I'd do fucking anything to make you happy. *Anything.*"

"I know," I whisper, tightening my thighs around his torso, automatically.

A whimper slips free at the sheer deliciousness of having his solid body against mine. I can't even think straight when he's this close.

His eyes darken.

"You turned on, Princess?"

I bite my lip. This isn't how this is supposed to go. I'm supposed to have a clear head. I have so much to think about. I haven't stopped thinking since I left his place this morning.

"Does it make you wet knowing I would rip a grown man apart for you?" Denver asks.

"No." But I tremble inside his arms, giving away my lie.

His eyes darken and he shoves my dress up around my waist with one hand and pushes a hand between my thighs. I take a couple of deep breaths, making my breasts rise against his chest in the small space between us.

My panties are soaked through, there's no hiding it from him.

A rich murmur of approval rolls from his lips as he presses his fingers against the damp fabric and circles my clit.

"Denver," I whine.

"You need me to fuck you until you understand it? Until you believe it?"

"Yes," I whimper in response, heat burning through my veins as everything else ceases to exist. There's just me and him. Two racing hearts. Two pairs of desperate, hungry eyes staring into one another.

He grabs his belt, yanking it open and tearing at the waistband and zipper of his pants. My panties are ripped to the side, and then the smooth, fat head of his cock is sliding through my soaked flesh.

"I'm a fucking wreck for you," he groans as he thrusts himself to the hilt inside me.

I throw my head back with a cry, my body rippling around him.

He pulls almost all the way back out, then thrusts back in.

"I think of you every damn minute," he hisses, forcing himself deeper.

I dig my fingers into his shoulders for support as he holds each of my thighs and pushes them wider, pinning me between his body and the wall.

His fingers push into my flesh as he pulls back and starts to pound into me, driving his hips with rough, deep grunts.

"I fucking crave you, Sinclair. You make me lose control. I'm supposed to protect you."

"You do," I gasp as he fucks me so hard my eyes water.

I'm so wet that he easily pumps deeper each time, his balls hitting my skin with force.

"No," he snarls. "Anyone could get to you when I'm like this."

I hold his eyes, which have taken on a wild sheen. They flare with the untamed primal urge to fuck as he sinks inside me again with a clenched jaw.

"Look at me," he grits. "I'm so fucking lost, buried deep inside your perfect cunt, feeling nothing but you stretching around me, seeing nothing but your eyes as you give yourself to me. Anyone could walk right up to us when I'm like this and I'd be useless."

He fucks me so hard that the elevator shakes.

"Denver... Denver, *please*."

"Tell me what you want, Princess."

"Oh my god." My nails rake over his neck, hot, sticky

wetness pricking at their tips as I pierce his skin, struggling to hold on.

"That's it, fucking mark me as yours."

My mouth drops open as I stare back at him. He looks scary as hell. All giant muscles and dark, burning eyes. He doesn't get it. He thinks he can't protect me like this because he's too focused on me. But if someone were here, they'd literally have to go through him to get to me. His body is broad and solid, curled around me like a human shield.

They'd have to go straight through his back to get to me.

He always has to sleep closest to the door. He always sits between me and the entrance to places. He's always on high alert.

And when we have sex, he prefers being the one in control. He wants to be on top of me, or behind me, pinning me beneath him. He loves to watch me ride him, but never for long. He has to get back into a position where his body is a physical barrier between me and anyone else.

He's sacrificing himself for me all the time.

He never puts himself first.

Ever.

"Denver," I mewl, the pleasure getting too much to bear.

"Come for me," he urges, the rough tone of his command so damn sexy that it's only a couple more thrusts before I do exactly as he says.

"Yes, good girl, that's my good fucking girl," he groans as I come apart, my body hugging his in tight waves as it fights to steal his pleasure for itself. "Fuck," he growls, thrusting harder. He presses his forehead against mine and his pupils dilate as he comes inside me with a grating curse. "Sinclair, Princess... fuuuuckkk."

I grab either side of his face, crushing my lips to his as his wet heat spills inside me.

"I'd do anything to make you happy too," I say as I press kiss after desperate kiss to his soft lips. "*Anything.*"

I kiss him until his movements slow and he stills inside me.

"Denver," I whisper, searching his eyes. "I love—"

His cell rings, loud and angry.

"Get it," I breathe, pressing another kiss to his warm lips.

He hesitates, frowning.

"It might be important," I say.

I hook my legs behind him as he shifts to hold me with one arm. He reaches into his jacket pocket and pulls out the blaring phone.

"Sullivan?" he answers, his dark eyes holding mine.

"Denver? Can you talk?"

I clench around him without meaning to, and he narrows his eyes at me in warning.

"Yes."

"Okay..." Sullivan's exhale is ragged, the sound so unlike him. I'm not used to hearing him sound flustered.

"What is it?" Denver asks.

"Tate," Sullivan says.

I widen my eyes at him. I knew cookie-baking Tate was more than just a friend to my brother.

"Listen, can I count on your discretion?"

Denver's jaw ticks as his still hard dick shifts inside me. "You wouldn't believe how good I am at keeping secrets," he rasps.

"Good. Because what I need you to help me with isn't exactly legal."

"Don't tell me anymore until I get there," Denver grunts. "I'll come to you now."

"Thanks," Sullivan clips.

Then he's gone.

"What's wrong? Do you think whoever this Tate is, is in trouble?"

Denver frowns, pocketing his phone. "I don't know. But I need to go."

"I know, I understand," I say, stroking the tense lines that have sprouted across his brow. "He needs you."

"You need me," he says, resting his forehead against mine.

I press a kiss to his lips. "I'll be okay," I whisper. "I promise you; As long as you're okay, then I'll be fine… now go."

40

DENVER

What Sullivan needs me for takes me away for the entire evening and late into the next day. But the slimy fucker who crossed this woman Sullivan seems intent on helping won't be a problem to her anymore. Not unless he really doesn't value his pathetic existence.

It's already ten p.m. when I'm riding the elevator up to Sinclair's place, and I'm as unstable as a nuclear fucking warhead from being apart from her for so long.

I smirk. I never thought I'd turn into one of those sappy fuckers, pining for their girl. It's something I used to rib Rick about all the time. But truth be told, I was always envious of the relationship he had with Lizzie. It would have been nice to have had a girl waiting for me at home. Missing me. Writing to me. *Loving me.*

Sullivan and I were in an area with bad signal. And Sinclair hasn't replied to the text I managed to get delivered, or if she did, the shit service meant it never came through.

The lack of contact with her has meant I've been losing my fucking mind.

I open up the tracking app on my phone. Monty's location puts him with Sterling and Halliday. But Sinclair's puts her at her place. Why would she be home without Monty?

I don't have time to consider the reason, because the second I stride out of the elevator, my senses heighten, jumping to full alert mode. The hallway leading to Sinclair's door is pumping with a deep bass. Her front door is vibrating with the volume of the music. Laughter spills out, along with it.

She's having a fucking party?

I know I'm not assigned to her anymore, but did she not learn a damn thing from our time together? Me, Killian, and Jenson have all been busy. She shouldn't be having a fucking party without at least one of us here to keep an eye on things. And in her own damn apartment? Anyone could plant a device. Her private conversations would be splashed all over the press. Damn it, a secret camera could already be in her fucking bathroom, primed and ready for some creep to jerk off to her in the shower.

I wrench open the door, anger sparking inside me like a lit fuse. She didn't lock it, let alone bolt the damn thing. Any sick bastard could be in here under the guise of a partygoer.

Heat hits me as the scent of warm bodies and liquor spills out in a cloud.

"Jesus," I grit.

The inside is a sea of writhing bodies, dancing to the pounding music. All the shades have been closed and it resembles an underground rave club. There's even a professional DJ station set up with a row of glaring lights. A red one circles the room, lighting up the throng of people.

But none are Sinclair.

"Sinclair?" I yell, stomping in. I'm going to spank that perfect ass of hers for putting herself at risk like this. "Sinclair!"

The Rule Breaker

My voice is lost to the music as I push my way into the crowd.

"Hey, Handsome," a girl coos, wiping her hair back from her clammy forehead. She gives me a tipsy smile as she pushes her tits against me and tries to entice me to dance.

"Where is she?" I growl.

The girl pouts up at me. "Who?"

"Sinclair. The woman whose place this is."

"Oh..." She tilts her head with a flirty smile as she snakes her arms around my neck. "Last time I saw her, she was going into one of the bedrooms with a guy. I'm sure there's another one we can talk in, if you don't fancy dancing?"

I pull her arms off me and place them by her sides. She throws me a look of disappointment as I step away.

I don't bother trying to weave through the crowd, I plow right through it.

My shirt clings to my back as sweat beads run down my back. It's a fucking spectacle in here. What the hell was she thinking?

"Get the fuck out of my way!" I bark at anyone who doesn't have the sense to move before I crash into them.

They part in a wave, immediately swallowing up the gap behind me as I move forward.

"Denver!"

I snap my head to the side and meet Zoey's wide eyes. She moves, positioning herself between me and the hallway that leads to Sinclair's bedroom.

"Where is she, Zoey?"

She flinches at the venom spilling from my voice, her eyes widening as the beat changes and a strobe light turns on. There's a collective whoop from the hundreds of people squashed into the living area.

"Um..." Zoey's eyes dart around like she's looking for someone to help her.

But I already know where Sinclair is. Her best friend wouldn't be standing here, in my way, if I wasn't about to walk right into whatever shit Sinclair's trying to pull.

"You don't want to go back there, Denver."

I glance down at Zoey's hand that's appeared on my chest, a token attempt at holding me back.

"Move your hand, and step aside," I say calmly.

"Denver," she pleads. "She's not... she's... trust me, please. Now isn't the time. Come back tomorrow. Talk to her. You can work this out, I know you can. She's... she's not in a good place tonight."

I level my eyes with her frantic ones, and she shakes her head, screwing her face up and turning away. Her hand drops from my chest, and I slide past her.

"Thank you," I say.

I pause for a nano second at Sinclair's bedroom door, dragging in a deep breath.

Then I boot the fucking door in.

"Fuck!" A body shoots up from beneath the covers of her bed. "What the hell, man? This room's taken."

I freeze.

Brad Garrett-Charles stares back at me, shirtless.

Blonde hair flows across the pillow behind him where he tries to position his body so I can't see her.

"Move!" I bark, stepping closer.

He scrambles up and slams back against the headboard, eyeing me like I might rip his head off. But all I care about right now is seeing who's lying next to him.

She sits up, swaying a little and the sheet drops to her waist, exposing the oversized T-shirt she's wearing. Her hand goes to her face clumsily and she pushes her hair back from her face.

Ice slithers up my spine and my heart ceases to beat.

"Sinclair?" I whisper.

Round green eyes anchor themselves to mine and for a second she just stares at me with her mouth open. Her makeup is smudged, and there's a glassiness to her gaze as she tries to focus on me.

"D-Denver."

She pulls the sheet up, trying to cover herself.

Trying to hide from me.

"Did you get her drunk? What the fuck did you do to her?" I roar, advancing on Brad and hauling him out of the bed with a merciless hand around his neck.

He's still wearing his underwear, thank god. But the hardness of his pathetic cock nudges against my thigh as I crush his windpipe.

"No!" Sinclair stumbles from the bed. "Denver, stop! You'll kill him."

"He deserves to die if he touched you," I snarl as Brad's eyes roll in his head.

"He didn't do anything! I asked him to come in here with me!"

Her cried words as she tries to prise me off him have me whipping my eyes to hers.

"What?"

"Please, let him go." She pulls at my hands.

I toss Brad to the side like trash, and he falls to the floor, curling into a ball on his side, wheezing.

"What the fuck do you mean?"

She gasps as I turn to her, my eyes dropping over her body. The T-shirt is huge and comes to her knees, swamping her. I can't tell whether she has underwear on beneath it.

"It was my idea for us to come back here," she says. Her eyes have a liquor-induced sheen to them. She licks her lips, the scent of something strong, like whiskey, hitting my nostrils as she breathes. "I'm not drunk, before you say anything," she slurs. "Not enough to not know what I'm doing." She wraps her arms around herself, making her look tiny in the ridiculous T-shirt. I scowl at it, wondering if it's Brad's. But the thing is huge. No way would he fill that out.

"And what exactly the fuck are you doing?" I hiss.

Her pulse is firing rapidly in her neck as she swallows. But she doesn't move back to give herself more space. Her eyes flick up to mine beneath her lashes, guiltily.

"I'm sorry, Denver. I just needed to know," she whispers.

"You never forget your first," Brad pipes up as he staggers to his feet behind me. "Isn't that what you told me, Sin?"

She winces, tears filling her lower lids as I pin my eyes to hers, searching for the truth.

"I'm sorry," she chokes, the tears spilling free as she blinks.

We stare at one another as Brad's voice takes on a cocky arrogance. "She tried you out, Buddy. But we both know a supermodel isn't going to run off into the sunset with a bodyguard." He snorts like the idea is absurd. "She's way out of your league."

I ignore him, giving every cell of my body over to focusing on Sinclair. "You chose to do this with him?"

Her chest shakes as more tears spill from her eyes. She rubs at them, smearing mascara across her skin.

"Tell me you didn't, Sinclair," I say, my voice a choked breath as I struggle not to break apart in front of her. "Tell me you didn't."

"I..." She clamps a hand over her mouth as a sob shakes her. "I can't."

"How the fuck could you? After everything," I say, not caring if I sound weak. Not caring about a fucking thing anymore.

Except the truth.

She cries harder and lifts a trembling hand to reach for me. But her outstretched fingers curl into her palm and she lowers it before she touches me.

"It counted," she whispers so quietly that I have to strain to hear her.

Blood rushes in my ears, my teeth clenching until my jaw feels like it might snap. "It what?"

"That first time with Brad..." She swallows, wincing like she's in pain. "It... it counted."

All sense of control abandons me.

It fucking counted?

"It is yours. You were my first, Denver."

"I fucking love you!" I shout.

I can't make out her eyes anymore. They are two swollen patches of black as she sobs.

"I know. And I'm so sorry... I... love—"

"Don't you dare say it," I snap, making her cry harder. "Don't you fucking dare."

I drag in a breath that makes my lungs feel like they're filling with shards of broken glass. She stands in front of me shaking, and it takes everything in me not to wrap my arms around her as I witness her distress. As it breaks me apart like a bomb went off inside my chest.

"Tell me nothing happened," I whisper.

She shakes her head.

"Princess?" I choke. "Tell me the *truth*."

"I..." She starts, then has to stop to compose herself. But she can't stop herself from shaking as she looks up at me. "We were fun, Denver. And for a while, I really believed we could be happy... I..." She swallows, her lower lip wobbling before she pulls it into her mouth. "I..."

"Don't," I rasp. "You have a choice. Don't make the wrong one."

"I'm so sorry." She turns her face like she can't bear to look at me anymore. "You should go."

Despite myself, I take a step toward her.

She sucks in a sharp breath and steps backward, away from me, creating a distance between us. "You should go."

"You don't mean that."

I realize my mistake the moment the words leave my mouth. Everyone tells her what to do. She hates having her choices taken from her.

But she's chosen this? She's really fucking chosen *this*?

She squares her shoulders like she's pulling together every ounce of strength she has. "I know what I mean! Don't tell me I don't. This is what I want, and you aren't listening. You said you'd train me on how to get out of situations I don't want to be in."

I stare at her, silently begging her with my eyes not to do it. Because if she does, that's it. I'll have no choice.

"This thing we got into together is one of them, Denver."

She looks me straight in the eye as she lines up her kill shot.

Her lips part and her whisper carries one word that shatters my entire soul, tearing us so far apart that we're no longer existing in the same universe.

"Mitt."

41

SINCLAIR
ONE WEEK LATER

"You should eat something." Sullivan grunts in disapproval, eyeing my mug as I lift the coffee to my lips.

I drop my eyes from his, no energy left to have the same discussion with him again. I swallow the liquid, ignoring that it's too hot, instead savoring the sweet tinge as it burns its way down to my stomach.

Vanilla.

It's all I've been able to stomach since he left. I try to convince myself that the aftertaste on my tongue is the ghost of one of his kisses. That there's still a part of him that exists within me somehow.

Denver left six days, twenty-one hours, and seventeen minutes ago.

And a part of me died.

I feared he might have tried to kill Brad after finding us together. But he didn't. He just turned and walked away without looking back. The second I said that one word to him, he was gone.

My safe word.

He took himself out of my life, just like I knew he would. But the fact I pushed him to it doesn't make living in the aftermath any easier. In fact, it's worse. Because I'll have to live my life wondering about the what-ifs. About what could have been if I'd chosen differently.

Being selfish or being selfless.

Either way he would have ultimately been the one who paid the price. And I'd have been the cause.

"What are your plans for today?" Sullivan asks, still eyeing my coffee mug like it's the root of all evil.

I balance it in one hand, stroking Monty with the other. He has his head resting in my lap, looking up at me with sad eyes as I sit on my sofa. Animals always know when you're hurting. I wish he could understand why Denver left, and that it wasn't his fault, it was mine. Because I know by the way he runs to the door every time someone knocks on it that he's hoping it's Denver.

It never is.

It's Zoey, Mikey, Halliday, Sullivan, my father, Uncle Mal. Everyone else whom I love, all taking it in turns to come and check on me since they noticed I've not been myself. It's as if they have a rota planned out to make sure I'm getting out of bed each day.

But never him. Never Denver.

I shrug instead of answering my brother, and he exhales with an exasperated sigh, planting his hands on his hips, curling them around the midnight blue fabric of his suit pants. He has a meeting with the giant London-run company who provide business insurance for Beaufort Diamonds today.

I glance at my watch.

He'll have to leave any minute now unless he wants to risk being late.

"You need to do something."

"I'm taking Monty for a walk later. And I'm going to the

store to get ingredients to make cupcakes with Molly for her sleepover."

Sullivan bristles, rolling his lips as he gives me a terse nod. "I'll drop her over by six."

"I'll look forward to it," I answer, holding his eyes for a beat before he looks away.

I still don't know what was so important that he had to call Denver that day and ask for his assistance. All I know is that it involved the mysterious Tate, and that Molly said she doesn't come round to their place anymore. Hence why I'm going to bake with Molly today to try and cheer her up. Because Sullivan is off on another overnight work trip to visit one of our stores and check in with them. This time it's San Francisco. Last week it was San Diego. I've never known him to go as much as he has recently.

I drop my head back against the couch. "We'll go for red velvet cupcakes. Molly loves—" I swallow hard.

Sullivan's gaze returns to mine, and I swear his ice blue-colored eyes he shares with my father soften a touch. "You're right, she does love them. So did Denver, from what I recall."

I shrug. "I wouldn't know." Sullivan watches me as I try to keep my tone uninterested. "Have you heard how he's getting on in LA?" I ask, unable to help myself.

"Spoke to him this morning, actually."

I whip my gaze to his face, ignoring the sudden slice of pain across my chest that my brother gets to speak to him and hear his voice, ask how he is, but I don't.

"He sounded like he always does. Serious, getting on with his job. You know Denver... or perhaps not. I guess you were never really a fan, you hardly spoke to the guy."

"That's right," I sniff. "I didn't."

"Well, you don't need to now. He's gone."

I hide my wince at Sullivan's clipped words. I know he's testing me. He's not an idiot. My newly acquired self-pity and hibernation inside my apartment began the moment Denver walked out. I hadn't even gotten the last unwanted guest out of my place from the party before he'd been to see my father, handed in his resignation, and boarded a plane to LA.

"Plus, you're free of needing a bodyguard, which is what you wanted. So at least try to look happy about it." Sullivan sighs.

"I am happy," I lie.

Sullivan shakes his head, muttering.

"Don't." I glare at him.

"Didn't say a word, Sis," he clips. "You want to stay in your apartment and tell yourself you don't miss him, that you didn't wish he was still here, then that's your choice. But don't expect me to fall for your bullshit."

"I don't know what you're talking about," I mutter, looking into my coffee as I swirl it inside my mug. Anything to avoid meeting his eyes.

Sullivan grunts. "Yeah. Just like you didn't know that Denver wouldn't accept any extra payment Dad offered him for being assigned to you."

"What?" I reel back, almost spilling the coffee. Monty lifts his head from my lap, looking at Sullivan too.

Sullivan's eyes narrow. "He wired it all back before he left. Personally, I think he should have asked for double."

I ignore his jibe and stare at him, my heart hammering. "Denver didn't take the money he earned from being my bodyguard?"

"Not a cent," Sullivan says, turning toward the door. "See you at six."

I slam the coffee mug on the floor by the couch and jump, bundling Monty into my arms as I race after him to my front door.

"What did Dad say when Denver told him he was leaving?" I ask in a rush.

Sullivan opens the door and steps out into the hallway. He turns back to me with an assessing gaze. "What do you think he said?"

"I... I don't know."

Sullivan's eyes narrow. "What exactly happened between you and Denver?"

I push down the sudden rising tide of emotion that threatens to shoot up and spray out, drenching us in its messy, heartbreaking truth.

"Nothing," I say, forcing my voice to sound dull and emotionless. "He just did his job. I was his job."

A muscle ticks in Sullivan's cheek, and he purses his lips, his eyes holding mine like a penetrating spotlight. I can see why the Beaufort Diamond staff shit themselves when he isn't happy about something. Jenson's enjoyed telling me a tale or two about fainting employees and ones who throw up just knowing my brother has called a meeting.

He's unnervingly calm in his Tom Ford suit, eyes like lasers, pinned on me. But he's also my brother, so he doesn't intimidate me no matter how much the look he's giving me might make any other person wither on the spot.

I hold his eyes, arching a brow in challenge.

"Suit yourself," he says finally. "See you later."

He turns and walks off, and my eyes drop to my fingers and the tremble in them as I close the door behind him, securing the bolt in place.

Two weeks later

"You doing all right, Sunshine?"

I look up from the bridal magazine I've been hopelessly

trying to concentrate on in my father's kitchen. "Sure. Why wouldn't I be?"

Uncle Mal slips onto the bar stool next to me, a soft chuckle deepening the creases at the corners of his eyes. Before my mother died, they were signs of a lifetime of laughter and happy memories, worn with pride on his face. But after he lost his sister, grief turned them into deep shadows created by the loss of the light she brought into his world. He took their loss hard. I worry about him more than he'd want me to. He has us, we're all family. And he has his wife, Trudy, although they never had their own children.

But some days, he seems more lost than any of us.

"Did you and Dad get the work done you wanted to?" I ask.

"Yeah. Just going over some things that Ade brought up on my visit. Your father's finishing up in his office," he says, running a hand around his jaw as he stares into space.

Ade is Beaufort Diamonds contact in Botswana who manages the mining operations when Uncle Mal isn't there. And seeing as Sullivan is on another trip again today—LA this time—and won't be back until late, he's been updating my father on his last business trip.

"Okay," I say, abandoning the magazine.

I came over to discuss planning details with Halliday. We managed to get a lot discussed until pregnancy tiredness won over and she took herself off to have a nap. I was about to head home, but Monty decided to join her. He likes to lay his head by her stomach. Halliday says he does it when they mind him for me. It's as if he's already protective over the new addition to the Beaufort gang.

"It'll be strange all of us going back there together," Uncle Mal says.

I follow his gaze to the open magazine and the article on beach weddings. "It will," I agree.

It'll be the first time since the accident that we'll all be near Cape Town together. Dad spent a lot of time there to begin with. And Sullivan went over with him a couple of times, more to try to talk him into coming home, I think. Which he did eventually.

But I haven't been back since.

"Not a day goes by that I don't think of them," Mal says quietly.

"Yeah." My throat thickens. "Me too."

I close the magazine, my fingers still trembling, the way they have been for the past two and a half weeks.

Calloused fingers close around mine until they stop shaking. "It's not easy, losing people you love," Uncle Mal says.

"No," I whisper, the weight of his hand on mine bringing some comfort. "It's not."

Before I can stop it, a tear slips free. It runs down my nose and drips off, leaving a wet splodge on the glossy cover of the magazine. The smiling bride hit by it seems unbothered, her smile still stretching up to her ears like a taunt.

A reminder of what happiness looks and feels like.

I swipe the tear off her face, but it's quickly replaced by another one.

"If we fall in love, then does that mean we have to climb our way out of it once that person is gone?"

My uncle pats my hand and sighs. "I don't think you ever get out of it, Sinclair. But as much as it hurts, imagine feeling nothing at all."

"I think nothing would be my preference," I reply.

"Hmm." He smiles sadly. "We need to feel it. The love. The loss. The guilt. We need to live with it. As hard as that is. Anything else would be too easy."

I look sideways at him. "What if it's our fault we lost it?"

His face contorts like he's lost in a painful memory. "Then I think it's even more important that we remember."

"Look at you two." My father's voice is like a fresh blast of air entering the room and lifting the somber mood. "Getting more wedding ideas?" he asks as he spots the magazine in front of us.

"Yeah, tons." I force my voice to sound brighter. He deserves to be surrounded by happiness. He and Halliday need to have a magical day, and I'm going to do everything in my power to help them have it.

"It'll rival any royal wedding with this one helping to plan it." Uncle Mal chuckles as he gives my hand one final pat and rises from his stool.

"I've no doubt," Dad comments, his blue eyes crinkling. "What are you doing today, Sweetheart?"

He says it so casually, like it's innocent. But I know they're all talking about me to one another behind my back. He's checking I'm actually doing something that doesn't involve wallowing in my apartment with only Monty for company. It's out of concern, I get it. But I wish they'd all back off.

"I'm going to a meeting with Julian," I reply. "We're going to discuss taking the foundation public."

My father's brows shoot up his forehead. After Denver left, I decided to come clean about what I've been doing. Having one less secret from my family seemed important. And they've all been amazingly supportive about it. I should have told them a long time ago.

But that's another choice I made that I'll have to live with now.

"That's fantastic. I'm proud of you, Sweetheart."

"Thanks." I shrug away my father's compliment, a nausea caused by guilt swirling in my gut. He still doesn't know I've been lying to him for weeks.

Denver's gone. It's over.

But the deceit that makes it hard to hold my father's eyes is still there, as strong as ever.

"What changed your mind?" Uncle Mal asks.

"Something someone said to me. About how I could do more good if I did it."

My father's gaze narrows as he studies me. "Sounds like someone who gives good advice."

"Yeah, I guess," I mumble, flicking the corner of the magazines pages with my fingertip.

My father picks his suit jacket up from where it's draped over the back of a stool. "I'm going to say goodbye to Hallie, then I need to head off."

"You want me to come and sit in?" Uncle Mal asks him.

"Please," my father replies. "We can't hire just anyone. They have to be..." He shakes his head.

"They can't be as good as him, so don't say it," Uncle Mal says. "But we'll get the next best."

"Hmm." My father grumbles.

I flick my eyes between the two of them. They're interviewing for Denver's replacement. Usually my father would have had him replaced immediately. But he's waited all this time, hoping he'd come back.

He hasn't.

I hang my head, shame pulling like a weight around my neck. It's not just me who was affected when he left. I know my father thought of him as a friend, *more like family*, than an employee.

But like Denver said himself, Lizzie and Dixie are his family. He needs them. We only got to have him for a while.

And the sooner I accept that, the better.

Three weeks later

"Did you order the bridesmaid's dresses yet?"

I lift my eyes from my coffee to meet Zoey's gentle gaze, grateful that she's trying to distract me. I've been the worst company for weeks.

"Yeah. They're arriving next week. *Sterling silver*," I muse.

She laughs. "Halliday chose them, I'm guessing?"

"She did." I smile genuinely. "She's so in love with my father, it'd be weird if they weren't so cute together."

"They are cute," Zoey hums in agreement. Her eyes drop to my travel mug that the barista of the small coffee place we're sitting in put my order into.

Black. Hot. A splash of vanilla.

"I know," I mutter. "I need to get a new choice of beverage."

"No, you need to eat." Zoey fixes me with a serious look. "No supermodel has ever been told by her agent that she needs to *gain* weight."

I rotate my hand in the air like I'm waving a tiny victory flag. "Yay for me. I am the chosen one."

"I don't want to see you getting sick, Sin." She leans over the table, lowering her voice. "He's gone, honey. And I know that's what you said you wanted, but—"

"I don't regret it," I answer with an air of finality, like I will actually believe my own words if I say them out loud often enough. "He'd have stayed if I'd asked him to. Then where would that have left us?"

"Ten pounds heavier and a whole lot less miserable." Zoey sighs. "You can't keep going like this. Why don't you call him? See how he's doing?"

"No."

"He's in LA, not living on the moon. You guys could work something out."

I chew on my lower lip. I considered the same thing in the

beginning. I have the money to fly over there to see him whenever I want. My father has a private jet I can use. And so does Halliday. I could even have a permanent suite in a hotel over there set up for me, like Sullivan has his fuck pad at The Lanceford.

And each time I left him and said goodbye, I'd feel the familiar and unbearable ripping inside me, like I'm being torn from my body.

I've said too many goodbyes over the last three years. I can't handle anymore.

"He deserves more than that. Besides, my family is here, and his is there. One of us would have to give them up eventually. And I can't be the reason that one of us has to make that choice. I can't do that to either of us."

"The way he thinks that you and Brad, though, I..."

"I know." I screw my face up in disgust at myself for that Oscar-worthy performance. Maybe I should have a word with my agent and branch out into acting. "But it's the only way I could think of that would make him leave."

"Sure did that." Zoey exhales, leaning back in her seat.

"So, your bachelorette?" I say, moving onto topics that don't include heartbreak, lies, or absent bodyguards with gold-flecked green eyes.

"I'm thinking Rio." Zoey claps her hands in delight, and I grin at her, eager to step into her excitement. I'm her maid of honor and best friend. It's time I pulled myself out of my self-induced downward spiral and acted like it.

"Ooh, yes. Theme?"

"I don't know," she muses, gazing out at the street through the window we're sitting in front of. "Nothing too crass."

"No inflatable dicks, got it." I lean my chin in my hand and listen as she talks excitedly about what we can do there, and how Ashton will probably want to go and play golf or something that sounds equally boring. I'm so glad I'm not *his* best man.

We sit and chat for ages until Zoey's attention snags on something behind me. "Pap at twelve o'clock," she whispers.

I keep myself from turning around. They're entitled to come in for a coffee. This place has a well-earned reputation for the best beans within a fifteen-block radius. But I'd still rather not today. Some have a certain level of respect when you're inside somewhere. Out on the street you might as well have a flashing sign over your head inviting them to hound the heck out of you. But inside, drinking a coffee with your friend, you'd like to think some have a modicum of decency.

"Sinclair Beaufort?"

Not this one, it seems.

I turn and offer him a polite smile. He's doing his job, I get it. He probably has a wife and kids that he wants to put through college.

"Now I believe the hype over the coffee here, seeing you drinking it," he says, looking between Zoey and I with an easy smile.

I glance down at the camera on a strap that's slung over his arm. He makes no attempt to get it.

"It's as good as they say it is," I tell him.

"Listen." He clears his throat. "I don't want to disturb you any longer, but..."

I brace myself, waiting for it.

"... Can I have a quote?"

"Sure." I brighten. "About the foundation?"

I've been getting questions about it since going public a couple of days ago, and it's the one topic I'll happily talk about for hours.

"Yeah."

The reporter listens as I reel off some of the publicity spiel

I prepared with the new publicist I've hired to help run it with me.

"Thanks," he says, sounding genuinely grateful when I've finished. "No bodyguard anymore, then?" he adds casually as he hovers by our table.

"No. Not since..." I tip my head.

"Since Theodora Rielly was uncovered as the one leaving you anonymous threats." He nods in understanding.

"That's right."

"Rumor has it Mr. Layne's working for Jenessa Falcon in LA."

I keep my lips pressed tightly together at the mention of LA's latest sweetheart and Oscar winner. She's twenty-nine and looks like a walking TikTok filter, one of the ones that makes you look stunningly, unrealistically hot. Only with her, she actually looks like that. *Without makeup.*

"Bet the guys over there won't land a shot of her with him like this, though?" The reporter scrolls through the images on his camera and swivels the screen in my direction. Denver's holding the door open for me, one hand resting on my lower back, his eyes on my face.

And I'm gazing up at him like he came up with the cure to end all childhood cancers.

"Thought I'd struck gold there." The reporter chuckles and then clicks a button on the camera. *Delete.*

"Just a guy doing his job." I offer him a polite smile before he leaves.

"Jenessa Falcon?" Zoey's nose wrinkles in disgust.

But I know she's only being a good friend. There's nothing remotely concerning about Jenessa that's ever been reported on. She's Hollywood's darling.

She'll probably treat him better than I did.

But I still make a mental note not to watch her latest movie that just released. Every time I see her face now, I'll be picturing Denver's hand on her lower back, his eyes on her face as he opens the car door for her.

Her being the sole focus of his attention.

"I need another coffee," I declare. "You want one?" I ask Zoey as I rise from my chair.

"Yeah." She nods, her eyes softening with empathy as she stands with me. "But this time, I'll get them."

42

DENVER

THREE WEEKS EARLIER

"Do you like it? Mommy said we can paint it daffodil yellow."

My heart squeezes as Dixie takes the photograph of Lizzie and Rick out of the packing box and places it on the nightstand in her new bedroom.

"I think it's a great room," I say, resting my elbows on my thighs as I watch her unpack. "And yellow's a good choice."

"Daffodil," Dixie corrects, always a stickler for details. She gets that from her father.

My eyes settle on the frame on her nightstand, and I'm lost in thought, transported back to the day I took it.

"This one's a kicker," Rick says, his face breaking in half with a grin as he rests his hand over Lizzie's stomach.

She laughs and looks up at him.

That's when I take the photo, capturing the look of excitement between them.

None of us could have ever known it would be the last photo taken of them together.

"You've got that look again."

I glance up at Lizzie standing in the doorway, her hip cocked as she leans against the frame, watching me.

"What look?"

"That sad one." She spins her finger in a circle, gesturing to my face.

"No sadness," Dixie trills, happily skipping around her new room as she adds another trinket to a shelf.

They're both incredible. I don't know how they do it every day. But they do. Lizzie's never been one to let life get her down, and Dixie's inherited her positive nature. Losing Rick was one of the worst things to happen to them, but Lizzie's always told me that she's grateful for the time she had with him. And grateful that he gave her Dixie, despite him having to go before he even got to hold his own daughter.

I plaster what I hope is a less morose expression onto my face and Lizzie snorts.

"I guess that's an improvement."

She walks over and sits on the bed beside me. We watch Dixie together in silence for a few minutes as she happily continues unpacking and setting her new room up how she wants it.

"She's excited to start her new school Monday," Lizzie says quietly as Dixie runs from the room, saying she's going to get another box.

"Yeah? That's great."

"It is," Lizzie muses, a soft smile gracing her face. "I'll send you a photo of her before I drop her off. And she can call you after to tell you about it."

"Call me?"

Lizzie bumps her shoulder against mine in a move that's so comfortable and familiar that a lump forms in my throat. "You're not staying, Denver. You know it. I know it. Dixie knows it. I appreciate you flying over to help move us in. But—"

"But it's time I took my ugly ass back to New York?" I arch a brow at her.

She sighs. "I appreciate you more than I'll ever be able to tell you in words. And Rick would be so proud to call you his friend."

I clear my throat, willing the thick, aching lump in it to give me a fucking break.

"But we're okay. *We'll be okay.*"

"I've always been close to you both," I say.

"I know. And you can tell yourself you stayed in New York all these years because of us if you like. But we know that's not the only reason."

"You're my family," I rasp.

Lizzie rests her head on my shoulder, the weight a comfort that makes my chest burn. "We are. And we always will be. But you didn't just stay for us, and you know it. You stayed for her."

I swallow at the mere thought of who she's referring to.

"You saw someone as lost as you felt, and you didn't want to leave until you knew she was okay. I saw the stories about what happened to her family. Dixie and I... we've been doing good for a long time... But Sinclair... She's why you've stayed in New York all this time, and that's okay," Lizzie says softly.

I stare at my hands, letting her words soak in. "How did you know?"

Lizzie laughs gently. "The way you ran out of your apartment half-dressed after she knocked on your door and saw me there? Come on, Denver, you've never run after a woman in your life."

"True."

"You love her?"

"Yeah," I rasp.

"Then she's lucky to have you. You're an amazing guy. It's time you had some happiness of your own."

My mind flits to Brad Garrett-Charles and his tiny hard prick as I hauled his ass out of Sinclair's bed and my shoulders bunch up with tension.

"You're going back, aren't you?" Lizzie asks, lifting her head to study me.

I don't answer.

"Mommy? Can you help me?" Dixie calls from the other room.

Lizzie pats my thigh and stands. "I'm needed, Big Guy. Back in a minute."

I nod at her, then pull my phone out of my cargo pants as she leaves the room. I bring up the tracking app that I've been looking at multiple times a day. Monty's small blue dot is at Sterling's place again. But the larger one has disappeared.

I go to my contacts and hit call.

"She asked me to disable it." Killian's regretful confession comes the second he answers my call, sensing what I'm about to say.

"And you fucking did it?" I snap.

"I had no choice. She watched me until I did."

I let out a low curse. "Sorry," I mutter. "It's not your fault."

"No problem," he says, giving me more grace than I deserve.

"How is she?" I ask, clearing my throat. I can't bring myself to ask after her using her name.

Killian's pause has me screwing my eyes shut and balling my free hand into a fist.

"She's... I've seen her look better," he admits.

"Jesus," I rasp, squeezing until my knuckles turn white.

"What happened between you two?" he asks.

My eyes roam over Dixie's new bedroom and my heart pangs at how excited she is about moving here and having a new adventure with her mom.

"Everything," I confess. "Fucking everything."

Two weeks earlier

I pin Molly's picture to the cabin's refrigerator and lean back against the kitchen counter to admire it. Sinclair's hair takes up half of the paper as she holds Monty's leash, and I look like a black blob with a giant frown. She's even given me a mono-brow, drawn on with thick brown crayon.

I fucking love everything about it.

Even down to the smoothie sticker I have stuck on my head like a hat.

You want a peach of me? it reads, across the smiling fruit.

My eyes drop to the one sticking to the side of the now empty takeaway cup I picked up this morning. *Orange you glad to see me?*

"Pull it to-fucking-gether," I berate myself, pushing off from the counter and heading outside to chop some wood for something to do.

I thought I'd come here for the night to check on the place. But the second I walked through the door, she was here. Smiling at me in the kitchen as I made her breakfast. Lounging in front of the fire, rubbing Monty's belly as she chatted to me with an easiness she never had before.

Looking up with her trusting eyes beneath me on that damn gym mat.

Dropping to her knees for me in the shower.

Resting her head against my chest as she slept in my bed.

Even her damn panties from that first time are still here, tucked away in a drawer next to my bed, like a secret love note.

They still smell of her.

It's the first thing I checked when I found them. I couldn't get that tiny scrap of lace to my nose fast enough. I was a suffocating man given air with seconds to spare before his life would have ended. I bet I looked crazy as fuck sinking to the floor as I held them to me, groaning her name.

I can't fucking escape her.

Nor do I want to.

I head outside and take out my frustration on a log, building up a sweat before discarding my T-shirt, and going back at it. The sound of approaching tires rolling over the dirt track makes me look up.

"Buck said you were back," Georgia calls with a smile from her blue truck as she kills the engine and hops out.

"News sure travels fast around here," I say, laying my axe down.

She used to do this, show up when I was here. We fucked a few times, three, maybe four. I can't remember, yet it's a low enough number that I *should* be able to remember them all. She knew it was casual, I told her enough times. I didn't want a relationship. My job came before all else. And that meant the Beauforts. That meant Sinclair.

Her eyes drop over my heaving chest as I get my breath back.

"Girlfriend not come this time?"

"She stayed in the city," I reply, grabbing my water bottle and downing half of it.

Georgia doesn't even try to keep her tone polite. "Best place for her. She was out of her depth here; a city girl like her. She's a model, right?"

"Yeah," I clip, knowing she must have looked Sinclair up since we were last here.

"Didn't have you down as going for that type?"

"Really?" I say, uninterested as I screw the lid back on my bottle with a little too much force.

"Yeah, you know." She shrugs. "The one's without much going on up here." She taps her temple.

"You're right," I agree, tossing my bottle back down onto the tree stump I had it on. "I used to mess around with those bitchy types. The ones who put other women down."

Georgia falters, then breaks out into a laugh. "Denny, you're funny."

I level her with a look that makes her laugh die. "Sinclair's smart. And compassionate. And yes, she's beautiful, so sometimes people miss the other things about her and just judge the outside."

Georgia bristles, picking up the cold detachment in my eyes as I look at her. "She's also in Manhattan while you're here. Alone. Didn't she have time in her busy schedule to come and be with you? Or was one trip away from Fifth Avenue enough for her?"

"I'll tell her you stopped by and asked after her," I say with a tight look that is far from friendly.

Then I pick up my axe and split the piece of wood I have set up clean in half.

◆

One week earlier

My coffee's going cold, sitting untouched in the center console of my car. I haven't been able to take a sip for the past hour. I've been too focused. Just like all the other times over the past three weeks.

But this time it's different. This time I've gotten reckless and positioned myself so close that I don't know how I've not been seen. Then again, people don't always see what they're not expecting to be there.

My phone rings and I hit the speaker button, my eyes remaining fixed on target.

"Denver?"

"Sullivan?" I reply, running a finger over my lips as another person enters from the street.

A woman with a toddler. Low threat.

"How's LA?" Sullivan asks.

I purse my lips. "Warm, I expect."

"I'm calling to ask you to come back," he says, missing what I just said.

"I can't do that."

"The guys Dad is interviewing are shit."

"I can send you some recommendations," I say, not biting.

"Fuck off." He exhales. "He doesn't need some guy that's *like* you. He needs *you*."

My lips curl up. Sullivan can get straight to the point when he wants something.

"How's Sinclair? She still working out with her trainer?" I ask, not bothering to work up to obtaining the confirmation I want from him.

If he's going to get straight to it, so am I.

"Brad Garrett-Charles? That jerk?" He scoffs with disdain.

This time, my lips really do curl up. I've always liked Sullivan.

"She hasn't worked out with him since before they tried to snatch Monty. And she won't again. He's moved to LA. His new girlfriend has some reality TV show she's filming there, or something. Sinclair didn't even go to his leaving party. Told me she was bathing Monty that night."

My breath rumbles in my chest like a purr. "Good."

Sullivan sighs. "My meeting's about to start. Same fucking time tomorrow?" he grits.

I smirk. "Same fucking time. Same fucking answer."

He curses me as he hangs up.

Our daily calls are always the same. He asks me to come back from LA. I tell him I can't.

Because a person can't return from a place they never moved to in the first place.

The door to the coffee place opens again as a young couple enter. My line of sight is obstructed for less than a second. But it's long enough to have me tensing and sitting forward in my seat.

Blonde hair comes into view as they move out of the way, and my shoulders relax with my rough exhale.

"There you are, Princess," I rasp, taking in the anguish on her face as she talks to Zoey. The sight of it is like a thousand swords to my heart.

But I know her, and she isn't ready yet.

Almost. But not quite.

"Not much longer now," I say, my eyes drinking her in like I haven't spent the past two hours watching her like a hawk. "Not much longer, Princess. I promise."

43

SINCLAIR

The second I walk into my apartment, I can sense something is different.

"Monty, wait," I instruct, hovering in the doorway, my eyes darting down the hallway toward the open-plan living area. I tilt my head and listen but there are no other sounds except my heartbeat in my ears.

I pull my phone from my purse and bring up the app Denver installed after he informed me he'd increased the security at my place. He showed me how to use it, but I didn't think I'd ever need to. He was with me all the time.

I fumble with the settings until I find the camera footage for the past couple of hours. Monty and I are leaving for his walk, so I speed past that until I find what I'm looking for.

My throat goes dry.

I drop Monty's leash, and he races inside, barking.

That's what's different. I should have recognized it immediately.

The tinge of mint and herb in the air.

Him.

"What the hell?" I squeak as Denver walks into my apartment with purposeful strides.

There's no mistaking that it's him. I'd recognize his broad shoulders and that painfully strong beautiful profile he has anywhere.

He looks at the camera in the hallway, knowing exactly where it is. His eyes darken with intensity as he stares at it for a few seconds, like he knows I will see this.

Like he's looking right at me.

I clamp a hand over my mouth, tears pricking at my eyes. He looks incredible, dressed in his usual black suit and tie and white shirt. Three weeks has made me wilt and fade. But every pound I've lost, he seems to have found, in muscle and pure raw manliness.

"What are you doing? Why aren't you in LA?" I whisper as I follow him on the cameras through the living area and into the kitchen. He opens the refrigerator and places something inside.

I pause the footage and run to the kitchen. Monty is going mad, racing around the place, nose glued to the floor as he tracks the trail Denver must have left.

Flinging open the refrigerator, I see what he's left for me immediately. It's hard not to. I have almost nothing inside. Why does a girl need food when all she can stomach is coffee made the way the man she loves and pushed away likes it?

My fingers tremble as I close them around the cold cardboard, taking the smoothie cup out. There's a sticker on the side with a whole fruit basket on it, and the text:

You better get juiced to my jokes.

I sob out a half cry, half laugh as tears spring free and race down my cheeks.

Why would he come in here and leave this for me?

I put the straw in my mouth and suck. Flavor bursts across

my tongue and I screw my eyes shut, swallowing down the first fresh thing I've tasted in days.

I drink the entire thing within a minute, crying the entire time.

I play the camera footage again and Denver walks into my bedroom. He puts something on my pillow and his lips move. My fingers are clumsy as I rush to rewind it and turn the volume up so I can make out what he's saying.

"I never gave you this back. I'm so sorry, Sinclair. Sullivan had it tested. It's not him."

My eyes are blurry as I stumble into my bedroom.

The diamond is glinting against the white silk, its chain like a thin golden snake curling around it. I pick it up and let it dangle from my fingers as I sink onto the bed.

Monty comes and sits by my feet, whining as he looks at it twirling around in a circle.

"It's not him, Monty," I whisper, my voice so small it's almost nonexistent.

He paws at my leg, and I reach down to stroke him, curling my fingers around the silky tufts of hair on his ears. I knew the moment Theo so cruelly told me that these weren't my brother's ashes that she was telling the truth. I don't know how, I just did. But it hasn't stopped me from missing the weight of it around my neck. It's been the one thing I've held on to for so long, desperately trying to maintain some kind of connection to him.

The chain slips through my fingers and drops to the floor.

"We've lost both of them," I whisper to Monty as I play the footage and watch Denver walk out of my apartment without looking at the camera again.

"We've lost both of them."

44

DENVER

The security guy who answers the door at Seasons eyes me up and down.

"Denver? What are you doing back, Buddy?"

I clasp his hand in mine, and we shake. "Just come to talk with Sterling."

"He's interviewing for your replacement."

"Still?"

The guy chuckles. "Apparently he thinks you're hot shit or something, because none of these chumps have measured up yet."

I tilt my head at the door further down the hallway behind him that leads to Sterling's office. "Can I?"

"Go ahead. I think they'll all be glad of a break. Sullivan and Mal are in there with him," he adds.

I nod and stride down the hallway, opening the door at the end. There are three guys in dark suits sitting on chairs, lined up outside Sterling's closed office door. All six eyes flick up to take me in, assessing me for the level of competition I pose.

One of them clears his throat as I walk past the empty chair beside him and head straight to the door.

"I wouldn't interrupt them," someone else pipes up as I lift my fist to knock on the door. "Last guy just about pissed himself when he walked out."

I turn and my eyes connect with Killian's as he walks in from the direction of the main bar.

"Bet Jenson would have loved cleaning that up," I reply.

Killian breaks into a grin and pulls me into a hug. "You're a slippery beast. Anyone else wouldn't have gotten away with it," he says low enough that only I hear.

"I'm impressed," I say, clapping him on the back.

"What can I say? I was taught by the best."

I pull back and look at him. "The others?"

He gives a swift shake of his head. "If they know, then they haven't said a word. Neither have I."

"Appreciate it," I say, holding his eyes.

"I don't know how you fucking did it. There's no way I could have spent three weeks watching the woman..." He glances at the guys waiting to be interviewed, then leads me farther down the hallway, away from them. "I couldn't have spent three weeks watching her the way you did. I'd have gone crazy and needed to speak to her."

"She needed space. And time," I say. And the fact is, I've spent years keeping an eye on Sinclair from afar while working for her family. It was my job.

And these last few weeks, it's become my salvation.

Watching her. Seeing the way she's been without me. Knowing for a fact she hasn't seen that fucker Brad Garrett-Charles once since the night of the party. My girl has been walking around, heartbreak as clear as day in every move she's made.

She loves me.

She just chose wrong. And I understand why she did it.

"You come to get shit out in the open, then? Got to say, I

don't envy you for having to go in there with all three of them."

I press my lips together, refusing to let apprehension slip in.

"I was always going to have to tell him. If it wasn't me, then there would have been a day she met some other guy and I'd have had to tell him why I needed to leave."

"Good luck. I'll come to your funeral," Killian says.

I walk to Sterling's office door and three pairs of eyes bounce to me again as I knock heavily on it.

It opens and Mal's brows shoot up his forehead as he takes me in. His eyes drop over my suit and tie.

"Here for the interview?" he asks.

"Sure am."

He grins.

"Position's been filled!" he barks at the three guys waiting on chairs. "Killian will show you out." He inclines his head, calling over his shoulder into Sterling's office. "Thanks for coming, but you didn't get it."

A big guy steps out as Mal stands to one side to let him pass. He looks me up and down with an unimpressed grunt, muttering something about how I must be fucking superman to be picked.

Mal holds out an arm, inviting me in. "About time. Whatever shit you've been up to, couldn't you have done it faster? I've done so many interviews my brain's ready to pack the hell up if I have to ask one more fucking question." He snorts out an amused chuckle as I step into the room, and he closes the door behind us with an ominous thud.

Two pairs of blue eyes immediately pin onto me like laser targets.

"Tomorrow's phone call's canceled then?" Sullivan clips.

"Yeah, it's canceled," I say, glancing at him.

"About fucking time," he mutters, leaning back in his seat, his ankle resting over the top of his other leg.

Sterling runs a hand over his jaw, studying me from his seat behind his large wooden desk. I don't take a seat. I don't step further into the room as Mal walks over and throws himself into a chair with a sigh. I don't move an inch.

I wait.

"How was your flight back?" Sterling asks finally, his eyes narrowed and calculating. "Admire any sights while you were there? Bet there's a lot to look at. A man can probably spend hours sitting around... watching."

I consider my answer as he holds my gaze without an ounce of discomfort.

He knows. I suspected as much. I've worked side by side with him for years. He knows me as well as anyone can. And the man misses nothing.

Sullivan and Mal remain silent, but both of their eyes track between Sterling and I, no doubt sensing there's a hidden undercurrent to his words.

Outrage. Admiration. Pity?

I haven't figured out which.

The night I called him and said I needed to see him, he didn't hesitate to open the door of his home to me. He never asked why I was turning up in the middle of the night to hand over my resignation for a job I've dedicated my entire existence to for years. He didn't ask why I was so mad my hands wouldn't stop shaking unless I kept them clenched into fists.

He didn't ask a single question.

He just said one thing.

"Thank you."

He thanked me for everything. He didn't need an explanation.

He trusted me.

He's always trusted me.

"I'm in love with Sinclair," I say into the silence of the room.

"What?" Mal scoffs.

"Fucking hell," Sullivan mutters.

Sterling leans back in his chair, a picture of complete calm and authority. "How long?"

I inhale slowly, my nostrils expanding. "Long enough that I no longer know what it feels like not to love her. Nor do I want to know."

"So you aren't back here to get your job back?"

"No, sir."

"You're here for my daughter? The one I asked you to protect?"

"That's correct."

Silence engulfs the room until he tips his head, thinking. "And if I don't give you my blessing?"

I can't stop the way my eyes hold his, burning into his gaze as every cell in my body goes on high alert. My fingers flex by my sides and a cracking of the bones inside them echoes around the room.

Sterling narrows his eyes at me and they gleam with amusement. "You think you could take me?"

"With respect, I *would* take you. If it was for her, I would take every last damn man breathing, and not even break a fucking sweat."

Sterling chuckles, but Sullivan and Mal remain deathly silent, watching the two of us.

"I must say, Denver." He sighs. "I'm disappointed."

The air leaves my lungs like I've been punched in the gut.

"I'm sorry that I didn't tell you sooner," I say with a sincerity that I feel in my bones.

He shakes his head. "Not saying the words to me, doesn't mean I didn't know. You might think you know Sinclair better than anyone. But she's *my daughter*.

Remember that. I will always be the man who loved her first."

The room is so fucking silent you could hear a pin drop.

There's both a threat and acceptance in Sterling's words.

And I hear and respect both.

I clear my throat. "Yes, sir."

"You should have damn well come to me sooner," he growls.

"Sir," I repeat, standing firm and unmoving, waiting for him to make his next move. He still hasn't indicated whether he's considering running me out of the States, making sure I never work close protection again, or worse.

"Like I said, I'm *disappointed*," he says again, dragging out the word like a knife across my throat.

I hold his eyes, refusing to back down. He can say what he wants to me. He can tear me the fuck down with words. But I'll stand here and take it without blinking if it means I'm one second closer to getting back to her.

"Disappointed that it took you so goddamn long to act on it." His eyes glitter as I frown in confusion.

"My daughter is special, Denver. I wasn't going to assign any man to be her bodyguard. To spend all that time with her. To be the one she placed her faith into. The one she would grow close to."

I thought that my time in the military and undergoing mock hostage training would have made me unshakeable. But it takes everything in me not to curse out loud in shock. I blink in rapid succession, my heart banging against my ribs as I look into his unwavering gaze.

"I trust you with my life. Now I'm trusting you with my daughter."

"Jesus, Dad," Sullivan rasps.

"You sly old fucker." Mal chuckles.

Sterling's eyes crinkle at the corners, still glued to mine.

"My daughter hired a dating coach all the way from England to find her father love. And now I have Hallie and a baby coming and feel like the luckiest man in the world. You know what I asked her?"

"No, sir," I reply, my mind still reeling that he knew. All this time, he had set us up.

And we thought we were the ones keeping a secret from him.

"I asked her why she didn't hire Hallie to find love for her. Because we all damn well know how much my daughter has needed someone these past couple of years."

I force a swallow, but my throat is so thick even breathing is tough.

Sterling runs a hand around his jaw again, his eyes softening at the memory. "She told me seeing the people she loves being happy is more important to her. That she would be happy knowing I was happy."

"She's incredible like that," I say, my voice coming out with an uncharacteristic crack to it, that I mask.

"She sure is," Sterling says, before pausing. "She won't put herself first, Denver."

His statement hangs in the air. I know what he's asking, no, *telling* me to do. I know, because it's been my main objective ever since I first laid eyes on her, long before she ever looked at me with anything other than indifference in her eyes.

He doesn't need to worry.

It's like I told Sinclair, that's what I do.

And it's what I will continue to do while there is life in my body.

I'm the asshole who will fucking die for her... and not because it was once my job.

"She won't need to. I'll do that for her. She will always come first. I swear on my life. I won't let—"

"—me down?" Sterling clips. "I damn well hope not."

I shake my head. "Her. I won't let *her* down."

"Better." He smiles.

"I should have known," Sullivan grumbles. "You played sleeping fucking lions."

Mal snorts and looks at me. "No way."

"Practically threw his gun at me to get down on the floor with my sister," Sullivan grunts.

I keep stock still. Any movement I make, anything I say, will risk my composure cracking. Because the mere mention of her and the floor brings me right back to that moment I pushed inside her for the first time on the gym mat.

The minute I knew there was no fucking going back. That I had to have her no matter what.

And the blood on my dick after was the confirmation I'd known all along.

Sinclair belongs with me.

She always has. She always will.

"You're a sucker for punishment taking on my sister. She pulls some shit," Sullivan says.

"Don't fucking speak about her like that," I warn on instinct.

Sullivan glances at me with growing respect as though I passed some secret test he's set me. Then he smirks at me and tips his chin. "Good luck. You'll need it."

"Welcome to the family." Mal leans back in his seat, chuckling like he could sit here all day, drinking this in. His eyes travel to Sterling's, and they exchange a look of amusement.

And beneath it is complete solidarity.

These are the Beauforts.

They're one of the country's most powerful, influential families.

And regardless of blood, now they're mine. But even though Mal might have been the first one to say it, Sterling made it known that first day, when he gave Lizzie and Dixie the new start they needed.

When he helped out my family and grew his own, all at the same time. Because no matter what else could have happened after that day. I would always have been grateful to him, connected to him.

"Now get the hell out of here." Sterling smirks.

I nod. "Yes, sir."

"Excuse me?" He lifts a lone brow and my lips curl.

"Yes, *Boss*," I reply.

"I expect you in bright and early tomorrow, Denver. Don't think you'll get special privileges just because my daughter likes you," he says.

I can't help myself.

I take my first real deep breath since I stepped over the threshold into his office.

"*Loves* me," I correct.

He holds my eyes, his glittering.

"Yeah… damn well loves you. Now get the hell out of my office." He flicks his fingers at me, chuckling.

"Yes, Boss," I say again, doing exactly as he says.

45

SINCLAIR

THE KNOCKING AT MY DOOR DOESN'T REGISTER TO begin with. I place my smoothie cup down on the kitchen counter to answer it. Monty flies past me, almost knocking me over.

"It'll be Sullivan," I tell him with a sigh. It's been heartbreaking seeing him race to the door every time someone calls. He's always pleased to see whoever it is, but I know he's hoping it's Denver. And since I found my necklace on my pillow three days ago, a small part of me has still held out hope that it could him too.

But it's not.

He'll be back in LA now. When I told Killian he'd been here, he looked at me and shook his head. *"Sorry, Sin. He was just here tying up some loose ends."*

He came all the way back to New York, and he didn't even want to speak to me, or see me face to face. I can't blame him. He probably thought I'd be with Brad.

Monty's barking and scratching wildly at the base of the door. He can probably smell Molly if she's with Sullivan. He adores her.

I open the door without checking the peephole and Monty flies out.

"Hey, Moll—"

My eyes are cast down at the height I'm expecting my niece's face to be. But instead of her, there are two black suited legs, and a large hand fussing Monty as he scrabbles against them like he's trying to climb up to their face so he can assault them with licks.

"Go on, Boy. Sit," a deep, authoritative voice commands.

Monty does as he's told and backs through the doorway, his butt wiggling side to side as he sits beside me, obediently.

My throat goes dry as my visitor lifts his head, straightening up to full height.

And then I'm staring into gold-flecked green.

"Denver?" I breathe.

He doesn't react. His eyes give nothing away as he stares at me with a cold detachment that has my heart falling to my feet. I curl my hand around the door for support, willing myself not to give in to the burning tears threatening my eyes.

His eyes drop, scanning over my body ruthlessly in my vest and sweatpants. I feel naked and exposed as his attention snags on where I've had to roll the waistband over itself to keep them up where I've lost weight. His brow furrows like he's pissed.

He continues his inspection of me, and I shiver, goosebumps pricking up over my arms as I drag in a shaky breath and the scent of him fills my senses. I breathe in quickly again, just to convince myself that it's real. That he's really standing in front of me.

"Den—"

He lifts two fingers in the air, silencing me.

His eyes leave my waist and move up my chest. Air puffs from between my lips in a soft pant as my nipples pebble painfully beneath my vest at his attention. His eyes glide over them swiftly, and my stomach drops as he displays no interest.

Jaw set firm, his eyes dark and closed off, all muscle and solid strength. His gun holstered at his hip, just visible beneath his open jacket.

He looks downright terrifying.

Finally, he looks at my face. *Really* looks. He stares at my jaw, at my trembling lips, at my hair falling against one cheek.

Then he looks into my eyes.

I don't move. I don't *breathe*.

"I'm going to ask you once. And this time, you tell me the truth," he says, his voice a rough, deep gravel that I desperately cling on to, taking in every note after weeks of silence.

I nod. "I promise."

His eyes pinch at the corners a fraction, the tiniest fragment of emotion flashing through them before he blinks it away. "Brad Garrett-Charles?" he says.

The air leaves my lungs in a rush, and I lean into the door, my nails digging into the wood to hold me up. "No," I sob. "What you saw at the party... he *never* touched me."

"You knew I was coming, didn't you?"

My voice shakes as I nod. "I called Sullivan, and he told me you were on your way back. I knew you'd come here."

"You wanted me to walk in and find you in bed with another man."

"Yes," I whisper, my heart breaking in two at my confession.

"Not just any man, Sinclair..."

My breath catches as he says my name, and I clamp a hand over my mouth, willing myself not to throw up.

"... Brad Garrett-Charles," Denver hisses.

His voice is so low, so dangerous, that I can barely keep my eyes on his. But I have to. He's come here, demanding the truth. Lying to him the first time broke me. I can't survive it again.

"I knew he was the one y-y-y..." I drag in a shaky breath. "The one who y-you'd hate to find me with the most."

"Damn fucking straight."

I blink as I hold his gaze. There's no warmth in his. Nothing to ease the churning inside my gut at what I did to him. The way I let him think I would throw everything we had away like it meant nothing.

I hurt him. I thought I had to. But the second I did it and saw his reaction that night, the doubts started. And they've clawed and scratched at me ever since.

"How are Lizzie and Dixie?" I ask, a pathetic part of me needing to know that he's happy. That they're all happy and living in the sunshine together in LA. That I made the right choice. Because him hating me would be worth it, knowing that he has that.

"Keep talking!"

The venom in his voice makes the tears welling in my eyes spill over. I wipe them away with the heel of my hand. I can't cry in front of him. Not when I did this. I *chose* this. I made him look at me in the way he is now—like he despises me.

And I have to live with that decision.

"Brad called over to see me that day I met them at your place," I confess. "I was thinking about them moving away without you... and I was crying and he... he offered to help me. I knew you'd never leave New York if you knew how much I wanted you to stay."

"Tell me about the party, Sinclair," Denver prompts.

I swallow, hating the business-like brusqueness of his voice.

"I asked him to go into my room with me, so you'd find us together. He wasn't supposed to take his clothes off. He did that himself. Maybe he thought..." I screw my face up, before I continue. "I had a full body support set on beneath that T-shirt. He'd have needed industrial shears to get me out of that thing if he'd dared to try."

"Support set?" Denver clips.

"Yeah, it's—"

"I know what it is," he grits.

"Oh."

Silence stretches between us as I soak in every second of having his eyes on mine. Because this might be the last time I ever get to see them, to admire their beauty. To sink into the feeling of safety they've given me. Nothing else has ever come close to making me feel that way in years.

"I thought you believed it," I whisper.

"No."

That same response of his.

One word. Nothing more. So simple. Straight to the point.

"But you were so angry. You yelled and then you stormed off."

"Because I knew exactly what you were doing."

"I..."

"I know you, Sinclair. I know you better than you give me credit for. Tell me, what do you hate people doing for you?"

"Making decisions for me."

"Making decisions for you," Denver repeats. "And yet there you fucking were, willing to make one for me when I didn't need you to. I told you I was staying. I told you I *loved* you. What else did you need?"

"I'm sorry," I choke. "I'm so sorry. I know what it's like to lose your family. I couldn't be the reason you lost yours."

"I wasn't losing them. They were moving on with their lives, that's all. And I'm happy for them. I thought I was moving on with mine too. *With you.*"

"But they're your family, you told me yourself that they stopped you from drowning."

"No longer drowning can mean you're still only floating. Going nowhere. You gave me something to swim toward, Sinclair. I have loved you for so long. And I've been waiting for you to understand that."

"Is that why you've not come back in all these weeks? You wanted to punish me for what I did?" I sob.

I would deserve it if that's what this has been, some carefully planned retaliation to teach me a lesson. But it doesn't mean that it doesn't cut deep, stinging my flesh knowing that he would willingly put me through it. I haven't been able to sleep or eat. I've barely been human.

"No, Princess," he breathes with the first hint of tenderness in his eyes since I opened the door.

My chest caves in a giant whimper as I grab on to that sliver of softness, praying he doesn't snatch it away again.

"I gave you the space you *needed*. I couldn't come back until you knew what it was like to be apart. I needed you to understand what it'll be like to live without each other. I needed you to be sure."

"I hate it," I confess in a haunted croak. "I hate not waking up next to you. I hate not hearing your voice. I hate not feeling your a-a-arms around me." My teeth chatter and I swallow hard to get control back over my body. "*I love you, Denver.* I love you so much.... so much that I couldn't risk the chance you'd look at me one day and resent me for making you stay here."

"You love me, Princess?"

My heart leaps into my throat. "More than anything."

His expression softens and I suck in a breath, willing myself not to collapse into a heap on the floor at the way his eyes roam over my face.

"I'm coming inside now," he breathes.

"Okay," I squeak.

I stand back and let him enter. His scent follows him, and it takes a lot of effort to close the door with my trembling hands behind him.

I wipe my palms on my sweatpants as I look at him, standing in my hallway, all big and broody, and *real*.

"I'm glad you're here," I say, hovering by the door, not knowing whether to move or not.

Monty is sitting by my feet and the gentle swish of his tail side to side against the floor brings a calm to me that I desperately need. Because I want to ask Denver if he's here for good. If he's staying. Or if this is just a visit. Because as much as I want to grasp onto what he just said about giving me time, he hasn't actually said—

"I love you, Sinclair."

I blink at him as he steps forward and pulls me to him, one hand curling around my hip, and the other taking hold of my neck.

His touch is gentle and strong. But burning with possession.

"I fucking love you, Princess."

He slants his mouth over mine and kisses me.

A sob unfurls in my throat, and he holds me up as I cry into his mouth, a whimpering wreck as he undoes the damage that weeks apart has done with each stroke of his tongue.

"Don't ever put yourself in danger for me again," he rasps, dragging his lips over mine before he surges forward and kisses me again, stealing the air from my mouth.

"I wasn't in any—"

The warning growl vibrates up his chest, and I swallow it down with his kiss, my words ceasing immediately.

"Don't ever pull a fucking stunt that involves another man, or any damn thing that is designed to make me leave you, got it?"

"I'm sorry," I choke.

My lips tremble against his as he holds me in place with his palm around my throat. His thumb gently traces the edge of my jaw as he licks his lips, the tip of his tongue grazing my tingling ones and making me moan.

"Because, Sinclair," he rasps, his whisper so hoarse and delicious that it sets butterflies swarming in my core. "... nothing you do will ever stop me from loving you. It'll never make me leave you, got it? I know you've said goodbye to too many people already. I will *not* be one of them, understand?"

My throat presses against his warm palm, and I dissolve into chest-wrenching sobs. "I-I-I'm sorry."

"Ssh," he soothes.

"Are you moving back?" I ask, not caring that I sound desperate. He's right. He does know me. I can't hide from him. And I don't want to even try anymore. "Denver, are you coming back?"

"Princess, I never left."

"What do you mean?" I search his eyes and they burn into mine.

"I helped them move into their new place in LA, then I flew straight back."

"You've been here this whole time?"

He frowns like he can't believe I ever thought he would really go. "You belong with me, like I belong with you. There's no way I was taking my eyes off you for a second longer than absolutely necessary."

I stare at him as I make sense of his words. "You've been here? *Watching me?*"

I lean back so I can study his eyes. His pupils blow wide as doubt creeps into them.

"That makes it sound—"

"Creepy?" I whisper.

His brows knot. "Sin—"

"You never left me?" I say in awe, shaking my head. "I don't find it creepy. I find it insane and kind of hot that you're that obsessed with me..." I tease, my pummeled heart coming back to life for the first time in weeks. "But... *You never left me.*"

"No," he breathes. "I couldn't."

"You couldn't leave me," I repeat, my eyes dropping to his lips. "I love that you went all secret stalker Brute on me."

"Sinclair," he bites with an edge of warning, "I wasn't stalking you. I was—"

"Kiss me again," I order, feeling emboldened by his confession.

He never left me. He couldn't physically leave me.

His mouth is back on mine, and this time, my hands stop shaking and they sink into his hair, grabbing it and pulling him closer, remembering who I am, remembering who he is.

The man I love.

The only one I've ever loved.

"It didn't count," I gasp between his all-consuming kisses as he keeps me pinned in place with his strong hands, melding my body to his, exactly how he wants it. "I lied when I said it did. You were—"

"... your first," he growls, nipping my lower lip between his teeth. "I know, Princess. I own all of your firsts. They're mine."

"They are," I whimper, kissing him again, my head tilted back so he can devour my mouth from where he's towering above me.

Heat pools between my thighs at his possessiveness over me.

I love it. The way it makes me feel treasured, desired, *safe*.

"Did you watch me in the shower?" I ask.

"What?" he snaps, breaking our kiss. "Fuck no, I wouldn't do that without you knowing."

"Okay," I say, unable to stop my pout. "So you didn't watch me naked? You didn't miss me that much?"

"Such a fucking princess," he scolds, pulling my lips back to his for another searing kiss.

It's like I've been brought back to life, each kiss of his injecting energy back into me again. I kiss him with a matching fire as he pieces me back together, making me stronger than before. Reminding me of who the woman he fell in love with is.

"Denver? I need…"

"You need me to prove to you I'm not lying when I said I won't ever leave you?"

I shiver as his words roll over my skin and his lips travel to my neck, pressing gently beneath my ear, over my pulse.

"God, yes, *please*."

"First you tell me what you want," he rasps, peppering kisses down my neck toward my collarbone.

I close my eyes to the toe-curling sensation of having him here with his arms around me and his mouth on me again.

"Start talking," he tsks, kissing his way along to the top of my shoulder.

"I want you to stay," I say, letting out a moan as he uses one finger to slide the strap of my vest off my shoulder, before he kisses the inch of exposed skin left behind.

"What else?" he murmurs, moving to the other side and repeating the move.

The fingers curled around my hip flex, and he lets out a groan as I writhe in ecstasy from having his mouth on me, making my hipbone rub over his hard dick in his pants.

"I want you to open the door for me and get moody when I try to do it myself to wind you up."

He dips his head lower and sucks the swell of my breast above the neckline of my vest, an amused grumble leaving his hot mouth as I arch into him.

The Rule Breaker

"Keep going," he husks.

"And I want you to hate all of my footwear and glare at it in that way that makes you look so hot and moody that I want to sit on your face, so you take your frustration out between my thighs instead."

He yanks my vest down with a rough curse and pulls my nipple into his mouth.

"God!" I cry, tipping my head back and soaking up the ecstasy that's pulsing through my veins.

"What else?" he asks, sucking on it until it's on the brink of being painful.

A surge of wetness soaks my panties.

"I want to be able to taste vanilla coffee again from your lips when you kiss me. Because I hate the way it tastes from a mug. It makes me cry when I taste it from a mug."

"Princess," he soothes, "you'll never have to drink it from a mug again, I promise." His touch softens as he switches to my other breast and rolls his tongue around my nipple in slow, sensual circles.

My voice catches in my throat. "I want to love you, Denver. I want to just be in love with you and tell you every day. Because I do... I love you *so much*."

"That's my girl," he breathes, rising up to kiss me on the mouth again. "Anything else?"

"I want to get Monty a girlfriend. I think he feels left out."

Denver's brows shoot up and he whips his head to the side, his eyes connecting with Monty, who's still sitting exactly where he told him to stay.

His tail wags faster as he gazes at us with bright eyes.

"You need a girlfriend," Denver says to him seriously, pulling my vest up to cover up my breasts.

The move makes me giggle. "Monty doesn't care if we're naked."

"No way is he watching, Princess. I want you all to myself."

Denver grabs my hand and strides off. I follow him into the kitchen where he goes straight to the cabinet where I keep Monty's special treats; the chews that take him hours to get through.

Denver holds one out in his hand. "Here, Boy." He hands it to Monty, then points to the living room. "Off you go."

Monty trots off happily and I stare after him. I have him well-trained, but that's something else.

"He really likes you," I say.

"You're right. He never liked Brad Garrett-Charles though."

I smile at his gruff moodiness. "No, you're right, he didn't."

I turn back to meet his eyes, but they're lowered, studying my sweatpants.

"You're wearing too many clothes," he grits. "Bed. Naked. Now."

I don't move. His nostrils flare as he bundles me up into his arms.

"I can see I've got three weeks of spoiled behavior to fuck right out of you."

I wrap my arms around his neck, biting back my grin as he takes us into my bedroom and kicks the door closed behind us. My clothes are dragged off me in seconds, followed by his.

I lie on the bed and stare at him as he kneels between my thighs, drinking me in.

"You're beautiful," he rasps, his eyes roaming all over my body.

"Everyone says I've gotten too thin," I say, suddenly self-conscious.

Denver's green eyes lift to mine and the adoration in them makes my heart skip a beat.

"You. Are. Beautiful," he repeats. "And now that I'm back, I'll make sure you eat properly, Princess. I'll cook for you; you don't need to worry."

"You saying I can't cook?"

"I'm saying you won't cook because I will. I want to take care of you, and you're going to let me."

He brings his body down over mine, sealing his mouth over mine in a kiss that sets my heart racing.

"Yes," I whimper, arching up to get closer to him. I'd agree to pretty much anything he wants right now. I just need him to touch me and never stop.

"Good girl," he murmurs. "But it wasn't a question. I take care of what's *mine*. Now hold on."

That's all the warning I get before he grasps one of my thighs and pushes it wide, thrusting into me in one swift move.

"Denver!" I grab onto his shoulders, sinking my nails into his flesh.

He tuts. "So fucking greedy and wet for me that I didn't even need to touch you and you're taking every inch of my cock straight away."

I mewl as he pumps his hips, sliding into me with deep, delicious, pump after pump.

"I love you, Sinclair," he says, leaning down to kiss me again.

I wrap my arms around his neck, holding him to me as he sinks his body into mine over and over.

"I love you too."

He pulls back far enough to look into my eyes as he slides a hand between our bodies until his fingers brush my swollen clit.

"The things I'm going to do to you tonight, Princess. But first I just want this."

"This?" I whimper, gazing into his eyes as he rubs my clit and my pussy clenches around him.

"Yeah, this," he murmurs. "You looking into my eyes and telling me you love me as I make you come. *I've missed you.*"

I almost do exactly as he says on the spot just from the look in his eyes as he watches me. They're so full of dominance and heat... but most of all, total and utter devotion.

"I love you," I whisper.

His pupils dilate and the green of his irises burns brighter. "Yeah?" One of his dark brows hitches.

"Yeah." I nod, unable to tear my gaze away from his.

He strokes my clit in skilled circles, pulling my orgasm closer and closer to the surface.

I part my lips and pant as pressure builds inside me.

"That's it. Let it go, Princess."

I look into his eyes as he works me beneath him, his huge body the same enormous shield of carved and sculpted muscle that he uses to protect me.

To love me.

To keep me safe.

To never leave me.

"Denver," I whimper.

"Let it go, Sinclair," he urges. "Let it go."

I hold his eyes, drowning—no *swimming*—in deep emerald green. Swimming toward those golden flecks of land that offer hope and love, and every dream I've ever had of feeling happy again.

A place where grief isn't vanished, but it also doesn't consume me anymore.

"Denver!" I cry as my body hands everything over to him and I come in deep, pulsing waves around him.

"Good girl. That's my good girl. I love you, Sinclair," he says, his lids hooding as he thrusts faster. "I love you so much."

I hold his face between my palms as he comes deep inside

me with an animalistic groan that stretches on and has warmth spreading all through my body at the same time as he spills his liquid heat inside me.

"Denver," I moan.

His lips crash to mine and he kisses me through the rest of his orgasm, his body driving into mine over and over.

"Fuck," he curses.

He takes his time, gradually slowing our kisses as our bodies settle into a gentle rhythm, before stilling completely.

I'm breathless as I gaze up at him, a million emotions bubbling inside my chest.

I stroke his cheeks with my thumbs as though I need to reassure myself that he really is here, and I didn't just dream all of that.

"You said you had to stay away because you needed me to be sure. What did you mean? Because I am sure about loving you. That's never been in question," I say, needing to know what he's thinking in this moment more than ever before.

His brow creases and his eyes fall closed briefly with a sigh. "I need to know that you want this with every part of you."

"I do."

He opens his eyes, and they burn into mine.

"Not just this." He taps his finger from his chest to mine. "I meant that I needed to know if you're ready for all the stories the press will want to write about you falling in love with your bodyguard. We're a cliché, Princess. A fucking cliché that they'll eat up."

He looks at me, his face serious.

I can't stop myself. I break into laughter. "You... you made a joke."

His eyes glitter and a smile paints itself over his face, making his mouth look ridiculously kissable. "You're laughing, so I guess I did."

I stroke his cheeks, gazing up at him. "They will totally eat it up," I whisper. "I might even need some extra private security until it dies down."

"Killian and Jenson are busy for the next decade." He grunts.

"They are?"

"I'm their boss again, so yeah, you bet your ass they are. No one is opening car doors and carrying your bags except me. I promised you I wouldn't do it for anyone else. And that goes both ways."

"You're going to be my bodyguard again?"

"I'm going to be your boyfriend, Sinclair."

He turns his face and catches my wrist in his hand, bringing it to his lips so he can press a kiss to it.

"We really need to tell my father," I say, guilt pulling at my chest. I want to bask in this moment, soak in the beauty of having Denver back again. But the knowledge that my father still doesn't know gnaws at me.

"He knows," Denver says.

"What?" I gasp. "You told him? Was he angry? Was he...? Oh my god, he must have been so shocked!"

I swear Denver's lips twitch, but his voice remains serious. "He's... getting used to the idea faster than I thought he would. I'm just thankful he chose me and not Killian or Jenson."

"If I recall, he said you were the best. Although, Killian is interesting, and Jenson's funny," I muse.

He flashes a warning look at me, and I bite down on my lower lip as I smile.

"I like your jokes better though, Brute," I whisper, trailing my fingertips along his sinful lower lip.

"Yeah?"

"Yeah."

"Come back here and kiss me," he rumbles.

"That an order?" I arch a brow, my pussy tingling at the way his eyes darken.

"It's a fucking order, Princess. Now come here."

I squeal as he pins me to the mattress beneath him and his cock thickens inside me again.

His eyes soften and he presses the gentlest of kisses to my lips, letting them rest against mine. "*I love you*," he whispers, and then he starts thrusting again.

46

DENVER

"You can take your eyes off her in here, you know? There aren't any paps about to jump out."

Jenson sniggers as I throw him a shut-the-fuck-up-before-I-punch-you look.

For the past two weeks, the press has been everywhere Sinclair's gone, the story of her falling for her bodyguard apparently being worthy of front-page news. Every chat show between New York and LA want her to go on and tell her story. But my girl's refused every offer. She released one statement saying she's taking a few weeks off work to enjoy being 'close' with her 'hot, close protection officer'. Those words alone were enough to whip up a media frenzy with pictures of us together trending online, and the so-called body language experts dissecting every photograph of us together to pinpoint exactly when our relationship changed.

But whoever claims they can tell is wrong. Because they're focusing on the photographs of after I became her bodyguard.

The real truth lies in the ones taken years ago.

Because, like I told Sterling, I don't recall a time I didn't love Sinclair. Whether I knew it or not.

My eyes slide back to her playing on the floor inside Seasons bar area with Molly, Halliday, Monty... and the tiny wrinkly pink addition she's named Mabel.

"You sure it'll grow some hair?" Jenson asks, eyeing the Chinese crested puppy.

"About as much as Monty," I reply.

"Wow." His brows lift. "No shit, that much?"

"Idiot." Killian chuckles.

The three of us all greet Sterling and Mal as they walk over.

"Boss," I say, noting the way his face seems drawn like he's got a lot on his mind.

"Denver." He nods. "Take a seat." He gestures to the low table, and we all sit down. He opens his hand, palms wide. "Let's make this quick. I know Sullivan has something he wants to discuss."

I glance over at where Sullivan's playing the piano, his head hung as deep, heavy notes ring out like he's pressing down on each ivory key with all the force he can muster.

Sinclair's eyes flick to me and she gives me a worried look as the classical piece carries around the room.

"Neil's gone," Sterling says.

"About time," Mal mutters.

I turn my head back toward our table and nod. Not long after he claimed that he saw a man walking away from the yacht the day of the accident, he upped and left New York. He's now staying in Chicago, caring for a sick brother.

It's as though once he offloaded what he needed to, he saw no reason to stay. I can't say I'm not relieved. I didn't like him being anywhere near Sinclair. But we've still got eyes on him where he is now, just in case.

"We do have that new lead to look into, though." Sterling looks over at Halliday and I understand the reason for his tight expression.

The more we dug into Neil's claims, the more evidence we

unearthed to suspect he's telling the truth. We found a new witness working at the marina that day who claims to have heard a guy shouting for help minutes before the fire started. And a previously hidden donation of an eye-watering amount to the now-retired port service manager who was on duty that day has come to light. It was paid to his sister, not him, so we only uncovered it recently.

It could all be unconnected.

But I don't believe in coincidences.

"I'm going over there to see what else I can find out. Poke enough shit and you'll find some flies," Mal says, clasping his hands as he leans forward over the table, keeping his voice low.

"Jenson, you go with Mal," Sterling says, running a hand around his jaw.

"Yes, Boss." Jenson's eyes light up. I know he's made up about catching up with some of his buddies he's made in Cape Town.

There's a loud crash of uncoordinated notes as Sullivan curses and slams at the piano keys, then stands in a rush, making a beeline for our table. He stalks over and slumps into an empty chair. The table is silent as he sits, sucking in sharp breaths, making his nostrils flare.

"She's fucking back," he spits.

My eyes flick to Sterling. He's already filled me in on this latest development. We were holding back, waiting to see what her next move would be.

Sinclair storms over to the table, hearing his raised voice. "Who?"

Sullivan looks toward Molly, but she's still engrossed, playing with Halliday and the dogs as Halliday shoots Sterling a concerned look.

"Natasha," he spits.

Sinclair's eyes widen. "Molly's mom?"

"Do you know any others?"

My fists clench against my thighs at the way he snaps at her. Sterling's eyes meet mine, and I exhale, forcing myself not to react. This is Sinclair. She can stand up for herself where Sullivan's concerned. She doesn't need me punching him in the face. And anyway, I get why he's so concerned.

"Don't speak to me like that." She smacks Sullivan up the back of the head and his eyes bug out.

I bite back my smirk. She's about the only person in the world who can get away with doing that. I've seen grown men cower when Sullivan Beaufort walks into a room.

Sterling winks at me as I look up.

"What does she want?" Sinclair asks.

Sullivan rolls his lips, tension radiating from him like he's one touch away from going postal. "Molly. She says she wants to take Molly."

"What?" she shrieks. "She can't! Tell her she can't."

"I did fucking tell her that," Sullivan says. "But she's her biological mother and—"

"And she's also an addict who can't look after herself, let alone a little girl. She *left* her on your doorstep in a fucking *box*, Sullivan. For God's sake, what kind of mother does that?"

"I know," Sullivan mutters, scrubbing a hand down his face, his eyes red-rimmed.

"She gave up all rights to be her mother when she did that," Sinclair says. "We'll fight her, won't we, Dad?"

She looks to Sterling for support, and he nods. "You bet your ass we will, Sweetheart. Molly isn't going anywhere."

Sinclair's shoulders soften. "Just slam some DNA tests at the courts along with her failed rehab stints. Then she can crawl back to where she came from."

"DNA results?" Sullivan echoes.

"It'll show you're her biological father, won't it?" Sinclair folds her arms and stares her brother down.

"You know it will, but it's not that simple—"

"You're her father," Mal says.

"You are," Sterling agrees.

"I know." Sullivan leans his head back and blows out a breath. "It's just the last thing I needed right now."

Sympathy fills my chest as I look at him. I know what it's like to be apart from the woman you love. And seeing as he hasn't mentioned this woman, Tate, again since the little jaunt he had me going on well over a month ago, I can't see that his situation there has changed.

"Okay," Sterling says in a calm voice that has everyone breathing again. "We all know what's going on. And we've all got each other's backs. We're family. And family look out for one another. We'll get this all sorted."

"Yeah," Sullivan says, pushing his thumb and forefinger into his eyes and rubbing. "Thanks, Dad."

"You're okay, Son. It'll all be okay." He reaches over and squeezes Sullivan's knee.

"It will," Sinclair agrees, sliding onto my lap and snaking her arms up around my neck.

I stiffen immediately and clear my throat.

She giggles. Fucking *giggles* as she bats her eyelashes at me.

"And that's our cue to leave," Uncle Mal says, clapping his hands.

Sterling chuckles and stands, and the rest of the men follow him, leaving the two of us sitting at the table alone.

"I'm working," I grit as her fingers walk up my tie.

"Uh-huh," she muses.

I glare at her, but it only encourages her. She flicks her finger over my lower lip until it makes a burbling sound.

"Stop it," I huff.

"I love you," she murmurs, doing it again.

My hand slides to her thigh, and I grab a handful of it with a tight grip. "I said, *stop it*, Princess."

"You know I find you sexy when you're mad," she breathes, replacing her finger with her lips and kissing me.

My fingers dig into her flesh, and I groan as I kiss her back briefly, unable to resist.

"You're so fucking spoiled," I tease, making her gasp. I take the opportunity to nip her lower lip between my teeth and then haul her out of my lap, setting her on her feet as I stand. "You know when I'm working, you can't do that."

She pouts, and I can't help myself. I grasp her face and give her cheeks a little squeeze, making her lips purse further.

"Make it up to me later?" I growl.

Her eyes light up and she nods happily inside my grasp.

I shake my head with a smirk. I know her. She pushes my buttons on purpose, because she likes to pretend that she's 'making it up' to me when she's on her knees sucking down on my dick like it's tastier than those damn favorite smoothies of hers.

I should buy shares in that truck. I'm there every day, either with her, or picking one up for her. But it's like I told her, I'm going to look after her. And she's already looking healthier since I practically moved into her place with her.

Close protection at its most personal level.

Because now I do watch her in the shower every day like she asked if I would.

Or I join her.

I slide a hand down and curl it around her hip.

"I love you, Princess," I whisper, pressing a light kiss to her lips, knowing no one is looking anymore.

She rises on her toes and looks into my eyes, a beautiful serenity in her green gaze.

"You okay?" I ask softly.

She smiles. "I am now."

Then she presses her lips against mine.

"I love you too, Brute. So much."

47

EPILOGUE – THE WEDDING
SINCLAIR

Five months later

The sunlight sinks into the diamond, picking up the golden hue and making it glow like the dying embers of a fire.

I smile at the irony.

Warm hands skate down my bare upper arms from behind and I shiver, leaning back against his solid chest, my eyes never leaving the small stone as it spins on the end of its chain.

"You okay?" Denver breathes softly, pressing a kiss to my shoulder.

"Yeah," I say back softly, wiping another stray tear from my cheek.

We came to watch the sunrise at the marina, on my request. Something about being back here for my father and Halliday's wedding told me that this was the right thing to do.

That this was the right place.

"All these years and I thought I had a part of him still with me." I sniff.

"You'll always have a part of him, Sinclair. You don't need to be able to touch it or hold it. You just need to be able to feel it. In here." Denver taps two fingers over my heart, and I sniff again as more tears fall.

"Who do you think he was?" I ask, staring at the diamond Sullivan made for me.

We know the ashes used to make it aren't my brother's. But we weren't able to find out who they really belong to. The morgue in Cape Town where my brother and mother's bodies were sent were unable to explain the mix up. They apologized profusely, likely worried of the huge court case that my family could fund against them, should we wish.

But we're all so tired. And it wouldn't bring either of them back. Nothing can.

Uncle Mal and Jenson spent weeks over here trying to find out more about what happened that day after Neil's claims. But it's been almost three years now. People here have moved on. Recollections have faded. Our family's story is just a tragic accident that is recounted by the locals from time to time.

Maybe it's time we accepted that asking questions that might never give answers isn't any way to live.

"I don't know, Princess," Denver says, kissing my temple. "But whoever he was, you gave a home to someone's loved one, and you cherished their memory for them."

"Who knew such a Brute would have such a beautiful way with words?" I say, turning to gaze up at him.

His green eyes soften. "I have a reputation to uphold, Princess. My romantic side is strictly for your eyes only."

"I like that." I smile and tilt my chin up so that he'll press a kiss to my lips.

I sigh as we break apart, and Denver nods in understanding. "It's time."

"It is," I agree.

I turn around and step out of his embrace. My toes stay one inch in from the edge of the old, weathered, wooden boards that are the farthest point of the marina. In front of us is wide open ocean, stretching out to the horizon.

I smile as Denver grunts and his large hand slides onto my hip, securing me in place so I don't slip. The grumpy look on his face when I pulled on a pair of high, wedged sandals to come here was priceless.

I knew he'd worry about me falling in.

I take a deep breath, curling my fingers around the necklace so that the diamond sits inside my palm. Then I bring my hand to my lips and kiss it.

"It's time to say goodbye. I hope you have someone who loved you as much as we loved him," I whisper.

Then I pull back my arm and throw it as far as I can, watching as it sinks beneath the crystal water.

DENVER

Piano music plays as the guests sit on chairs set out on the sand, waiting for Halliday to make her entrance. There isn't a hint of nerves on Sterling's face as he stands at the top of the aisle beside Sullivan, both in matching tuxedos. In fact, he's smiling as he says something to Sullivan and claps him on the shoulder.

My eyes skate past Vincent, sitting at the white grand piano, and over to the guys wearing earpieces, who are dotted around, trying to blend in.

"Will you relax?" Jenson says, from his seat beside me. "You helped pick them."

"I know that," I reply, keeping my eye on the security detail brought in for the wedding today.

Killian snorts, next to Jenson. "Baby face is right. They're good guys. Relax, Denver. You're a guest today, you're off duty."

My teeth grind together. I'm never off duty. Sinclair's mine to protect. Her and the Beauforts. Killian and Jenson.

They're all my family.

And family comes first.

"A hundred bucks says this baby face gets me laid tonight." Jenson smirks at Killian.

"With who?" Killian asks.

Jenson's face takes on a look of intense concentration as he looks around at the guests. It's a small, intimate wedding, but that'll not deter him.

"Maid of Honor is out," Killian says quietly, his eyes scanning the guests too.

Halliday's friend from London, Sophie, who brought her husband, Drew, and their baby twins with her is playing that role. Drew watches Sophie the way I watch Sinclair. Jenson's not stupid enough to even attempt to go there.

"Then you've got Sterling's nieces," Killian says, nodding in the direction of Sterling's two brothers and their families, which comprise of more than a few women in their twenties.

Jenson throws a flirty grin at one as she makes the mistake of glancing our way.

"Touch the daughter of a Beaufort and you'll be eating your wedding cake with the sharks later," Killian says.

"Denver got away with it," Jenson says.

"You're not Denver." Killian snorts, finding the whole thing amusing.

"Any tips, Buddy?" Jenson elbows me in the ribs.

"Here's a tip," I growl. "Shut the fuck up."

He chuckles as he sees what's got my attention.

Sinclair has arrived at the start of the aisle with Molly. She's wearing a long silk dress in a silver color. It wraps around her curves in a way that means she can't wear panties with it. I know because she stuck her head back around the door as she carried it out of our room to get ready with the girls and told me with a smug smile on her face, knowing exactly what she was doing.

My dick has been fighting its way to a giant fucking boner

ever since, and it's taken every part of my mental training to talk it down so I can walk around with a modicum of decency.

They stand and wait for Halliday and her father to catch up. I can make out Halliday approaching through the tree line in my periphery, but my attention is fixated on Sinclair, crouching and smiling brightly at Molly in her flower girl's outfit, giving her a pep talk. Molly nods seriously, her lower lip poking out as she grasps a basket of petals between her palms, which have a distinct purple hue to them.

Sinclair's eyes catch mine and she gestures to Molly's hands, rolling her eyes with a smirk. It'll have something to do with the case of purple candy Sterling had me guard.

"She looks... wow." Jenson exhales, his eyes dropping up and down Sinclair's body as she stands.

"She does," I agree, my chest swelling with warmth. "And that's the first and last time you ever look at my girlfriend like that unless you want me to break every bone in your body."

Jenson laughs but stops the second I flick my eyes to him. "Got it," he says, clearing his throat.

Sinclair walks around the edge of the seats, her eyes on me as she passes our row. They twinkle as I gaze at her. She slots into a row near the front, next to Mal and his wife, Trudy, saying something to Sullivan.

Vincent starts playing a new song and the guests all turn collectively, an 'aww' rumbling through them as Molly starts her walk, ahead of the bride.

It takes everything in me to tear my eyes away from Sinclair and watch.

SINCLAIR

"Thank you for being here to celebrate with us," my father says, pride and happiness oozing from him as he stands, holding his glass up in a toast. "I'm sure you're all aware of how we met. But I promised my daughter, Sinclair..."

He chuckles as I wave from my seat. Denver's hand clasps my thigh protectively beneath the long table.

"... that I would give her credit and tell the story again..." my father continues.

I part my thighs a little, placing my hand on top of Denver's and sliding it higher so his pinky grazes my pussy.

"Princess," he growls under his breath.

A rumble of laughter passes along the table at a joke my father makes.

"Move your hand if you don't want it there, Brute," I whisper in his ear, giggling, and he tenses, his eyes flicking along the table at the sea of faces.

Everyone's attention is fixed on my father and the way he's radiating love as he lifts Halliday's hand to his lips and kisses it.

"Those three words were... *She's your gift*," my father says, reciting the words I told him when I hired Halliday to find him love.

I take Denver's free hand in mine and clap with it, throwing him a little wink. He glowers at me, and I giggle again. He could have moved his hand and clapped with both of his if he'd wanted to.

We lift our glasses, toasting my father and Halliday. Warmth blooms in my chest at how happy and perfect they look together.

"Look at the way he looks at her," I murmur. "He's so deliriously in love."

"Mm-hmm," Denver murmurs.

"You're not even looking," I say with a smile, feeling his gaze burning into my cheek.

I turn and am captured by glittering green.

"I'm looking, Sinclair," he rasps, all deep and sexy and *him*.

"Yeah?" I bite my lip, staring at him as heat pools between my legs. I've been with the girls getting ready ever since we got back from the marina this morning. We haven't been alone together for hours.

His fingers flex against my skin, and he slides them higher, turning his palm so he can swipe the tip of one through my arousal.

He curses quietly.

"You want to pretend you're helping me with something?" I whisper in his ear as chatter breaks out around the table and serving staff come to refill glasses.

"We can't leave together. Everyone will know what we're doing," he whispers with a tortured groan.

His eyes scan the table, snagging on something.

"What?" I breathe, following his gaze.

My father is leading Halliday away from the table discreetly. She's gazing at him in adoration.

"I'm incredibly happy for them both, but now you have to sneak me out of here and do deliciously filthy things to me, otherwise I'll be thinking of what my father is doing right now." I laugh, pulling his face to mine so I can kiss him.

He gifts me with a scorching kiss full of promise that leaves my lips tingling.

Then he stands and pulls my chair out.

His eyes darken as he gazes down at me, and I blink, not even trying to hide my eye-fuck of him in his suit.

"Let's go," he says quietly.

I stand, glancing up and down the table at our family and friends who are all chatting away, love bouncing around the table in every smile and laugh.

"Sinclair," Denver warns as I pause.

He's right, he does know me. Because before I can call out to our guests that we'll be back in a bit, his mouth slants over mine, muffling my words.

But I don't care.

Because his lips are on mine, and I'm kissing him as though my life depends on it.

A cheer erupts and someone calls out about ours being the next wedding. I grin against Denver's mouth as he mutters out, '*Princess*', like he's pissed.

But as I dust my lips back and forth over his, he smiles.

"Sinclair Layne, or maybe Denver Beaufort," I muse, giggling as his dick presses against me, getting harder by the second.

"Move," he growls, his hand sliding to the base of my spine as he marches me away from the table.

I lean into his side as we walk away to a wolf-whistle, which I bet was Jenson.

"This spoiled princess loves you." I laugh, wrapping my arm around him.

He grunts. "I hope so. Because this Brute loves her enough to die for her—"

"Because it used to be your job?"

He presses his lips into my hair, kissing the top of my head, as his voice softens. "Because she's everything to me."

My insides go all gooey, melting like butter on hot toast.

"Everything, huh? You want it all. Now, who's spoiled?" I stop walking and turn to look at him from beneath my lashes, lust working its way through my veins and heating my blood as he lifts his hand and dusts his thumb over my lower lip, his pupils flaring as the tip dips inside my mouth and grazes my tongue.

"You saying I'm spoiled now?" He arches a brow, and I have the urge to suck on his thumb, but he moves it before I can, curling his hand around the side of my neck and gripping it in his signature way.

Strong but so gentle.

"Yeah." I smile. "You're a spoiled Brute now. Who knows what you'll be demanding next."

"Demanding?" he rasps, the depth of his tone sending a shiver of anticipation skating up my spine. "How about I demand you stop talking and kiss me?"

I flick my gaze to the table of guests behind him. We're far enough away that they can't hear us, but we're still within their sights if they were to look in this direction.

"Public displays of affection growing on you? What will you be into next?" I tease.

He steps closer, his jacket brushing my nipples and making them pucker to attention beneath my dress. "The same thing I've always been into." His eyes roam over my face and my breath hitches at the intensity in them. Everything around us fades into a low hum. The sound of chatter, glass clinking, the ocean waves. He breathes in slowly and exhales his next words like a soft prayer. "Sinclair Beaufort..." His eyes drink me in again, like he's looking at me for the first time. "The woman I love with everything I am."

Fireworks erupt low inside my stomach. *I love intense romantic Denver.*

"The one you'd die to protect," I whisper, emotion catching in my throat and making me need to blink.

"The one I'd die to protect," he says, "because she is *everything* to me."

My lips sink into my lower lip before a goofy smile takes over my face. "Say that again."

Denver's gaze heats as he tilts my chin up. "Now who's demanding?"

The first soft press of his mouth against mine is like those first rays of warm sun in spring, telling the earth that it's time to grow things again. It's time to bloom.

That it'll all be okay.

"I love you," I tell him as he pulls me into a kiss that I never want to end.

We're two people who know loss too well, finding happiness in each other when we feared there would be none.

He tells me he'd die for me.

But he needs to know what I'll do for him.

I pull back far enough to break our kiss, but not far enough that his warm breath doesn't entwine with mine in the tiny slice of air between us.

"I live for you, Denver Layne," I declare, stroking his jaw. "I live for your vanilla coffee tasting lips, and your giant brutish arms around me. I live for your insistence of opening my door for me, which you know I secretly love, but will pretend not to. I live for the way you sleep with your gun under your pillow because you're worried about losing someone you love again."

His eyes shine as his hand wraps around my hip, holding me close.

"And I live for every time you tell me it will be okay... because the only time I've ever truly believed it has been when it's you saying it."

"Sinclair," Denver breathes, wiping away a tear that's rolling down my cheek.

"I love you," I say again, wanting to tell him over and over. "Thank you for being that one solid in a world where everything felt like it was spinning and nothing was safe."

The tender smile that graces his handsome face sends sparks bursting through me, like little shots of magic.

"Thank you for letting me be that person." He strokes my hair back from my face. "I love you with every part of me, Sinclair. You're everything to me."

I sniff, fighting back happy tears, before deciding to embrace them. Who cares if our sexy sneak-away has turned emotional? I intend to soak up every second of it. I've cried too many tears of grief.

I welcome the wetness on my cheeks now as Denver looks at me like I'm his entire reason for existing.

"Just everything?" I pout, more tears falling.

"And more, Princess," he rasps.

"How much?"

His rare chuckle washes over me as he leans closer, his lips hovering over mine.

"More than every shoe of yours I'll find fault with. More than every door I'll open for you, secretly loving that you try and fight me over it, because you toying with me is the highlight of my day. More than the way you love those smoothie stickers that have better jokes than me. And more than I'll ever be able to tell you, even if I said it again and again until my final breath."

He rests his forehead against mine, waiting.

"Hm," I muse. "It'll do as a start, I suppose."

He purses his lips, his expression serious, only given away

by the way his eyes are glittering. "I better up my efforts," he says.

The next second the stars dotted against the inky sky flash past my eyes as he pulls me up into his arms, my body pressed against his chest, my legs flung over his arms. Like he's about to sweep me away somewhere with urgency, bodyguard style.

"Sounds like a plan," I say, pulling his lips to mine.

He kisses me, a deep groan building in his chest. "Time to execute the next phase," he groans.

"Does it include that thing you do with your—?"

He cuts me off with another kiss.

"Such a fucking princess," he scolds. "Trust me, okay?"

"Always."

"It'll be okay," he says. "Everything will be okay."

And as he strides off with me in his arms, I gaze at his profile, my heart lifting every other second as he glances down to check on me, a smile playing on his lips.

I believe him.

Because now that I have Denver, I know, whatever happens now...

It'll all be okay.

DENVER
BONUS SCENE

"Why are you wearing that?" I ask, my eyes glued to Sinclair as she waltzes past me in a skintight cream bodysuit that comes to her mid-thigh.

"Do you like it?" She twirls.

The thing is so tight, I don't know how she got it on single-handedly.

"You said you wanted to work out," I say, staring at her as she saunters around the gym mat, giving me a show.

"I do." She stops directly in front of me and looks at me with a glint in her eyes.

"In that?"

"Uh-huh. It's my support set."

She pouts, and the urge to pull her over my knee and spank her is almost too much. I narrow my eyes, licking my lips as I drink in her curves again.

"You want to play, huh... *Baby*?" I tilt my head, assessing whether I read her cues correctly.

Her eyes light up like the Fourth of July and she bounces on her toes. "If you think you can handle me?"

I shake my head with a smirk. "All right, you asked for it."

I lift her straight up into my arms and bring us both down onto the mat, her on her back beneath me.

My favorite place to have her.

She bites down her grin, trying to look serious as she starts to wriggle and thrash.

"Get off me, asshole!" she yells, pushing at my chest.

I pin her in place with my hips, forcing my rapidly hardening dick against her inner thigh. "Aww, don't be like that. I know you like it really."

"As much as I like the idea of being eaten alive by rabid rats," she spits.

I run my nose up the side of her face, breathing in her scent. The low growl of appreciation that leaves me has her panting beneath me. I snag her neck between my teeth, giving it a gentle nip. Her body trembles in response before she recovers herself and yanks a handful of my hair.

I can't help smiling. It's been weeks since we've managed to make it out to the cabin. This is the first time since Sterling and Halliday's wedding that we've been here. But the way Sinclair's hot body is fighting beneath mine as her nipples pebble against my chest make it feel like only yesterday that we were here.

Since that first time I made her mine.

"I'm the only one who's going to be doing any eating around here," I murmur in her ear, spurred on by the way she shivers at my words.

I move back onto my knees so I can look down at her.

Her movements halt as she gazes up at me, her chest rising and falling with fake angry breaths.

"Did you think this choice of attire would save you?" I ask, running a finger down her body, over one breast, toward her navel.

She arches into my touch, like she's fighting to get closer and feel me better through the stretchy material.

Denver

"You'll lose your eyes before you get me out of it," she says, her voice full of fire.

"Really?" I smirk, and her eyes widen as I reach into my sock and pull out my Swiss Army Knife.

I pull out the blade and trace a slow line up from her pussy to the neckline of her bodysuit. The tip snags on the fabric, making a scraping sound as it goes.

"You forget how well I know you," I say as I turn my wrist, flicking it just enough to pierce the edge of the fabric.

"That's cheating." Sinclair huffs as I close the knife and toss it to the side.

I shake my head as I curl my fingers around the damaged edges of the suit. "I told you, Baby. Assholes don't play fair."

Her eyes gleam as I wrench my biceps apart. The bodysuit tears right down the center, all the way to her naked, glistening pussy.

I wondered what she'd done with the thing after she told me it's what she wore when Brad Garrett-Charles... fuck, I still hate to even think of that guy's name. He's been gone months now and not tried to contact her. Probably one of his more intelligent choices.

I knew she was up to something when she told me she wanted to change for our workout. I couldn't conceal that knife fast enough, hoping that this was what she had planned.

My girl loves to toy with me.

I survey the shredded material. The sight of it, torn open and exposing her especially for me makes my already solid dick leak at the tip.

Sinclair gazes up at me with flushed cheeks, her tongue sliding out to run over her lower lip. I hold her eyes as I tear the bodysuit down each leg until only the shoulder straps remain in place. I should let her remove them, throw the damn thing away.

Denver

But I'm already pushing my shorts down and grabbing my dick in my fist, my need for her outweighing everything else.

"You ready for me, baby? I can't wait to feel this pretty cunt stretch around me."

"Mm, not bad," she muses, looking down at my pre-cum dripping off the head of my cock and onto her pussy. She parts her legs wider, her lips spreading so the glistening drops land on her clit. "Let me guess… You want to show me what it can do?"

"Admit you're as desperate for me to fuck you as I am to stuff you full of my dick," I rasp, rubbing the crown up and down between her lips, covering it in her slick arousal.

"I dunno." She shrugs, as she continues her assessment of my cock. "I guess I should test it out seeing as it'll be the one I'll be getting from now on."

"It will," I groan, circling the tip against her entrance. "The only fucking one. I'm going to marry you and then you'll have to call me husband as I sink inside this sweet cunt every day, baby."

"Marry me?" She snorts. "Well, you'll need an amazing ring. My family own a diamond company."

I look up from where I'm rubbing my cock against her and catch her glinting eyes. "Do they really?" I arch a brow. "Such a spoiled *Princess*."

She bites her lower lip, letting a suppressed whimper out as I break character and press down to kiss her.

Her hand threads into the hair at the back of my head, and she kisses me back, moaning as I feed the head of my cock into her and her body greedily accepts it without hesitation.

"You called me spoiled." She pouts.

I nip her lower lip, drawing her into another kiss.

"I did," I growl. "But I should have said ruined. Because I'm going to ruin you all over this mat."

She giggles against my lips, but it turns into a gasp as I thrust, burying myself to the hilt inside her.

"Fucking beautiful," I grit.

"Show me what it can do," she teases, clenching around me.

"What it can do?" I growl.

Her smirk turns into a gasp, then panted cries of my name as I pull back and thrust... and thrust... and thrust...

I'm a man possessed as I rail her into the mat, spurred on by the way she's mewling and clawing at me, her cunt clamping down onto me so hard that I know she's aching to come.

"Oh my god, fuck me, Denver!" she cries, throwing her head back as she bucks beneath me, lifting her pussy to meet my cock, so fucking eager for it that I have to grit my teeth to stop myself from coming.

Her breasts bounce up and down as I push inside her with rougher, deeper thrusts.

"Yeah, you like that?" I groan, reaching up to hold one breast, my thumb flicking over her pinched nipple.

"Yes," she moans. "God, yes!"

Sinclair's eyes glitter as she gazes at me. I'm pretty sure mine are doing the exact same thing as we both absorb the moment.

Us. This.

Being back in the exact same spot I first touched her.

Fuck, I love her so much.

She gasps as her body quivers.

"That's it, Princess. Come on my cock. Good girl, that's it."

My eyes are glued to her face as she trembles and comes hard, her body milking my throbbing dick like a fist made of iron.

"Fuuuck," I hiss, holding her eyes as I fuck her, driving her through another cunt-fluttering orgasm before I finally let myself release inside her.

"Sinclair," I groan, my forehead falling against hers as my dick pumps inside her, rendering me useless for anything else other than bracing myself over her as I fill her full of cum.

I can't speak. I can barely breathe.

My abs convulse and my cock swells with each surge.

And she looks into my eyes the entire time, clenching around me until I come back into my body.

"I love you, Brute," she whispers so gently I almost don't hear her over the thundering of my heart.

"I love you too." I pull her face to mine, slanting my lips over hers in a breathy kiss.

I plant one hand on the mat next to her as I ease back to look at her. My palm presses into the fabric of the bodysuit that's flapped open.

"Let's burn it next," she says, her eyes lighting up.

I smile, maneuvering us both so I'm sitting and she's straddling me. I hold her eyes as I slide the straps from her shoulders, one by one, leaning forward to kiss the area of skin beneath.

She sighs happily, her soft fingers sliding over my cheek as I kiss my way up her neck to meet her lips again.

"What do you think my father will say when that day comes?"

"The day I ask you to be my wife?" I ask, sliding my hand around her jaw and pulling her lips back to mine for a kiss.

"Uh-huh," she murmurs against my lips.

I kiss her, hiding my smirk. I imagine Sterling might say the same as he did when I admitted to him that I was in love with his daughter.

"What took you so long?"

Or maybe he won't.

Because I've waited years for Sinclair to be ready for this. For me. For us.

And I don't intend on waiting much longer.

"Maybe he'll be grateful to me for willing to take on such a handful," I say, earning myself a pout.

"Was that supposed to be a joke?"

"You didn't laugh, so it can't have been."

She turns away, rolling her eyes, pretending to be pissed.

"Hey, Princess?"

She turns, her eyes narrowing as I do a stellar job of mimicking her sulky little pout.

"No, I'm not falling for it…" She huffs, looking away, then eyeing me again. "I'm not…"

I lean forward, losing my pout and kissing her.

"You're not funny," she breathes, kissing me back.

But as her hands sink into my hair and she holds me close, her lips part, and she laughs.

"Not funny, Brute," she repeats.

I kiss her harder, sliding my hands down to grip her hips. Her laugh turns into a gasp as I lift her and bring her back down onto my rapidly recovering dick.

"Shut up and fuck me, Princess."

"So rude and bossy," she tuts.

"Shut up and fuck me, *please*," I growl.

And this time, she really laughs.

The End.

Ready for Sullivan's Story?
Get your copy of The Love Hater here:https://books2read.com/BBthelovehater

If you enjoyed Sinclair and Denver's story, please consider leaving a review. It helps authors so much.

Denver

Thank you,
Elle x

ALSO BY ELLE NICOLL

The Men Series

Meeting Mr. Anderson – Holly and Jay

Discovering Mr. X – Rachel and Tanner

Drawn to Mr. King – Megan and Jaxon

Captured by Mr. Wild – Daisy and Blake

Pleasing Mr. Parker – Maria and Griffin

Trapped with Mr. Walker – Harley and Reed

Time with Mr. Silver – Rose and Dax

Resisting Mr. Rich – Maddy and Logan

Handling Mr. Harper – Sophie and Drew

Playing with Mr. Grant – Ava and Jet

(Also available, **Forget-me-nots and Fireworks**, Shona and Trent's story, a novella length prequel to The Men Series)

Beaufort Billionaires Series

The Matchmaker - Halliday and Sterling

The Rule Breaker - Sinclair and Denver

The Love Hater - Sullivan's Story

Book 4 - Coming Soon

ABOUT THE AUTHOR

Elle Nicoll is an ex long-haul flight attendant and mum of two from the UK.
After fourteen years of having her head in the clouds whilst working at 38,000ft, she is now usually found with her head between the pages of a book reading or furiously typing and making notes on another new idea for a book boyfriend who is sweet-talking her.
Elle finds it funny that she's frequently told she looks too sweet and innocent to write a steamy book, but she never wants to stop. Writing stories about people, passion, and love, what better thing is there?
Because,
Love Always Wins
xxx

Website – https://www.ellenicollauthor.com

Made in United States
Cleveland, OH
20 July 2025